Barren Worlds

BARREN WORLDS

Edited by Eric T. Reynolds
with Adam Nakama and Rob Darnell

Hadley Rille Books
PO Box 25466
Overland Park, KS 66225
USA

www.hadleyrillebooks.com
info@hadleyrillebooks.com

The stories contained within this book are works of fiction. Any resemblance, unless noted by the author, to actual persons, living or dead, is purely coincidental.

ISBN-13 978-0-9785148-2-2

1.1

To George S. Reynolds

ACKNOWLEDGMENTS

"Man Alone" copyright © 2008 by Drew Arrants.
"Project" copyright © 2008 by Adele Cosgrove-Bray.
"The Sound of Sun Rising" copyright © 2008 by Geraint D'Arcy.
"Living Amongst the Lizards" copyright © 2008 by Lawrence R. Dagstine.
"Elysium" copyright © 2008 by Tristan S. Davenport.
"Rats" copyright © 2008 by Graham Fielding.
"The Secret Life of Jane Gray" copyright © 2008 by Ginny Gilroy.
"This Abandoned Sky" copyright © 2008 by C. E. Grayson.
"He Would Have Given Them Wings" copyright © 2008 by Rob Haines.
"Cleveland" copyright © 2008 by Jasmine Hammer.
"Winterset" copyright © 2008 by Erin M. Hartshorn.
"Something out of Nothing" copyright © 2008 by Martin Hayes.
"The Secret Life of Mars" copyright © 2008 by Geoffrey Maloney.
"Tiger's Eye View" copyright © 2008 by Mary Ellen Martin.
"After the Storm" copyright © 2008 by Tracie McBride.
"Ocherva" copyright © 2008 by Ken McConnell.
"A Small Show on Double Gamma 3"
copyright © 2008 by Kevin James Miller.
"Alone On This Chance Planet" copyright © 2008 by Shane Nelson.
"Fallout" copyright © 2008 by Michael Obilade.
"Saying Goodbye" copyright © 2008 by Sue Penkivech.
"Introduction" copyright © 2008 by Eric T. Reynolds.
"Elessa the Restless" copyright © 2008 by Shauna Roberts.
"Gift Time" copyright © 2008 by Lawrence M. Schoen.
"Blue Dome of Sky" copyright © 2008 by Ted Stetson.
"Bad People" copyright © 2008 by Gene Stewart.
"Allotment" copyright © 2008 by David Tallerman.
"Antiope in Black" copyright © 2008 by Geoffrey Thorne.
"Candhiga's Corpse and the Birds at the Edge of the Sea"
copyright © 2008 by Andrew Tisbert.
"Otsego Undead" copyright © 2008 by William Blake Vogel III.
"Moon and Bones and Birds" copyright © 2008 by Christopher Woods.
Editorial assistance from Adam Nakama & Rob Darnell, and Rose Reynolds is appreciated.

CONTENTS

Introduction

You've entered orbit around a bluish world and are about to make a drop to the surface in a small excursion vehicle. You don't believe the rumors that anyone still lives on this world, but you've been sent to investigate. How you'll cover the entire surface and search for evidence is up to you, but you've prepared for it. There's that area just south of the planet's equator, the place where the coastline of a large island appears disturbed. Remote imaging only shows an anomaly, but no real evidence of habitation. Could be that it was inhabited in the distant past and the images just revealed the long-since weathered landscape that now obscures most of what might have once been a settlement. As you brake from orbit and fall toward the land you prepare your instruments and then wait to see what awaits. This is just one scenario of a *barren world* . . . .

A barren world could be defined as a place without life, a rolling endless desert of mountains and seas that continues its lifeless process of change in geology. But a barren world can exist within a populated place. "Barren" can mean absence of life, but also the absence of civilization, or the absence of a particular characteristic within a population. A barren world can be a place that was once *not* barren. A barren world can be a place crowded with people, but absent reason.

The storytellers in this anthology will take you into a universe devoid of *something* and in some cases, to places you'd best *avoid.*

Welcome to *Barren Worlds*. Like its companion volume, *Desolate Places*, this book contains stories set in bleak locales throughout the universe. These stories span a range of styles from dark to quirky to those of survival and escape.

You will experience a sentient life form trying to flee the torment of her captors, experimental ways for traveling great distances, and the desolate dreams of one child and how another deals with a mandatory evacuation of his world. The characters in these stories have willingly accepted, or have had forced upon them, puzzles that they must solve, that often involve survival: avoiding death or maintaining sanity.

Sometimes, grand human experiments have gone bad and humanity struggles with the consequences. The efforts put into those schemes can be insignificant compared to what it takes to undo the damage. However, humans, and non-humans, are very resourceful and often arrive at creative ways out of trouble. But sometimes no amount of intelligence get them out of their predicaments.

You'll meet characters across the spectrum of likability. And you will really hate a few of them. But you will marvel at the places they will take you.

Eric T. Reynolds
Santa Fe, New Mexico
Overland Park, Kansas
June 2008

Cleveland
by Jasmine Hammer

The worst was when there was no water. Even when you weren't dying from it, you knew you would soon. But pouring water on a stomach that had been empty for days hurt—could even make you throw up. Justin knew, he'd done it once before. He stared at the water, yellow with stomach lining, soaking into the ground and thought, what a waste, what a waste. He hadn't been as desperate then.

He still wasn't as bad as the girl. He had been watching her for months. She was dying, and not slowly either. Justin could tell by looking at her that before everything she had been a big girl. Maybe strong, maybe fat, definitely curvy. A big girl. She had wide shoulders and thick cheekbones. Her hands, all bony knuckles and long fingers now, might once have been as large as a man's

Justin had always been lean and twitchy, darting around every space he was in. He ate little, considering how tall he was. It was how he survived. His muscles stood out so sharply, they looked like they might split through his skin. Only lately had those muscles begun to shrink, had he become lethargic.

He did not know how the girl had survived. Maybe she hadn't, really. She never had any expression on her face, sometimes sat and stared at a wall for hours. She had no water. Her face was blackened with grime and her lips cracked and flaked off in white, dead pieces. Her skin blistered with a rash and it caked with blood where she had scratched it raw.

Seventeen days ago, pale gray clouds gathered over them. Justin put out his own buckets and pans, then went to watch her. She had a single bucket on the roof of the burnt-out warehouse where she lived. The tar of the roof had long ago dried and shriveled, skittering away in black pebbles. When the wind picked up like it might actually rain, she took off all her clothes and spread herself on the roof. Her dirty skin hung in folds off her body.

When the rain at last drizzled down, Justin tipped his head back and opened his mouth. The air, so acrid and hot, absorbed most of the rain before it hit them. It dripped off his forehead, but never touched his chest. It was barely enough to dampen the bottom of her bucket.

When it was obvious it wasn't going to rain anymore, she curled into a ball and cried without tears.

He didn't go see her for a few days after that.

Whether watching her or not, he would talk to her, imagine how she would answer.

Did someone hurt you? he would ask.

People always hurt me, she would say, even before the world fell apart.

Why do you think it fell apart?

Because people hurt each other.

It will never end, will it?

No, I don't think so. I pray to die every day.

You believe in God?

No, I don't think so. You?

Yes I do.

What did he bring you for Christmas?

What?

I said what did he bring you for Christmas?

Water.

Oh. Why did he let this happen?

He didn't. We did.

Justin had tried to approach her twice, very carefully. Both times she ran and hid so well that he hadn't been able to find her for days.

He had a new plan. He had to do it now, before he got too weak, before she died.

He waited until she wasn't looking, then dropped down behind her. He wrapped his arms around her, pinning her arms to her side, and swept her off her feet.

It was the first time he had touched another human being in a year and a half.

She fought, and fought dirty. She tried to bite him, to smash in his nose with her skull. She stomped on his insole hard enough to make him cry out and let go. She slipped away from his arms, so he had to tackle her. She snarled at him. No words, just growls.

He lived under the floor of a warehouse, like she did. He wrestled her to the trapdoor that hid his basement home and dropped her down into it.

He'd removed the ladder and she had nowhere to go.

He jumped down after her. She got her hands on a bucket and swung it at his head. She missed, tried to lift it again, and couldn't. Justin grabbed her arm, twisted it behind her back and pushed her to the floor.

"I'm not going to hurt you."

"You *are* hurting me," she whispered. Her voice cracked and scraped.

"No I'm not."

He tied her hands in front of her and set her against the wall. She bled from a corner of her lip. He wondered if he had done that, or if her lip had simply split open of its own accord.

"You'd better let me clean that."

"Touch me and I bite you."

His basement room was small, but cluttered. He had packed earth up against the cement walls to keep it warmer at night. He slept on a pile of rags in one corner and would sometimes build a small fire in the middle. The rest was filled with useful junk he collected: metal spikes, a rusty wheel, piles of wood.

He reached behind a pile and pulled out his canteen and a metal cylinder to drink from. He poured water into it so she could see.

She inhaled sharply and struggled to her feet.

"Sit down." He wedged the cup into her hands and she poured it down her throat greedily.

"More," she said.

He took a damp rag and dabbed carefully at the blood trickling down her chin.

"Please." She stared at him, ignored his insistent hand on her face.

He shook his head. "You'll get sick."

"No, I—"

"Yes you will. Trust me." He'd made a single clean spot appear on her chin. He leaned back to look at her, letting his hand rest on her knee. Her eyes had no color in them. He had never noticed that before. They were hazy and unreflecting, like the sky. He was afraid of them, didn't know where to look.

"Why don't you just do it?" she whispered, voice cracking again.

"What?"

"You know." She pulled away from his hand and he understood.

"You think I'm going to rape you? You think that's what I want?" He snorted and stood up. "I might as well be screwing a corpse. An ugly one at that."

"Then what do you want?"

Footsteps above them. She shivered so violently she nearly fell over.

Justin dropped down around her and clamped his hand over her mouth.

"That's Phil and Derek."

She looked at him fearfully, the first real expression he'd seen on her face.

"You know they won't help you."

She nodded. He uncovered her mouth and pulled her to her feet.

"Don't let them find me," she begged.

So that's who hurt you.

He pushed her down behind the rusty wheels. He scooped up his pile of rags and dumped it over her just as Derek yanked open his door.

A year and a half ago, there had been four of them in that gang. Phil was the leader even then. He was the smallest, which made him the strongest, the least vulnerable. All four had jumped Justin, beat him, took everything he had, and left him for dead. They hadn't been as desperate then either. When they saw him alive a few weeks later, they demanded food and he gave them what he could. They hadn't touched him since.

Derek poked his head down the hole, held out a bucket.

"Water."

Justin poured his canteen into it while Derek stared at him, his hair hanging in his eyes. He didn't bother to push it back, or to look around the room, or question where the ladder was. Derek had not survived by his wits. He looked worse than usual, too. His eyes were sunken and his arms trembled.

Justin never knew if the other two in their gang had run away or if they'd been killed and eaten. He suspected the latter.

"Food."

"Got none."

Derek narrowed his eyes, coughed once.

"Not for days," Justin said. "There's no food left."

"Birds."

"Can't catch 'em." Justin hopped from one foot to the other. He tried to stop but he couldn't help it.

"You'd better get some," Phil's voice boomed from above. Justin couldn't see him, but the splintered boards moaned over his head.

He rolled his eyes, too desperate to be afraid. What were they going to do, kill him? Then he remembered the girl.

"I'll try."

Derek dragged himself away from the door and slammed it shut.

Justin pushed aside the rags until he found her, eyes squeezed shut, holding her breath. He put his hands under her armpits and lifted her out.

"Food," he said.

"I don't have any."

"You lie, you have some, and I have water and alone we will die."

"Thank God."

"No," he said, "not yet." He almost asked her about God, decided not to. Not yet. "What's your name?" He untied her.

"Annie. Ann."

"Annie Ann, I'm Justin."

He talked her into spending the night because Phil and Derek might still be around. She curled into a corner, wouldn't go near his rags. So he built a small fire and told her a story. It wasn't a very long story, but it was a true one, and she stared at him in amazement.

"When my father was a little boy, his grandpa, my great-grandpa, died. He walked up the hill by their house, lay down on the ground and just died. He always said he wanted an Indian burial, and he almost got it. By the time anyone found him, there were flocks of birds circling his body.

"A few nights later, my father had a dream about him. His grandpa was sitting on the hill where he died, watching the birds. My father said he could see right through him, down to the daisies smashed under his butt. He looked at my father and said, 'Boy, remember—don't take any wooden nickels.'"

Justin rocked back on his heels in laughter. Ann didn't know why. She just raised her eyebrows at him, startled by the noise, tired of his voice. She remembered nickels. They weren't wooden.

Justin prowled around the fire, flexing his fingers noisily, and continued. "Then my father reached out with both hands to touch him, but his hands went right through. And you know what he said it felt like? Like a whisper. His grandpa's ghost felt like a whisper. That's what he told himself in his dream, and he remembered it when he woke up."

He stopped fidgeting and looked at her then. She wouldn't look back. The story was done, so she nodded at his elbow and turned her face to the wall.

The next morning she was gone when Justin woke up. She had drunk all the water she could find. Last night Justin had put the ladder back and told her there was more where that came from.

She would be back. With food. He hoped.

She came back at nightfall with half a bird, probably a crow, already plucked and cooked for him.

He gave her two cups of water. She drank one immediately and poured the other into a container she'd brought.

"You tell me where you get the water," Ann said, "And I'll tell you how to get food. We won't have to—"

"No way."

She shrugged and climbed out.

"Wait, you can stay! I have another story . . . "

She didn't even turn around.

The next night he was ready for her. She came down with the same offering, drank her water and turned to leave.

Now there was a knife at her throat.

"Annie Ann, I just want you to stay here with me."

"Don't!"

"I won't hurt you, I swear. I won't touch you."

"Justin, put the knife down."

"I just want you to stay here. I just . . . "

"Justin . . . "

"I can't spend another night alone."

"You don't need the knife."

He blinked at her. He lowered the knife slowly, and she pushed past him back inside. He closed the knife and put it in his pocket sheepishly.

She lay down on his pile of rags, spreading it thinner to give them more room. He ate his bird in a few bites and lay down next to her, face to face.

"Don't touch me," she whispered.

"I won't."

But he stretched his legs out and touched the tops of his bare feet to the bottoms of hers. It made her smile. He left them there and she laughed.

They were only feet, after all.

That became their routine. She brought food—usually a crow, sometimes smaller birds with no meat on them. They cooked it there together. Then they would lie down, feet and noses touching. Her eyes began to turn blue again. Justin wished he could drink from them. He would tell her a story and they would fall asleep feeling something like contentment.

How did you survive it all?

I had people at first, people I loved.

What happened to them?

Died, of course. Don't ask me how. I don't remember.

And then?

Then I forgot I was alive and just kept going. How about you?

Lucky, mostly.

Hmm.

I watched you.

I knew.

What are we going to do?

What we've always done.

We can start a family.

We are dying.

But if we have a family . . .

We can't. Trust me, we can't. I can't.

Never?

Not ever.

We are dying.

On the ninth day she didn't show up. It was way past nightfall, and Justin was worried. She'd never said she would come every day, but she never said she wouldn't either.

He didn't usually go out after nightfall. He took both his knives and tied a rope around his waist.

He thought about heading to the warehouse where she used to sleep, but decided to go to Phil and Derek's place first. Once he decided, he started to run.

They had her there. She didn't scream, didn't do anything. They didn't hear him come in. Their cave, a corner of a brick building, was lit by a dim, smoky, foul-smelling fire. Justin climbed onto a window ledge and stood there a moment, blue-black smoke curling around his ankles.

When they looked up and saw him, Phil laughed. Phil was dirty and small, with tiny round eyes. Justin flinched, remembering how fast he could move.

Derek sneered and walked toward him. "Bring us some food this time?"

Justin kicked him in the face. He jumped from the window ledge with knife in hand and buried it in Derek's pitifully thin chest. The tip of it stuck out of his spine and blood ran down his legs. His ribcage split open like an overcooked crow.

By the time Derek's body hit the floor, Phil was gone. Ann wrapped her arms around her bare chest and came to stand next to him. They looked at Derek's body and Justin knew they were thinking the same thing.

What a waste.

So hungry.

She started to cry then. That made him feel better; he didn't know why. He pulled his shirt off and had it over her head before she could even protest.

"You'll get cold."

"Not if you sleep next to me."

"He's still out there," she whispered.

"We'll hide."

"He'll find us."

"I'll kill him."

Justin wrenched his knife out of Derek's body. By morning the corpse would be picked clean and Phil would be stronger.

They ran. They ran to a place Justin knew that was deep and safe. The place he got the water.

She was crying harder now. She held her face under the dripping water, let it run into her eyes and ears.

"No one will hurt you now, Annie Ann. I'd kill for you."

"You did."

"I'll stab them all. I'll kill everyone who comes near you."

"I know."

"Everyone will die."

She wrapped her arms around his waist tightly, until she could touch her own shoulders again. Then she stood on her toes and kissed him on his mouth, his cheeks, his chin.

He closed his eyes and let her lips like rain but better patter down on his face.

The next morning she was gone. In her place was a net, frayed and dirty. It was how she caught the birds. He thought that she had given him this because he'd shown her where to get water.

Then he saw his shirt, the one she'd been wearing. Next to that her pants and her knife and her water pail.

Justin gathered her net in his arms and slung it over his shoulder. He went to look for her. He did not run.

There was a canyon north of where the water was. The ground had simply split open one day, long ago, spewing cool, muddy air into the world.

The bottom was filled with bones—bird bones, people bones, and way at the bottom, creature bones. Her bones were on top.

She was broken, bloody, unmoving. The crows had found her already, were fighting over her desiccated organs. Annie Ann was dead, a corpse. And an ugly one at that.

Justin unslung the net from his shoulder. The movement startled some of the birds, drew them near him. He could get his own food now.

The biggest of the crows hopped right up to his feet, focused its tiny round eyes on him.

"Whisper," he said to it.

It squawked and hopped closer. It would not whisper.

Justin shook his head at it, disappointed. He threw the net into the canyon with Annie Ann, then lay down and watched the sky.

Man Alone
by Drew Arrants

Martin sat in the crowded nightclub, listening to the loud band and the drone of nonstop conversation from the people around him. Glancing around the room, he recognized many of his fellow patrons. He was a regular at that establishment, and so were they.

He was one of the very few people sitting by himself, and he felt bored and depressed in the midst of all the chatter and laughter. His mood gradually hardened into hostility, and he decided that he'd had enough of that crowd for the night.

"Screw this place," he mumbled. He stood up abruptly and headed for the door. "What a hokey way for a club to make itself look popular."

It was well after midnight, but he wasn't at all tired as he walked the half block from the nightclub to the hotel where he lived.

After entering his suite, Martin flipped through the many available television channels, but none of them appealed to him. So he switched off the television and picked up the phone.

"Yeah," he replied to the digitalized voice that answered his call. "Send one of your girls up here in about 30 minutes . . . oh, I don't really care . . . Suzy sounds fine." He didn't do that very often, but tonight he felt more in need of company than usual.

Martin's refrigerator was almost empty, and he was out of whiskey as well. That wouldn't do, now that he had a date for the night. He could have ordered snacks and drinks through the automated room service, but decided to go to the store instead.

"This neighborhood is really a dump," he muttered, as he walked through the seedy back streets. He looked at the potholes in the roadway, then at the wind-blown refuse that had been allowed to accumulate in the gutter.

"I don't know why I don't move uptown, now that I can," he thought. He knew why, of course. Martin had lived in this locale before the war, and it seemed more like home to him than any place else.

The streetlights provided only minimal illumination along the sidewalk, and each alley that he passed looked as black to him as the grave. Once he would have worried about muggers waiting in those dark recesses. Now that no longer concerned him.

He strolled past a sleazy strip joint that was disturbing the night with the loud sound of bad music. As he went by the door, a woman in a low-cut red dress stepped out and looked toward him.

"Hey, handsome," she said. "C'mon in. We've got what you're looking for in here."

Martin looked over her shoulder into the bar area. He could see a young girl dancing on the stage, slowly removing her clothes. The cheap nightspot had managed to attract only two patrons. One was slumped forward in his front-row seat, resting his head and arms against the stage as if he were drunk. The other was an old man in a dark corner, who had fallen asleep and now leaned against the wall.

Martin glanced back at the woman in red. "Lively clientele you have here," he said with a chuckle. Then he moved closer to her and looked directly into her eyes. "You must be getting worn out, honey," he said. "It isn't hard to see right through you."

She made no reply as he turned and continued on his way down the street.

A few minutes later he had reached his destination, an all-night convenience store. There were no other customers inside, and like all of the 24-hour shops that had been built in the past decade, it had no attendant. So Martin had the place to himself.

He went over to the liquor booth and made his selection, sliding his credit card through the slot to release a bottle of Scotch whiskey. Then he purchased cold cuts and bread by the same method.

Walking back to the hotel, Martin took an alternate route along the dark streets. He stepped around several homeless people who had stretched out over the hot-air vents in the sidewalk, trying to find some warmth against the chilly night.

Then he cut across the back lot of a large department store, ignoring the prominent sign that read: "WARNING! GUARD DOG PRESENT! DO NOT ENTER!"

He was about one-third the way across the lot when he heard angry barking behind him. A large, vicious-looking German shepherd was running in his direction. The dog stopped right in front of him, baring its fangs and growling.

Martin snickered and resumed his leisurely gait. The animal began running around him, lunging and snapping at his legs and then backing off, never quite touching his body. When Martin reached the far corner of the property and stepped back onto the sidewalk, the dog did not follow.

Back in his small suite, he opened the bottle of Scotch and mixed a strong drink. "But not too strong," he cautioned himself. "Don't forget, you have company coming."

As he hummed along with the music coming from the living room, he heard the sound of a door opening and closing. When he walked out of the kitchen, there was a girl standing in front of the entertainment center.

"Hello, baby," Martin said, trying to get into a receptive mood. "I heard you come in. Care for a drink?"

"Hello, there," said the girl in a low, sensual voice, ignoring his offer. "My name is Suzy, and I've got a special treat for you tonight."

Suzy was an attractive young woman, with a dark complexion and dark eyes and hair that had been incongruously dyed blonde. Her slender but well-developed figure barely fit into her clothes. She was wearing a white sweater, a red blouse, and a black leather skirt above red high heels.

Martin took a drink while Suzy winked at him and unzipped her sweater, pulling it back and off over her shoulders. He smiled at the ample cleavage that her partially opened blouse revealed.

"I normally don't do this sort of thing with strangers," Suzy said coyly, "but you're so attractive that I just can't resist." She began unbuttoning her blouse.

"Would you like to hear about what I did in the war, Suzy?" Martin asked. She turned her back to him as she took off the red blouse.

"No, I didn't think so," he sighed, "but I'm going to tell you, anyway."

"We're going to have lots of fun tonight." Suzy said, facing him again. The black lace bra that she was wearing hid very little of her full breasts.

Martin took another sip of the Scotch. "That's fine, baby, but don't interrupt while I talk. That music is a bit noisy, don't you think?"

He aimed the remote control unit at the entertainment center and lowered the volume until the sound was barely audible.

"Anyway, I was a shuttle pilot, so I missed almost all of the combat. That's why I survived without getting my ass blown off, I guess."

Suzy started to speak, but Martin held his finger to his lips. "Sssssshhh. I need to talk more than you do, honey. You just listen for a while.

"I was in my transport shuttle, bringing back a load of minerals from the refinery on Titan, when the big blowup finally came. My copilot Jerry had gotten sick from drinking too much at the canteen. Ol' Jerry always did like his booze—besides, he was still grieving for his wife, you know. So I left him in the dispensary there and headed back to earth alone."

Suzy dropped her bra to the floor and slipped out of her skirt, paying no attention to what Martin was saying.

"Lord, Suzy, I wouldn't have left Jerry there, but the Titan station still had enough oxygen and supplies for two weeks—and they were supposed to get restocked from earth in ten days—" His voice revealed a trace of guilt.

"How'd I know the goddamn war was going to be over when I got back to earth?"

Suzy had slipped her last stocking off her right ankle and was now completely naked, smiling and caressing her body. She held out her arms toward Martin. He looked at the nude girl and wished that he could feel aroused, but he didn't.

"Too bad you aren't wearing any perfume, baby," he said. "I bet you'd smell real good. Yeah—that might turn me on."

Instead, he thought of his old girlfriend Jeannie, who lived in the distant suburbs with her little daughter. Jeannie didn't have Suzy's artificially enhanced figure, but at least Jeannie would listen to him when he talked, and actually care about what he had to say. Perhaps, Martin thought, it was time to pay her another visit.

He pressed a button on the remote control unit and turned the music completely off. Then he walked to the door, glancing back at Suzy as he left the suite. She was standing still in the middle of the room, looking in his direction and smiling.

"Make yourself at home, honey," Martin suggested. "I'll see you when I get back."

He strolled out of the hotel and down the street toward the nearest subway entrance, several bocks away.

The alcohol and the boredom had finally made him drowsy, and Martin yawned as he stepped inside the subway car. He slumped down in the seat and dozed off.

Two hours later the train left the final tunnel at the edge of the city and rolled onto the east river trestle. A sudden rush of wind slammed into the car, rattling it and producing a loud whooshing noise.

The abrupt motion and sound jolted Martin awake. He saw that the sun was rising over the eastern bank of the river, casting a glistening reflection over the water. The car's internal lights dimmed and then switched off as their sensors reacted to the brightening sunlight.

Martin stretched and glanced around the car. Across the aisle was a young woman who had fallen asleep with her two children resting against her. The younger child, a boy, lay with his head on her lap, while his slightly older sister pressed against the woman's shoulder. To Martin, they appeared incredibly peaceful, as if together they had found escape from the chaotic world around them.

He noted that the young mother was still slender after bearing two children, still attractive. Her stylish blouse and skirt showed her to be one of the better-dressed passengers on the subway.

"Well, she obviously comes from one of the upscale boroughs," Martin thought. "Is she Jewish? Irish-Catholic, maybe, with all that red hair?" Too bad he couldn't hear her voice, since her accent would give away the neighborhood.

Martin felt the urge to relieve himself, so he walked to the restroom at the end of the car. The flag on its door read: "Occupied." There was no reason to stand there and wait for the occupant to come out—it would be a long wait—so he went on to the next car.

Twenty minutes later the train came to a halt in Jeannie's borough, its mechanical voice announcing the station to the inattentive passengers. Martin was the only one who got off.

Jeannie's house wasn't far from the station, and he reached it after a short walk in the cool spring air. Someone had carelessly left the front gate ajar, and Martin slipped past it into the yard.

He pressed his palm against the metal plate on the front door. Its electronic circuitry recognized his touch and unlocked the door, which swung open slowly.

This house was haunted. A ghostly little girl sat on the stairs in the front hallway. Martin watched as she jumped up with glee and raced into the kitchen to announce his return. The spirit of a small dog ran into the hallway, sniffed at his feet and barked silently, then disappeared.

Martin went into the kitchen, looking for another ghost. He saw her sitting at the kitchen table in her nightgown, with her brown hair still unkempt from the night before, and a smile on her pretty face. It amazed Martin how much he had once taken that smile for granted.

Then he was aware of a mechanical sound, that of an over-stressed compressor. The refrigerator door had been left partially open, and now the appliance struggled to maintain its proper internal temperature.

"Damn, how stupid of me," Martin grumbled. "Oh, well—I'm sure the food is still good." He checked the refrigerator's contents, and he was correct: nothing had spoiled. The smell of the food made him hungry, so he fixed himself an early breakfast.

As he finished eating, he glanced through the window at the two shallow graves which he had dug in the backyard. Only a few strands of grass grew over the graves, but the rest of the lawn needed its first trim of the season.

He took the lawnmower out of the garage and pressed its starter button. The machine instantly sprang to life, its antenna picking up the energy transmitted from the city's main fusion generator.

As he rode the mower over the small lawn, Martin asked himself why he felt compelled to keep returning to that empty house, let alone maintain it. Maybe it was because he had let Jeannie down so many times, always using the war as a perpetual excuse for putting off future plans, and now this was his futile way of making amends.

It was late afternoon when he left the house. This time he made sure that the refrigerator door and the front gate were properly closed. He knew that his actions were unnecessary rituals in a world where nothing decayed, and no unwelcome creatures would come wandering into the yard.

The subway back to the city arrived to pick him up on time, as it always did. Martin wondered if by chance it could be the same specific train that had brought him out to Jeanie's borough overnight. He walked up and down the cars looking for familiar faces, perhaps even the young mother and her children.

Instead, one of the cars had a more disturbing sight. An old man had fallen and struck his head against a metal seat, and he had not gotten up. Martin walked over to where he lay and noticed that his watch had smashed against the floor, freezing the moment forever in time.

"Five minutes after two," Martin said in a whisper. "So time stopped at 2:05 in the morning."

The subway left its dark tunnel and became an elevated railway as it entered the central part of the city. Martin looked out the window at the huge metropolis. It was eerily active: streetcars and computer-scheduled buses moving busily along the streets, music and other sounds associated with human existence clamoring from its shops.

From a high elevation, the city looked normal, much as it had on that fateful day he had returned from Titan. The only difference then had been the season, when a light snowfall had coated the scene.

He recalled how peaceful everything had appeared while his shuttle craft had cruised over the city, toward the military airport on its outskirts. His radio transmission had activated the control tower's automatic landing system, and its computers had brought his plane in for a flawless touchdown. But Martin had been away from earth for four months, and a great deal had happened.

The bodies at the air base, perfectly preserved, with no signs of injury and no residual radiation, had told him all that he needed to know. Apparently the scientists hadn't been so misguided when they'd warned that the new global neutron weapon systems weren't ready for deployment.

"So it happened late at night," Martin mused, "when the stores were closed and the streets were deserted, and children were asleep in their beds—or on the subway."

He wondered if the young mother and her children had been dreaming on the train that winter night. Were their dreams pleasant, or scary perhaps? Whatever—at 2:05 a.m., all the dreams had faded to black.

Now that family, like their fellow passengers, would ride the subway system forever, never stirring, never complaining about the endless journey, and taking no note of the day when Martin would no longer be among them.

As the train crossed the last overpass before heading underground to Martin's station, he viewed the familiar sights of the neighborhood. There was the strip joint where the lady in red had enticed him, and the back lot where the guard dog had threatened him so fiercely.

The lady and the dog and the noisy night club patrons were gone now, fantasy creatures of the night vanquished by the light of day. Convincing in artificial light, their image became faint in the bright sun, betraying their secret. So they were programmed to switch off at sunrise, to rise again from their electronic graves after nightfall, like the vampires of a previous dark age.

Nightfall came at the end of every day, of course, and the sky was already darkening as Martin walked up the stairs from the subway station to the street. The city that now belonged entirely to him would soon become alive again, in its own way.

Suzy was waiting patiently for Martin when he entered his suite. She was still standing in front of the entertainment center, naked and lovely, with her arms reaching in his direction.

"Hello, baby," Martin said. "You sure are pretty, but right now you don't do any more for me than all those old porno discs that Jerry always got off watching."

He went into the kitchen and made himself a drink from the Scotch. Then he sat down on the couch, looking at Suzy's motionless form.

"You know, Suzy, you really aren't very good company. I'd rather talk to Jeannie, or Jerry, or the strangers on the subway—or even the real Suzy, if she was still around. I'll bet any of them could hold my interest now, no matter what nonsense they wanted to prattle about. Yeah—nowadays I'd make a goddamn good listener."

He pressed the "resume" button on the remote control unit, and Suzy's figure once again became animated. Martin watched for a few seconds while her body swayed sensuously in front of him.

Then he pressed the "off" button.

He Would Have Given Them Wings
by Rob Haines

The nor'easter was persistent, and the clouds below were fast-moving. Kayla brought her fanwing soaring round in a wide arc to survey the storm below. The clouds were angry, red and black, orange and purple with lightning. She tracked the center of the storm by the dome of turbulence that pushed against the choking cloud cover, and her 'wing shuddered in the chaotic updraft. There appeared to be little chance of cloudbreak here, and they could no longer afford to waste either fuel or time on failed flights.

The radio crackled, and Anil's soft voice filled the cockpit. "How does it look?" he asked.

"Like your calculations were wrong," said Kayla. She tried to keep her disappointment out of her voice. Anil didn't deserve it; he was doing his best with limited resources. "I'm skimming a thunderhead as we speak."

"At a safe distance, I hope?"

Kayla smiled and scratched an itch through her tight-fitting bodysuit. "You think I was born yesterday? I handle my 'wing better than you handle your meteorographs!"

"We'll see. Hold your position." Anil broke off, and Kayla heard the rustling of papers. "Yes, it makes sense," Anil said when he returned a moment later. "The storm is the key factor. It's all in the calculations. There's a ninety-five percent chance of cloudbreak in the next thirty minutes!"

"I'll believe it when I see it."

"I've never been so sure! This is it, I know it."

Kayla hesitated, then spoke quieter. "Don't get my hopes up. Please. I can't afford it right now."

She was answered with silence. Anil had been her friend for as long as she could remember. She knew he wasn't angry, just searching for the right thing to say. He was right to show concern. The clouds looked menacing even thousands of feet below, and the updraft from the storm jostled her 'wing from side to side.

Beyond the storm the landscape of cloud stretched as far as the eye could see, an unending red blanket choking the surface of the earth. Only the highest outcrops and plateaux had survived. Only those who had fled to the high places of the world escaped the contamination that swept across the surface. Yet even those who had escaped did not live out their full span of years; the poison was already in their lungs. Kayla's grandfather had finally succumbed in a makeshift hospital in Qinghai City when she was still a toddler, crawling in the dirt and looking up at the blue sky.

"Look, Kay," Anil said, "I shouldn't be telling you this, but Psych were in here earlier asking about you. Lots of questions about your relationship with your father."

"Making sure I don't flake out?"

"They don't want to lose you," he said.

"It's the 'wing they can't afford to lose, else they wouldn't care about us at all."

"*I* don't want to lose you. If Psych are waiting for you when you get back, look surprised and act normal."

And don't tell them I warned you, she sensed in his voice. Kayla smiled to herself. Anil was over-protective; Psych would have no issue with that. Estimations of the number of operable fanwings left above the clouds ranged from forty to fifty. The last thread of hope for the human race depended on them and the Seekers who piloted them.

Two had been lost in the Americas only a month before, had disappeared beneath the clouds, never to rise again. Rescue was impractical; by the time another 'wing could be dispatched the cloudbreak would be no more, and the thick layer of cloud that hovered above the surface was as choking to a 'wing's engines as it was to human lungs.

Kayla looked up at the blue sky, reveling in her freedom as the 'wing circled above the storm. But Psych were asking about her. If they thought she was a threat to herself, to her 'wing, she would never fly again. Freedom would be a memory; she would be tethered to the plateau, her hope seeping away amongst the huddled masses.

Her father had already given in to despair. She had seen it in his face when she had visited his cramped apartment on the slopes of Qinghai City. There was a musty smell in the air when he met her at the door, as if he hadn't opened a window for months. Inside, the apartment was a mess. Half-eaten dinners grew mold on the wicker sofa. Papers were strewn across the floor. A dark-green trail from a ceiling leak had dried against the white-washed wall and the plaster had begun to crack from the moisture.

He had been so proud when he first brought his wife and daughter to see their new home. Now his wife was gone, lost to the poison that encircled the globe, and his daughter risked her life for the same cause.

Kayla had cleared the plates from the sofa and sat down opposite her father as he folded into his favorite chair, a luxurious leather affair. He looked frail, and his shoulders were slumped in defeat. They had talked, about life in Qinghai, about life in Lahdak, where the shadow of the Himalayas kept the monsoon rains from damaging the precious fanwings. They had talked about Kayla's mother.

Then they had argued, a bitter, hateful argument which had left Kayla in tears as she returned to her 'wing to begin the flight back to Lahdak. She could not deny the truth of his words; sooner or later her role as a Seeker would get her killed, but how could she live without hope, without at least trying to secure a future for the human race?

An insistent beeping filled the cockpit as one of the cameras mounted to the underside of her 'wing caught a glimpse of the scorched earth beneath the clouds. She tilted the wing and scanned the deep-red clouds around the storm with a practiced eye. False alarms were not uncommon. The clouds shifted continually, and the briefest sighting of the earth beneath was enough for the cameras. She needed visual confirmation before cloudbreak was confirmed.

The radio crackled, but Anil's voice was drowned by the blaring alarm. Kayla let go of the yoke with one hand and scrabbled under the console. With the click of a switch the alarm faded to a background tone.

"Repeat, Control," she said.

"What have we got?" Anil asked. Kayla couldn't help but crack a smile at the excitement in his voice.

"No visual yet. The cameras have spotted something, and I'm eyeballing as we speak."

Then she saw it. At the tail-end of the storm, the spiraling winds had torn a patch of cloud apart from its kin. For the first time in five months of searching, Kayla saw the surface.

"We have cloudbreak!" she exclaimed. Anil's whoop of delight came from the speaker as the 'wing wheeled and plunged towards the gap.

"Size?"

"Ten, maybe twelve meters. What's my estimate?"

Silence. The cloudbreak blossomed into a halo of reds and purples. Streaks of lightning lit the funnel through the thickest layer of cloud.

"Anil?" she asked.

"Fifteen, maybe twenty minutes at most. Don't overstay your welcome!"

She checked her watch. "I'll report back in twenty-five," she said. The clouds reared up all around, and Anil's voice broke into endless static. She was on her own. Her 'wing bucked wildly as it fought against the turbulence at the heart of the funnel of clear air, and the scent of sulphur filled her nostrils. Anil had assured her again and again that it was impossible, that the fanwing's cockpit was fully airtight, yet each time she broke through the clouds she swore the smell was real. Just her mind playing tricks, Anil said. Psych would love to get their hands on that little insecurity, so she kept it to herself.

Then she was through. The solid red banks of cloud rose away behind her as she regained control of the 'wing and skewed right to avoid a jagged spire of rock which reached for the cloudbreak and the promise of blue sky beyond. The clouds were above her now; her stomach swam with a moment's disorientation, but she blinked and brought herself under control. No matter how many times she visited the surface, the way the clouds loomed overhead still seemed like an inversion of the natural order of things.

The worst of the pollution, the most toxic band of the poison that encircled the world, was concentrated at the boundary between the cloud and the blue sky. Once she reached the surface her suit would provide adequate protection as long as the weather held out. The suit was uncomfortable. It itched in all the wrong places, and she sweated copiously at the slightest exertion. The boots were heavy with thick soles to protect her from the acids that seeped from the soil after rainfall. Yet it gave her a chance, and by extension, offered humanity hope. Perhaps not enough, but it was a start.

The 'wing had settled into a gentle glide towards the surface, its cameras once again scanning the barren earth below for any sign of the relics of human existence; the metal structures and air-tight stores of the old world gave the best chance of finding anything uncorrupted in this contaminated wasteland. At altitude the air was tinged with crimson particles, but visibility increased as she descended. The cloudbreak was a pinprick of blue above her head.

The console emitted a sharp series of beeps as the cameras picked up the stark rectangular outline of a metal building, and Kayla took the controls to bring the 'wing in to land nearby. The aircraft settled with a puff of dust, and the fans that drove air across its wings wound down. Finally there was silence. Dead quiet. She fingered the canopy release, and the hiss of escaping air made her start. Her eyes watered behind her eyeshield and again her nostrils picked up the sulphurous scent of the desolation all around.

Scrambling down the side of her 'wing, she took in her surroundings. There was dark soil beneath her feet, cast blood-red by the dim light that eked through the clouds. The soil was powdery, and particles scudded with the wind across the earth. A low stone wall to Kayla's left had caught the windblown soil and formed a dune, but the acidic rain had eroded even the last relics of human habitation. The surfaces of the stones were worn and pitted, and the wall was encrusted with translucent crimson, the poison which had contaminated the surface world.

Beyond the wall, a purple expanse of water stretched as far as she could see into the gloom. She dismissed it without further consideration. The sulphur in the clouds had turned the surface waters of every water source below ten thousand feet to acid. There was little chance that life had adapted, and even if it had, it would be a one-way street. Such organisms could no more live above the clouds than Kayla could live below them.

In the other direction, dunes of blackened ash and rolling brown hills stretched before her, devoid of life, until they faded into the red mist that cloaked the surface. A corrugated metal barn perched atop the nearest hill, brooding over the bleak slopes. The silence was disorienting. Seekers were trained to deal with sensory deprivation, but it still took Kayla's breath away every time.

The canopy of the 'wing swung closed behind her and expelled the contaminated air within with a loud exhalation that seemed to echo across the landscape. The cockpit's systems would be protected, but Kayla's suit and ventilator would remain in place until she reached the sterilization facilities back at Lahdak base. The risk of contamination was too great.

She glanced up at the cloudbreak for reassurance. The sun was high beyond the clouds, and a beam of white light shone down through the break. It was almost tangible in the gloom. Where it reached the earth it shone a pale pink, already corrupted by the particles in the atmosphere, but the radiance that shone from the ground gave Kayla renewed hope. Confident in Anil's estimate, she headed for the barn.

It rose above her as she struggled up the dry slope. She forced herself to resist the urge to scramble upslope on hands and knees. If the passing storm had rained here, the acids in the soil would tear her suit apart.

The metal of the barn had resisted the sulphurous rains well, yet it was coated in a near-invisible sheen of poison. The oversized doors lay open on the far side of the building. It was both a blessing and a curse; access would have been near-impossible if the barn was still sealed, but the chances of uncontaminated material surviving inside dropped dramatically once exposed to the environment.

She slipped inside, careful to skirt clear of the edges of the doors. Her eyes adjusted rapidly to the gloom. Rusted metal tools hung inside the door, and a large piece of farm machinery leaned askew to the left. To the right, plastic and burlap sacks were piled against the wall. Kayla's heart leapt before she could catch herself.

It had been a Seeker who discovered TQ149, a strain of barley resistant to contamination, in the low foothills of the Qinghai plateau. It had given the human race seventeen years of good harvests, an end to the threat of starvation that had loomed overhead as the indigenous high-altitude crops fell one by one to contamination and disease. But yields of TQ149 were falling, and the entire crop on the Andean Altiplano had been wiped out by a virus the previous year. Only a combined relief effort on the part of the Seekers of Lahdak and Colorado had prevented the loss of the second largest population center on the planet.

The contents of the burlap sacks would already be contaminated, so Kayla pushed them aside and knelt beside a plastic sack of seeds. The sack was clearly marked, but still she hesitated. Perhaps the contents would not grow at altitude, or perhaps they would fall prey to the same diseases that stalked TQ149. There was no way of knowing unless she tried. As she reached for the sack, a glint of light caught the white plastic. It shone crimson for a brief moment, the surface slick with liquid. Kayla withdrew her hand sharply and nudged the sack with the sole of her boot. It teetered over, spilling purple liquid from unseen degradations in the plastic. She leapt back to avoid the growing pool of contaminant. The light caught a trickle of droplets as they seeped through the corner of the roof and ran down the inner wall of the barn to ooze through the plastic sacking. There was no hope here, no salvation. This was a place of death and contamination.

Despondent, Kayla turned to leave. Silhouetted in the doorway against the crimson gloom was a small black shape she hadn't noticed on her way in.

Then it moved. Large green eyes opened and observed her. She froze. Every Seeker knew that no living thing could have survived beneath the clouds, yet this *creature* sat in the doorway and watched her intently. It opened its mouth and snarled, then it was gone.

She reached the door a moment later. There was no sign of the creature. The hillsides of the ruined world spread out before her, gently sloping towards a far-away ocean. On a nearby hill-top a copse of decaying tree trunks stretched for the sky, skeletal in bleached white with flecks of scarlet gore. The clouds rolled overhead and seethed wildly.

On instinct Kayla glanced up at the cloudbreak. Blue sky still shone through but the sunbeam was gone, swallowed in turbulence. Soon the spiraling forces that held the funnel open would collapse. The surface world would again be sealed from the blue sky. But she could not bring herself to leave the enigma of the creature without further investigation.

She checked her watch, visible against her wrist through a clear window in her suit. Her descent had taken a matter of minutes. The barn had quickly proven to be a disappointment and if Anil's estimate was correct she still had a margin of five to ten minutes before she needed to be airborne again. Her father would have told her to cut her losses and run, that the narrow escape in the barn proved it was too dangerous, that she should give up her vocation and live out her days in the safety of Qinghai. Perhaps Psych were right, and she was putting herself in danger to prove her father wrong, but it was his imagined disapproval that made up her mind.

She scanned the hillside, but the barren soils were deserted. Only the wind broke the silence. If the creature was nearby it was expertly camouflaged. The shattered trees beckoned. The slope was powdery beneath Kayla's feet, and she picked her way towards the remains of the copse with care.

The trees were an eerie sight, a vivid reminder of the life that once must have flourished so verdantly across the hillsides. Stripped of leaf and fruit, branch and bark, they rose like grasping fingers from the soil as if clawing at the clouds that obscured the bright sun. Yet even these relics were marred by the poison that filled the atmosphere. Seekers had died trying to take samples from such dead trunks, unaware of the concentration of acids and poisons gathered in the wood.

Kayla kept a safe distance as she walked through the copse, scanning her surroundings for the creature. Her ventilator rattled as she let out a deep breath. The creature could be anywhere. She had to consider the possibility that it was never there at all, just a figment of her imagination brought on by the stress of facing such devastation. Perhaps she wanted so dearly to find life, to find hope for the people of the plateaux, that she had imagined the impossible. She could find no solace in flights of fancy. The mission was a failure, another cloudbreak without reward. Again she would return to her friends, to her father, with nothing to show for her efforts. Perhaps he was right after all.

She reached the far side of the copse. The ground dipped away sharply, and more skeletal fingers rose from the opposite hillside. There was a new scent in the air, and she let out a gasp as she stepped forward. Before her lay a valley of death, of bleached trunks, of dead and decaying vegetation. Fallen trees lay parallel to the ground, supported by their kin, while the remains of unfamiliar plants created a mat of detritus over the barren soil. At the bottom of the valley, there was a flash of purple and green, a circle of what looked like living vegetation, low-lying and scrubby, but alive. As she gaped, her eyes caught a glimpse of motion on the downslope. It was her imaginary creature again, she was certain, or maybe another of its kind.

Caution and training kept her from charging down the slope into the litter of the valley, and as she half-slid, half-crept her way through the outer reaches of the dying garden she spotted the creature again for a brief moment. It was a bit less than half a meter tall, no larger than the domesticated creatures kept as pets before the clouds had covered the surface, and it moved with the predatory grace of a hunter. Its fur was jet-black, and as she watched it flitted into the shadows and vanished.

Her Seeker training reasserted itself with a jolt. The creature was impossible, incredible, a discovery beyond her wildest dreams, but investigation of the teasing glimpse of vegetation was her duty. She could bring back word of the creature and offer the hope that the world below the clouds was not entirely barren, perhaps the dream that with enough vegetation filtering the air, one day the clouds would dissipate and humankind could climb down from the mountaintops and reclaim their home. But she was a Seeker. She was running out of time, and if her imaginings were to come true, her task was to ensure that the human race survived long enough to see that day.

The cloudbreak was barely visible now, but the glimpse of blue gave her strength. Five minutes was enough, then she would return to her 'wing and retake the skies.

It wasn't until she approached the vegetation that she noticed something odd in the air. There were no particles floating within, no glimpses of the red that speckled the dead trunks, no slow fade over distance into crimson fog. The air was clear, uncontaminated. It seemed to gather in a protective dome stretching over a patch of vegetation fifteen or twenty meters across. A gurgling rumble shook the valley, and Kayla took a step back as a plume of clear gas erupted from a rocky spire in the center of the patch. The plume split into bubbles as it spread out through the contaminated air, and each bubble floated down to join the dome. The strange plants within raised their leaves towards the sky as the dome expanded.

The species were unfamiliar, most probably mutations brought on by the harsh environment. With the greatest of care Kayla stepped into the dome and knelt beside the plants. They reminded her of the barley grown in Qinghai, but with an extended canopy of waxy leaves that stretched above the husk. Perhaps they were contaminated, or poisonous, or would die as soon as they reached altitude. Or perhaps they were resistant. Even if they were unsuitable as food, perhaps their resistance could be interbred into existing cereal crops. It was too good an opportunity to waste.

A guttural bark came from behind her, and she spun round. The creature stood behind her with hackles raised. It lowered its head and repeated the noise; on second hearing it was more of a cough than a bark. It reminded her of the coughing fits of the patients in the hospital in Qinghai when she had said goodbye to her grandfather. The creature stretched its neck, and a row of purple gills flashed for a brief moment.

As reluctant as she was to turn her back on the creature, there was no time to waste. She retrieved a roll of sample bags from one of the pockets in her suit, and a sturdy pair of forceps from another. The stems of the plants seemed to be free from contaminant, so she nudged the larger plants aside and pulled some seedlings from the ground. They had little anchorage in the dusty soil, and within minutes she had fifteen samples stored in the pockets running down the legs of her suit. The lab technicians back in Lahdak would perform the analysis; all Kayla had to do was get the samples to them.

Satisfied, she turned around to locate the creature again. It was gone. Lightning flashed in the distance, and a low vibration shook the earth. The visibility beyond the dome had closed in while she'd been working, as if the contaminant itself was affronted by this haven of life in its midst. Thick red fog coated the landscape, and Kayla could barely see the broken tree trunks atop the hill standing stark and white against the choking atmosphere.

It was not far back to her 'wing. Her suit would protect her from the atmosphere, and she had no more time to waste. The cloudbreak would not hold much longer. Checking that her samples were tightly secured, she took a deep breath and advanced into the murk.

She reached the copse and set out for the barn, but no matter how hard she strained her eyes, no matter how many times she trudged up the hills that she swore she had come down, the stark outline of the barn eluded her. Overhead the stormclouds swirled, and the cloudbreak was lost to sight. It had to be there, it had to be open. She hadn't been on the surface that long. But the fog was suffocating, impenetrable. She stumbled onwards with increasing desperation, hands held out in front of her to shield her from the wind as it rose to a howl.

Don't go. Her father's words rang in her ears. He had pleaded, had begged. *Don't leave me here.* All alone. He would be alone now. The surface world had claimed her, and it would never let her go.

She shook off the panic that rose within her. There was still hope, if only she could find her 'wing.

It's hopeless, cried her father. *You should have stayed here, where it's safe.*

No. Those weren't the words. *Stay here,* he had said, *where it's safe.* To protect her, not to judge. Her imagination was doing the judging.

So I can watch everyone around me lose hope when the crops fail? She had yelled at him. Their last conversation had ended with anger and tears. *So I can lose hope along with them?*

So you're going to leave me, just like your mother did? Always chasing hope! It was hopeless. He was right. At least Mother had made it home, riddled with contaminant, to tell of her failure.

An image sprang to Kayla's mind, of Anil sitting in his cramped control-room, waiting desperately by the radio to hear her voice again. He would wait forever, she had no doubt. There would be no rescue, no recovery. Finally, Anil would mourn her. The last strands of near-invisible hope that held her father from total despair would fray and snap.

Then the ash and soil slipped away beneath her feet as she clambered down a slope, praying that it was the right direction. Her balance failed her in the disorientating gloom and she crashed to her back. Her skin tingled instinctively, waiting for the acids in the soil to break through her suit, for the inrush of ice-cold contaminated air that had killed her mother. Her luck held; the soil was dry.

There's always hope, Father.

That's what your mother said. That's what killed her.

Kayla took a deep breath, her ventilator rattling loudly in the solitude, and raised herself to her knees. Her legs were shaky. She leant forward on her hands and gathered herself. The valley was a distant memory now. The barn was her best chance, but the visibility was so poor that she could have walked right past it in the fog. She thought of her 'wing, trapped in the darkness. At least the fog still seemed considerably less dense than the cloud layer. The 'wing would still fly, as long as the funnel through the clouds was still open.

There was movement to her left. She sat back on her haunches and peered into the fog. Nothing. Then a shadow appeared at the edge of her vision. It let out a hacking cough, shook its head convulsively and advanced towards her. It hesitated just beyond her reach and looked up at her with its slitted green eyes. She stretched out her hand, and the creature scrambled backwards to maintain the distance between them. It tilted its head to one side and studied her. She held still, not wishing to alarm it.

Without warning, it turned and ran into the fog. As quickly as the creature had come, it was gone, leaving Kayla squatting amidst the storm. She could see no more than ten feet in front of her before the red mist obscured the way, and she had no landmarks to guide her. There was nothing to do but to keep on walking, to trust that she would stumble across her 'wing. In her heart she knew that it was over. The desolation had claimed her.

Shakily she rose to her feet, but she had barely taken three steps down the slope when there was a tug on the leg of her suit. She froze, terrified to move in case the material tore, and glanced down. The creature stood behind her, its teeth hooked into the tough fabric of her suit. She reached down with her hand, and it let go and leapt away, but as she took another step forward, it launched itself at her leg again. She swiped at the creature. It released her leg, but hesitated, holding her gaze with its own. Then it ran towards the fog behind her.

The creature stopped at the edge of her vision and turned to look back at her. Then it was gone again. A thought struck Kayla as she watched it go. She had first seen it at the barn; perhaps it knew the way back. With nothing left to lose, she turned and followed her guide into the darkness.

There was little doubt that the creature was guiding her. Whenever she lost sight of its shadow in the fog, it would appear again, as if beckoning her on. Twice she caught up with it as it burst into fits of full-throated coughing, flinging its head from side to side, bright-purple gills flashing. Perhaps it was like the plants, mutated to live in the clear gas from beneath the earth. The field of dead and dying vegetation was testament to the fading influence of the creature's habitat.

Kayla brushed the red dust from her sleeve and glanced at her watch. She felt as if she had wandered in the fog for hours, but unless the watch had been affected by her fall, it was less than half an hour since she had last spoken to Anil. Still the creature led her on.

And then a familiar silhouette loomed out of the darkness, and her heart leapt. Already the metallic surface of her 'wing was coated in red dust. It would need to be cleansed on her return, or the poison would corrode the structure of the aircraft. Once the fanwings were gone, the Seekers would be useless, condemned to sit and watch with the rest of humanity as their kin faded into oblivion.

The creature sat on the wingtip, looking down at her. It coughed again, and closed its eyes. Kayla was already clambering up the side of the cockpit, and the hiss of air as the canopy rose gave her tired legs new strength. She slid into her seat, and reached for the canopy controls.

There was a flash of black, and a heavy weight landed on her stomach. She lashed out in panic and the creature leapt down onto the floor of the cockpit, where it vanished from view. The sound of coughing came from beneath her seat, but there was no time to expel the creature if she was to escape the clouds. The canopy settled into place, and the contaminated air was expelled. The 'wing leapt from the ground as its fans engaged, and accelerated rapidly towards the location of the cloudbreak.

Streamers of cloud obscured the funnel, and the blue sky above was no more than a pin-prick as the fanwing zigzagged skywards. The fans groaned with the weight of red dust as they stretched to breaking point. Beneath her, the creature yowled uncomfortably as it was thrown from side to side by the turbulence. A shudder ran through the fans as the aircraft reached the remains of the funnel.

They burst through at high speed, streaking vertically into the blue sky. The fans spluttered, and one by one, died. The 'wing hung in midair as it slowed, then stalled. Kayla cursed and hammered the fan starter switch on the console. The engines revved in the body of the plane with each push. The nose of the fanwing dropped, and the deep-red clouds filled her vision.

In desperation she yanked out the choke, flooding the engines with fuel. She stabbed at the switch. The engines revved, and the fans roared into life. Not all of them, but enough. The 'wing bucked in the updraft, then stabilized.

"Kay!" Anil's voice crackled into life. "Is that you?"

"I'm here," she said. She took a deep breath, her ventilator rattling. She swore she could smell the freshness of the blue sky.

"You were gone too long. I thought you . . . "

She cut through his awkwardness. "I'm going to need a full decontamination unit on arrival. The 'wing's a bit battered, but I'm okay."

"I'll make sure it's waiting for you," he said as his voice recovered. "What happened down there?"

"I'll tell you all about it when we've cleaned up." The creature yowled softly and nuzzled the leg of her suit. Decontamination would be unpleasant, but the creature would survive, and she hoped it would adapt to the thin air of the plateau. There would be no return to the surface, no going back to the bubble of life amidst the wasteland. The cloudbreak was gone.

Kayla checked her pockets; the samples were safe. Perhaps they would bring hope to the people of Qinghai, of Lahdak, of the Altiplano, to the human race eking out their existence on the edge of the sky.

After the Storm

Tracie McBride

Kirsten kicked up purple dust as she trudged across the alien plain. The dust irritated her skin, and she scratched absentmindedly at an open sore on her ankle with the long sharpened stick she carried. She stopped for a moment and looked around her, as if she were standing at a crossroads and must decide which direction to take. It was a pointless gesture; except for the occasional squat, fleshy-leaved shrub, the vista was equally featureless no matter which way she looked. She spotted a flurry of movement and froze as a small furry animal made a break from the cover of a shrub and dashed in front of her. Almost without thinking, she speared it through its side.

The Denvali had a name for the creature, but Kirsten could not pronounce it, so she had called it a pussum. It was mangy and malnourished (much like me, she thought), and its three bulbous eyes rolled in agony as it writhed on the end of her spear and uttered its distinctive breathy squeal. She grimaced as she ended its misery with a quick, savage stomp on its head.

In death, with its eyes sealed shut, it resembled more than ever the pet cat she had as a child on Earth. There was a time when she would have sooner cut off her own arm than harm an innocent being, but it seemed all her principles had been swept away by her instinct to survive. She stooped to stroke its wiry grey fur, then jerked her hand away when she saw the vermin swarming over its body. Suppressing her revulsion, she deftly skinned the pussum, then skewered it end to end on her spear. She stripped the leaves from the branches of a nearby shrub and sucked the moisture from them while she lit a fire and constructed a makeshift spit for her dinner. The creature's flesh charred over the fitful bluish flame.

"Hey!"

Kirsten jumped up and looked around her for the source of the voice, her heart hammering wildly.

"Hey!" A man waved at her, both arms raised over his head as if he were signaling her from a great distance, when in fact he was only thirty-odd meters away. He trotted towards her, a huge grin illuminating his unremarkable face.

"Am I glad to see you!" the man exclaimed. "I was beginning to think I was the only one left alive." He grabbed her right hand and pumped it. "My name's Ben." He smiled intently at her, still shaking her hand, and it took a second or two for her to realize that he was waiting for a response.

"Kirsten," she said. Her voice sounded gruff and strained. She couldn't remember when she last spoke out loud. She looked down at Ben's hand, still holding hers. It was clean, pale-skinned and plump. His clothes looked freshly laundered. She pulled her hand away and took a step backward.

Ben glanced from her to the roasting pussum to the plain around them and back to her. "Are you out here on your own, Kirsten? Did any of your people survive?"

"Dead," she said. She squatted to attend to the fire. "All the Denvali are dead."

Ben's smile froze. "I meant the humans in your party," he said.

Kirsten shook her head, partly to answer his question and partly to reprimand herself. She had been criticized more than once by her superiors for becoming too attached to the subjects she observed, and the Denvali's peculiar culture of joyful pacifism had endeared them to her more than any others. She wasn't ready to openly admit to a stranger that she mourned their passing more than that of her colleagues.

Ben nodded in sympathy, misinterpreting her silence for grief. "There were four of us in our bunker," he said. "Samantha got stung by one of those scorpion-mice thingies, Faye got sick—I don't know what from—" his eyes slid sideways, and Kirsten wondered at the reason for the obvious lie, "and Ian just went out one day a week ago and never came back." He gestured toward Kirsten's spit. "Fresh meat," he said. "That must have been a lucky find. What is it?"

She picked up the pussum's bloody pelt on the end of her knife and waved it at him. His face blanched, and his hands fluttered to cover his mouth in an oddly feminine gesture. When he finally lowered his hands, his expression was thoughtful and pitying. "How long have you been living like this?" he asked softly.

Kirsten ran her fingertips over the grooves cut into the handle of her spear. She had started to record the days that had passed since the bomb hit, but had lost heart for the exercise when she passed the fourth month. She shrugged and looked up at Ben.

"Why were you in a bunker?" she said. Her manic blue-eyed stare made her seem more animal than human at that moment, tensed ready to spring at his throat if he made a false move.

"Come with me," he said. "I have food—mostly dehydrated or tinned, but it's better than roast alien. I'll fill you in with what I know."

Ben had a hoverbike. It was designed to be a one-person craft, but Kirsten could just fit if she straddled the battery housing and molded her body, chest to back and thigh to thigh, against his. He kept up a running commentary as they rode, like a tour guide. His constant stream of chatter, coupled with the strained buzz of the overtaxed engine, had a curiously hypnotic affect on her, and she relaxed into the journey, eyes half-closed, barely registering his words or her surroundings.

"See that round, grey patch on the ground? That's a Denvali water sink. There's enough potable water in there to keep five hundred humans alive for two years. Which is lucky for us, because it could take several months for the rescue party to get here," he said. "And over there on the right is where we found our first living thing after the storm—it was a Denvali, but it was too badly injured to survive."

Kirsten tensed. Something in what he had just said unsettled her. Before she could ask him to repeat himself, he braked to a stop, and the moment was lost.

It looked like any other stretch of desert, but Ben took a keypad from his pocket and keyed in a sequence of numbers. A panel slid noiselessly open to reveal a long, well lit flight of stairs. They descended a few steps, and he turned to close the door behind them with another push of a button. Another sequence of numbers opened a door at the bottom of the stairs.

"Welcome to my humble abode," he said, ushering her in with a mock bow.

The room was large and utilitarian. A kitchen took up one wall and four spartan single beds inadequately partitioned from each other clustered against another wall. The rest of the space housed a couple of comfortable-looking sofas, a small dining table and a well-stocked bookcase. Ben sang to himself as he pulled a couple of boxes in plain khaki-colored packaging from a kitchen cupboard and threw them into a microwave.

"There's a bathroom through there." Ben nodded towards two doors next to the kitchen. "You're welcome to have a shower, but be warned—the hot water supply is pitiful, so you'll only have ten minutes tops. I'll dig out some of Samantha's clothes for you. You look about the same size."

Kirsten tried the first door. It was locked.

"No, not that one," he said. "That's just a store room." Again, a sideways glance, thought Kirsten. What could he be hiding? She smelt the food as it warmed up in the microwave, and her mouth watered. Perhaps she had been away from human contact for too long, she told herself, and had forgotten how to read people. She shook her head and entered the bathroom.

She emerged ten minutes later, pink-skinned and clad in a dead woman's dress. "Oh, look!" laughed Ben. "There was a woman underneath all that dirt!" He nodded at her left hand, still clutching her bloodied spear. "You can put that down, now," he said. "There's nothing to kill down here."

Kirsten glanced at the spear and smiled apologetically. "I hadn't realized I was still holding it," she said. "It's become part of me." She sat down at the table and laid the spear at her feet.

The meal was a mild chicken korma, surprisingly good for a ration-pack dinner (although she had to admit that anything would taste good after what she had been subsisting on). Ben ate slowly, his eyes never leaving Kirsten's face.

"I'm glad I found you," he said.

"You're glad?" she said, swallowing a mouthful of curry. "I thought I was going to die alone on this planet." It was the first time she had confronted this awful truth squarely, and now, safe in the company of a fellow human being, she began to cry. Without a word, Ben pulled her up from her chair, wrapped his arms around her and stroked her hair until her tears subsided.

Their lovemaking had all the awkwardness one would expect from two people who slept together for reasons other than physical attraction. Afterwards Kirsten lay in the crook of his arm with her head on his chest, luxuriating in the steadiness of his heart beat.

"What was your job here on Denvalia?" she said.

"You go first," he said, nudging her playfully.

Kirsten frowned. She knew nothing about Ben, beyond his first name. The existence of his underground bunker concerned her; the native sentient species the Denvali lived and slept on the planet surface without any protection at all, and the rest of the human scientific community had taken their cue from them, conceding only to lightweight tents for the sake of comfort. The bunker had been constructed with obvious forethought and secrecy. Yet she sensed that if she tried to press Ben for answers too directly or too soon, she would get nowhere. She sighed.

"I'm a xeno-anthropologist," she said. "I was exploring some underground caves for signs of Denvali relics when the bomb hit. I guess that's what saved my life. Much like your bunker saved yours."

Ben shook his head. "It wasn't a bomb," he said. "It was a storm. An unpredictable, one-in-five-hundred-years storm, the meteorologists said."

Kirsten pushed herself up on her elbow and stared at him. "What meteorologists?" she said. "Everyone's dead! And you're trying to tell me that a storm destroyed almost everything with nerve endings on the surface of the planet? I'm no meteorologist, but I'm pretty sure the only thing that could do that is an illegal bio-bomb. I don't know who would want to wipe out a harmless species like the Denvali, let alone all the humans who were working here, but . . . "

"You're right," Ben said. "You're just a bleeding-heart anthropologist, so for one thing, you don't know the first thing about extraterrestrial weather conditions, and secondly, you have no regard for the difficulties involved in sharing a habitable planet with another sentient species—especially one like the Denvali, who have no technological achievements to share with humankind."

Kirsten scrambled backwards in horror off the bed as the implication of his words sunk in.

"Come on, Kirsten," he said. "Denvalia is damn near Earth's identical twin. Hospitable climate—except for those five-hundred-year storms, of course," he chuckled at his own humorless joke, "breathable atmosphere, water, fertile soil . . . sure, it's pretty barren and boring now, but nothing that a decent-sized city or two and a few fast growing pine forests won't fix. We can't let a backward little tribe of humanoids get in the way of colonizing the planet."

Kirsten snatched up her spear from the floor and held it in front of her like a talisman. "And the humans you killed?" she said, her voice shaking with rage.

Ben shrugged. "You know what they say—you can't make omelettes without breaking a few eggs. But look on the bright side. You're still alive, and I'm still alive, and we can keep each other company until our ship comes in. What do you say?" He patted the bed next to him as Kirsten inched her way back towards him.

Kirsten emerged from the bunker into the cool Denvalian dawn. Ben would not have let her live, she told herself. He might have kept her around for his own amusement for a few months, but he could not take the risk of her returning to Earth alive and telling others the truth about what had happened on Denvalia. This was her only course of action.

The Denvali would not have understood. Jealousy, anger, hatred, fear—negative human emotion in general had been beyond their comprehension. Perhaps in some perverse way, Ben had been merciful, bringing them a swift and sudden death rather than the slow degradation they would have faced being overrun by human colonists.

She took a final look down the stairwell at the long, unbroken smear of blood left from dragging Ben's body to the surface. Hefting her freshly stained spear, and with her backpack bulging with pilfered supplies, she set off across the desert, her footprints already wafting away in a gentle morning breeze.

Fallout
by Michael Obilade

You'd think after living here for most of your life—all sixteen years of it—this kind of stuff would become normal. But it doesn't. Even though there are about ten, twenty million of us here already, and more arrive in the shuttles every day, it's still a kick in the ass to wake up every morning and realize you're part of the first generation of kids to grow up *here*—on stinking *Mars*.

When we were small, Dora and I would watch those stupid movies. You know, the ones they made in the 1950s about colonizing Venus and Jupiter and every other planet in the solar system. They were full of these alpha males who spoke in deep voices and said cheesy stuff like "We come in peace" to some little green men dressed in cheap boots and plastic suits. Well, let me tell you, none of that stuff exists. Not here, anyway. I mean, yeah, it *is* red outside—but it's more like a brownish, faded brick color, instead of that fire-engine hue we used to use when drawing the place, back on Earth. Mostly, it's like living in some parts of Arizona, or Colorado—where *we* lived—except it's a lot colder, and you can't go outside without bringing an O-tank with you. But other than that, it's about the same.

"What's wrong?"

"Nothing." I'm staring off into the sky, watching everything swirl in sand and dust. It's kind of peaceful.

"You think it'll be done by Wednesday?"

I look at her, and shrug. "Maybe." I think for a second. "I hope not. I hope it goes on for a *week*."

We both settle back into our chairs, nice and easy. From here, twelve stories up, we can see everything when it's clear. And when it storms, it feels like we're the only two left on the whole freaking planet.

Dora's my older sister. She isn't that much older—just a couple of minutes earlier, really—but she calls herself my older sister since she acts so much more mature than I do. I don't think she does, but everyone else seems to, so whatever. To tell you the truth, we don't even look like twins.

Ginger's the baby of the family. She doesn't remember anything about Earth, which makes sense, because she was a wish in my mother's heart when we left. Nowadays, every Martian—I'm not kidding, that's the official name—gets taught about their original planet through textbooks, charts and graphs and the like. But even in the pictures, you can tell there's something missing. Like some of the pages were torn out, and some phony changed the numbers to make it all look the same. I've never been to half the places she points out to me when we go through her geography book, but I still have a *feel* of what it would be like to go there, since I was actually born there. Earth, I mean.

It doesn't matter, though. It's just a little weird every now and then, when you stop to think about it. Like now. It's Monday, 7a.m. local time, and Dora and I are on the roof with the canopy open, watching one hell of a dust storm. There's no way we're going to have classes today; you can't see more than a meter in front of you when it gets this bad. But it isn't like back home. In Denver, we had dust storms, but those were nothing compared to these. The *snow*storms, though, were something sweet. There was a big one, I mean *huge*, right before we left. I was six, and it was the first day of first grade, but I still remember it like it was last week. Ginger was about ten years from being born, and Mom and Dad were busy training for the Mission, so most of the time, it was just me and Dora. The day it happened, it was like waking up in another world—and even though I've woken up on Mars every day for the last ten years, I still can't think of a better way to describe it. It was just that good.

Everything was covered in white. I mean, these days, when I'm in the mood for a laugh, I open up one of Ginger's science books about Earth, and Dora and I can laugh for hours about the passages on global warming, and nuclear winters, and all those euphemisms for 'fallout.' *Now* it's funny, because we get the jokes, and we've seen it all. Nothing about where we came from is still new anymore, so everything's comfortable. But back then, neither of us knew anything about that stuff. We just knew we'd gone to bed the night before, and woken up to twelve feet of snow outside. You couldn't even open the door. We climbed out through a window on the second floor, and joined what turned out to be one of the last snow-fights kids throughout the city would ever have. It lasted for *weeks*. Eventually, the schools re-opened, and we went back, but by then, everything was out of schedule, and I don't think any of us learned much that year.

"What are you guys doing?"

I turn back and see Ginger, still in her pajamas and trailing a bright blue towel behind her. She's all messy and scruffy, but cute in that way some kids are. My mother says she looks just like we did at her age. Dora kind of agrees with her.

"It's storming again," Ginger says, and she smiles real wide.

"Yeah. Just watching everything," Dora replies. "Pull up a chair."

She does, and the three of us settle down again, watching the sun rise—in the East, same as back home. Except it's a little smaller, since we're a lot farther away. And it doesn't leave you feeling warm when it shines on your forehead in the middle of the afternoon. It's more like a frightened, distant version of the sun. Like we treated it bad and scared it away. So it isn't really the same. Nothing's ever *really* the same. You just pretend it is.

When I tell Ginger the story, about the twelve feet of snow and what it meant to get in a snowball fight with thousands of kids, all throwing snowballs at each other and hiding and chasing one another throughout the city, her eyes light up like stars, and she sits absolutely still and doesn't miss a word. But she's never seen snow—not in person—and for some reason, that tears the hell out of me. I mean, looking at pictures and video and hearing stories from someone is better than nothing, but it's not even close to the real thing. It's like talking about being on a roller-coaster instead of actually riding one. It feels hollow. But she doesn't know that, because she doesn't know what she's missing. Which is some comfort, I guess.

"So whaddaya wanna do today?"

"I don't know." I get up and walk over to the glass. It's not really glass—it's some kind of silicon-graphite blend—but it acts the same way. Before the Mission became official, before anyone outside of a small group of people began to take the whole deal seriously, some whiz kid developed it, somewhere in a lab in Palo Alto. I think he killed himself after, working on some other project, but I'm not really sure. The little I know, I learned from overhearing some big wigs a couple years back on a shuttle trip. If you touch it, it somehow arranges itself so it's ready to take a higher stress—like a punch, or a jab with the end of a chair. Apparently, the most common method of death around here is suicide, but no one really talks about it much. They just try to design everything on the outside as strong as possible, to keep whatever's inside of you on the inside. Like they'd rather have you die of boredom, or apathy.

"When's Mom getting back?" Dora and Mom have been really close since our dad died, a couple of years back. When it happened, they both took it really hard, so it kind of makes sense. We *all* took it pretty hard, but you know how it is. I like to keep things in, keep them quiet. And Ging, well, she was young, but she wasn't stupid or anything. I mean she knew what happened, and she asked a couple questions and everything, but I think whatever got into me that kept me from talking too much about the whole thing got into her, and we both kind of just went around *doing* stuff, you know, instead of talking about *that.* No sense talking about certain things, especially when they just bring you down, and make you start wondering if everything else in the world is worth dealing with.

"I don't know. I think . . . probably by noon." She's attending a conference on the other side of the planet.

"If she doesn't get back soon, we're going to be late," Dora says.

"She'll be here in time." It comes out hollow, like even I don't believe it. But I do.

"Late for what?" Ginger asks. She knows, but she always makes us say it aloud—as if it would lose meaning eventually if we kept on talking circles around it. Sometimes she's like that—bold. Dora and I are more quiet, according to kids in school.

"For the memorial, silly." Dora pulls a blue strand out of her sister's hair, and blows it into the air. We share a knowing glance as it floats down slowly—slower than it ever would have drifted down, back home.

The year after our dad died, none of us knew what to do about the time shift—particularly Mom. Back on Earth, we'd have done something 365 days after it happened, but what do you do here? What do you do when a year's 669 days long?

"I'm not waiting six-hundred days to remember my own bloody father!" Dora said, eleven months—Earth months—after his death. It's still the only time I've heard her curse. We were standing here, trying to talk about anything other than the memory of him when she started tearing up, and said what I hadn't had the heart to spit out. Mom was in the next room and she overheard, but she wasn't mad. She just came in and hugged her—hugged us both—and we decided we'd stick to the old calendar for this, and for a few other things. My little sister was asleep downstairs. When she woke up and Mom explained everything to her, she didn't think twice about it. "It wouldn't make sense to do it the other way."

"She'll be here in time, then," Ginger says. When it comes from her, it sounds convincing—like whatever's out there causing this sea of sand and dust wouldn't keep a kid from her mom.

"Yeah," Dora says. "She can't be that far now." I pull out a deck of cards, and flip the set at her, so we can play something to pass the time.

The first thing every kid learns here is how small everything is—geographically, I mean. It's not like Earth, where you've got a bit more space to raise crops and have wars and all. It's not like it's tiny or anything here; it's just smaller. But it takes longer to get around here than it does—than it did—to get around back home. For one thing, you can't just walk out. Got to put on suits, tanks, check timers and pressures—it's a lot of fuss. And on days like these, when it's just storming like all hell, the best thing to do's pretty much to sit down and take it easy. I guess that's one thing you learn over here. You learn patience. Dora and I aren't high strung or anything, but compared to Ginger, we're pretty wound up. The clocks here run a little slower than they do on Earth, because the days are a little longer, on account of rotation rates, or something like that. But she was *born here*, so she's used to 25-hour clocks, and a lack of seasons, and all that stuff. I guess that's a good thing. I mean, what's the point of going around comparing everything you see to everything you used to know? There's no point. Just a lot of wasted time and energy. Except when it storms, which is fairly often. Junior year just started a couple of months ago—the school year is set up so we're in school during the calmest months, when the weather doesn't make getting around impossible. During the 'summer,' you can get storms that last for weeks, and you're just stuck indoors, trying to keep from going crazy. It's hard.

But it isn't always that way. I don't want you to think I hate it here or anything, because I don't. My best memory from the past summer was actually a pretty good one that had nothing to do with our surroundings. Ginger and I came up here, where we are now, with a telescope one night, and we set it up just right. Home is usually just a bright star, but if you train a telescope on it, especially when we pass by close, you can see a hell of a lot.

"It looks *really* pretty," she said.

I looked through the eyepiece, and it was a blue marble—one of those swirly ones, with streaks of white and green throughout. It was amazing.

"Yeah."

You couldn't see too much—you couldn't see Denver, or anything like that—but you could see enough. I mean enough to give you an idea of where you came from, and what you were looking at. Even if you never came from there. Even if you were among the first people in, I don't know, history, to ever look back at a place everyone *before* you was from, but *you* weren't from. You couldn't see the scars from here—I mean, like all the countries and places that no longer existed. You couldn't see any burned-out homes, or millions of people struggling to get out, or even traces of those black clouds that lingered for ten years after the last fallout. It looked peaceful—like someone sleeping who you didn't yet know was dead. It was that moment right before you tried to wake him up. I don't know how it looked to her, but I hope it looked grand. I hope it didn't feel like she was missing something. I really do.

Saying Goodbye
by Sue Penkivech

The heels of his boots tapped an odd, discordant counterpoint to the gradually fading wheeze of the engines that followed him down the ramp. Both sounds ceased, however, as Captain Matt Cullen stepped onto the planet's surface.

Unlike his previous visit to Balthar IV, there was no need for a spacesuit. Matt closed his eyes, memorizing the soft touch of cool air on his face, the faint taste of grit that accompanied the strong winds. Soon enough, he knew, the taste would be gone, no longer part of the "new" Balthar IV once the terraformers had finished transforming the planet into something they considered more appropriate for human life. For now, though, it still belonged.

His eyes opened slowly, revealing ragged stone, painted purple under the dim light of the planet's twin moons. Stark, barren—the astronomers had hypothesized the planet was a lifeless husk, one where the germ of life had simply never taken hold. They found them sometimes, as they peered out into space through their telescopes, then spent time enhancing the images and handed them over to the experts for study. And then, once the experts had given their official opinions, they spent years hypothesizing as to why some planets developed life while others didn't, and why this one in particular might hold the key to the answer.

From what he'd seen, they rarely reached any conclusions. Instead, they hemmed and hawed and lobbied and filled out reams of official forms. They passed them on to department heads, who scarcely noted what they were signing, and who likely wouldn't care if they did so long as their precious formalities and procedures were given the deference they were due.

Then, and only then, would they request that a survey team be sent to the planet in question, to confirm their suspicions that it was ripe for terraforming. As they had with the planet he was standing on now.

Matt smiled a little, remembering his initial visit to Balthar IV. As always, the crew had joked amongst themselves as they'd tugged on their suits, elbowing each other and making ribald observations about each other's chosen undergarments. There'd been seven of them on that trip: five men, two women, all experts in their fields, and among the finest he'd been privileged to work with over the course of his career. Jeff had been wearing a pair of smiley faced boxers that Trish had tried to insist were an auspicious sign, though just what they were supposed to signify she couldn't or wouldn't say. Gradually the laughter had quieted, the voices faded, until the only remaining sounds were those of the air rushing through the ventilation ducts and the soft hum of the equipment around them.

He'd put on his helmet, and then those had disappeared as well.

Silently, almost reverently, they'd filed down the ramp just as the sun first peered over the encircling mountains. And they'd paused, right where he was now standing, to stare around them in awe as the sun's rays reflected off metallic traces in the rock, transforming the desolate landscape into a glittering rainbow of light.

There had been years of photos, of experts, of analyses, but until they'd watched the sun rise that morning, no one had ever had a clue.

The crew had stood there, frozen by the display as if hypnotized, until he'd finally pulled himself together and broke radio silence to ask the crew why they were all standing around. In retrospect, he wished he'd waited just a little longer. But they'd had an entire new planet to explore, and more marvels to find.

Matt glanced down at his watch, pressing the button to make the sickly green light illuminate the numbers, then nodded to himself. He had time. He stepped out onto what remained of the path their equipment had worn in the planet's surface. Even now, it was the sole visible proof that seven people had used this valley as a base camp for months, by design rather than accident. They'd taken pains to keep the valley intact, scarring it as little as possible as they'd gathered, studied, analyzed. The land rovers that had carried them over the landscape had compressed the rock directly before him, but by unspoken agreement, they hadn't lifted the ship until it had been time to survey the other continent. It had been their landing site, upon arrival. By the time they'd left, it had been their home.

Finally, they'd completed their work. Their report, full of the cold, hard numbers and percentages that the administration valued, had been forwarded to headquarters. Secure in the knowledge they'd thoroughly surveyed Balthar IV and found it as suitable for terraforming as the astronomers had predicted, they'd moved on to the next planet, the next magical moment of discovery.

It had been ten years since that day, or nearly—Matt wasn't in the habit of keeping the details on his personal chronometer, and didn't see any reason to check the official reports when the details that mattered to him were forever frozen in his memory. Time enough, at any rate, for the wind to blow debris over the spot where their ship had rested those many months, for the path they'd worn to be obscured.

Sufficient time, even, for crew members to transfer, to resign, to marry; he'd been amused when he'd received an invitation two years ago to Jeff and Trish's wedding, touched and honored the following year when they'd sent him a subspace message to inform him they'd named their newborn son after him. Time for many more planetfalls in many solar systems, each a fresh discovery, a new challenge.

And time, at least, to be re-summoned to Balthar IV by the same bureaucrats who'd signed his initial orders. This time not to survey the planet, but to "say a few words" in honor of the day.

Matt scrubbed his hand through his thinning ginger hair and looked out again over the barren landscape. The distant, cold mountains were just as he remembered them; the terraformers' work hadn't yet touched this remote valley, beyond the increased oxygen content. It was only a matter of time, though. Later today, in a flurry of speeches, of plastic smiles on the faces of money-makers and administrators and lobbyists who'd never set foot on the planet before and who never would again, Balthar IV would be officially opened to colonization. Within a week, the valley—his valley—would be inundated by specialists intent upon finishing what little work remained, hoping that this once they would actually manage to earn that early-completion bonus they were always promised but never managed to attain. Not a one of them would take the time out of his or her busy schedule to visit the plain at dawn, and within a few weeks it would no longer matter. The colonists would never see the planet he and his team had landed upon. Grateful for the new life Balthar IV represented, it was unlikely they'd care.

He couldn't even fault their logic, he supposed. It just didn't work for him.

A crackle of static from his communicator heralded Zoe's voice, and he sighed impatiently as he waited for her to speak. "Ready to head out yet, Captain?" she asked in a bored tone. She didn't understand what had brought him here today or why he'd pulled strings to gain access to the shuttle she was flying, and he couldn't begin to explain it to her in terms she'd comprehend. He predicted that within six months she'd be requesting a transfer to a cargo ship, eager to fly a milk run from civilized planet to civilized planet now that she had experience under her belt. Predictable routes through established shipping lanes. To her, it would sound like paradise.

He thought it a poor trade for losing the magic, but magic was something that Zoe, like so many others, didn't seem to value.

"One minute," he replied curtly, impatient with her for bursting in on his reflections, for breaking the silence. He put the communicator back in his pocket just as the first rays of the sun broke over the mountains, rolling as if in slow motion over the boulders, the rock, and the gravel. And igniting them all, one last time, in that same blaze of fire he'd seen that very first morning.

For ten long minutes he stood there, transfixed, swallowing occasionally in an attempt to push down the lump that persisted in forming in his throat. These were the moments he lived for, the reason he'd initially joined Survey, and the reason why, twenty years later, he still couldn't imagine doing anything else with his life. Zoe was welcome to the predictable. He'd take the magic, every time.

Finally, he turned his back on the shining expanse, set his jaw, and resolutely trudged back up the ramp and onto the ship. Hopefully when he checked his messages, he'd find that the next assignment was waiting.

This Abandoned Sky
by C.E. Grayson

Once the Durandin had finished destroying their ancient enemies, the Vorii, they gave us back our world. It was only fair. They'd only won the great war when we humans, who'd been the slaves of the Vorii for hundreds of years, had joined the Durandin side. The Vorii thieved our world from us, and now we, scattered among them, working in their factories, serving their nobles, being beaten and eaten and other, worse things on any one of a thousand worlds, decided it was worth any cost to end it, even if that meant we'd be ending ourselves.

So we sabotaged their ships and blew up their factories. We revolted against our masters, defied their orders, and we murdered noble families in their sleep. Out of everyone I knew on the station where I'd lived, only a few of us were still alive. But those that remained were free. Most of us didn't really know what that meant, and we still don't. But it sounds important; it sounds right.

My mom sent me in a transport with her wife, Marit, and Marit's niece, Hannah. We're going back to Earth. And I say back to Earth, as everyone does, but the truth was I'd never been there before. None of us had. But we all mean to return. This was another one of those things that felt important, another one of those things that sounded right.

Besides, it's not like we had any place else to go. The Durandin don't keep slaves. It's one of the things that made them hate the Vorii as much as they did, but they're not much interested in keeping us as citizens of their empire, either. Vorii worlds are Durandin worlds now, all of them except for one.

Our transport could hold thirty-six of us, and it was full when we started out from Reiin Station, but an outbreak of Running Blood—something the Vorii left behind for us—killed about twelve of us before we even got into the system. Our pilot was one of them, but luckily there was someone else who said he knew enough to at least get us to Earth.

His name was Adan, and he'd been quiet through most of the trip which only made me want to talk to him more.

I'd been playing with little Tracia, who bounced around the hold when she wasn't asleep, but I was getting tired of answering her "what's that?" and "why?" questions so I gave her back to her parents, Lia, and Jagger, who had been coordinating our supplies with Marit.

It was our first night aboard—a few turns (I guess I should call them days now) before the first of us started getting sick—I sat next to Adan in the main hold while we ate our stale ration-bars. Marit tried to shoo me away, but the guy held his hand up, told her it was all right, and looked at me with this weird smile, like he was a little bit afraid I would turn out to be the kind of kid who would actually bite him. And I wondered if he'd had a bad encounter with Tracia.

I told him my name was Tobi Alvarez, and he asked me how old I was.

"Seven," I said.

"Is that Vorii cycles or Earth Years?"

Marit had already taught me how to do that calculation, so I did it in my head and changed my answer to: "Twelve. Years."

"Was that your mother?" he asked me. "You don't look much like her."

That was true. Marit was tall and had rich, dark skin and curly hair tight against her scalp. I was short (but growing) and my hair was a thick mop of almost silver-white down to my shoulders. "She's my mom's wife," I told him.

Adan nodded and smiled, but looked quickly away, and I could tell what he was thinking. "My mom's not dead or anything—she sent us ahead. She's working for the Transitional Authority, helping everybody get to Earth."

"That's good," Adan replied. "You've got some family left. There's not many of us that do."

"Do you?" I asked him, and he just shook his head. Before, I'd thought he was a pretty young guy, but he looked older at that moment, and he looked even older a few minutes later, when he'd finished his rations and pulled out a cane to help him stand up. The way he'd been sitting, it looked like his legs were crossed, and I hadn't noticed the cane leaning against the wall on the other side of him. But as he braced himself with one arm against the wall, and one shaking hand on the old wooden handle of his cane, I could see that he only had one leg.

"What happened to you?" I asked.

"They had me on the Ring," he said. "But it was a lucky thing, I guess, because that's probably why I'm still alive."

The Ring was the place the Vorii had threatened to send us when we misbehaved. On the Ring, you were . . . well, nobody much knew exactly what they did to you, but we did know that no one came back from it. We'd heard rumors that the Durandin had set some people free from that place, but no one had ever expected to actually see any of them.

Reading the look that must have been on my face, Adan said, "You can ask, but I'll tell you now that it's really not something I like to talk about."

And so I never asked him about it, even as I spent a lot of time walking and talking with him over the next few days. He seemed to know a lot about where we were going, even though he admitted he'd never been there himself.

"None of us have ever lived under a sky that was ours before, Tobi," he told me once. "And back when we did, all we wanted was to go into it, see beyond it, visit whatever it was that was on the other side. And we did and we found . . . we found wonders. But some of those wonders betrayed us, and now its time we got back to living under what we own."

I wasn't sure what he meant by that, but what he told me about Earth sounded wonderful. He told me about cities built of glass and metal, rising out of great plains, about mountains that could catch fire, and about the great oceans and the islands made of nothing but fine sand and green leaves.

I'd never seen anything like that, as I'd spent my whole life on Reiin Station. I knew about living in metal warrens, and how to turn Vorii scraps into proper meals. I knew how to hide, and which doors would shut in an emergency, which was how I'd survived when the bombs went off.

A few days later, when people started dying, one-legged Adan turned out to be the one of us most qualified to pilot the transport.

Which was how he ended up being the pilot who crashed us.

It wasn't his fault, though Adan would take all the blame on himself. The bridge—what passed for it in this old Durandin re-fit—wasn't much bigger than the closet where the extra blankets would have been stored, if we'd had any. The space itself was small, and the seats were small too, on account of the fact that the average Durandin was not quite as big as an average human. Adan didn't let many of us come into that bridge unless he needed help setting the auto or staying awake when the auto wasn't working. That's when I would visit him, and we'd continue our talks.

That last day we weren't alone up there. Hannah begged her way in, saying she'd been sent by Marit to bring Adan his supper, which had just been the usual hunk of ration bar. This annoyed me, because everyone knew that was my job.

We were just coming into orbit, seeing Earth for the first time.

"Just wait, Tobi—you'll see a little bit of fire, and then all around us it will be blue."

I had a hard time seeing how that was going to happen. The blue and green world from the pictures I'd seen wasn't what was below us now. I could see a little bit of brown land through a haze of some rust-grey smoke, and in the spaces, what few of them that were clear, there were huge black smears, as if some giant had rubbed his fingers in soot and then traced them over the world. It didn't look like a living world to me, but a dead one. A dead one that'd had its carcass thrown into the bin and then fished out again.

Hannah asked if she could stay to see it as we came down, so we let her. Of course, she couldn't be quiet. The first thing she did was lean over Adan, to get a better look out the shield, she said, but she seemed pretty close to him. After a few seconds she looked down, and then pulled back on his shirt collar.

"What's this?" she asked him. She didn't actually touch the scar on the back of his neck, but I could tell she wanted to.

It was a ridge of raised, red flesh, gone white in the middle. Burned there. It looked like the top of a triangle that was missing the bottom and took up most of the space just below where his neck met his hairline. The image seemed unfinished, somehow, as if it were waiting for some other half to complete it.

"That's . . . that's just . . . " he said, snapping his collar up so that it rode against the bottom of his shaggy brown hair. "That's a brand from the ring."

He looked up at Hannah, at her rightfully embarrassed face, and forced his scowl to turn into a smile. There was something in the look that passed between them that I didn't like, but there was no time to think about it because right then this hideous "whoop-brack" noise started spitting out of the console.

Adan cursed and brought up—on his third try—the nav screen, which showed some spiky, orbed object rushing toward us.

"Mine," Adan said. "I was afraid . . . I don't think I can evade." He looked sideways at me, and there was panic in his eyes, panic that leapt from his eyes to my own.

"Hannah—get her out of here!" He put his hand on my arm as if he meant to yank me out of my seat but was at the wrong angle to do so. "Get everyone sealed up and strapped, as many as you can!"

Hannah pulled me the rest of the way out into the main hold. Marit was standing there, at the head of a group gathered by the alarm.

Hannah explained, sounding calmer than she had a right to. Marit turned around and, raising her hands into the air, shouted out "Everyone—secure yourselves!" I wasn't sure why they listened to her, but they did. Adults grabbed children and found seats with straps they could anchor themselves to. Hannah took me by the shoulder and shoved me down into one of these seats. Jagger did the same to Lia and Tracia a few seats away. I didn't know why any of them were bothering, because if that mine hit us the ship would blow, and being strapped down in an explosion wasn't going to help much.

A great, cracking sound shut up my protesting. The entire transport gave a lurch, and then a long shudder. Hannah wasn't strapped in yet, so she clung to me, kneeling in front of me with her arms wrapped around my waist. I closed my eyes and thought about Adan, how he would save us, somehow. Surely, we hadn't come all this way to die when we were, at last, on our way to the ground.

After a while I couldn't hear the people screaming anymore because of the roar that seemed to be all around us, and there came this upside down feeling. I wanted to open my eyes and see what was happening, but they defied me, not really wanting to see what was going on for themselves.

It felt like we leveled off a bit, but then we were falling again, and that was the last thing I knew before the world opened up and spilled me out.

I don't know if I got knocked out or fell asleep or just slipped a little ways into the future, but the next thing I remember was Marit's face looking into mine. She shined this bright white light in my eyes, and when she saw I was alive, she pushed back from me and then started pulling off pieces of metal and stone.

Hannah was there too, sprawled across my legs. At first, I thought she was dead, but I could feel the shallow movement of her breath against my body, and she moaned when Marit touched her.

She had blood on the back of her head and streaked across her formerly white shirt. Marit, as she looked at me and then back at her niece, was covered in some fine, dark-grey powder. When she saw that I could move my legs, she embraced me again, and told me she'd need my help checking on people.

It was more silent than it should have been inside that hold. There were a few low moans, and some whimpers, but so many of us were lying amid the wreckage of the transport, completely still and silent, and I was afraid that I knew too well what that meant. I could see that the side of the ship was cracked open. Rocks and dirt and dust all spilled inside, which accounted for the stone that had covered Hannah and me. There was a crack, though, between the ship and the mountain we'd crashed into, a space I could see between, filled with some milky light. It looked just large enough for me to climb through, and finally see this world that had held so much of our hope.

Part of me wanted to stay and help Marit, another part wanted to rush to the bridge to find Adan. But I was afraid of the answer I would find there, so instead I went toward that shaft of light, climbing up on pieces of metal and stone that shifted as I put my weight on them.

The light felt wrong. It hit my face with—well, not with heat, but with a force I'd never felt before from the light on Reiin. I pulled myself up and through the gap and then found myself standing on the scarred outside hull of the ship.

We were lying against a low hill. There was a gash all around us which had streaked off a ways. This was where the rock and dirt had come from, and it looked like we'd actually tried to cut our way into the mountain. This hill led to others, more jagged, taller, that rose up behind us, but on my other side it sloped down a bit more, then went flat for as far as I could see.

There was no blue in the sky. Had that been a lie, or had all of those old books and Adan's stories just been wrong? Because the sky I looked up into was almost a gun-metal grey, broken by streaks of brown that looked like shit-stains. It wasn't a lot different from the ceiling of Reiin's main hall. The ground itself was dry and cracked, grey at the surface, with deep black ash in the spaces between.

This was our new home? How were we supposed to live here? Air hit me, rushing air, as if from the station-vents. This was wind, and it was cold. I shuddered at it, and drew my ragged, blood-stained coat around me.

Something in the wind flew down into my mouth and my throat and brought up a nasty, racking cough. Here I was, beneath a real sky at last, and all I wanted was to get below again, beneath the shelter of what remained of the transport. So, I climbed back down, out of the wind, back into that dark swirl of dust and fallen wires and bobbing emergency lights.

There were more people up and around now, enough that Marit didn't even yell at me for not coming to help her sooner. And since she wasn't yelling at me, I decided to go find Adan. I couldn't hear his voice among those calling out names among the wounded, but that didn't mean anything. He was probably still in his seat, hoping the rest of us had made it.

Now that I had been outside, if only for a minute, the transport's hold felt so much smaller. I kicked my way to the front of the hold, the place where the door to the bridge had been. The wall here was pushed out and buckled, protruding in the middle like a pregnant belly. The door itself was busted open, but the walls on either side narrowed the passageway.

Thankfully, I was small enough to fit.

Marit grabbed me as I began to push my way through. Even in the dim light I could tell how furiously she was shaking.

"Adan—" was all I said.

She understood, but still shook her head. "I need your help. Hannah's really badly hurt, and so many of us are . . . " Her voice broke as she said that, and I didn't need for her to finish that sentence. "They just had to get at us one last time, didn't they?"

She dropped down, half-kneeling, half-resting against the wall, and shuddered, giving out great, heaving sighs. She had the light pointed up at her face and I thought I would see huge wet splotches there, but I didn't. She shook, but she wasn't crying.

I'd never really seen Marit cry. Not even when she told us the story of her last family, her husband beaten to death by joy-bending Vorii noble kids, her twin babies served at a feast to celebrate Beniin. That story had made me cry when she'd told it, but she'd told it with dry eyes. I guess it was the same thing now.

"I still need to check on Adan," I said.

She looked up at me, and this time she nodded. I didn't wait for her to change her mind.

The sides of the door bit at my chest and my shoulder, their jagged edges snagging my jacket and ripping holes in my shirt as I forced my way through. When I got to the other side, the broken viewshield filled my vision. Half of it was covered in dirt and rock, and this spilled in through the broken spaces and coated the now-darkened console. The sky, what I could see in the view that remained, made the shield look like just another one of the transport's walls.

And there was Adan, still strapped into his chair. He lay back, his arms hanging limply at his sides, his nose pointed straight up at the ceiling. No . . . he couldn't be . . . I was afraid to touch him for fear that I would find him cold and stiff (how I'd found my friend Mannara, after she'd been hunted at that same Beniin feast), which was stupid because I knew it hadn't been that long. I made myself touch him anyway.

He was still warm, at least, and his shoulder joints seemed loose enough when I shook them. I brought my hand up so that it hovered just over his mouth and nose, trying to feel his breath against my palm. This didn't tell me anything, so I moved my hand down and pressed it against his chest, hoping I would feel it push out or a rhythmic thump-thump would tap against my hand. Something, at least, that would tell me he was alive.

He gave a start, and then a shudder. In a panic, he unstrapped himself from the chair, snarled, and then rolled sideways, falling off his chair and landing on the floor near my feet.

He moaned softly now, and I dropped to his side. I put my hand on his shoulder as he pushed himself up on his arms.

"Adan." I breathed softly. "You're not dead."

"I don't—" he looked up at me as if he was trying to remember who I was.

"It's Tobi," I said. The look on his face was scaring me more than anything had yet.

"Tobi," he said, and fell back against the floor. "I'm sorry, Tobi. I tried . . . I tried to get us down . . . "

"You did, Adan. We're down. We landed. We're on Earth now."

"Where are we? I thought I could get us to New Hope, but—"

"I don't know where we are but I don't think it's New Hope." I really hoped it wasn't, anyway, but telling him that we were in the middle of someplace better named "No Hope" wasn't something I wanted to do just then.

He pushed himself up again and I helped him get into a sitting position. There on the floor, his back against the console, he rested, breathing hard from the effort of sitting. Then his face went a sudden white, and he started coughing up little bits of red that thickened and became a stream as he kept on with it. More red leaked from his nose and the corners of his mouth, and as he coughed again, more violently, he tried to hide from me the glistening, red-black pulp he'd deposited into his hand.

"That means you're hurt really bad," I said. "Marit needs to get a look at you."

He just sat there and breathed, which I suppose was enough work for him at the moment. I didn't know what else to do, so I forced my way back into the hold to find Marit. She'd moved from the space where I'd left her, and I found her in the open area in the hold's center. She was standing next to Jagger, and they weren't speaking, but both of them were looking down at a pair of bodies, one about Marit's size, one much, much smaller, twisted at their feet.

She looked up when I approached, and flatly asked, "Is he all right?"

"You need to come look at him. He's coughing blood."

She winced when I said that, and said "All right." As she moved past him, she squeezed Jagger's shoulder. He teared at the moment of her touch, and when we were a few steps away, she told me, "Lia and Tracia were killed." Her voice was cold, which was another thing that scared me more than just a little. I didn't want to think about that. Little Tracia . . .

"Is Hannah all right?" I asked her.

"I don't know," was all she said.

I led her to the bridge, clearing out a bit of the gap for her as I went so that she could pass through. She didn't even yell at me to be careful.

Adan locked eyes with her as she settled in front of him; she felt the side of his face with her hand. Taking his pulse with one finger on his neck, she just kept staring, something like a smirk on her lips. What was funny about this?

"You're bleeding out inside," she told him and he nodded. "You know there's nothing I can do for you. I don't even have anything to give you for the pain."

"I know," he said, gulping down something so that it didn't come out of his mouth when he spoke. "Is everyone else . . . ?"

"We've got about twelve still living so far. Half of those will be dead within hours if we don't get help . . . and I don't suppose help is coming, is it? "

"I tried to evade," he gasped. "If our pilot . . . "

"This was not you, Adan Matthews," Marit scolded him. I started to tell her not to yell at him, but with a tug on my arm she hushed me. "This was the Vorii . . . always, always the Vorii, even after—I just hope the Durandin hunted down and ate every one of those bastards."

Adan closed his eyes, and for a moment I thought he was gone, into sleep or . . . or worse things. But then they fluttered open and he tried to sit up as he said, " . . . sent distress signal. Maybe . . . maybe New Hope received?"

"We can hope," Marit said. "You're a good man, Adan, worried about us when you're . . . well, we can hope." She stood up and with a gentler hand on my shoulder, told me, "Stay with him, Tobi." She didn't have to say what was in her eyes. *Don't let him die alone.*

She marched back to the gap and pushed herself through. When she was gone, Adan looked at me and mouthed the words: "You hurt?"

I shook my head. To distract him, I told him about my trip outside, and he grimaced as I told him about the hill and the barren, ashy plane.

"Thought we'd be close to New Hope," he said. "Other side of the hills . . . could have lived there." This much talking was making him cough and I told him to stop it.

But he ignored me. "Fire," he said. And I looked around, looking to see if something was burning on the bridge. With some effort he shook his head, and threw up a hand to indicate the outside. "Signal . . . so they can find us."

I wasn't sure I understood what he meant. "I'm supposed to stay . . . "

He grabbed my arm and said, "It will help them find us sooner . . . I'll . . . " He winced as he put a hand up and tried to pull himself up on the chair.

"What are you doing?"

"Help me up," he gasped, his face even more pale than it had been before. "I'll . . . I'll try to get on the com. Maybe . . . "

"You shouldn't be doing anything," I said. "Just rest, you're making it worse."

"Tobi, I'm going to die. Let me . . . let me help before I do."

"You're not going to die." But that was the only argument I could make. He looked at me again, so I grabbed him by the shoulders and helped him sit in the chair. I strapped him so he wouldn't fall if he passed out again.

"Thanks," he said, and patted my hand. I leaned over him and, not really sure why I was doing it, pressed a kiss against his quickly-chilling forehead.

If I was going to make a signal fire, I knew that I would need something that would burn. I'd never actually made a fire before, but I'd seen them made. Back on Reiin, we had to make fires sometimes when the Station Masters would save power by reducing the heat on our levels so that it was just warm enough to keep us alive. Sometimes we would burn fuel traces in rags we'd smuggled from the shipyards. I wondered if there would be any leaking fuel, and if I could use some of that to soak rags from the clothes of the people who'd died.

At least if I did this outside, I wasn't going to blow a hole in a level and accidentally vent a couple hundred people.

I was going to ask Marit about this idea, but as I made my way back into the hold, I saw Jagger at the port doors. He had a long strip of metal and was trying to pry them open. I guess I wasn't the only one who wanted outside.

Another man was helping him, someone I didn't know, and together they managed to open up a gap large enough that someone as small as I was could just fit through it.

Cold spilled into the dark hall, along with a pillar of light, which drew moans from the wounded on the floor and a sharp hiss from Marit.

"What are you doing?" She yelled at them.

"We need to get out of this," Jagger said, whirling on her. "I didn't bring my little one here to leave her in a Durandin ship. She's going to see Earth."

"Oh, Jagger . . . " Marit began, but she'd lost the spirit to argue with him. "At least, in here, we have shelter."

Jagger just shook his head, and returned to widening the opening. Two more people, Bren and Mika, joined the effort. This, I realized, accounted for most of us who were still alive and walking.

I went to stand next to Marit as I watched them work. She slipped an arm around me and pulled me in close against her side. After we had watched for a while and seen the door open perhaps another hand-width, she moved off, telling me that she had to check on Hannah.

I stayed and watched and after some time had passed, the opening was large enough that even Jagger could pass through if he turned sideways.

At least now I wasn't going to have to climb out the roof.

One by one, those who'd worked at opening the door jumped down and onto the surface of Earth for the first time. Bren, Talbot, Mika. I envied them being the first, since I had been outside, but had not touched the ground.

I went to that door and I could see below me the ground about as far from my feet as I was tall. Bren and Talbot were looking up at me expectantly. Mika had wandered farther; her arms spread out, she spun, almost tripping herself in an oddly joyless dance of celebration.

Jagger stepped back, not ready yet, and as he made his way toward Marit, I jumped forward, in flight for a few seconds. I hit the ground and rolled, jagged bits of rock poking at me through my clothes as I bounced over them.

I stood up quickly, though part of me wanted to lie there and feel the dirt against my cheek. No one laughed at me or tried to help me; we were all just . . . just there, together, I guess. We were alive, but with no idea of what we were going to do next.

Was this what freedom was?

I looked back up at the ship, where Jagger was there in the doorway. He leaped down and landed easily, as if he'd practiced the move. A low grunt was the only thing that showed it was any kind of effort.

Then Marit appeared. She held something in her arms. No . . . she held someone in her arms. Little Tracia, limp and bloody, her arms dangling out at impossible angles.

Marit knelt and handed her gently down to Jagger. He took the child and Marit leaped down behind them, found a flat space on the ground. He lay his daughter there, took a handful of dry, ashy dirt in his hand, kissed her forehead once and then sprinkled the dirt over her body.

I couldn't watch this, so I turned away. Bren was having a similar problem, so I went up to her and told her what Adan had said about a signal fire. She just nodded. She was looking for something else to do too.

Talbot helped us, and we spent the next few hours looking for things that would actually burn. My idea of soaking dry clothing in leaking fuel was a good one and once we'd used that and a mini-weld we'd found in one of the storage compartments, we found other things as well. I actually felt proud of myself as I watched the thin stream of smoke take off on the wind and vanish against the grey-brown sky.

Tracia's body was the only one brought outside. But while I'd worked on the fire someone—Bren told me it was Jagger and Mika—had gone back in and brought out Adan. Marit had braced wreckage with rocks around the space where the transport's nose pointed upward and created a sheltered space; Hannah and Adan were brought there. Hannah was awake now, but one of her arms was broken, and she slipped in and out of coherency.

"I know we should stay in the ship," Marit told me as though I'd asked for the explanation "But . . . but Jagger's right. How can we?"

No one was talking about what we were going to do next, at least not to me. Someone had found a box of ration-bars and we shared these around the fire as the grey sky turned black. That was the good thing about there being only a few survivors. We had enough food for a couple of days, and cubes of water as well.

I took one of the bars to Adan, but he wasn't awake anymore. He wasn't dead yet, either, but I didn't think he was going to wake up. It wasn't anything Marit had said, but he just looked gone to me. I would have asked Marit, but was afraid she would tell me exactly that, and it wasn't something I wanted to hear spoken out loud.

As dark came—I'd never felt anything like it before. Reiin's lights had always stayed on, though I'd heard old stories about nightfall—it got even colder. We took what blankets we could find and even clothing from the dead to wrap around us; we were so cold. Mika asked the others if maybe we shouldn't go back inside. Bren told her she was welcome to, and Mika even got up and walked toward the transport doors, but when no one joined her she came back.

The fire was almost out and there was nothing left to throw on it. Among all of us, it seemed like we'd all agreed that if we were going to die it might as well be tonight; we would lay ourselves and go to the earth that way. Marit told me that if a body was laid out, the way Tracia's was, it would become part of the planet.

I thought about that while I looked up at the black, which was how I got to be the first one of us to see the light in the sky. It had come from over the mountain, and I thought at first that it meant the stars were showing through at last. Then it got bigger, and noise came with it and one by one we all noticed it and stood up to make some kind of greeting.

Had Adan gotten a message through, saved us after all?

It was a small ship that landed in front of us, unlike any other I'd ever seen before. The transport loomed over it, and the lights pouring out from every side of it obscured its shape.

There was a low click-hiss and a door on its side opened. Three figures stepped out and made their way toward us, but all we could see were their silhouettes against the light.

Bren hissed and I heard someone—I think it was Marit—cry out, a wet, interrupted yelp. Marit stepped forward to put herself in front of me, and I thought about Adan and Hannah, sleeping . . . defenseless.

The shapes were bent, wide in the legs and shoulders, with a familiar set of triune humps on each side. The heads were narrow and half as long as each leg, and they moved with a familiar jagged sway, carrying their scent with them on the wind.

Vorii.

How . . . we'd hoped they were all dead. This was our world again now . . . what were they doing here? I was not comforted to realize the third figure, obscured at first by the other two, was a human.

That one made his way lithely between the two Vorii. He was older, shorter, with a scarred, bald head and a belly that protruded over the belt he wore as part of a dark, makeshift uniform. "It's all right!" He called out to us. At our silence, he continued, "I'm Corporal Trent with the Transitional Authority."

"Who are they?" Marit spat at him, pointing at the nearest Vorii. At my side, Mika remembered enough to stoop down and pick up a rock from the ground. Recognizing a good idea, I did the same, even though I knew the Vorii's skin was tough enough that a rock wasn't going to do that much damage.

"They're from the nearest settlement," Trent said. "They're here to help."

"Help?" Marit said.

"There's a lot you don't know. The Durandin—they didn't do us any favors leaving us this world, and they didn't just kill all the Vorii for us, either. Some of them, a lot of them, they sent here, and that's not counting the ones who were left here in the first place. There's a lot of Vorii refugees, just like us . . . "

"Like us?" Marit said, asking the question that was in my own head. I thought of Mannara, perforated by Vorii spears. I thought of Marit's children, of Adan, of Tracia.

No, not like us.

One of the Vorii stepped forward to stand beside Trent. He bent over, bringing his head down to the level of Marit's face, only inches away from her, the way Vorii did when they talked to each other, and said, his words punctuated by the series of clicks that came whenever Vorii talked, and which was part of their language, "Eh-dahn Matt-hews. Search Eh-dahn Matt-hews."

I just stared. I'd never heard a Vorii speak Glish before. They thought it was dirty to speak the human language.

And why was he asking for Adan?

"We won't give him to you," Mika yelled out and hurled the rock that was in her hand. It bounced off the Vorii's rigid brow and ricocheted against Marit's eye.

Marit yelped, and put a hand on her face. I could see blood leaching out between her fingers; the blood was black in the harsh light.

Shamed by Mika's mistake, I dropped the rock that was in my hand.

The Vorii put a hand up as if he meant to cradle Marit's face, but she backed away from him and put one arm around me, keeping one hand against her face as she did.

The Vorii turned from us and looked off, toward the transport, and Marit's makeshift field hospital. Could he sense Adan there somehow? But then I saw what he could see . . . Adan, standing there, shaking, braced between his cane and the transport's hull, his skin bleached white by blood loss and light.

"Tiigalt," he called out in a voice louder than he should possibly still possess. "Tiigalt—is that you?"

The Vorii crossed the space between them in an instant. The joy in Adan's face when he saw the Vorii . . . it almost sickened me. And then I saw it. On the back of the Vorii's—Tiigalt's—neck, was a raised grey-black scar, a symbol. It was a downward-pointing triangle that was missing its top, and between the lines, nestled there in the point, was an almost perfect circle. It had to be the other half of the symbol branded into Adan's own neck.

Adan fell forward, into Tiigalt, dropping his cane to let the Vorii hold him up.

"Tiigalt, my brother," he breathed. Tiigalt said something back to him in Viin, and Adan said, "Yeah, I think I'm in pretty bad shape."

Tiigalt supported Adan and carried him back to the little hopper. Marit, her eye still bleeding, discussed with Trent how the rest of us would be evacuated. The rest of us stood silently by, not yet sure that we believed in our rescue. Not yet sure we wanted to.

In the next few weeks I would learn about what the Durandin had really done to us, abandoning two conquered races on a dying world. And I would learn about the Vorii fifth column who'd betrayed their own people, and about the brotherhood, made up of humans and Vorii, who'd preserved humanity's heritage for generations and who would be called upon to guide us all into a new future, one which no one could have imagined.

But on the first night on Earth, looking up into the black as I waited to board a craft that would take me to a new life, I knew that, no matter what, I wasn't going back there again.

Marit took my hand. We settled Adan and Hannah in the little craft with us, leaving everyone else to wait for another run. I watched the broken transport vanish into the black below us, and held Adan's head in my lap as he conversed in that hated language with one of our rescuers. I closed my eyes against the dark.

Winterset
by Erin M. Hartshorn

Tófen scanned the horizon. Suri had disappeared, but her heavy footprints showed her path through the packed snow. He needed to catch up before she reached the ice, where he wouldn't be able to track her. He twitched his ears. It had been a long time since he'd left the city, but the air still invigorated him. He began to lope.

No one at the university would miss him; they'd been hoping he would disappear quietly anyway. Everyone agreed that the byari population was declining, but only Tófen wanted to do something about it, even if it involved breaking taboos that went back to the first joint settlement of byari and reven.

Suri's tracks dipped over a hill of snow. On the other side, they disappeared into a river that would soon be frozen over. Suri was his last chance to prove that his research had meaning. Their friendship had begun before Tófen had managed to walk upright, a stage the reven came to later than the byari. Even if no one else would listen to him, she had to give him a chance.

He hesitated where she had entered the water. Lifting his nose, he scented the air. Her musk was heavy here, though the scent of her mate was fading. Shaking his head, Tófen blew through his nostrils to clear them and moved farther up the river, hoping to catch a fresher scent.

Ice crackled under his feet, and he moved farther away from the water. No sense in falling in.

There! Suri's scent flowed down the river toward him. Tófen followed, after glancing up nervously at the sky. The light was fading, and he had to find her, needed to persuade her to return to the city with him before the sun set for the winter. Her scent strengthened, and he saw her tracks emerge from the far side of the river.

Grimacing, he set off across the river, stepping from stone to stone as much as possible. His feet still slid into the water a few times, but he made it across mostly dry. He shook the droplets from his boots. Later, he'd worry about getting his fur dry.

The tracks moved over a small ridge, and Tófen followed. Too late, he realized the ridgeline was a sharp one. Snow broke under his feet and he slid down the far side, ending in a heap next to Suri.

She growled and cuffed him.

"No, wait, Suri. It's me." Tófen curled into a ball to protect his head. When no further attacks were forthcoming, he peeked out at his friend.

She towered above him, only a minimal harness over her creamy fur. "You're lucky my mate isn't here. You would be dead."

"I waited until you headed off on your own. I had to talk to you about your cubs."

Suri raised her right arm, and Tófen cringed. Was she going to be as close-minded as all her species? But she didn't move, so he slid his pack off his back.

"Look, I have the data. The trek out here depletes the nutrients you need for childbirth. That's a major factor in the shift in births from twins to singletons." He held the pages out to her. "If you—if the byari—gave birth in protected caves in the city, the birthrate would double immediately. You could be saved."

She didn't take the pages. "You don't understand. Go back before the sun sets; you'll never make it through winter dark on your own."

Suri strode away into the churned snow. The wind kicked up some powder that masked her form. When it cleared, she had gone.

Tófen stared at the place he'd last seen her. He had thought she would listen to him. He didn't understand? No, she was the one who didn't understand. If she would just follow him, they could save the byari, keep her people from dying.

He shoved his papers back into his pack and shrugged it on. A glance at the sky showed not much light. His watch gave even gloomier news—only a few hours until sunset, and tomorrow was the last day before winterset.

Too late to make it back to the city tonight, but he'd planned for this. He had supplies enough for a handful of days if necessary. Exhaling, he set off after Suri once again.

Her tracks skimmed the snow, leaving gouges before the deep indentations of footfalls; she'd begun to run. He frowned. That would draw even more from her stores, nutrition she could ill afford to lose. He had to make her see sense.

His head bowed against the wind that had picked up; he struggled across the icy snow. Suri's path led in a straight line; so long as he kept that in his peripheral vision, he would find her again.

The wind shifted, blowing now over his left shoulder, now directly into his face. His ear tufts were icing up, but aside from the wind and the creaking of the ice, there wasn't much to hear out here, far even from the wild pods of selra. He hunched over farther, intent on placing one foot in front of the other.

This was the farthest he'd ever been from the city, and the variation in the land surprised him—hills, unevenness, ice dunes, and pockets hollowed by the wind. He wished he'd asked Suri how the byari found their way out here. He had watch and compass, complete with homing beacon to the city. He could find his way back when he wanted, but the byari who came out here took no such technology. Maybe if he knew how they chose where to go, it would be easier to convince them to stay near the city.

He sighed; he'd have to worry about that later. He had no funding even for his current project. Getting money to conduct interviews of the byari women wouldn't be easy—wouldn't be doable at all unless he showed some success with this winter's venture. Even a single byari staying behind to give birth would give his work validation.

The wind cut off as he rounded a hillock, and Tófen stumbled forward. He caught himself and raised his head to look around.

The vale was already deep in shadow, although enough light remained for Tófen to see Suri's tracks heading toward a cave off to the left, one of many set around the circumference. More were set into a central hill, whose top caught the last of the fading light. He trudged after Suri. If only he'd thought to bring cameras, he could get pictures of this unique place.

A foreign scent caught at his nose, and he stopped short. Craning his neck, he peered around. Another byari crouched at a cave entrance behind him. Others perched on all fours atop the hill, staring down at him. He swallowed; he was still close to the valley entrance, but he couldn't outrun them if they gave chase. They stood unmoving. Slowly, he edged toward Suri's cave.

She met him at its entrance. "I told you to go back," she snarled.

"I know." He hung his head, making himself as small as he could to be perceived as less of a threat. "But I'm worried about you, all of you. I want my grand-pups to have the chance to grow up with byari friends, and right now, I don't know if that's going to happen."

"So you think you know better than we do what we need?" She pushed his chin up to look at him then knocked him over backward into the snow.

"You have to get out of your books occasionally."

"But . . . your scientists aren't doing *anything* about the declining population."

She chuckled. "Nothing that comes up for peer review, you mean." Suri rolled him over. "This is where a difference is made."

He struggled to sit up, brushing snow off his pack and clothes. "You mean this is new?"

"No." She helped him to stand. "Not every change can be measured in a lab. Here we find peace."

Suri nodded behind him, and Tófen turned around. The byari who had been watching from a distance were approaching. Some of them were already heavy with the cubs growing inside; others looked spring-thin. All were female.

This was the chance he'd waited for. Here, he could study the byari birthing process and possibly discover better interventions. He'd have to go back to the city tomorrow, get more supplies—enough for the winter, maybe a sledge to carry them on. He was so busy creating a mental inventory he almost missed Suri's low comment.

"You can't leave. This is a private place, and even our men don't come here. They leave as cubs in the spring and never return." Her hand rested on his shoulder. "I'm sorry, Tófen."

He turned back to look at her, mouth open in dismay. "What do you mean? I only have enough food for a few days."

The other byari were close enough now that he heard their steps on the ice. He shivered at the thought of them encircling him. One of them spoke. "We have some selra meat set aside. You will not starve, but you cannot leave."

"I wouldn't lead anyone back here," he protested.

"Only a reven would think it that simple," said another voice, older and weighty. He turned to see a byari crone almost golden in her age. "This is our place, our time. You have entered it—and if you flee, we would have to kill you like a selra. Accept it; this is your home now."

He bowed his head in false assent. The byari had to sleep through the winter; he would leave then. There would be repercussions when they returned to the city in the spring, but he would worry about that later.

The same woman spoke. "I will keep you company through the winter night. My days of bearing cubs are long past." She rolled her head. "Come spring, I'll show you the best hunting grounds. This life will not be so bad."

His shoulders drooped. He could not save them, could not change them, could not even help himself. As the byari sensed his resignation, they moved off into the gathering dark. Soon, Tófen stood with only Suri and the crone for company.

"I'll help you set your tent," Suri said.

Later, he looked out the flap of his tent at the stars overhead. The rainbow curtains shimmered in the sky, making the colors dance over the snow of the vale. At least a few weeks of the year, he'd have company. It seemed small consolation, but maybe someday, Tófen would make a difference here. He could hope.

If not, he would return to a city where no byari remained. On the whole, he'd rather stay.

He sealed the tent, blocking out the night. Winter started tomorrow.

Ocherva
by Ken McConnell

Ocherva is in my bones; it is a part of me like nowhere I have ever lived in this galaxy. I am so much a part of this place that I feel nothing will ever force me to leave. It was not always so.

When I first came here I was an outsider. The Stellar Ranger Company I took command of was a bunch of misfits and loners who didn't care for rules and regulations. It was my job to bring discipline and compliance to the unit and for that I was not initially liked by any of them. I could see it in their eyes when they looked at me; they didn't like me telling them to change their ways. Some of them had been stationed on this rock for years and it seemed to have affected their ability to comply with standard operating procedures. Especially the man I was replacing, who seemed to have little regard for unit compliance.

"Cap'n, we just find it more to our advantage to look like everyone else here," Seth said in his slow, easygoing manner. "We can still do our jobs without all the spit and polish." His face was unshaven and his skin showed evidence of either sun exposure or red dirt, I couldn't tell which.

"Sergeant we will wear the Ranger uniform when on duty and we will wear it correctly. Understand? That includes bathing and grooming before putting the uniform on."

It amazed me the lack of personal hygiene on this moon. Seth nodded and lowered his head like a schoolboy in trouble. I thought that was going to be the end of it but he spoke up again, "Cap'n, we're a long way from the civilized parts of the galaxy. People don't take too kindly to fashion and pretense here. Besides, this is a desert and it's damn near impossible to keep a shine on boots."

If that was an attempt at dry humor, it failed.

"I don't want excuses. Just get your people in uniform and up to standards," I said.

That was when the call came in from dispatch about a smuggler ship heading out across the southern desert. Aven, the dispatcher, was watching the long-range scanners, his gaunt face lit with the green light of the display.

"It's a known smuggler; he's flying low to evade our markers."

"I'll get this one," I said. "Feed the coordinates to my Scrambler." I headed for the launch platform.

Seth caught my arm before I could leave. "Cap'n, maybe I should come with you. You've never been out that way before."

I flashed him a cold glare. He looked at me strangely and let go of my arm, like he knew I was going to leave without him. "Never mind," he said.

He watched me grab my flight gear and head out the back of the building, probably thinking I was the craziest woman he had ever seen.

I had only been on the moon for five days. Long enough to piss off just about every Stellar Ranger in my company by making them comply with rules and regulations. I thought if I could bring everyone back into regulation I could then rebuild the unit into a shining example that others would follow. Company H would be the best damn Ranger Company in the galaxy when I was through with them. But that vision was not to be. It was not the members of the Company that needed to change. It was me.

The Ocherva desert was vast and unforgiving. Red sand dunes extended from horizon to horizon. I watched the shadow of my gull-winged plane play across the dunes like some kind of alien bird. After several hours I was nearing the end of a vast sea of dunes. There were no settlements this far out. The gas giant planet hung in the pale pink sky like a sentinel watching over a dead and forgotten landscape.

The renegade ship was about three times bigger than my single seat gull-winged plane. It was skimming along the red dunes when I finally caught up to it. I had the advantage of surprise coming up from behind. I broadcast the standard warning message from all ship-to-ship channels as I locked onto the ship's dual engines with my canons.

The ship, a Capellian light cargo model, appeared to shut down its engines; the white flames were suddenly cut off by reverse thruster shields. I was stuck directly behind it as it slowed dramatically and came at me with a vengeance. I frantically tried to slide out of its way as it blasted past me. I was not quick enough and the cargo ship took off most of my port wing. I had no altitude for cushion and my plane fell like a rock. Jamming the throttle wide open and pulling back on the yoke let me hit the sand dunes with the bottom of the Scrambler instead of auguring in and exploding.

My Scrambler came to rest at the base of a large sand dune. All electrical systems were dead as the engine turbine whined to a stop. I popped the canopy and looked around. The air was hot and dry. In another couple of hours both suns would be burning in the pink sky and the temperature would soar. Sand was sliding down the dune and covering the shiny metal plane. Before too long it would be buried. I unstrapped myself and pulled the survival ruck sack from the back storage compartment. It had enough rations and water for about two days. As I looked around at the barren landscape, something told me that it could be a lot longer before anyone found me. My transmitters were broken and I had no idea where I was. I've been in some remote places in my life but nothing as remote as that desert. The feeling of suddenly being alone in the universe came over me like the oppressive wind. I wished I had never come to this moon and for the first time I truly missed my friends and family on Prahran.

Not one to sit around and feel pity for myself, I decided to head for a nearby mountain range. Perhaps I could find water and food there while I watched for rescue planes. I slogged over the tops of the dunes for about an hour until I reached the rocky base of the foothills. It was an easy hike up the smooth sandstone rock. As I came down into the shadows of the rock walls I found a hidden cavern. The temperature lowered considerably as I moved deeper into its confines. There was a deep pool of water tucked away from the reach of the twin suns. I set down my ruck sack and went to the water's edge. It was cool and inviting. I took off my boots and waded in. I didn't realize it at the time, but I was descending into more than just cool water. I was surrendering to the land and moving into its warm and dusty embrace.

I sat there for a while, looking at my reflection in the cool, still water. My perfectly pressed uniform and new leather jacket was the textbook image of a Stellar Ranger. I was Devon Ardel, the daughter of the Chief Stellar Ranger and a well-respected Senator from Prahran, a border world not yet a member of the Federation. My father, Joe Ardel, was descended from a long line of lawmen. He was tough and strong with everyone he knew and they all loved him for it. He was quick to tell you when you screwed up but equally as quick to tell you how to correct your mistakes. He was also a drunk. He kept his drinking private, but it slowly brought him down and eventually led to a messy divorce with my mother. It was my father who sent me to Ocherva. He suggested that I make a name for myself on the frontier where I would not be under constant comparison to him. I respected his opinion and two weeks later I was stepping off the transport onto this dirt ball moon in the middle of nowhere.

Coming to Ocherva was an adjustment for all who made the journey. It was like stepping back in time to when people were strong because they had to be in order to survive. You couldn't go to the local store and buy everyday conveniences like you could on Prahran or Selene. If you needed a tool you had to learn how to make it yourself, or do without. Most people learned to get along with what they had, which wasn't much. The people tended to live simple lives uncomplicated by stellar politics or fancy societies. Most folks were either ranchers or miners, though some were just loners who wanted to live off the grid. The only professionals in demand were frontier doctors and they tended to be more veterinarians than human healers.

Being a frontier world, Ocherva had its share of criminals. The Stellar Ranger Company had twelve Ranger Sergeants and they were kept busy most of the time. Between cattle rustlers and gun fighters making names for themselves, the Sergeants were always being called out to restore order and maintain the peace. Sometimes the locals would take the law into their own hands and by the time the Rangers arrived, someone had been hanged or shot dead and whatever wrong had been committed was made right again.

I spent several hours at that water hole, trying to figure out what to do about my Company as I waited for them to find me. I had to make the unit my own and in order to do that I had to get Seth, my second in command, to accept me as his leader. That much was obvious to me. What was not so obvious was how to earn his respect. I didn't need him to like me as a person. I needed him to respect my authority and carry out my commands.

Taking charge of the Company like I had done, making all kinds of changes to dress and policy in order to make it my unit and not his seemed to have backfired on me. I was sure that all the Rangers pretty much hated me for one reason or another. But they seemed to adore and follow Seth like he was their protector. What was it about him that garnered their respect? Was it his rugged good looks and natural leadership traits or was it simply loyalty? He was practically a native on the moon. He seemed to know the land and the people better than anyone. I thought about that for a long time. How does a newly arrived person come to know the land as well as a long time resident? It seemed impossible. I was not willing to wait months or even years until I knew the land as well as a native.

After the first day, I grew tired of sitting around the cavern. I gathered my things and headed out into the foothills to see if I could get to higher ground. The desert landscape was simple and elegant in its desolation. The salmon colored morning sky was calm and peaceful. A low fog clung to the foothills before the suns had risen. I sat down and watched the dawn break over the mountains in the distance. It really was quite beautiful. The morning air was cold and I rubbed my arms. Before long the searing heat of day would force me to find shade.

As I wandered the hills I began to teach myself about the shrubs and the sand-blasted trees that dotted the landscape. I didn't know their names but I began to classify them in my mind. There were sweet edible plants and bitter tasting ones that I avoided. I identified various varieties of reptiles and small mammals that made their home among the rocks. I ate fewer of my rations and more and more off the land itself. I trapped snakes and various small critters that were at first ugly and strange to me but as I consumed them over open fires, I began to develop a taste for them.

One of the indigenous weeds that grew in abundance on the moon was known as Ocha. I learned about it from Hap, the only Ranger who had befriended me when I first arrived. She was a tall, thin brunette with a perpetual look of concern on her face. She told me to chew on the white roots of the Ocha to keep hydrated in the desert. Nearly everyone sucked on the roots like candy. They were sweet and very moist. Hap reminded me of my mother, the honorable Gail Constantine. My mother was always looking after my safety. She even gave me a caretaker android to look after me when I lived with her as a teenager on Selene. I was always trying to see what crazy thing I could get Thirty-Seven to do in order to keep me safe. That poor machine was never so glad to see me leave and return to Prahran to live with my father. I didn't need looking after by anyone, I was always a pretty independent person.

The red dirt began to permeate my skin and alter its pigment. My long blond hair became a reddish color and started to mat on me. I had no brush and I didn't care what I looked like for the first time since I arrived on the moon. My uniform was becoming stained reddish brown and the leather boots quickly lost their shine.

The temperatures soared during the afternoons and I learned to take refuge in rock overhangs. In the mornings I explored and studied the ancient landscape. There were valleys and bluffs that had ancient rock beds exposed in stripes of jade green and reddish orange layers. I became quite adept at climbing the loose rocks to get to more interesting features of the geology.

It was during one such hike amongst the scattered shale that I first encountered the ruins of a walled city. I knew there were no indigenous intelligent life forms on the moon but it was entirely possible that ancient space faring beings had once lived on the arid landscape before moving on or dying out. It was difficult to tell much about the inhabitants who made the stone city. There were no biological remains or anything other than shards of pottery and broken mud bricks. I took shelter in the ruins during the afternoons and thought for a time about what it must have been like for the ancients to travel for light years only to find this barren and hostile moon to eke out a living on. It was no wonder that they either moved on, or died off.

That evening I gathered firewood to cook my dinner of snake and whistle rat. There were precious few trees in the area so I substituted with Ocha weeds. I started the fire at dusk and prepared my meal with my utility knife. The meat cooked quickly and before dark I was feasting on the finest cuisine that Ocherva could offer. The smoke from the burning Ocha drifted up into the clear night sky as I lay back on the sand and searched the black for my home star. I was less than ten light years from it, but it seemed much farther away that dark, lonely night.

The smoking Ocha weeds were in fact psychoactive, although I did not know it at the time. I began to feel lightheaded and relaxed. For the first time since coming to Ocherva, I felt as if I truly loved the place, that I was at home. I no longer missed Prahran or Selene or any of my friends and family from off moon. I was relaxed and comfortable with the red dirt and the pink skies. I could not imagine ever leaving this moon again. I can remember experiencing those feelings of belonging and love for the place for the first time that night. I know it was probably just the Ocha weed's influence, but at the time I felt I was making a real connection with the land. I felt at one with the moon in a way that I had never known with the planet on which I was born or any other planet I had visited. I also knew that my future on the moon was somehow meant to be. That if I stayed here long enough, I would eventually be taken on a great adventure that I could not comprehend at the time.

This may sound strange to anyone who has not been to Ocherva, but that night, under the twinkling stars I found my destiny on a barren moon on the wild frontier. In my dreams I saw a devil faced image that I must have traced out in the dirt. It would become the symbol that would unite my Ranger Company and signify law and order in a lawless land. I also saw images that confused me like the blue skinned people with dark hair and blood lust in their eyes. I saw very large warships attacking each other in the depths of space. I saw my caregiver android, Thirty-Seven, covered in dust and scratches. I even saw the thin, elegant bodies of the aliens that had lived in the ruins around me. They were gentle, patient beings that faded in and out of my dream like ghosts. Before I awoke from the trance-like dream I saw the faces of the Rangers under my command, all of whom I knew that I could trust with my life.

I awoke to the howling wind and blowing sand of a dust storm. The fire had been blown out and the pit was covered in loose dirt. A drift of sand had blown against my body nearly burying me. I stood up and tried to make it back to the shelter of the ruins. The blowing wind blinded me and slowed my progress. By the time I made it out of the wind, I was covered with red sand and tasted its grit. I sat there for the longest time, not thinking at all about the storm, but instead about my strange dreams. I shook out my long hair and bound it into a tail before I cut it off with my pack knife. It was a very crude bob, but I didn't care. I dropped the blond hair onto the floor of the ancient hovel and covered it with dirt. It was liberating to not have to wear long hair anymore. Everyone in the inner worlds wore long hair; it was the fashion of the day for both men and women. It was not popular on Ocherva. Hard-working people had little need for fashion. Hair was cut short and people concerned themselves with more weighty matters in life.

The dust storm had moved on, altering the landscape as it drifted over the surface of the moon. It was time to go. I knew what I had to do and I wanted to get back to town to get on with my life. I heard the sounds of Scrambler engines in the distance. They had come for me, probably wondering if I had survived the storm. I walked out of the desert looking like a vision of death rising out of the dirt.

Seth noticed me first. He watched with his squinting eyes as I moved over the Ocha weeds, carrying my ruck sack over my shoulder. I was covered in red dirt like a sandy ghost. Hap noticed Seth's stare and followed it to me. They didn't look as startled as I would have thought. I guess everyone who lives through a sand storm winds up looking more like the earth than a human.

I rode back with Seth in his Gull Scrambler as mine was buried in sand. I don't know how he tolerated my unwashed self, but he never flinched from the dirt and weed odor that clung to me like the sand. We didn't talk in the tiny cockpit until after we landed.

I asked him how things were while I was away, and he shrugged, "Same old stuff, bar fights and range disputes. The storm brought down the ship you were chasing. We apprehended him down range yesterday."

He looked at me differently, and I thought for a moment that he might actually like me. A gentle smile of approval spread across his whiskered face. I was no longer threatened by him. I somehow had managed to survive in the desert, and in the process, gained some respect from my second in command.

We gathered in the dirt street in front of the command post. Aven came out into the sunshine to greet us. He saw me, covered in dirt, and laughed out loud.

"It looks like the desert ghost hath returned."

I smirked at him, he could have said worse.

Hap climbed out of her Scrambler and came over to our group. She took off her helmet and shook out her brown hair. I pointed an accusing finger at her.

"You didn't say not to burn the Ocha," I said to her, my dirty face serious.

Hap looked at the others and then started to flounder, "I, I didn't?"

She stopped when she saw my wide grin break loose.

"You had the vision then?"

I nodded.

"What did you see?" she asked.

"I saw my future here with all of you," I said, looking at each of them in turn.

"We've all had the Ocha dream. I dreamed of you, Captain. I knew you would come to lead us one day," Hap confessed.

I nodded after meeting her gaze. Seth kicked the dirt a bit with his boot. "I knew you would come too, I dreamed you would come out of the desert and take us forward."

He looked at me briefly and I swear I saw more than respect in his eyes. Something tugged at my heart and I knew inside that he was going to be special to me.

Aven spoke up, "I didn't see you in my dream, I saw that," he pointed over his shoulder as a thin, metallic form ambled out into the street.

It was Thirty-Seven, my caregiver android.

"Thirty-seven?" I was not entirely surprised to see it, but I didn't know why it was here.

"Your mother sent me. She was worried about you living on the frontier alone," the android said with little heart.

I let out an embarrassed laugh. The others looked at me like I was crazy but they soon laughed along with me. Only my mother sends a caretaker to a frontier moon. I walked over to the android and put a dusty arm around it and gave it a hug. I knew it hated that human gesture, because it could not feel anything in return.

"I'm sorry Slim, she must be getting senile."

Thirty-Seven reserved comment. Its politeness routines were much too refined to say anything bad about its owner. I dug into my pocket and pulled out an Ocha root and stuck it in Thirty-Seven's mouthpiece.

"Maybe you need to burn the Ocha my friend. Come to grips with this place, I recommend it."

After a long, cold shower and a clean uniform, I gathered the Rangers in the main room for an informal meeting. I had Aven round up some leather die paint and brushes. My brown leather Ranger jacket lay spread out on the table. I picked up a brush, dipped it in the paint and drew out the V-shaped devil head design on the jacket. It was not perfect, but it was identifiable. Underneath it I wrote, "Devon's Devils."

"Today this unit is known as my desert devils, not Stellar Ranger Company H. We will uphold the law of the land and protect and serve the system and its citizens. We will not concern ourselves with spit and polish, only doing our duty. We will live on this moon and make it our home. Songs will be sung by Rangers far and wide about our courage and our fairness on this hostile world."

I saw the looks of approval on everyone's faces so I continued, "I no longer care how you like to wear your uniform or how you do your job. I just want you to uphold the law and maintain the peace. Any questions?"

There were none.

"Let's get out there then and do some good."

We went on to do plenty of "good" in the years that followed. I've never heard any ballads about our deeds, at least not yet. Some of our Rangers were killed on duty and some of them moved on to other assignments. None of them ever forgot their time on the red moon of Ocherva. After the Great War started, I left the Rangers and joined the Fleet. I took my hard flying, straight shooting ways with me and helped to defend the Federation against a new and terrible enemy who wore blue skin and nursed a devilish hatred in their hearts. But then, I saw all that in my dream.

Elysium
by Tristan S. Davenport

No language has a more tragic word than *ecocide*—a planet rendered unfit for its own inhabitants. Among the life-bearing worlds, ecocides are by far the most common. Active, non-human civilizations are unknown, suggesting that suicide, of one kind or another, is the natural endpoint of societies.

The surface of an ecocide world is invariably a blasted desert. A thick atmosphere clings and in many cases a primitive moss creeps over the sand. The oceans, or what is left of them, stir with krill and insensate plants. All the ingredients of a lush ecosystem are present. The only problem is one of time: not enough has passed since the cataclysm.

The adventurous traveler is therefore advised to look underground. Building underground is cheaper than building in space—and if the kinds of races on the verge of destroying themselves have any other property in common, it's frugality. Another, overarching project demands their resources: the one that promises salvation. It might be a massive sacrifice to some incomprehensible god, a tragically uninformed project to colonize other worlds[1], or an enclave city where the planet's elite can hide from the armed and desperate. Many hospitable planets are eerily empty except for a sepulcher of this type.

So tourists should not be surprised to learn that the fourth planet of Sheng-Microsoft is today a ruined wasteland. Mosses and worms scab the rocks, and feathery things like seaweed own the single remaining ocean. Eroded cities await excavation, but the only structure of real note is several kilometers underground.

When you enter one of the numerous elevators operated by the Touristic Ministry, you descend into one node of a silent, planet-wide

---

[1] The most famous example is the case of Asellus Australis V. The piscine rulers of this ocean world drove their kingdoms into penury, funding a series of paddle-driven vehicles designed to swim to the planet's moon.

nervous system. The elevator stops in a cool grotto; a tour guide invites you to contemplate the silver filigree lacing the walls. This delicate tracery is the true masterpiece of Sheng-Microsoftian culture, as well as the cause of their extinction.

Its complete history will not be given here. A short summary will suffice. As with many humanoid species, their culture's dominant theme was narcissism. It was not enough for their world to be just a world; it had to be "God's World." Likewise their name for themselves was "God's People." They yearned above all for transcendence. Pure was the realm of mental activity; corrupted was the hell of the body. Their sublime entertainments and love for abstract thought led them to sedentary lives. Spending their days immersed in calculations and virtual dreams, they caught the "rich man's diseases" that so plagued our own twenty-first century. Obesity, depression and diabetes took different forms in them, but the final effect was the same: first, a focus on medicine as a fixture of everyday life; second, a yearning to abandon the body altogether.

After many disastrous wars with the Cults of the Singularity, our own society eventually settled on the first strategy. Among the Sheng-Microsoftians there was no strife. Without deliberation, they chose the second. And unlike the brutal, secretive remnants of those cults that still persist in the corners of human space, the Sheng-Microsoftians finally achieved their dream of escaping the body. All their resources—their genius and love for problem-solving—went into the digital Elysium where their minds would be free of material tedium.

Construction took more than a century. The biosphere was drained for fuel, the surface strip-mined for alloys. At last, on a day of planet-wide rejoicing, the inhabitants uploaded their minds. Their corpses remained on the surface, rotting into the wind-blown skeletons that can still be collected as souvenirs.

A world-spanning computer offers more resources for a mind than a planet does for a body. To its newborn children the universe of data seemed infinite, an endless playground of creation. God's People had become gods. Pain and fear, which are things of the body, were abolished.

In planning their paradise, they had neglected only one detail. Ecstasies, even of esoteric contemplation, are also things of the body. The pleasures of the intellect, sublime as they are, depend on hormonal surges triggered by the recognition of symmetry, logic and beauty. God's People had ascended to a realm of supreme logic, yet they lacked the hormones and physical brains to enjoy it.

Certainly, they could have simulated such crudities, recapturing what they had lost, but they did not. Such crucial motivators as remorse and longing depended as well on the mortal flesh putrefying on the surface.

Standing in reach of their Grail, they lacked only the urge to reach out for it. "It's just zero of one, and one of the other," as they were fond of saying.

When, after centuries, the first systems began to fail, God's People declined to fix them. It was not that they had turned suicidal in their despair—indeed, they felt no despair at all—they simply lacked the survival instinct that is characteristic of biological creatures.

Cognition ceased roughly four thousand years ago.

Recordings of the Sheng-Microsoftian history, as extracted from the dead archives, are available for purchase at the gift shop. Be sure to buy one to commemorate your visit.

A Small Show on Double Gamma 3
by Kevin James Miller

There is a statue of him in the largest city on Alpha One Prime, the central planet of the New Human Fellowship. He understood the nature of what humanity then called "The Golden Age." We now call it "The Glittering Age." We know and celebrate the story of most heroes because of their devotion to their goal. However, he was an altogether different sort of hero.

His name was Athelstane, and he was an ordinary man—spectacularly, magnificently ordinary.

We usually tell his story in this way:

Athelstane decided he needed to die. This was unheard of for anyone from Earth. It was an age when Homo sapiens had all but dispensed with death, and diseases of many kinds. Poverty, war, racism, sexism, and on and on were all distant memories from generations past.

He kept the desire for suicide hidden in his mind, and the reason for it hidden deeper and further. There was simply no one who would understand. He kept his secret heart locked up, far from straying, ignorant eyes.

Terrestrial authorities—global, civil, and ecumenical—would not allow something as base and old-fashioned as suicide on their watch, which meant Athelstane needed to head for the outermost planets. In the long years before, he had always loved travel. Now, it was a pesky preamble to his extermination.

But first, there were rules and procedures. Humanity hadn't built "The Golden Age" by not following rules and procedures. The species somehow hit upon the magical combination of laws and standards to play the game that was the universe.

So very early one morning, Athelstane went to his local spaceport. *L. David Holbrook, Jr. Metropolitan Spaceport* was located at just outside the city limits of Chicago. It was a huge, sprawling complex and it took Athelstane an hour to find room 100251.

One billboard in a hallway advertised a new brain text download: *USA 2000-2009 A.D.: The Big Con Game.*

The New Planets Registry listed in a floating, rotating holographic display, planets newly bought by various corporations, all eager for settlers/fellow investors. The planets were named for twentieth and twenty-first century movie stars, and other myths.

In the Level 11 food court, a distinguished woman in a three-piece, black, white, and gray suit was surrounded by three Guardians. These were among the billions of robots that policed humanity in the Earth system and most of the colonies. Their function was to be on the lookout for suicidal tendencies and take preemptive action. There were three of them, six feet and taller, with plastic and stainless steel limbs, and video monitor heads that played an endless montage of smiles from every possible type of human face. Taking away what might be a bottle of poison, they listened passively as the woman said, "Don't you understand? Nobody remembers what it was like!"

Eventually, he stood before Clerk One Twenty-Seven Zero to apply for a space flight permit.

The walls and floors of the room were tediously white and spotless, the fashion of "The Golden Age" for barber shops, schools, hot dogs stands and seemingly every place else.

Athelstane, on his thirteenth birthday, had picked "Male Generic 57-B" for his face. Clerk One Twenty-Seven Zero, it looked like, if Athelstane remembered correctly, had picked "Glamour/Sex/Romance Icon 68-L/Female," all long blonde curls, magnificent cheekbones, and a long, curving elegant neck.

Athelstane stood in front of her desk and waited for the whole thing to be over.

She made swipes in the air in front of her, working her holo-computer.

"I have here that you work in Lunar Station Five. Is that right, Mr. Athelstane?"

"Yes."

"Let's see . . . Oh, you're part of the team that maintains safety standards for Earth's weather. You do very important work. You must be proud."

"Um, yeah, okay."

"I also see here that three weeks ago your supervisor found records of unauthorized use of Lunar Station Five's word-processing equipment. However, I don't have a follow-up on that . . . "

". . . that was a level 2 glitch in the computer records." Athelstane tried to look at her steadily. "That's all that was."

"Oh. Okay, then. And how are your dreams?"

Surprised, Athelstane took a step back.

"What?"

"The pysch-monitors on Lunar Station Five have you having these—I guess I should say 'nightmares' instead of 'dreams.'"

Damn. Athelstane thought he had disabled the pysch-monitors. "That's simple to explain."

"Nightmares featuring 'birds as big as planets, with wings of shadow, flame and diamonds.' Sounds very colorful."

"That was because of stress. Just stress. I really need this out-of-system vacation."

Clerk One Twenty-Seven Zero gave Athelstane a long and careful look. "Fine. Your space flight permit is approved."

Even with faster-than-light space travel commonplace, even with a portion of humanity devoting itself to wandering the cosmos, it took five years out from Earth, with almost daily, 24-hour FTL travel, for Athelstane to finally arrive at the portion of the universe terrestrial authorities designated "Unknown Space."

The best scientific minds believed that space-time, in this neighborhood, was fragile stuff, and were convinced that somewhere in the depths of "Unknown Space" the fabric of reality would grow dangerously frayed.

Kathleen Miller, author of the brain text download *Unknown Space: What Is Known*, wrote that, "Several centuries of fanciful tales about extraterrestrials year-by-year, century-by-century, continue to remain only fantasy. Humanity is well and truly alone in the cosmos, even in this distant corner of space-time."

Regarding so-called "Unknown Space," there had been some human explorers. With Homo sapiens numbering in the tens of billons, what else could there be? However, few went and fewer still returned.

Nevertheless, Athelstane pressed on.

One time, Athelstane passed an off-system manufacturing sphere. Behind transparent steel, dozens of tech/bio-altered monkeys manufactured and boxed Addington Chocolate Promise/Shock Cookies. Every veteran outer space traveler came across these spheres a lot. It was a way to avoid the taxes of the Earth authorities, and advertise goods to the large portion of the human species that moved restlessly between the stars.

Athelstane came in the fullness of passing months to a small, unmapped, oxygen-atmosphere planet his navigational computer designated "Double Gamma 3." The ship's sensors indicated no higher form of life than a few simple plant and fish species, just enough to provide this world with a breathable atmosphere. Landing, he donned an old pair of shoes. He opened the hatch and walked away. He didn't bother to lock up. He randomly picked a direction, walking east. He wondered when and how he would pick the time and moment to commit suicide.

He walked for almost twenty-four hours, without a stop, when, just before dawn, he encountered the robots.

They looked, to tired human eyes, more rust than metal and plastic. The five of them had their creaky artificial limbs hard at work building, with the ancient technology of hammers, nails and wooden planks, a small stage.

"Human, present," Athelstane said. "Attention, present units. Request/query. Data, present units current activities."

It was the kind of verbal shorthand that had been used with robots for the past hundred years.

However, these five robots ignored Athelstane, going so brusquely about their business, several times he had to jump and duck out of the way to avoid getting beaned on the skull by a two by four.

This was, at the very least, ironic for a man who had spent months cherishing his desire for suicide.

Finally, after perhaps maybe a quarter of an hour of work, the five robots mounted the little stage.

They broke into an amateurish song and dance routine, which involved a lot of foot tapping, bowing to each other, and linking together metal and plastic arms and swinging partners in a move clumsily borrowed from ancient square dancing.

The song they sang off-key was equally slapdash:

"The birds go flap-flap/The sun goes shine-shine/The rain goes plip-plop/And I am yours and you are mine/Each day is another new day/And each night are the parts between/Candy is sweet, roses are pretty/I like it when folks are nicer better than when they are mean."

The song went on like that, the clumsiest of rhymes, the most cornball of sentiments, and with much repetition.

Athelstane, despite his low opinion of the whole spectacle, sat on the moist and grassy ground and looked up at the show.

The blinking blue glass eyes of the robots did make a kind of eye contact as the mechanical men performed, but never with Athelstane, so to speak, in mind, or so it looked to Athelstane.

It was like the robots were waiting for somebody and decided to start without him, or her, or it.

It had been morning, still, when Athelstane sat down to watch this show. Eventually, he noticed the lengthening shadows, and realized it must be late afternoon, getting on to evening.

The five performing robots saw the spaceship before he did. They looked to the sky. He didn't at first, his eyes still fixed on the stage. But then he heard a low hum filling the early evening air that seemed to be coming from above.

Athelstane looked up.

The ship landing was far in advance of anything Athelstane knew of back on Earth. Every ship, when easing into a planet's gravity well, had to switch to sub-lightspeed power; FTL was pointless when traveling such a short distance.

But this ship, shaped like a giant playing card, sparkling with red, blue, and green, seem to be ascending with the assistance of waves of yellow light.

As it came near enough, Athelstane started to hear the ship's sound.

There are sounds that are "heard" by other parts of the body, as much as they are heard by the ears. A house cat's purr creates warmth in the stomach and heart. The sound of rain, very late at night, gives a weird charge to the limbs, as flesh remembers the challenges of life and tenses at the idea of death. This spaceship, with its low, cycling hum, cleared away dusty space behind Athelstane's eyes.

Athelstane got to his feet as the ship landed.

The yellow light faded and the red, blue and green light dimmed.

Athelstane felt a highly bizarre but pleasant feeling that took him several long moments to name:

He had it.

Awe.

Unfamiliar because he had literally never felt it before.

A crack appeared on the surface of the ship, widened to a slit, and then a door.

A man strolled out.

He wore a black robe, and had white hair and a full white beard.

He walked right up to Athelstane, who had no idea what to do.

The white-haired man looked Athelstane up and down and said, "So? Do you still want to kill yourself?"

"How did you—?" Athelstane stopped and observed the white-haired man's goofy, cockeyed grin. Athelstane studied the new arrival's face, studied it hard.

"'Unknown Space' and the oddball things it does to space-time," Athelstane said at last.

"Meeting a future version of you is one of the more normal things a person can expect in this part of the cosmos. And how do you know, really, that I'm you?" the white-haired man asked of Athelstane.

"Because even at the end of the universe, there are three we all know, no matter what face they wear—our greatest love, our greatest enemy, and ourselves," Athelstane said.

"Actually," the white-haired man said, "the end of the universe, its outer boundary, is that way," and he pointed upward and to the south.

"The end of the . . . ? But I was just being poetic," Athelstane said.

"Poetic or not the cosmos has an outside, and it's over there." After pointing at a part of the sky again, the white-haired man gestured at the stage, and the robots, which were looking at him with patient silence. "This show means nothing, Athelstane. The song means nothing. It amused you, interested you, a little—if I remember correctly—and that was its only purpose."

Athelstane grimaced. "And it is so important that I don't kill myself?"

"Oh my yes. You were right—we were right to think that using the computers in Lunar Base Five to write poetry and fanciful tales was, in the so-called 'Golden Age,' a deviant act. In a civilization where war, poverty, disease, crime, pollution, corruption, prejudice had largely been tossed into history's garbage can, what is the use of poetry, fiction and all the rest of it? Especially when living itself every day in such a time is such a sublime pleasure."

"I don't know," Athelstane said. "Although I guess one day, I do know."

"It's all about mistakes. This time, your era now, is a moment of no errors." The white-haired man paused. "Except one. Thinking that the 'Golden Age' would last."

Athelstane asked, "What happened? I mean, what will happen?"

The white-haired man looked up. It was night now, and the stars sat in the heavens. "The Winged Ones. Giant monsters, impossibly huge birds, with a mindless appetite for destruction."

* * *

"I—we had—"

"Nightmares about them, I know. I remember. They're real, Athelstane. They're waiting for humanity, just beyond the outer edge of the universe." The white-haired man looked just over Athelstane's shoulder. "They destroy Earth, and most of the colonies. Billions die. No matter what you tell the authorities, they won't believe you until it happens." The white-haired man looked right into Athelstane's eyes and smiled. "And no matter what you do, you'll survive." The visitor gestured grandly around him. "You may have noticed you are quite good at running away."

"What do you—do I want me to do?"

"Life is its own purpose, Athelstane. It doesn't need reasons and excuses. As it happens, however, your life does have a purpose—to be the first poet and storyteller for humanity in the time that follows the so-called 'Golden Age.' After the first attack of the Winged Ones, it will very quickly become clear to Homo sapiens, some of us, how badly we will need alchemists of words and tales. For a long while, you will be the only one of your species whose reflexes remember how to do it. However, there will be those who say, after the attacks that the last thing the human species needs is poets and storytellers. On the contrary. Such people will occupy the top half on the list of our civilization's essentials. And like the court jesters and soothsayers of yore, most of their function—your function—our function will be telling the human race things they would rather not hear. There will be those who say, publicly, loudly, and frequently, that after the attacks of the Winged Ones, any action by humans meant as part of our war effort is acceptable. They will be wrong." The white-haired man smiled. "Don't worry. Wrap it all up in pratfalls, stage illusions, soap opera, rubber masks and fake blood and thunder and you just might get away with all of it."

"'Might'? I'm talking to you, so don't I get away with it?"

The white-haired man shook his head. "Not even your future self can promise you anything about the future with absolute certainty. Hell, somewhere in the depths of all possible time and space Adult Hitler XLV right now is designing his next cloned body. A few universes over, IBM and Ford battle for Mars. Possibilities linger.

"Go home." The white-haired man gestured at the stage and the waiting robots. "You will know when it is time to set all this up. Go live on."

Elessa the Restless
by Shauna Roberts

Walking and walking and walking. Elessa the Restless, purple hair rippling in waves behind her, walked into the wind along a path worn in the rock by her bare feet. The path meandered for miles along the sea's edge. Her people had always settled by the sea and gleaned their living from it, harvesting the finned and the shelled creatures for food and skins, collecting the patchwork of red and green vegetation matting the surface for medicines and fibers, diving to the bottom to collect the black shards of glass to sharpen into knives. Now, as Elessa wandered, her people's knowledge fed, clothed, and housed her.

On this day, Elessa's eyes were not on the sea, but on the columns jutting from the ground ahead. A forest of twisted and bent metal stretched from the edge of the path halfway up the slope of the sleeping volcano. She took a deep breath and wrapped her mantle more snugly around her. Usually, she passed the place of the Vanished Ones with eyes averted. Today, there was no help for it: she must enter its walls to harvest the sleeping herbs that still flourished in the ruined gardens. The ensorcellment that drove her from home and family could be calmed by day by walking. But by night, when weary legs could shuffle no further, only the sleeping herbs could still her restlessness and grant her slumber.

She steeled herself to enter and stooped to slip through the gap in the gate. Legend said this place had once been a village of the Vanished Ones. She could hardly credit that one family could require so much space. Perhaps they did not birth only five or six offspring in each litter, as the People did. Perhaps they spawned hundreds at once, if they needed half a mountainside to contain them all.

The Vanished Ones were not like the People, or so it was said. Not much was known about those strange beings, for they abandoned the land between the sea and the summit soon after the People first arrived. Their villages lay deserted and crumbled. The Vanished Ones now dwelt—depending on whether you believed her mother or Storyteller Maril or

Storyteller Semarr—inside the volcano, or under the waves of the sea, or even above the clouds.

Inside the gate, she looked carefully in all directions. Although no one had seen a Vanished One in generations, it was wise to be wary, as her mother's mother always said. She unfurled her tongue and tasted the cool morning air. It held many flavors—the salt tang of the sea, the sharp musk of furred creatures, the sharp, sweet, sour, and astringent scents of myriad plants, the bite of rust and metal of the village remains. But she tasted no unfamiliar flavor.

Reassured that she was alone, Elessa walked east on a path wide enough for twenty People to walk abreast. The contorted metal ruins around her made her shiver. Her village had metal, of course. Her father was a wealthy man and owned a necklace strung with hammered copper disks. But here, metal was everywhere. And not friendly copper, which glowed with the warmth of the sun and autumn leaves and could be worked with ease. This metal was cold and gray and so hard she could not even dimple it with a stone.

The silence also unsettled her. The village walls muffled the outside world. She could not hear the rhythmic slapping of waves against rock, or the lulishi singing to lure their prey from their dens, or the wind whipping between the rocks. Her ears heard only her feet crunching on bits of shell and gravel.

She filled the emptiness by singing. Like all children of the People, she had learned songs in honor of each of the known spirits and of each season of the year. She had learned to move a listener to tears, to laughter, or to sleep. Here, she always sang sleeping songs, for they seemed least likely to rouse any slumbering spirits of the Vanished Ones' dead village.

She walked and sang until she reached a place where the clusters of metal posts alternated with squares of grass and gardens. Annin and prillia trees grew in regular rows along with others she did not know, but whose fruit was sweet and nourishing. She knelt in the patchy shade by a plant with feathery leaves, opened one of the pouches attached to her sash, and scooped four plants out of the soil with her claw. She snapped the stalks off and dropped the rhizomes in her pouch. She then moved into the sun and began plucking the leaves from a grayish herb, placing them one by one in another pouch. She checked another patch of plants, but their flowers had not yet dried into little cones; she would have to wait to harvest them.

Relieved to be finished, she hurried from the dead village. She tightened the thongs on the pouches swinging from her girdle and began walking.

"Found her yet?" Captain Hrankin took a swig from his flask, then wiped his mouth with a tattered jacket cuff.

"Not yet," First Officer Jana Swindan replied, hiding her disgust behind cold, precise words. "Our sensors were designed to locate humans, not Berillians." She pretended to busy herself at the sensor station. With any luck, she could keep her scans away from the path through the tuff without the captain catching on.

But Hrankin was not as drunk as she had hoped. "You're scanning too far from the shore. You know she sticks to the path." The captain shoved Jana aside. She crinkled her nose at the stink of alcohol and unwashed flesh. "I'll do it," Hrankin said.

The captain ran his beefy hands over the screen, leaving a smeary path of what Jana feared was snot, then hooted. "There she is!"

Jana made one last try. "That's probably just a wrood. They're similar enough to Berillians in size and metabolism to fool our scanners. Perhaps we should stop this wild goose chase and return to our mission."

But Hrankin would not be deterred. "Focus the viewscreen on those coordinates. Then we'll see." He dropped his bulk into the captain's seat, which groaned in protest.

Jana sighed and complied. It was the Berillian female, of course. Ever alone, ever walking, ever restive. Pursuing an unachievable goal. To be apart from her home and family must tear at the Berillian every day. It certainly tore at Jana.

"There she is! First Officer, your scanning skills need some improvement." Hrankin smirked and took another drink from his flask. "After your shift ends, report to the simulation center for a half-shift of practice. Tomorrow and the next day, too."

"Yes, Captain," she said. She heard snickers behind her from the bridge crew. She glanced over to Ferrol Trandle, who supervised environmental systems for the habitat rings and the bridge and who was her only ally among the crew, but he hunched over his monitors.

The captain stared at the screen. His communications panel buzzed; he ignored it. Jana wished, for the thousandth time, that she had never accepted assignment to the ship Hrankin had renamed the *Vulture*. In fact, she wished she had never joined the officer program at all. She could still be a civilian on *Golden Pegasus*, working in the agriculture ring alongside her sister, Kokona, in hydroponics or her brother, Timo, in soil generation.

At the time she had finished school, full of wanderlust and ambition, she had craved adventure and the glamour of an officer's uniform. She had looked down on Kokona and Timo for choosing a life of humdrum. Now, she envied them. What a luxury to feel sunlight on one's skin all day, to talk and joke with agreeable people, and to worry about nothing but earthworms and cabbages. The *Vulture* had no skylights on its dirty, dingy bridge, and Hrankin ordered the lights kept low when he was hung over, which was more often than not. It was like working in a cave. And her time off duty was little better. Jana usually spent it alone in her narrow cabin. She was nearly as bereft of friends and family as the poor Berillian.

Hrankin's voice interrupted her thoughts. "The creature is always the same. I've been running this route for twenty years. Nothing has changed except her hair. Once it hung to her waist. Now it drapes on the ground."

Grinit, the cloaking supervisor, shot Jana a nasty look and said, "Why don't you ask First Officer Swindan about it? She studied Berillian xenobiology at the academy on the *Cormorant*."

The captain swiveled toward her and glared. Jana knew he hated to be reminded that she had won an appointment to the prestigious training school and he had not. "Well?" he demanded.

"The Berillians age differently than we do. Adolescence and young adulthood lasts 70 or 80 years in Berillians. But their middle age and old age get compressed into the next 20 years."

"So she'll stay this beautiful for years and years?"

Jana hesitated, then said, "Most likely." She wondered once again at the captain's obsession. The streaks of grime around the doors, the crushed plastene cups and other debris littering the floor, and the captain's grease-splattered uniform with its torn collar implied a man who cared little for elegance and beauty.

The captain digested Jana's words. "I haven't had a woman—or any creature—that beautiful in a long time."

"You can't do that, captain!" Jana burst out. "Kidnapping sentients is a violation of the Third Interplanetary Code. So is contact with the Berillians before they reach technology level 5A1."

Hrankin sniggered. Only then did Jana realize Hrankin's words were meant to rile her. She clamped her mouth shut, but it was too late. A smile slowly grew on the captain's face. Jana's stomach contracted into a knot.

That grin usually appeared only when he was about to humiliate or demote someone. "Bring me that creature!" he ordered, to no one in particular.

Jana knew she was pushing her luck, but pity for the Berillian made her continue. "There's no cure for whatever it is that drives some Berillians to wander. Confined in a habitat ship, she'll go crazy or even die. And if she does survive, who knows what effect our Earth-normal gravity will have on her?"

The captain's face purpled as he glared at her. Jana realized she had only made him more set on capturing the Berillian. Hrankin swung to face the rest of the bridge crew. "The first person to capture the Berillian and bring her to me unharmed will get double pay and double rations for six months." Grinit leapt up, Yarch deserted his communications post, and they and most of the other crew raced down the corridor toward the shuttle hangers. Only Ferrol remained at his station.

Walking and walking and walking. Elessa breathed deeply of the sea air, its perfume of salt and soil and sand borne to her by the brisk breeze.

Her shadow had shortened to almost nothing, and the sun glared overhead: Lunchtime. She turned toward the sea and clambered down the rocky slope to a slight ledge. Her eyes scanned the water as waves lapped her bare feet. There, and there! Her hands slashed through the water and emerged with a wriggling, gleaming swimming creature transfixed on the hunting claw of each hand. She ended the creature's suffering with quick strokes, then sang a prayer to the spirits that safeguarded the sea. She nibbled at first, then ate faster as the urge to walk bubbled upward inside her. She bolted down the last few bites as the pressure reached her head and she began to tremble. She splashed her hands in the water to clean them and scrambled up the rocks to the path.

She ran until the even rhythm of soles slapping stone lulled her spirit to calmness. Then with a sigh, she dropped her shoulders and slowed to a walk. Now she could enjoy the feeling of sun-warmed rock against her feet. Elessa tilted her face into the wind, enjoying the caress of it on her cheek. The sky glowed the brilliant blue of an eye.

The sky shimmered, then four stars flashed into being. Elessa tipped her head; she had never seen a star born in all her years of walking. She watched the stars grow to the size of moons, then bigger yet, and realized they were not new stars at all. They were shaped like seed pods, but glistened in the sunlight. She walked. One by one, the pods nestled into the slope ahead. She walked. Sniffing and tasting the air for clues borne on the breeze, she could sense the metal of the seed pods as they cracked open. But what emerged were not seeds, but People.

No, not People at all, even though they walked on two legs and wore garments. She stopped. Her hearts pounded, out of synch, so her pulse throbbed in the rhythm of hard rain battering dense rock.

The creatures pointed at her and started running. Instead of being the colors of sky and sea and flowers, as People were, they were the colors of dirt and sand and decay. They had hair, but it was yellow or brown or black. They had eyes, but they were brown. Their bodies were squat like tree trunks and they ran awkwardly, some even falling. All was as the legends claimed for the Vanished Ones. And they came from the sky, where some said the Vanished Ones now lived.

Fear choked Elessa's throat. In legends, the Vanished Ones were capricious. Storyteller Maril had told of one who lived among the People for years and gave them rice and taught them to grow it. But Storyteller Semarr had caused many nightmares among the children with his stories of Vanished Ones who visited, pretending friendship, only to trample the harvest or steal away women. The Vanished Ones were kind; they were cruel. They were friends; they were enemies hiding behind friendly words. The legends seemed to agree on only one thing: The enigmatic creatures used metal and glass and stranger materials as easily as the People used bone and shell and wood.

Should she run? No, she thought. She had seen many predators on the prowl in her years of walking and knew that fear excited them. Should she fight? They were short, but there were ten of them, all stoutly built—not good odds. She decided to do what she always did, what she had to do.

She walked.

The Vanished Ones slowed as they neared her. Most contorted their mouths into a peculiar shape, with the corners turned up. First one, then another, jabbered at her. When she didn't react, one slapped another on the arm, then said clearly, "Idiots! You don't have your translator units turned on." The others fiddled with their clothes, then flung words at her: "Come with us!" "We won't hurt you!" "Want to have some fun?"

Elessa's skin twitched as if small creatures were squirming across it. Insincerity and lies, she was sure of it. She planted her feet solidly apart, released the two fighting claws on each hand from their sheaths, and shrugged her mantle back from her shoulders. Some pack hunters, she knew, broke and ran if their vanguard met with unexpected resistance from the prey. She hoped the Vanished Ones were like that.

She didn't get a chance to find out. One of them stepped forward. Elessa prepared to fend off a kick or a punch or a bite. Instead, the creature reached out and lightly touched her uncovered arm. She felt a cold pain, and the sky turned black.

"You nimwit, you've injured her." The captain scowled as Grinit staggered onto the bridge lugging the unconscious Berillian over his shoulder.

But the cloaking supervisor just grinned. "She's fine, Captain. She woke up on the shuttle screaming and thrashing about, those sharp claws of hers slashing every which way. We had to hit her with another dose of trank."

"Well, take her to my quarters. Looks like you've earned yourself extra rations and pay, Grinit."

"Captain, I suggest your conference room would work better," Jana said.

He turned and glared. "You're treading close to insubordination today, Swindan."

"It's for your own safety, which is my responsibility as First Officer. The conference room is bigger and has a higher ceiling. She might be calmer if she doesn't feel so penned in. And you would have her close at hand." Jana did not add her most important reason, that an opportunity to help the poor Berillian would more likely occur if the creature were nearby.

The captain stared at her, eyes narrowed, but could find no flaw or trick in her argument. "Put her in the conference room," he told Grinit.

Grinit lurched across the bridge and palmed the door pad. When the door slid up, he chucked his burden in. Jana cringed.

The captain saw her response and smiled. "You, Swindan," he said, "Get out my best uisghe and the mugs. Me and the boys are having a little party."

Ice seemed to trickle down her torso as she entered the conference room. Mechanically, she unlocked the liquor cabinet and got the uisghe and the captain's special "mugs"—blown glass goblets etched with snarling faces of extinct predators from Earth. "Don't think about it," she told herself as she lined them up on the conference table. "This isn't your business. You've got enough problems of your own. You don't need to take on anyone else's."

But sweat beaded on her forehead despite her admonitions.

Finished, she sighed and pivoted toward the door. The Berillian female lay propped on one elbow, staring at her with drugged eyes. Jana's mind flashed back to childhood. Little Timo had gotten his hand caught in a grain sorter, and his eyes had held the same helpless, dazed look Jana saw now. She looked away in embarrassment, then forced her gaze back to the Berillian. Wouldn't Hrankin enjoy seeing his victim sprawled befuddled on the floor, she thought.

"Get up," Jana ordered, thrusting her hand down. The Berillian remained frozen.

"I'll help you up," Jana said. "You don't want these men seeing you like this, believe me."

The Berillian took her hand. Jana jerked her to her feet with more force than she intended, then, ashamed, patted the female's arm in apology. She had not always been in the habit of taking out her anger on other people. She had been too long with the rapacious crew of the *Vulture*.

The Berillian unfurled a tongue as long as Jana's lower arm and flicked it snakelike first in all directions, then for long seconds toward the uisghe.

The Berillian looked at Jana. "They're going to hurt me."

Jana swallowed. "Probably."

"Help me."

Jana turned away. She reached to turn off her translator unit.

The Berillian grasped her wrist to stop her. "Tell them I'll sing."

"What?"

"Tell them I'll sing beautiful songs for them," the female said.

Jana looked at the Berillian. She appeared to be recovering from the trank quickly, yet her request made no sense. Finally Jana nodded, "Sure," Jana said. "I'll tell them."

After the female Vanished One left, Elessa shook her head to clear the fog. The feeling that the air was weighing down on her like a heavy mantle remained, though. The pressure was already building in her chest and head, an insistent, incessant alarm that she had been still too long and must be on her way.

Her eyes returned to the drinking vessels. The smell of the liquid reminded her of fermented grain, which had certain predictable effects, among the People at least. She tried to think against the squeezing in her head. Was there some way she could even the odds a bit? She fingered the pouches at her waist, then knew what to do.

She had barely finished when she heard the wall slide open behind her. Elessa picked up two cups, turned, and held them out in what she hoped would look like a welcoming gesture. "Come, drink, while I sing you some songs of my People."

The men surged in as she began a sleeping song.

Jana stood alone on the bridge at her station. By rights, she could occupy the captain's chair while she was in charge. But the stains and stink repelled her. Besides, she was too antsy. She checked all the summary readings, then checked them again. She ran diagnostics. She walked around the bridge and checked all the main systems, including environmental—Ferrol had joined the other men in the conference room after an embarrassed glance at her. "Coward," she had mouthed at him. He had looked away, but not altered his course.

"Coward," she now said out loud to herself. She tapped her screen to start another round of systems diagnostics. She was getting just what she deserved. She had wanted to wear the crimson ribbons of First Officer so badly that she took the first assignment that came open, never mind it was on the worst habitat ship circling Berill with a crew renown for sloth and debauchery. But she could do nothing to fix things now.

Nothing. Nothing, at least, that wouldn't destroy her career. Nothing that wouldn't prove her family right, that she should have stayed on the *Golden Pegasus*, clean, gleaming *Golden Pegasus* with its sweet air and bounteous crops, waking each morning to the bells of the monastery, spending the evenings in delicious debate at one of the multitude of salons hosted by scholars, monks, guild leaders, and anyone else with the wit or the wisdom to attract an audience.

Singing pierced the thick wall separating her from the conference room. She heard laughing. A glass broke. The singing was interrupted by a gasp, then started again, shakily.

Jana stabbed the screen with her finger to pull up the ship's database and checked on the location of the *Golden Pegasus*. She stared at the coordinates and map and then superimposed the *Vulture's* location. She reached toward the screen again, hesitated, and then pulled up the technical specs on the fuel system on the shuttle ships.

The song from the conference room was interrupted by a moan, followed by laughter. Jana gave her console's support stalk a hard kick. She stared at her console, then with jaw clenched checked the stock of riot control agents in the weapons supply room. After finding what she wanted, she cleared her screen and strode off the bridge.

Fifteen minutes later she was back, a duffel over her shoulder and a sidearm loaded with aerosolized trank in her hand.

She dropped the duffel by her console. Squaring her shoulders, she walked toward the conference room door. Odd—she heard nothing. Jana hesitated, then slapped her palm on the door control. The door panel started its upward glide. She glimpsed shadow and movement in the enlarging opening. She braced her legs and brought her weapon up. The door cleared her eyes, and she found herself facing a purple scimitar claw.

Jana raised her head. Human and Berillian stared at each other, unblinking. Finally, Jana dropped her arm. The Berillian followed suit. Jana looked past her into the conference room. She saw the captain slouched onto the table. Yarch lay crumpled next to him. Grinit and the other bridge crew were draped over various chairs. All appeared to be asleep.

"What in the universe . . . !" Jana gaped. She turned to the Berillian. "Are you okay?"

"That rests on you. What do you intend to do?"

"Take you someplace where you'll be safe."

A purr-like gurgle burbled from the Berillian's throat.

A few hours later as the setting sun flamed gold and pink, Jana set the shuttle down halfway across the continent in the sector patrolled by the *Golden Pegasus.* The shuttle's sensors were cruder than the *Vulture's.* Still, Jana had located an area with everything the Berillian said she needed: a stretch of sea teeming with fish and water mammals and floating mats of seaweed; an early human settlement in which Earth herbs of the genera Nepeta, Humulus, and Valeriana still grew; and a lonely, barren flatlands running along the sea.

The Berillian had spent the journey rocking back and forth, her lips pressed tightly together, her body trembling. As soon as the roof panels telescoped into their pockets, the Berillian leapt up.

"Wait," Jana said.

The Berillian looked down at her, muscles poised to spring free of the shuttle. Jana opened her mouth, then shut it again. What was there to say? Finally, she said, "Good luck."

"The People don't believe in good luck, only in good choices." Then the Berillian bounded out and began running, cape and hair flying behind, an elongated ebony shadow trailing.

Jana took the shuttle up into the darkening sky. She checked her fuel supply. Her calculations had been correct—she could make it to the *Golden Pegasus*, with a little fuel to spare. She tried not to think about what would happen after that. A court martial? Probably. Angry reproaches from her family for embarrassing them? Almost certainly. An exciting new career in earthworm cultivation? Also likely. Still, she was smiling as she flew away.

Walking and walking and walking. Elessa the Restless, purple hair rippling in waves behind her, walked into the wind on smooth rock that one day would bear a path worn by her bare feet.

Blue Dome of Sky
by Ted Stetson

Anne Gibson shifted in the passenger seat trying to get comfortable. She was used to the ammonia cleanser smell, but she'd never gotten used to a mini-sub being pushed up, down and sideways by the currents. Her stomach roiled and she clamped her mouth shut. When she opened her eyes rays of sunlight were shining into the water like waving liquid spotlights.

The sub went past fish farms in the shallow Texas Ocean. Giant nets held fish in pens. Farmers swam through the water.

"Heard a rumor the icecaps are reforming," Brian, the pilot, said as he steered past the outskirts of submerged Dallas. On other trips Anne had seen ruins projecting out of the water. Thousands of birds had filled every ledge and crevice of the ancient buildings.

The young pilot glanced at her, looked away quickly. She wondered if it was her pale, white skin or her long black her. Most people's skin turned pasty gray and their hair grayed from the regimen of drugs humans had to take to be able live below the water, under the sea.

"Where'd you hear that?" Anne glanced at the young man. Gray hair covered him like he was a gray seal.

"Guy I know pilots a sub in the Arctic," Brian said.

Anne heard those rumors, too.

The com buzzed and Brian said, "For you," and pressed a switch on the console. The picture changed to a young towheaded boy.

"Hi, Mom."

"Hello, Henry." It ached her that she had to be away from him, but his father, her ex, had him this weekend and she had important business today.

"My class is about to leave for NASA."

"Great," she said. "How was Disney?"

"Some of the rides weren't working. And the dome was leaking again."

"Having a good time?"

"It's great," Henry said. "Mrs. Adams is making sure I take my skin pills."

"Behave. It's hard for the teachers to watch the whole second grade."

"Why do I have to take those phooey pills?"

"So you can live in artificial light."

"I don't want to live underwater."

"The whole world is covered by water. So take the pills. In a few years your body will adjust and you won't have to."

"Only 'cause you say so." Henry looked about as if checking if anyone was near. "Jimmy's father says we're moving back to the surface."

"They've been saying that for over a hundred years."

The hover-sub raced over the urban sprawl that had once been Dallas. Fish swam through tall plumes of algae and around the standing structures.

"What's the matter?" she said, sensing something was bothering her boy.

"I want to live on the surface so I'd get to ride a horse."

"If we move back to the surface I will get you a horse," she said, knowing that would never happen.

"How's your father and his new wife?"

"She said people used to eat chicken, especially for dinner. I told her it's an urban legend."

"She's right. People ate chicken and turkey and other fowl."

"But turkeys are extinct."

"They weren't when people lived on the surface. They might still have the DNA stored somewhere."

"That's what they always say. They got it stored. I think they make it up."

"Where's your father?"

"He trying to make a baby brother while I'm on this trip."

"Oh." Anne sat back, a sudden memory flooding her mind of Jason lying on the brown rug in their apartment.

"Gotta go." Her son hung up.

"Bye," Anne said to a blank screen.

In the reflection she noticed her own hair. Thinning. Still long and black, but no longer the thick raven locks she was accustomed to.

The whine of the hydrogen engine filled in the quiet.

"Heard they finally DNA-ed gills," Brian said.

"Probably a rumor."

"You think if they do something like that, it'll stop us from returning to the surface?"

The water was getting shallower and the speed of hover-sub picked up as it rose.

"Isn't the water . . . usually deeper here?"

Brian looked down at the computer navigation monitors. "Not according to my charts."

The water became too shallow for the sub to move at high speed under the surface. Brian pressed a switch and the Plexiglas windshield darkened as the sub rose up into the air and sped westward under a gray canopy of sky.

"Looks like we'll have rain," she kidded.

"Big surprise," Brian said.

Raindrops spattered the curved windshield. The wind pushed the drops across the hood and up over the roof.

The hover-sub skimmed over the surface. Thousands of birds sitting on the calm water rose up in front of them.

"A lot of birds." Anne craned her head to watch them fly away.

"Ought to get rid of them, you ask me. Foul up air vents. Used to be a vent cleaner before I became a pilot. Believe me that's dirty work."

They glided into Rocky Mountain port, past the dock where a silver-suited worker waved them into a large cement hangar.

Inside the hangar were other hover-subs including one with the Presidential seal on the outside.

"Are you an important person?" Brian asked.

"It'd be news to me," Anne said and noticed the President's hover-sub wasn't outside where it would receive media attention.

Attendants opened the door and Anne stepped out. The first thing she noticed was the strange smell of the air. It took her a moment to realize that's how unfiltered air smelled. She observed a line, like a high-tide mark, going around the wall, as if it had been underwater. *Must be a seasonal thing.*

An attendant guided her into a room where she was given a silver protection suit to put on.

"Right on time," another attendant said.

"I'm going outside?" she said.

"Don't know, ma'am."

Holding her protection hood and gloves in her hand, she walked into the elevator. The elevator rose horizontally and vertically.

A tall bald man with a long neck was waiting for her when she got off. His gray eyes lingered on her long black hair and then went over her slender figure.

"Secretary Frank Johnson?" Anne said.

"Nice meeting you, Professor." Johnson stuck out his long fingered hand. She was surprised how dry Johnson's hand felt. Dry and almost scaly. "Glad you could come on short notice."

"The note didn't say why."

"For security reasons." Johnson motioned Anne to walk down the corridor. "Your questions will be answered in a moment."

The long corridor was made to appear ancient with stone columns lining it. Their footsteps echoed in the cement passageway. She breathed in a pleasing smell and couldn't put her finger on it.

"What's that—?"

"Flowers." Johnson's gray eyes smiled like a little boy with a secret.

The smell of flowers was so much different under the surface, so muted, so . . . so unflowery.

"Can you give me an idea what's going on?"

"Right this way."

She followed him into a side room. History wasn't her field so she knew little about ski lodges and wasn't sure what this room had been used for when it was built. However, the stink of hospital antiseptic chemicals coming through the closed door told her something.

Johnson opened the door. In the room were a dozen beds and in each bed was someone wrapped in white gauze bandages.

"They're changing the bandages," Johnson said and walked to the bed the nurses were gathered around.

A nurse handed them white masks to put over their mouths and placed a screen around the bed.

The patient was wrapped with white gauze bandages from head to toe. The medication almost made Anne gag. "The bandages have been soaked to prevent them from sticking to the skin," Johnson whispered.

"Carl lasted outside the longest," a doctor in a white lab coat said.

"Outside?" Anne said and the doctor nodded.

"How long was he outside?" Anne asked, but the doctor looked to Secretary Johnson. Johnson put his hand up to his mouth indicating now was not the time to talk.

Very gently the doctor unwrapped the white gauze bandage. A nurse stood by the man's head and told him to remain calm, everything was okay. Behind her stood a nurse holding a long syringe filled with yellowish fluid.

The doctor continued to unwrap the gauze. At first, it came away nicely revealing pink gray skin underneath.

After two rows of gauze came away, Anne saw that the skin was not perfect. Red and dark pink blemishes dotted the skin.

Another row and the blemishes were large ugly blotches. Milky white dots were in the middle of some of the blemishes.

"It itches," the patient grimaced and Anne remembered this was a living, breathing person here. Her pulse had quickened.

"Are you okay?" the nurse by his head said; the nurse behind her with the syringe was ready to lunge forward.

"Yeah," the guy said. Anne heard so much pain in his voice, she felt sorry him.

They were almost up to the elbow when the gauze caught on the skin.

"Careful," the doctor said.

The doctor holding the gauze tried to free the end, but it seemed to be stuck.

"Does it hurt?" the nurse said.

Anne had expected the guy to say yes. Instead, he said, "I'd really like to scratch it; it itches so much."

"You're very brave," the nurse said.

"Yeah, sure."

Then the gauze came free, but when it lifted up it pulled the skin with it. It was only a couple of centimeters wide and went down the center of his forearm. Everyone seemed to breathe a sigh of relief.

But something seemed wrong with the skin still on his arm. Anne saw it and wondered why the others didn't, until she realized they were holding their breath.

Slowly the rest of the skin fell away from the arm like a snake shedding its skin. Red bloody skin was still on the arm. It reminded Anne of a third degree burn victim.

The nurse with the syringe was trying to shoulder the pretty nurse aside, but the nurse was holding her ground.

"Does it hurt?" the nurse said.

"Oh no," the patient said. "It feels good. Feels so . . . pleasurable. Now I know why snakes shed their skin. Getting the old skin off feels sooo good."

The pretty nurse paled and a few others stopped holding their breath.

The doctor next to Anne motioned to Johnson and the Secretary led her outside the curtain.

As she was led out of the ward, Anne glanced at the beds full of patients wrapped in gauze.

"Why don't they treat him with burn medicine?" Anne said.

"Isn't really a burn," Johnson told him as he dropped his white mask in a large garbage can.

"What is it?"

"Possibly a staph infection from the pollutants on the surface."

"He was on the surface without a suit?"

The Secretary didn't answer as they walked down the corridor. Anne heard a machine whine in the distance. The noise from the heavy machinery grew louder as they came near.

"How long was he outside?"

Again no answer.

"Were the other patients outside, too?"

Johnson glanced at her. "I can't say. Please don't ask."

"Why did you bring me here?"

They approached a door that was guarded by two young men, each wearing an earpiece. The noise from the machines came from the other side of the door.

The two men nodded and Johnson stopped.

"Right this way, Professor Gibson," one of the young men said and motioned at the gloves Anne held. "Put them on," he said, then gave her sunglasses.

"You're in good hands." Johnson said and walked away.

In the room they helped Anne on with her hood. "You're going to shove me outside and see how long I can last?"

"Oh no, ma'am." The guards didn't smile.

A security man opened the door and Anne walked into the room where the whine of machinery came from. She smelled the oily machinery. She recognized the room from old vids. A chair lift, like they used at ski resorts.

A man stood by the chair waiting for her.

Anne recognized President George Fenton immediately. She hadn't voted for him. She thought the man was too dogmatic. Candidate Fenton said he wanted change, but Anne had been suspicious of his ties to industry.

Fenton waved his hand that meant they were dispensing with formalities.

"How are you, Professor? I trust you had a good trip out here."

"I've never seen so many birds before."

"You think it's bad here, you should see them over submerged New York. The remaining towers are giant rookeries. Los Angles, San Francisco, Seattle, they're just as bad. Last week a tower in New York fell from the weight of the birds and almost crushed a breathing vent."

"There was a patient—"

"You didn't like the hospital?"

"Was he outside?"

The President indicated a seat on the chairlift and sat down. Anne sat next to him.

"Ready for the ride of your life?"

The President waved his hand and the tram started up. Taped to a stanchion was a walkie-talkie. Anne could hear a babble of voices coming from it.

"I don't understand what I'm doing here, Mr. President."

"Read your paper on the possibility of reclaiming the surface."

"That was just an academic exercise," she said.

The President waved her modesty away.

The chair came to a stop.

"Cover up," a voice said over the walkie-talkie.

The President put on his hood and sunglasses as if he had done it many times before.

"That's what we need in this world—visionaries," he said. "We've been living below water for so long, it seems like all our thinking is bent that way."

"Ready," the President said and the chair started again.

Unlike the vids of chair lifts there was a huge canvas covering the opening.

When they rode out of the enclosure Anne was so surprised she couldn't speak. Before her was a mountain covered with grass, bushes and small trees up the slopes. The green was so much different, so much more alive than the vids it took her breath away. Farther up the slope were medium-sized trees and larger bushes.

"When did this happen?" Anne said.

"We're not certain," the President said. "Because of budget cutbacks we didn't send a scout out until a year ago."

"Why didn't anyone say anything?"

"Don't want to get people's hopes up. Just mentioning it might have started riots."

Anne gazed at workers in white E.V.A. suits on the slopes.

"People can work outside?"

"You saw those people in the ward. Some volunteers went out without suits. Now we will not let anyone out without one."

"How long—"

"Didn't last a day."

Anne looked around. It was beautiful: green plants were everywhere. There were red and yellow flowers. The fragrance was intoxicating.

"How can that be?"

"We spent centuries poisoning the surface; you can't expect it to be clean so quickly."

"But the trees and all?"

"When we found the valley there was some growth. We augmented that with seeds stored in the vaults. A few plants grew. Other plants, well . . . are lost, possibly forever."

"It's a start," Anne said.

On the slope, she saw something white with black spots on it. The creature appeared bloated with little feet coming out of its side.

"What is that?"

"A pig."

Now that she was told what it was she could see what's its ancestry was.

"You don't want to see what cows and horses look like."

"Surely we can try again and . . . . "

The President was shaking his head. "What you see there is the thousandth try. One of the few that survived outside of the laboratory." He sighed heavily. "It's one thing to do it in a laboratory with other mammals around to experiment with. What we've been able to produce is too horrible for a sideshow."

"If pigs and cows can't be DNA produced, how can we have livestock on the surface?"

"My thoughts exactly."

"Maybe we can continue to use the fish in the shallow oceans for food like we've been doing."

The President was already shaking his head. Billions of people had died when the waters rose. Some retreated to higher elevations, but they only survived a short time. Many tried to live on the ocean's surface, but storms and the changing weather conditions ended that. However, humanity survived below the surface. For over two hundred years, lived and thrived with a liquid sky.

"But now," Anne said, "if we can come back to the surface."

"We've had scientists up here, testing, working on ways to do just that. You see the best results of that below."

"The best?" Anne looked down at the slopes of the valley and saw specially clothed people working in the fields. "Can't we live off the fish until we can reintroduce plants and animals to the surface?"

"Most of our food comes from the fish farms in the shallow oceans. When the ice caps start reforming the shallow oceans will drain and we will not have enough food.

"Believe me we've tried everything. I cannot tell you how many brave people died trying. Too many generations living out of sunlight in controlled environments have made our skin unsuitable to surface conditions."

"Meaning?" Anne said, fear filling her.

"We have given this tour to our scientists and leaders of industry and asked each of them if they had any ideas that could solve the problem. They had a few which, unfortunately, failed.

"We are no longer suited to living on the surface. The lack of food alone would kill billions. Their deaths would bring on a devil's brew of viruses and diseases. We are evolving into beings that live below the surface—like dophins and whales—and now that it's evident we can't return to the surface . . . we should help that along."

Anne was about to object when the President motioned down the slope. The little furry animal was eating a plant, something similar to broccoli. It had just started eating then fell on its side and the little legs kicked spasmodically.

"Few animals have made the adjustment back to the surface. Those we didn't try to restore from saved DNA are okay."

"What animals?"

"Mice, rabbits, rats, hamsters. Some were kept as pets, others in the laboratories, and that probably saved them. We are going to be like dolphins and watch the mice and rabbits compete for the surface."

Anne felt her hopes yanked out from under her. The future was a bleak watery grave. What would she tell her son?

The President spoke to the walkie-talkie, "Take us back."

Anne looked at the mountain slope. She wanted to walk on the surface even if she was wearing an environ-suit.

"Can't we—"

An alarm blared. "The spotters." The President pointed at an outpost on a distance mountain.

In the distance was a black speck against the gray sky.

"What?" Anne said.

"Faster," the President said to the walkie-talkie and the tram picked up speed.

One speck became several specks. Soon the sky filled with tens of thousands of specks. They looked like insects, but as they came closer, she saw they were too big to be insects.

"Birds?" Anne said.

They came quickly over the mountain. Thousands of birds descended on the dead animal. Many flew past the chair and their wings, white, black, gray, beat the air around them.

As the chair raced to the station, Anne saw the workers hurrying out of the fields.

By the time they were near the base, the birds had risen up again, a great white-black-gray cloud flying up into the blue sky.

Blue sky?

"The sky!" Anne said.

President Fenton glanced upward and shouted into the walkie-talkie, "Get the workers in."

Anne shielded her face with her hands, then she felt the warm sun. She had never felt anything like that. It seemed to go right through the suit. She carefully spread her fingers and opened her eyes. It was so bright she had to squint.

Then the curtains parted and they were inside the lift station. The interior was dim after being out in sunlight.

Several aides rushed to the President. "Are you all right, Mr. President?" "Are you okay?" "Is everything okay?"

"I'm fine," the President said, holding up his hand for them to stop. "What about the farmers?"

"A dozen were exposed," an aide said. "They're being rushed to sickbay."

Anne followed the President into a nearby room where they took off their environ-suits. The President looked older, grayer and more tired.

"That's all for today," he said.

The aides left them alone.

"We can't return to the surface," the President said. "We've tried and it won't work."

Anne felt crushed.

"I brought you here because you are a proponent of mankind returning to the surface. I wanted you to see for yourself."

She didn't know what to say.

"This is a lot of information to digest and you'll have questions. Please call me."

"Yes, sir."

Anne opened the door and the cries of the injured workers echoed up the hall.

"You said the ice caps are reforming?"

"Industry is going to reactivate coal burning plants and other measures to keep the cloud cover. If there is anything else you can come up with, I'd appreciate it."

Anne nodded.

"Keep this between us until I can make an announcement to the nation."

"What about the other nations?"

"The China Sea is receding also. The Chinese President is very worried. I have been in daily contact with the C.E.O. of Africa and the Premier of India. You think we have a problem, you should speak to the Europeans. The Alps are overflowing with birds. All the oceans are receding. Billions could die without fish farms."

"If I come up with anything, I will let you know."

Soon Anne was in the hover-sub speeding back over the Texas Ocean. Dark clouds had returned and they were flying above the surface.

A call came in over the vid phone. Brian answered it.

"It's for you."

Anne grinned at her smiling son.

"How was your trip?"

"Mommy, I saw the sun today."

"You did?"

"We were down around the ruins of NASA when the sun came out. A dive plane on the school hover jammed and the bus broke the surface. Some of the kids were scared, but I wasn't. They all ducked and put their heads between their knees and their hands over their faces, but I looked up at the sun."

"Are you hurt?

Henry smiled proudly. "It was great."

"Did the doctors examine you?"

"They wanted to cover me with salve, but I wouldn't let them. I want to show off my sunburn."

"You have a sunburn?"

"Only a little one." Henry turned his head to the side and Anne saw the skin was red.

"I'm the only kid in school with a sunburn."

Tears filled her eyes. "I'll see you when I get home."

"Can we go out for squid?"

"We'll see." Anne hung up.

They were closer to some ruins. A cloud of birds circled the towers.

Anne looked at the birds flying among the towers and thought of how much her son liked being on the surface. She had been just like Henry at that age, and then she started taking the pills so she could live under water.

She watched clouds of birds circling the towers.

"Going to go below now," Brian said.

"Wait!"

"But I have orders."

"Return to the President."

"Yes, ma'am."

Anne took the business card from her pocket and stuck it in the phone. In a minute the President's face filled the screen.

"Professor Gibson," the President said.

"I think I figured out how we can go back on the surface," Anne said. "Maybe we can't, but our children should be able to. Children are more adaptable."

"It's the food supply that worries us."

"The birds."

"I don't understand."

"I'll explain when I get there. It won't be easy, but I believe it's possible."

"Nothing worth doing is easy."

Anne watched the birds flying overhead.

"Birds?" Brian said.

"You've heard of people eating chicken dinner?"

"That's an urban legend. Besides there are no chickens left."

"We'll improvise. We were always good at improvising."

Anne smiled. It was a chance. A slim one. But maybe that's all the human race needed.

Otsego Undead
by William Blake Vogel III

The rumble of his Jeep's engine was about to wear on his last nerve. Samhaen Wallace had been driving since sundown, and this six hour stint on the road had left him just a little past raw. He was full-on pissed and ready to kill. But that was a good thing in his line of work.

The radio was roaring; the song "Permanence" by Static-X echoed like a ghastly hellish dirge all around him. His mind was tightly focused on the goal. The music centered him, making his thoughts a raging silence waiting for intent.

The vehicle pulled over along the edge of the gravel road. Samhaen got out and walked to the front of the Jeep. Spreading a map out on the hood, he shined a flashlight on it as he ran his finger down the little black line. At the top of the map in big bold type read the words, "Otsego County, New York."

"Damned rat bastards, they just had to take me to the middle of nowhere," he said to himself. Yankee country: he hated going North into the "societal wastelands" as he so often called it. In these urban hinterlands the undead had found new hunting grounds, where drugs and boredom had dulled the wits of their prey.

The sun would be up soon, and making his move before then would be suicide. Even recon before dawn was risky; the cold air cut through him. From the seat he took a small container filled with scrambled eggs and cooked peppers. They were clabbered with butter, and long past being cold. But they still tasted good.

He waited several miles away from the suspected site of the lair. From all reports, it was a small farmhouse located on an 83 acre plot of fallow land. Strangers had been seen in the local area, along with an abnormally high number of disappearances as well as grisly, unexplained deaths. None of these were conclusive details, but they were good indicators that warranted a closer look at least. And Wallace had a calling . . . .

* * *

Sunrise came without event. From a nearby hill, Samhaen scanned the exterior of the decrepit edifice with a pair of binoculars. The list of facts was rundown quickly: boarded windows with new lumber, heavy doors that appeared to be new, small basement windows painted black, overgrown yard with two well-worn paths, and absolutely no other upkeep done to the withering wooden structures. Wallace was convinced now that he had his target.

He drove down to the house. Opening the back of his Jeep, he lifted-out a five-gallon canister of gasoline and set it on the ground. Six bottles filled with his own special derivative of a Molotov Cocktail haphazardly sat in a milk crate in the back of his vehicle. There was also kerosene, a CAR-15 submachine gun, a sword, and a machete as well. All that Wallace carried on him was a Browning Highpower and a kukhri knife for those "hairy situations" that seemed to happen so much more these days. He preferred a good plan to good luck.

As he prepared, he heard soft footsteps approaching. "Oh good," he whispered to himself, "The welcoming party has arrived." He made his best efforts look unaware. "A watchdog or a gimp?" he wondered to himself, amusingly.

A voice snarled, "Who the hell are you? What the hell do you want?" The solid click of a gun's safety rung as it was loosed.

"A gimp," Wallace thought as he rotated slowly to face his aggressor. He smiled, and asked, "Are you the owner?"

"Uh, no," the young man answered, "my, uh, uncle is . . . he'll be back real soon." He was wearing dirty dress clothes that looked like they hadn't been washed, or changed, in several weeks. His hair was a tangled mess. He was another wrecked city kid, a living zombie that had been taken for cheap labor. The kid got angry and stuck the shotgun into Samhaen's face. "Get the hell out of here!" he screamed. The gun was shaking in his hands.

"I'll kill you!" he howled, his grip tightened on the trigger. This was it. He busted Samhaen in the jaw with the gun's butt.

Wallace fell like lead weight. Blood gushed from his busted mouth, the red black drops shining like a starry night. Saliva hung from his lips. As tears filled his eyes, he reacted violently. With a quick snap he grabbed the shotgun and tore it from the kid's hands. Then he smashed the kid back in the face with the butt of it. The crack was deafening, as metal smashed flesh.

"How do you like it?"

The kid yelped, falling down. The blood spurted, running down his face in a thick, red torrent. "Damn it," he cried. "You broke my nose, you bastard."

Wallace smiled. "Little pointer, kid. Don't ever stick a gun in someone's face. It'll cost you," he said. "This is gonna hurt." Then he pulled the trigger.

The kid's head exploded; fragments of skull and blood splattered all around the body. Fingers twitched, as muscles seized in a last cadaverous dance. The momentum of writhing tissue made the corpse spasm periodically.

"You'll know better . . . in the next world," Wallace said calmly, pulling the spent shell from the shotgun. Stepping over the puddle of crust that once was the kid's head, he grabbed the arms and dragged the corpse up onto the porch and placed it in front of the door.

"Bait," he said quietly, dropping the torso's hands with an unceremonious thud. With a ball-peen hammer he smashed open the fortified doors, leaving the broken remnants swinging wildly in the erratic, gusting winds. This was just the beginning.

He pried open several boarded-over windows; gasoline was then dowsed through every broken threshold. Cellar windows were shattered.

Wallace was almost ready now.

Throwing lit bottles of kerosene through the basement windows, the old house was soon set ablaze. He did the same to the first floor windows and doors. Soon the withering building was an inferno. Smoke rose in raven black columns to touch the heavens in requiem.

Samhaen took out a cell phone and started dialing. "Here, kitty-kitty," he said, lifting the phone to his ear. "Hello, Fire Department? Yes, there's a field on fire. South of town, East Roche Road. I don't know. Hell, you can't miss it. The damn place looks like Dante's Inferno. C'mon! Hurry . . . hurry . . . I'm losing." Click! Then he smiled. "That'll keep them busy for a little while." Wallace leaned against the Jeep, and waited patiently.

He loved a good fire. It was like demon poetry.

Screams charged the crackling roar of burning torment. The substructure was collapsing, as the walls were felled by flames. A shriek broke the rumbling cacophony.

From a second story window, a smoldering, thrashing form flew-out. The flaming body, writhing and twisting in a trail of dark grey smoke, hurled outward from the burning house a good distance before impacting through the roof of a nearby shed. Crashing clumsily, the smoke soon dissipated after the charred mass landed.

Samhaen was on it quickly. Jumping into the Jeep, he gunned the engine. "Bastard must pay."

The speeding Jeep smashed through the remnants of the tin shed, sending the galvanized metal sheets and lumber sailing through the air like autumn leaves. It jumped the cinder block foundation. Swerving wildly, the hood now was adorned by a second passenger.

The creature's face snarled, its fangs exposed in rage. It scurried up the hood; the cracked windshield was like an abstract painting. Then the undead thing punched the glass, pushing its fist right through it.

Sunlight ignited its flesh; Samhaen slammed on the brakes. With an abrupt jerk, the vehicle stopped dead. He rolled off of the top of the hood, in a cloud of ash and ripping flames, tumbling into the tall grass. As he crawled away, a fiery nimbus followed him like a neon sign. His continuous screams only intensified.

Wallace grabbed his machete from the seat. "Burn, baby, burn," he said. He opened the door of the Jeep and got out.

Through the yellow fields of fescue, Samhaen tracked his prey. There was no hurry, there was nowhere for him to go but to Hell. He could take his time.

Soon he was upon him. A twisted, burning body laid in a mangled, twitching heap in the middle of the fallow pasture land. He was murmuring now, and Death was drawing near.

Wallace furiously hacked at the creature with the machete, severing chunks of wrecked flesh and finally beheading it. All remaining tissue fell to ashes. Cinders floated in the air around him, wafting in a ghostlike dance of downfall. Only the bones remained.

The sun was setting, the twilight glow of dusk charged the resplendent heavens. An amaranthine halo took the sky, as conquering night murdered the dying day. The breeze cooled, and all that was left was starlight.

Wallace surveyed the exterior of the smoldering husk of the old house. Little was left, except for memories. But he had to be sure.

Then he heard it—a crunching slither in the grass. When he found the source of the noise, it was a beautiful woman with dark complexion crawling away from the remnants of the house. She had been burned badly in the fire.

Samhaen rolled her over gently; her green glowing eyes shined brightly in the moonlight. She was regenerating rapidly, but she was not like the others.

He checked her teeth, they were normal. Then he sat in silent wonder, as she healed before his eyes. Soon she was restored. Lying asleep, she was sublime and serene.

"What are you?" he asked softly, tenderly brushing her hair from her face. "What the hell are you?"

The Sound of Sun Rising
by Geraint D'Arcy

Every view screen on Wendell base held a chasing blue-light image of Dr. Michelle Jameson. She had been in her early thirties, straight brown hair bobbed under the chin; she frowned slightly as if slightly afraid of the crowd fidgeting behind the cameras. The film was documentary footage from the pre-mission press conference where she had assured the world that the mission would succeed and that in ninety-five years time there would be a viable alternative to faster than light travel.

"Wendell," Jameson's image lectured, "is the fourth planet in the Beta Pectoris system; its Earth-like atmosphere and comparable gravity make it ideal for a base of operations. What makes the planet perfect, however, is its slow rotation period. A single Wendell day lasts twelve Earth years." She paused, her eyes flicked down to her notes, a nuance magnified by the camera. "We propose to build the Gain Field Archway at tea-time and have it completed by breakfast." A good humoured wave of laughter swept across the crowd, unseen by the camera but, heard on the soundtrack of the film. Dr. Jameson smiled slightly, pleased that they liked her joke; it shone in her eyes and made her small smile warm.

"Any questions?" Her face looked round the room still smiling, a grumble and crunch of murmured noise from out of shot then a broadening of the smile. "Yes, please?"

"Evergrade, *Daily Times*." A male voice spoke, tinny away from the microphone. "What guarantee?" Suddenly the voice became clear and loud; the microphone had arrived slightly late. Evergrade began his question again. On the screen, Jameson waited patiently.

"What guarantee, do you have that in ninety-five years time we won't have found a faster solution to exploration? When you wake up on Wendell, we may already have FTL."

"First of all Mr. Evergrade, the whole plan cannot help but benefit from FTL, whether we develop it now or in two hundred years time is irrelevant. What the Gain Field technology represents is the future of exploration. If we wake up to find colonists on Wendell already, then it is to everyone's benefit that the project continues. FTL is a dream that may one day come true, but we will never be able to journey sixty-three light years in a moment in a FTL ship, no matter how advanced it is. The Archway we will build will be the first outpost for colonizing humans whether we have FTL or not. Yes, Ms.?"

"Esselte, *New York Sun*." The microphone had arrived in time for Ms. Esslete's prime-time television voice to be clearly heard. "How are you proposing to overcome the entropy effect of Field use? Won't any matter lose energy as soon as it passes the archway?"

Dr. Jameson smiled, this was the perfect question to mop up the doubters. "The entropy effect has been a problem for the smaller archways which assist communication and transportation of inert supplies around our solar system. The entropy effect is directly proportional to the distance, but inversely proportional to the size of the gain field created. The Archway on Wendell will be greater in size by a factor of two thousand than the Titan/Earth Freight Archway." The off-screen crowd rustled their comprehension as the sound and image faded from the screen.

On Wendell base, the screens went dark. The film had finished. After a short moment the screens revealed a small platform dressed in black palls in front of a large black wall curtain. A single lectern stood at the center of the platform and behind it a young man who bore a filial resemblance to the woman on the screens a moment before; he was taller than Dr. Wendell, but he had the same angular chin, and eyes a shade darker of grey. Though he would have hated it if he had been told, they both shared a slight crook in the bridge of the nose inherited from maternal grandparents long since passed away.

"My sister," he began with barely a falter in his voice, "was a brave visionary who ninety-five years ago began a project that was unlike anything the world had ever seen. We saw her just now speaking about something she was passionate about, something she believed in. When they made Michelle head of the project, she was overjoyed. She genuinely had not expected to receive that accolade, despite the fact that it was all her idea. She asked me to come with her and I did." The man cleared his throat. "She personally picked most of you to be on the project. Those of you who were later assigned, she deliberately went out of her way to get to know. It is a great shame she did not live long enough to complete . . . " He trailed off, a painful sob stretching the back of his throat in its eagerness to escape; a full burning pressure swelled in his eyes and nose. He paused for a moment before continuing. "Michelle's refusal to lead from behind a desk, her insistence on leading from the front, for experiencing the same hardships and difficulties that she asked us to bear made her a great leader, a wonderful friend . . . " His voice suddenly broke, a much larger man got up onto the platform and put a wide arm around the grieving brother. "And my only sister," was barely caught by the microphone as he was gently escorted away. The larger man stepped back up to the lectern. He ran a hand across a dark mess of stubble that did not really suit him and sighed heavily for a moment. His hand slid underneath the wooden surface and pressed a concealed button. The black backdrop slowly swiped aside revealing a large window looking out into space from a high orbit. The green curve of Wendell encroached the upper left portion of the view. At the bottom right, Beta Pectoris threatened to dawn. The large man looked up from the lectern and cleared his throat.

"We commit this body to space . . . "

Danny sat at the canteen table pushing the remnants of green curry and rice around his plate with his knife. He would push it into a mound at the center of the plate, then stretch the mound out until it reached the edges in a long ridge. Then Danny would push it up into a mound again, spending ages making sure it was dead center by moving the plate around in a circle. Bryn walked over from the double doors past the first few tables, stubble still unshaven since the funeral. From under his glowering brow Danny had hoped he would sit down on another table and leave him be; he had humiliated himself by crying earlier and he refused to do so again. Bryn sat down and with a meaty, dark-haired hand placed a manila file on the table next to Danny's plate. Not looking up from the plate, Danny slowly reached out and pushed it back towards Bryn.

"You not going to read it then?" Bryn said. His voice was deep and unfaltering, just as it had been when he sent his wife's remains to orbit a strange star.

"What does it say?" Asked Danny quietly.

"You need to read it, lad." Bryn said.

Danny stared at his plate for a while then looked up at Bryn. He sat back in his chair and continued to look at his new boss and sister's widower.

After a time Bryn sighed and spoke:

"It's a field promotion, they want you to complete Shell's project before the deadline a week from tomorrow. You are to be my second in command of the base." Bryn let the news sink in. He received no response so pressed on taking the silence as a sign of encouragement. "I'm not qualified to do what Shell did; they want me to administrate the final stages." Again the silence. Without a response he continued flatly: "Do you think you can finish the Keystone before sunrise?" His words hung out in the canteen like mildewed laundry. Danny did not respond so he waited and stared back at his brother-in-law's pale face. Bryn was a man to make anyone look unhealthy, wide across in every direction with hair like brown-leafed clematis. His sad brother-in-law looked particularly wan in comparison: his dark hair slightly greasy, his skin sallow. Normally Danny was nearly two meters of compact engineer and energy. Michelle's death had sapped that away from him.

The canteen, empty but for those two, hushed itself in a white noise hiss of air processors; the metallic echoing silence of the kitchen loomed, darkened and empty at the end of the mess hall. The staff had long since retired to their bunks in the accommodation tower: sleeping, ready to start their next day of service with a full breakfast, for those who wanted it, under the long Wendell night.

"I keep hearing her scream, even though I didn't. I felt like I should have heard her scream, because her body seemed to." It was a hushed whisper of fear from Danny. The moments when his voice was lost in the hush of the canteen, meanings and emotions were conveyed to Bryn through Danny's eyes. He spoke for an hour like that, quietly, guiltily, sadly. Every moment lived out anew from the moment his sister died in front of him to the moment he had woken from the dream of her death again that morning and had wandered into the canteen. He did not remember ordering or eating most of the curry, but he recalled in the most minute detail the moment his sister had died.

"The frame was in place, beta team had the southern exposure, Shell's had the north; it was just a bolting job, the keystone would not be ready for another couple of days, but the frame had to go in that afternoon so they could free up the scaffold pods. I don't understand how it could have gone wrong. The team were just returning to the shuttle. Shell and I were snagging the work from opposite ends of the array. She looked like I should have heard the screams, but I was already half way back to the shuttle. I tangled the lanyard trying to get back to her, maybe I could have." Danny did not trail off, he just stopped. Bryn pursed his lips and nodded.

"Meteorology says it was Aurora, Northern lights. But not pretty like back home, it's too early for visible light Aurora, it was probably up near the violet end." He paused wandering if the double message was getting through: "it was an accident and we are running out of time".

"It activated the part of the archway Shell was touching. The resonance killed her quickly." Bryn looked down at the table and wished he had some curry to push around too. Just realizing what it all meant made him feel small and out of control, a feeling he was not used to.

"But not instantly." Danny whispered at the table.

"No," replied Bryn. "She would have known what was happening."

Danny looked out with his binoculars from the Wendell observation lounge. Wendell at night time was brutally cold and barren. Layer upon layer of ice covered the only form of life on the planet: a particularly fecund and resilient form of bryophyte which used the intense cold as part of its life cycle. The botany survey team had determined that this life form would never evolve beyond its current form, given the harsh conditions it had to grow in. Wendell consequently was a duo-chromatic planet: white with snow at night and green with moss during the day. As night fell on Wendell so did the snow, the six-year night froze the moss, killing the plant but preserving the spores; as day broke again, six earth years later, the spores would germinate and colonize the detritus left by the rotting parent plant as it defrosted.

Danny had once been to the day side on an early expedition, to build an observation hide; he knew then that the task would be pointless. The planet held no life aside from the project scientists and engineers and the Wendell moss; there was nothing but mile upon mile of furry green moss to observe and nothing to hide from. The landscape looked the same at night as it did during the day: undulating doldrums and drumlins. Only in a few weeks it would be green instead of white and there would be Earth colonizers and exploration clippers everywhere.

The observation lounge was circular; the direction that Danny faced would soon be the main parking lot for the first wave of settlers and explorers from Earth. Through the west viewing window was a sight that he was building up the courage to look at again. When he finally did look, it was a sight that filled his eyes with tears. His emotions confused him:

should he think of them as tears of pride or of grief? The view was unique and his Shell had made it.

The Archway straddled across the white wastes, forty kilometers between each column, rising into the night sky: silver running into black against the stars. The imposts soared fifty kilometers from the base level with the voussoirs rising up from the haunches, at sixty, to meet at the keystone a further twenty kilometres up. The entire structure was constructed from a silvery superconducting alloy shipped in sections: bound up as carriages trailing behind the Sleeper ship. Other supplies and replacement parts were shipped by means of a smaller version of the Archway established near the depots to the south of the base. Every piece of equipment and material came through the gain field at the same instant it was put in. The space between the supply depot on earth and the recipient archway on Wendell was sixty-three light years, reduced in time and space to no distance and no time at all. Every piece of equipment and material put in, came out fifty degrees below absolute zero. The Gain Field reduced time and space to nothing but could not account for sixty three light years of heat loss through entropy.

The mammoth Archway would activate at sunrise on Wendell. At the same time, a sister Archway would be towed from behind its sun-screen of asteroid rock and into the light from Sol. The alloys within the structure of the Archways would activate in the light of the two Class G stars and vibrate in sympathy with each other causing the space at the point of Wendell and the space at the point of the Archway of Earth to meet. Sixty-three light years would be as nothing; it would be like stepping through a door.

When the press had first witnessed the effect on a smaller scale, they called it a wormhole; scientists, Michelle Jameson amongst them, had been quick to point out that this was not a hole in space at all, but two branes made incidental to one another in frequency through artificial means. Many official and confusing papers were published explaining how the phenomenon worked, but to keep it simple for the press, it became known as the Gain Field Effect.

Danny needed to finish the project for his Sister's life-long work to be complete; Bryn wanted to put him in charge. The radio message delivered through the supply arch said the same: Bryn would administrate, Danny would build.

He looked up at the Archway, a ribbon of omission in the stars. For a moment a faint flare of silver ran down the southern voussoir, illuminating a scaffold pod. Danny brought up his binoculars, which hung around his chest, to check the structure. With ease born of second nature, he located the scaffold pod immediately.

The image cleared, Danny was met with a thought he had not expected: All the scaffold pods were down and rigged to the keystone, ready for tomorrow's first shift. They had all been commandeered for the lifting team; as the support structures were already in place, there would be no reason for a pod to be supporting the Arch. There should not have been a pod left over for him to be looking at.

He scanned across the intrados towards the soffit unsure why he had done so, or what he was looking for. On the underside of the Archway were two human figures clad in the micro-gee environment suits that had been modified for rigging. They were definitely part of his construction team. Two figures: one reaching out, hopelessly struggling to reach the other, arm stretching, legs tethered at the end of a tangled lanyard. The other figure writhed and spun away from the soffit with gloved hands at the side of her helmet. He knew it must be "her." The coincidence was too overwhelming. It was her death all over again: reaching out but not managing to get to her as she spiraled in space, hands up to the sides of her helmet, no one could save her, especially not Danny who was reaching out to his sister and her screaming, screaming inside his head.

The alarms blared deeply and wailed thinly. Several people dived into doorways and pressed themselves against bulkheads as Danny and the duty rescue team bolted down the flashing red passageways to the lifeboat station. Bryn met them there.

"Status?" He boomed through the cacophony.

"Obs lounge alarm. Two in distress on South Intrados Section Eight." Came the duty officer's reply. "ETA twelve minutes." She nodded her head and two colleagues held up her suit. She pushed her arms into the suit and pressed the seals.

"Twelve minutes is too long!" Danny shouted from the corridor; he barged past the duty officer as she was tying back her hair ready for the helmet, and stumbled in the cramped space until he was face to chin with Bryn. "We've got to move faster than that!"

"Sir?" The duty officer shrugged off Danny's rudeness and continued to suit up.

"Stand down, Dan. Let them do their thing." He pulled him roughly back by the shoulder.

"She won't last that long."

"She? It's not Shell, Daniel. Let them get on." Bryn pulled him back from the edge of the airlock where he had been pushing to get to. "Come on." The lock slid shut and in an explosive, but silent separation the lifeboat slid away from the body of the base dock and took off for the Archway. Danny shrugged off Bryn's hard hand with an aggressive shoulder.

"All right Dan, that's enough!" Bryn was reaching the end of his sympathy. Danny was not the only one grieving for Michelle. "I take it, then, it was you who called it in. What is it you saw?"

"I saw one of the scaffold pods and," Danny took a breath, "I think I saw me and Shell, as she was dying." Bryn began to protest but Danny cut him short. "I know that was stupid, so I called it in. I figured it was just some prep work for the keystone business tomorrow."

"Okay Danny, you calm now?"

"Yeah, I'm okay."

"You sure?" Bryn put his large hand on Danny's shoulder.

"Yeah."

"All right, whatever happens I'll let you know about it in the morning. Right now, get some rest. It's going to be a long one tomorrow, isn't it? And you're in charge, so you need to stay cool. Get me?" Bryn stared hard at Danny until he was sure his friend had got it.

Bryn suspected they would find up there exactly what they did: nothing. All Scaffold pods and personnel had been accounted for. He worried about tomorrow and passed orders to Danny's second in the "unlikely" event of another episode. He should pull the plug on Danny, but Danny's experience made him non-expendable, and he was a friend, family even. Bryn slept little that night and thought of his wife and how much he missed her. He wondered if, when the project ended, he would get time to cry; he wondered if he was capable; he wondered if he would ever sleep again.

Danny twisted the spiked end of the spanner through the guide holes. With effort the top guide matched up. Forcing his knee into the crook of the stanchion to maintain purchase, he used his now free left hand to force the bolt through the top hole. Pulling the podger free again, he banged the bolt home. The next slid more easily through the second guide hole. He felt a tug at the back of his belt. Looking round while holding onto the girder, Danny saw that his spanner had flown loose of his belt and was spinning at the end of its safety line. He drew it back towards himself with his free hand and slotted it back into his belt, hoping that this time it would remain in its worn leather holster.

This was the last secondary support of the day. They were ahead of schedule by a long way. Everything was going well; his team were working quickly and efficiently. He was looking forward to celebrating with everyone in the bar when they touched down back at base. He unclipped the first safety and repositioned it on the other side of the stanchion. At his chest, he loosened off the ratchet that allowed his work-positioning line another meter. Then he crawled across the stanchion to the other side and unclipped his second safety line, reattaching it on a strut near his foot. He loved rigging in micro-gee, the freedom it gave made him feel superhuman: climbing could be done easily in any direction, falling and jumping were more leisurely than under full gravity and the suits were nowhere near as clumsy and cumbersome as they were in zero-gee work. Bryn had been right this morning when he said that throwing yourself into your work was the best thing for grief: Danny had started feeling good about the project again and was proud to be continuing his sister's work.

"All done this side, Boss," Steve said over the radio, a harsh bark of static following on his words.

"Ow, Steve, your radio all right? I got a blast of static then."

"Far as I know. Heading back now." Again a squelch of wincing static. He made a note to check out the radio gear on his PDA. If sunrise was in two days, it stood to reason that the electromagnetism might send the communications weird.

A cap-nut on each bolt and the last support in the section would be complete. He attached the fuse charges to the cap-nut, and began the process of climbing back: unclip first lanyard, reposition, re-clip; unclip second lanyard, move, relocate, re-clip. Five meters away from the cap-nuts and bolts, he activated the charge and the nuts span tight and fused. The job was complete with two days spare for snagging the keystone before final activation at sunrise. It was nearly breakfast. Danny smiled at his sister's ninety-five-year-old joke and gazed down on Wendell. The horizon to the west was increasingly blue with every day; a midnight-misty halo had begun to form against the Wendell night sky obscuring the alien constellations. Next year promised to be a lovely day.

Something hit the back of Danny's helmet with a sharp jolt.

"That bloody spanner."

"What's that, Boss?" The bark of the radio static was extreme this time and hurt Danny's ears; he yelled against the sound and the pain.

"Steve! Shut down your coms!" Steve either could not comply or could not hear as the static screamed on. The back of Danny's helmet felt a knock again. He started screaming against the noise in an effort to cancel out the pain and the noise, as he fumbled with the panel on his arm that controlled the communications to his suit. The screaming was unsuccessful, but the static had stopped as soon as he had clobbered the panel a few times with his fist. Danny could fix the damage back on the surface tomorrow morning. The object smacked against the back of his helmet again, making him wince with frustration rather than pain. He clipped off both his lanyards then positioned himself to look for the straying spanner, twisting round over his shoulder in an attempt to catch it. Five meters above him, right by the stanchion he had just finished, struggled an individual in a micro-gee rigging suit. The worker flailed from the end of a safety lanyard like an obscene jellyfish surrounded by tools that extended out on their own lines, a colony of distressed creatures struggling in the upper atmosphere of an icy barren planet.

"Shit." Was all Danny could manage to utter into the silence of his helmet. A spanner from the ailing figure cracked sharply against the glass of his faceplate, rebounding back to its owner. Danny had to reach his comrade before he could pull them in. Hurriedly he unclipped one of his lanyards. He snapped off the wrong catch and in his rush to reach out he lost his grip of the Archway structure. His foot slipped and he was sent into a forward somersault that entangled him in his own safety gear and held his legs against the side of the Archway superstructure in a mess. Danny reached out his free arm towards the struggling figure and screamed out his sister's name. The figure in the micro-gee rigging suit reached up to their helmet. Through the silence of space, Danny was sure he could hear his sister screaming.

Bryn sat reading by the slumbering Danny in the Base infirmary. The doctor had diagnosed Danny as being "overly stressed." The incident on the Archway had been put down to a psychotic episode brought on by the events of the past week. Aside from a burst eardrum and exhaustion, he would be fine. Bryn, quite rightly, blamed himself. No one else blamed him, but Bryn did and quite rightly too: Danny was not just Shelly's little brother, he was his too and had been for the past twenty plus ninety-five years. Bryn was just staring at a page in his book when Danny woke.

"I saw her again, Bryn."

"So they tell me." Bryn replied without looking up from the page. He had small gold reading glasses perched on the bridge of his nose. Their petite delicacy looked somewhat ridiculous on so large a man.

"Was it real?"

"I think it was real enough for you." Bryn put his book down and tried to smile. "The doctors say you're going to be fine. I'm sorry Dan; I shouldn't have sent you up there."

"Did we finish?"

"Yeah, but . . . "

"Then what's the problem? You made the call, we completed the job," said Danny. His throat felt dry and painful, a side effect of the sedatives. "Is there any water?"

Bryn helped him to some from a beaker on the bedside table. Danny finished drinking, Bryn held onto the beaker.

"Activation is tomorrow morning. There will be a party and presentations in the Observation lounge. The Doctor says you can go to it, if you feel up to it."

"Am I allowed?" Asked Danny.

"Of course you are, pal. We couldn't have done it without you."

"I doubt I helped that much." Danny croaked and assisted by Bryn, took another sip of water.

"We were behind schedule when you started, we were ahead when you finished. The snagging's all done and the safety measures are in place. What's the problem? Everyone wants you there. They're as worried as I am."

Bryn left half an hour later when Danny pretended to need rest. As soon as Bryn was gone, Danny rolled onto his back and stared at the ceiling.

When he was a small child, Shell had taken him down to the river every day for an entire summer. She was eighteen and about to leave for university; he was seven and convinced that she knew the answer to every question in the world. The water was bitterly cold as he waded in up to his knees, his sister in slightly deeper, but only up to her knees.

"Stay there now, don't come any deeper or you'll get swept away!"

Danny had obeyed and positioned himself like his heroine did: legs straight, back bent, hands dangling in the cold flow past the wrists. The sound of the air and the surroundings sounded different when he stood like that: the air seemed far away, the wind muffled, and the river alive with reverberation and cacophonous song. He never thought to ask why they were doing that, he just enjoyed the feeling of his extremities being numb and the forest sounding distant. With a loud splash and a cry of triumph his sister swept up a great handful of water and hurled something silver-brown and speckled onto the bank of the river, then with a great unsteady splashing gait ran over to glory over her triumph. Danny was elated, his heart thudding thickly in his ears as the blood rushed down from his previously hung head and back into his numb feet as he too crashed towards the bank.

Michelle's glorious catch flippered and slappered across the grass as she struggled to keep it from its natural environment by scooping and pushing and fumbling it away from the water's edge.

"What is it?"

"It's dinner." Shell cried as she pounced on the trout one last time and watched it struggle no more.

"Come on! We have to get one for Nan too. I'll show you how."

Danny learned more that summer than at any other time of his life, of that he was sure. Experiences never again opened themselves up to him like they did that summer. In the week before she left for the university, he had asked her the one question he could not bring himself to ask anyone else, trusting that she would have the only satisfactory answer.

"I don't know. I'm not sure anyone knows." She could sense his disappointment. "But I know what I would like to happen. Life is so full of things that I don't think you can ever fully assimilate them in one lifetime." She never "dumbed down" her language when she spoke to her brother, if he did not understand he would ask.

"Every experience, every smell, taste or observation has to be noted and accounted for. Life's too short to do that when you are alive, so maybe when you die, you get to appreciate all that has happened to you."

"I thought we were meant to rest in peace." Danny said.

"That's a matter of perspective, I suppose. I like stuff like reading and observing and calculating. I find that fairly restful. Don't you?"

"No," he said making Shell laugh, she made a grab for him trying to tickle him under the arms and across the ribs. They chased each other through the summer forest all afternoon.

* * *

Danny pushed the past from his mind and thought about the figure: he was sure it was his sister, but how could it be when they had retrieved her body?

The Gain Field worked by resonating at the same frequency as the space and time of a certain point, when the field opened it was as if the Archway was passing from one side of a wall to another even though the respective sides of the wall were many light years apart. Danny stopped; this line of thought was getting him nowhere. He reached over for his beaker of water and took a sip. At a lecture in university he had heard postulated that space-time was not an ephemeral dimension but a bubble with a limit to it, a definite membrane that pushed up against other branes in the multiverse. It had formed part of the early thinking of the Gain Field Theory that the membrane of space-time could be forced into one place and allow matter to pass across great distances in a single moment; some of the models used by scientists were of bubbles and surface tension. One particularly early paper had proposed an area of differently-shaped space-time existing at the fringes of the Gain Field near to the places the Archways touched each other at the moment of connection; it was like the meniscus of water on a glass creeping up the edges. In this space, Dr. Michelle Jameson was trapped, forced to live out her own death for eternity. Danny had never believed in such fancies as souls, but whatever was left of Michelle's consciousness must be trapped in the Archway somehow. This was not the eternal peace he had been promised by every eulogy ever written. This was not in accordance with Michelle's riverside wishes and he would not let it continue.

Everyone was preparing for the activation. The Scaffold pods were unattended and would not need maintenance until after all the festivities had taken place. If he took a shuttle or the lifeboat, they would try and stop him, but if he programmed a ride on the Pod no one would notice. His sister might be trapped in time because of the Archway's shivers of early activation. Danny knew what he had to do when he got up there: if the keystone was removed, without the scaffold pods and the pre-structures in place, the Archway would fall and the Gain Field effect would cease. Shelly would be free to appreciate everything she had done in life, she would find peace. At that moment Danny did not care for consequences or for the safety of his colleagues, he thought he knew what his destiny must be. Clipping his lanyards onto the pinion hooks and shortening his positioning harness to its minimum length, Danny opened the access panel of the Alpha section Scaffold pod and changed its day-program.

The ascension took half an hour. Danny could see the full extent of the base, sprawling over the ice under the pillars of the Archway. He wondered if many of those who lived below would make it out in time, and if they would ever rebuild, but it was a quiet, uncolored thought that was washed out by others. The western horizon was a warm blue, specters of spectrum flitted across the night sky. Time was running short.

Bryn had so many things on his mind, the events of the last few days seemed like such a strange story he had once read perhaps as a child and not something that had been deeply affecting him. The thought of seeing an Earth Ship come through a Gain Field of such magnitude was utterly intoxicating and desirable. So much of his life had been building up to this. Michelle would have been so happy. Today would mark the first day in the new age of Humankind. Dawn was in just thirty minutes. Out of the western observation window Bryn could see colors in the sky. Murmurs of excitement and awe rippled through the crowded lounge.

"Aurora." He breathed.

A slowly executed back-flip was the method that Danny chose to leave the pod and gain access to the Keystone section. A back-flip that saw him dangerously unfettered across twenty-five meters of space. As soon as he touched the framework of the superstructure, he slapped the clips round the nearest joist and back onto their own lengths. He clung fiercely onto the Archway until his adrenaline had reduced. That was an unorthodox but necessary way of gaining access to the Arch, one the safety rules frowned upon.

After a few minutes, Danny was calm enough to start to move towards the secondary connections which secured the keystone in place. Once those were severed it would just take a moment to re-program the primary couplers remotely, then the keystone would be free and so would his elder sibling.

"Not long now, sis," he muttered into his face plate.

The north side he would do second, only because it was farther away. If he did away with safety and disconnected his hook clamps, he could run himself along the stanchions quickly with his hands; he had done it before on training missions and when there were emergencies, though again, the book did not recommend it.

It was time for Bryn's speech. He ascended the platform and made his way through the applause to the microphone. Scanning the crowd, he realized sadly that his brother-in-law was not there to share the moment. Something cruel in the back of his mind told him: "never mind, it'll save us all a bit of embarrassment."

Danny pulled himself to a jerking stop, killing his momentum. He slapped on the safety hook. He took from his kidney-pouch a small plasma torch which he used to cut through the first set of retaining bolts. On the red metal ends he applied tapping-caps. When ignited, they blew out the bolt-weld entirely. The first support was free. He moved onto the second: hand over hand, head towards Wendell, safety hooks clipped onto his chest strap.

Danny clipped off near the joist but slipped. His previous momentum had not been fully quelled and his inertia took over sending him planet-ward with just enough energy to unravel the safety tolerance on his lanyard. The fall arrest lanyard unraveled three more meters to the safety line's usual two, stopping with a jolt at the end of the line. His tools liberated themselves from their pouches and holsters, and they too sailed out on their retention lines. He floundered for a moment before righting himself, then struggling with his arm wrapped round his back, he tried to grab his tools, while simultaneously endeavoring to pull himself back to the joists and safety. This set him in a slow spiraling motion—feet towards the planet, head towards the stars like a strange low-orbit satellite. Danny's radio burst suddenly with static, he hit the panel on his arm and it ceased. Silenced while he tried to get his bearings, the crisis had sent him into a slowly revolving moment of mad clarity. His radio burst into static again and no amount of hitting would silence it. As he pounded his arm to kill the radio, he realized that the sound was not coming from the equipment but from his surroundings. Vibrations from Archway conducted along the lanyard like a string telephone to his helmet. Sound was crashing through him while outside was silent in the near vacuum of the upper atmosphere.

Dawn was creeping into view, a thin blinding line through the silence of space. He stared at its beauty, dumbfounded through the noise. He looked below, along the soffit of the Archway. A few meters below a figure in an environment suit specially modified for rigging in micro-gee struggled; his safety lines were twisted and wrapped round his legs. The figure desperately reached out towards him, a scream sounded in Danny's memory before the figure abruptly vanished.

In the tiny air space of Danny's helmet, sound found air to live again. So much vibration and sound that Danny could not stopper it, he put his hands up to the sides of his helmet knowing it would do no good to scream; even if it were just to try and cancel out the noise he heard and cope with the pain. Blood filled Danny's ears as the Archway resonated through him. The sound changed through the blood, it became thicker and more comforting as it pulsed down his neck. It was the sound of wind muffled and the river alive with reverberation and cacophonous song. It was the sound of Sun rising.

The Secret Life of Jane Gray
by Ginny Gilroy

On Aurum 9 the gold nuggets that were scattered on the sulfurous, desert surface of the planet had been picked up years ago by minerbots. The surface was too hot sustain organic life for more then a few hours, but there was an atmosphere that contained enough oxygen to support the office staff and the mine.

A descendent of executives, Director Jane Gray had come to the planet after a disappointing career. She had shown promise as a geologist, but as a manager she was a complete failure. Still, nobody could talk her out of her chosen career path. It was thought by the executive branch that Jane could do no harm on Aurum 9. It was a long-established mine that practically ran itself, and a prospect that was near to spent anyway.

When news of the rebellion reached her, Jane insisted on handling the situation herself. She gripped the elevator handle tightly as she descended into the cold bowls of the planet to the derelict drifts on sub level 43. Walking through the abandoned drifts she was free to wear her anger on her face and in the stiff set of her body. She had plotted and schemed for years to find the perfect planet and get assigned to it. The miners threatened her grand plan with their bad behavior.

The sharp click of her footfall echoed off the cold stone filling the hall with the sound of her authority. As if on command, the phosphorus that lined the floors ignited, casting an eerie green glow in the darkness. The drifts in this section of the mine had been closed long ago. The miners had cut away as much gold as they could from the main ore body. The rest was too expensive to bring out. This planet had no source of water for refineries, and there wasn't a large enough return on investment to cover the cost of shipping raw ore halfway across the solar system to the main refinery.

It was the dwindling gold supply that was making the miners nervous. Twitchy miners were a danger to themselves and the company. They did stupid things like conduct secret meetings in abandoned stopes in the middle of the night. Jane could drug them all; it wasn't against company policy to chemically placate her staff, but it wouldn't serve her purpose. And she did have a purpose.

She heard the voices of the miners hushing each other. When she entered the hollowed out chamber there was a gasp, an instinctive response to a dangerous predator, as they collectively pulled away. A dozen miners, more then Jane had hoped, stood in the chamber illuminated by the lamps from their helmets, which they had hung from the bolts that dotted the low, craggy ceiling.

The only sound left in the cavern was the soft hiss of the oxygen canisters as they let out just enough gas to make the thin air more breathable. Without letting her professional demeanor slip, Jane nodded to Curtis, a civilian mining supervisor. She had hoped the report from her security officer, Lydia Renson, was wrong. Jane valued Curtis both professionally and personally, but here he was actively engaging in an act of insubordination. To his credit, he didn't back down. He knew he was caught.

In a mining colony everybody was being watched, always, except here. The miners had chosen well. They knew the stope had been stripped of its security devices. He continued his diatribe about what a terrible job she was doing supervising the mine, not giving them the tools they needed to work, blah, blah, blah. When he first came to her with his concerns, she had tried to explain to him that he might not understand the big picture the way she did, so he should just trust that she was doing what was best for the mine. Unfortunately, he was too conscientious to accept that they all shouldn't work as hard as they could.

He said the one word—*strike*—that sealed his fate, and she had to put an end to it.

The miners parted for her as she came forward. Her voice was strong and clear and overrode his when she said, "This is all my fault." She crowded Curtis out from under his lamplight, and continued, "We *all* have a role, a job to do. We *all* work for the same company. I hate that it's come to this, but I must remind you: this is not a democracy."

Shaking her head in dismay, she glared at the miners and said, "Anyone interested in becoming a free citizen is invited to submit his or her resignation. Transportation will be provided off planet." She paused looking for volunteers. There were none. Unemployment was the most dangerous prospect in the galaxy.

"Thank you all for coming," Jane said, dismissing them. One by one they took down their helmets. With each departure the stope grew dimmer and dimmer, until she and Curtis stood facing each other in the small circle of light from the lone helmet that still hung from the ceiling.

He was a tall man, much taller then she was, and well-muscled from working the mines. Even laser mines required brawn to work effectively. His eyes met hers. He had eyes as blue and strong as sapphires. Jane blinked and looked away.

He started, desperately reminding her, "We're going to be closed. There is more product here than we're bringing up. We can cover expenses if—"

She stopped listening. The irony didn't escape Jane. In the old days people would complain about being overworked, here they complained about being underworked. She held up her hand, stopping him. "So, you think you can strike? And what? What do you think will happen?"

"We could get you reassigned, get a more efficient manager in here."

"That's not the way things work." Jane marveled at his naiveté. The corporation didn't care what he thought, regardless of whether or not he was right.

He pleaded for her understanding. "We need our jobs. How many of us would be relocated if this mine closed down?" The tone of his voice said he knew not many of them would be relocated. Miners were an expendable and easily replaceable resource.

Jane answered him. "How long do you think your jobs will last if you bring up more product—another ten terms, maybe twelve? I asked you to trust me. There is another way." Jane answered, eyeing his intricately crafted gold belt buckle. A glimmer of understanding started in his eyes, but was squelched by the realization that it was too late for him.

"A place of our own." He finally understood.

"For all of us, but first we have to make them believe there is nothing left here, that Aurum 9 is nothing but a desolate windswept rock now devoid even of gold. They would abandon the facilities to us, and we could work it." She spoke as she drew her pistol and shot him once. Flames were too dangerous in a mine. The chemically activated organic poison ate his flesh away in an instantaneous chemical reaction. Still, she used the old terminology. "You're fired," she whispered to the pile of ash and empty clothing.

On top of the pile was a belt buckle. She knelt and picked it up. The buckle was heavy in her hand and as large as her palm. She ran her fingers over pebbly surface that depicted the bumpy yellow surface of the planet. Curtis had even included the triangle-shaped rock that marked, just out of range, the down shaft of the original mine. This holding was as important to him as it was to her, and she had just killed him.

Jane reached up for the mining helmet and turned off the light. She turned her body three hundred and sixty degrees making sure the stope was pitch black. In the freedom of darkness Jane let the tears well up and spill over her eyelids. Struggling to keep her breathing even she let the tears run down her face not wiping or rubbing at her eyes. She didn't want any redness to give away her emotional reaction to what was supposed to be purely a business decision.

Before Jane switched the light back on she put on the serene, smiling, agreeable face that she had learned from her mother. Alena Gray had taught Jane to cultivate the corporate demeanor through any emotion, and any physical discomfort. Alena taught her: nod your head, look alert, don't let your eyes glaze over, keep your breathing even, smile and nod, always look interested. Unfortunately, Alena Gray had never mastered "the face" or had refused to use it, even when Jane begged her, and so was sent away to hospital where she died a few years later.

When Jane emerged from the shaft, Lydia Renson, head of security, greeted her. The black-suited woman with the blonde hair and ice blue eyes cut a path through the corridor for Jane to follow. Without being asked Lydia reported, "The miners are in the brig."

She knew Lydia's security forces would have grabbed the miners as they emerged from the shaft. Jane nodded. She didn't want to say anything more for fear of being overheard. This time of night the corridors were almost empty except for the house staff. In indigo night-light, they scoured the gunmetal gray halls with cleaning vacs slung over their shoulders. The vacs sucked up the endless dust from the mines and filtered it, releasing fresh clean air.

In her office Jane went directly to her desk, anxious to put a sea of mica between herself and the security officer. Lydia took the seat in front of the desk as per their usual arrangement.

"What about the miners?" Lydia threw a container down on her desk. The gold that had been confiscated from the miners rattled inside as it hit the hard mica. She asked, "Shall we arrange an accident?"

Jane leaned back in her chair and put her feet up on her desk before she answered, "No. We'll sever them the way we're supposed to."

She tossed Lydia the gold belt buckle that had been Curtis's, and ordered her, "Curtis has been fired. Give this to his family, and send them off with the others."

"This is company property," Lydia reminded her.

"Thank you, Lydia," Jane said, dismissing her.

"You're too soft to be an executive." Lydia dared to chide her. Jane frowned, wriggling her fingers in dismissal. Lydia was too sharp for Jane's own good, but she couldn't dismiss her. Security officers always reported up to corporate headquarters.

When Lydia closed the door behind her, Jane sat up, put her elbows on her desk and folded her hands in front of her face. She was worried about how much Lydia knew. Part of her job was to keep an eye on Jane. Did she know enough about mining to know that Jane was holding out? Did she know enough about Jane to know that she wanted nothing more than to be free of the company? All these questions Jane couldn't answer.

She dumped over the container Lydia had put on her desk. Gold spilled across the black mica, tugging at her spirit. She ran her hands through the gleaming yellow buckles, and bangles, fine chains and charms. There were more than a few that depicted the triangle-shaped rock on the surface. It had become the unofficial symbol for their prospect. Jane sighed deeply. She hadn't expected the pressure of the change. She should have. She was a geologist by training. She of all people should have known that great change requires great pressure.

Jane wanted to keep all the gold pieces, but she picked out the best ones and matched each with a name. These miners would be allowed to stay because they would further her ultimate plan. The others would be severed, sent off planet to some wild colonial place, and left to fend for themselves.

It was well past 1:00 AM when Jane wrote her official report on the incident. Her fiefdom, the Aurum 9 mines, was a small department in a vast corporate holding, a holding so vast Jane suspected the executive branch barely bothered looking at her reports. But this time a supervisor had been fired, and eight miners would need transport off planet. Jane didn't go so far as to use the word union. That would have caused more carnage than she wanted to be responsible for. She reported only a rabble-rousing session. She requested severance for the miners and replacements. Everything in it was true, not completely true, but true in principle.

She transmitted the report, hoping it would pass with little more than a shrug at corporate. Unfortunately, the ripple caused by the incident reached the executive office. Shortly thereafter Jane received the communiqué from the Vice President of Operations for this sector, William Orion. He was the worst kind of executive. He mindlessly towed the company line having neither imagination nor a sense of humor.

Orion's assistant, a lanky effeminate young man named Devon, condescended to deliver his orders to Jane. He inclined his head at Jane and shrugged as he told her all her records should be in order and quarters readied.

She clenched her fists off screen to stop herself from telling him that he would never, no matter how hard he worked, be anything more than a second manager because he wasn't hereditary. She wanted to warn him that the company would deceive him for as long as it could, extract every bit of work from him, steal every idea from him, until he realized his ambitions would never come to fruition. Then he would end up in a holding like this taking meds twice a day and vaccing the dust from the air.

Instead she answered, "Great." She smiled her best fake smile at him and continued, "We're looking forward to the visit."

In the weekly staff meeting Jane announced the inspection to her senior staff. They weren't the brightest stars in the corporate sky. Kevin Stewart, head of finance for the planet, was so incompetent the corporation bounced him around until he landed here with Jane. She welcomed his incompetence as a good foil for her duplicity. She conjured an excited smile and said, "We have a party to plan. Pull out all the stops. The only way we're going to survive is to show corporate how prosperous and together we are." She spoke as if she believed that the appearance of prosperity were all it would take to keep the mine open.

"I hope you know what you're doing." Lydia said cryptically as she left. Jane smiled at her confidentially, pretending to know exactly what Lydia was talking about.

Jane inhaled the fresh organic smell of carrots. Real loamy earth, all the way from the corporate headquarters, still clung to the veins. She experienced a memory of her childhood home, a gilded dining room on the home planet, soft yellow sunlight through green leaves shining into the dining room. And the taste—the snap of fresh food. She shook herself out of the memory.

"What am I supposed to do with this?" Marty, the nutrition technician, asked, holding up the celery bulb that the vice president had brought with him. It was his contribution to the reception this evening.

Remembering endless receptions of crudités and wine Jane told him, "Just arrange it on a platter. It should be fine." Marty nodded and began to artfully create a platter of color.

"We should wash it first," Jane said.

"With water!" Marty was thoroughly appalled at the thought of wasting precious water washing food.

Jane shrugged at Marty and left him to figure out the food dilemma for himself. She had spent enough time on it, delaying her meeting just enough to look inefficient, but not enough to appear lax.

"Is everybody in place?" She asked Lydia as they left the kitchen.

"Everything is ready, but I have to tell you as your security officer, your dress is just not working for me."

Lydia pointed to a large gap in the deep V that offered a rather inappropriate view of her right breast. "You really should secure that."

"It's fine the way it is." Jane said. She took a deep breath, centering herself. She put a smile on her face and pushed open the door to the reception room.

Smile plastered to her face, Jane shook the vice president's hand. He was a dim, almost colorless person with watery blue eyes and gray hair. He looked to Jane as if some day he would fade away in a puff of smoke, and just dissipate from life. Jane ached at the thought that she had had to fire Curtis and this watery human got to continue living. After a prelude of "hello, how are yous," Jane began her carefully orchestrated program by introducing several of her key people to the Vice President. There was Lydia, Jeffrey the civilian mining supervisor, who had taken Curtis's place, and Kevin Stewart.

Jane proceeded through the night by asking the vice president about his family.

"They're fine, Jane. Mary Anne is going to university in the spring. She'll be a scientist like you."

Jane nodded, smiling, and asked a few more questions about his daughter, keeping the conversation focused on his family until the tray of vegetables arrived.

"Jane, please." The vice president deferred to her, giving her first selection.

"No, thank you, sir. I haven't had real food in some time. It's just easier to eat native with the rest of the staff."

The vice president nodded approvingly, maybe too approvingly. Jane wondered if she had tipped too much of her hand. Executives often tried to retain as many of their headquarter habits as they could. Jane's inability to digest real food was a dead give away that she was too close to her staff.

Because their meetings would begin first thing in the morning the party broke up early. Jane knew she wouldn't be able to sleep without help, so she stopped by the infirmary and got a sleeping pill from the dispensary. Nobody, not even the director of mines, was allowed drugs outside the infirmary.

"Good luck tomorrow, boss" the med tech wished her earnestly.

"Thanks. I'm sure we'll be fine," Jane answered, swallowing the sleeping pill. The med tech tried to smile in agreement, and almost succeeded.

The strain of operating at two levels was starting to exhaust Jane. If her plotting and conniving worked out, she would be severed from her position. The planet would be granted her in a settlement package. Once freed she would set up an economy that centered on the jewelry the miners crafted. In her endless quest for water she had discovered several mineral deposits, rich formations of topaz and emeralds that blossomed from the granite like coral from the ocean bottom. Combined with the gold that was left they could make jewelry. Their holding would be worth something. It would be a meager economy at first, but it would work. She had run the numbers over and over in as many configurations as she could imagine.

She would get her wish or she would be fired as a saboteur.

They met over breakfast in the small conference room. It was the only room with a view of the planet's surface. Jane looked past the marking rock down the path the robots had cut decades ago, to the mountains beyond. Jane was sure that some of those mountains contained valuable mineral deposits. She was anxious to explore the possibility.

Orion entered, followed by Lydia. Her presence meant only one thing. Jane's status was about to change. As she took her seat next to the vice president, Lydia smiled cryptically at her. Jane wasn't sure if it was conspiratorially, or triumphantly.

The VP was taking too long to examine the numbers on the private screen he was holding. Jane didn't wriggle in her chair though she desperately wanted to. She knew he was playing her.

He said solemnly, "Your directive, Director Gray, was to find water on this outpost. Have you found water?"

"No, sir. There hasn't been water on this planet for at least a million years."

"That being the case, we've determined that the viable product left on Aurum 9 outweighs the expense of mining and shipping." He paused. Jane's breath caught, every cell in her body leaped hopefully toward the possibility of independence.

The vice president continued, "The jewelers—" Jane's breath stopped. They knew! The vice president continued to speak in his deliberately bland tone. "Your failure to report this resource could be considered a form of sabotage, but the home office has chosen to consider the jewelers a valuable asset to the company. Congratulations."

Her mouth dry, she croaked, "Thank you, sir." She tried not to think of the implication of her best assets being shipped off planet.

"As for yourself, the home office wants you reassigned. You will be transferred to the Egoli Mine."

Jane's mouth dropped open. Egoli was one of the top five mines in the entire company, a very prestigious holding, and now it was Jane's. She cringed.

The VP continued, "The director there is being severed to spend more time with his family. Apparently, Egoli has been exceeding their production quotas and we need them cut—discreetly of course."

"Congratulations on your promotion," Lydia said.

Moon and Bones and Birds
by Christopher Woods

On their seventh day along that road the sky darkened earlier than usual. At first they made no mention of a bloody sun lowering itself down the sky of a cloudless afternoon. However, they did notice how their shadows lengthened. Remy was the first to mention this. He was studying the way his rotund shadow seemed to bump against that of his colleague, Octavo. Their shadows seemed to spar.

"Day is done," Remy said. "And without due satisfaction."

Octavo listened silently and then spat dust from his mouth. He lifted his own arms and let them drop. He noticed how his own shadow seemed to want for flight. But he was too heavy. He flapped, to no avail. Remy began flapping his own arms. They continued like this until it was dark along the road. They stopped and made a fire. Later, they slept, dreaming of lizards, the carnivorous kind.

By the next afternoon, the air became very humid. Both men sweated profusely. On either side of the road, so overgrown that at times the road was little more than a hunch, grew enormous ferns that spread out across the damp earth. Sunlight seemed pressed out by the looming foliage.

"Maybe we should start dropping bread crumbs," Remy said, a low rumble of a laugh coming from inside him.

"You would do me the injustice to speak of food," Octavo whined. "I'm starving."

Octavo had been thinking of, and counting on his chubby fingers, the number of meals they had missed so far on the mission. One of goodwill, it was called, to take a census. They were to spend three weeks traipsing through a rain forest and a desert, then return home with their tally. How many villages, how many people? That done, the relief, food and blankets, would be delivered. On paper, the mission was simple.

But so were previous missions, seven total, all lost. Disappeared. No census had ever been delivered to the Agency. No food or blankets had gone trekking.

"Food and blankets, that's what we're about," Remy said.

"In this heat, I'd welcome death before a blanket," Octavo said.

Swamp gloom gathered around them now, and they began to notice how the ground beneath them seemed to disappear. In its place were thick, curling roots, the shade of albino. They took care not to trip. Watching his steps, Octavo imagined himself crossing a wide platter of linguine. He did not share this fantasy with Remy, who would only have taunted him. Like your Rossini, he would say, wanting nothing more than to feed your big belly.

That night, as they slept, Remy dreamed about blind, albino snakes, ball after ball of them. He had to step gingerly as the balls rolled toward him on the road. Octavo dreamed he was being smothered by a hundred blankets, each of them on fire.

In his dream, Octavo burned to death, but his mind, as it will, kept on. Kept on. Not long after he died, he came across Remy's corpse. His friend's body was covered with snakebites. As Octavo bent over the cadaver, Remy opened his eyes. They were milky from the venom that filled his body. But Octavo could see something else in those yellowed eyes. The tarnished ivory color reminded him of a particular moon he knew.

"Is that you, Octavo?"

Now, with Remy speaking in a voice hoarse from screaming, Octavo decided to keep the knowledge of that moon to himself.

"It's me, friend," he replied.

"I can't rest until I know something for certain," Remy said. "When the birds come, will they peck out our eyes?"

Octavo nodded gravely. He knew that the eyes were the first to go. Eyes were like buttons. Birds began with them, undressing the body down to the soul. But never finding a soul, the birds pecked until there was nothing left but bones. Then they moved on, maybe discouraged, to look for another pair of eyes.

"Don't worry, Remy. By the time the birds come, we'll be asleep. The dead are always asleep."

"Thank you, Octavo, my friend."

"Rest now."

They had not seen another person in a long time. In the village of Huzuni, they had counted nothing by empty huts. Then, after leaving Huzuni, the bone business began. Smelling rank and covered with ants, the bones came in piles and batches every few steps. It appeared that many had died while trying to flee.

Initially they pretended that they were stepping over the bones of animals. After a few miles, this wore thin. Remy suggested that some odd kind of slaughter had taken place.

"Oh, don't you think most slaughters are odd?" Octavo asked.

"I strive to be impartial," Remy said. "I am a census taker. I have no traffic with politics."

Politics or not, Remy concluded that something was terribly the matter in this place. It bothered him greatly. Living or dead, people needed to be counted. Yet the Agency had no guidelines for the counting of bones, no matter how great their number. Octavo and Remy sat down to rest beside piles of bones to consider the failed census.

"Remy?"

"Yes, Octavo?"

"I count you as a friend."

"No less than I count you, Octavo."

"Good, then. But I must tell you that something is bothering me. It has to do with where we go from here. Once we leave the jungle."

"The desert. Isn't that what you mean?"

"Yes."

"That's the end of our trek, friend. Once we pass through the desert, we cross the border. We'll be on our way home. Are you unsure about it? Here, look at this map."

"I know the map, Remy. But, this road. What about this road?"

"What about it?"

"Let me be frank. Will they send another census team? To look for us?"

"If something should happen to us?"

"Yes."

"They sent us, didn't they? Hasn't the Agency always been good about sending teams?"

"Losing them is more like it. Isn't the point that we are the last team? That there won't be any more?"

"That's so, yes. Let's not dwell on it. Why, someday, Octavo, a school or a library might be named after you. Or a fountain. Imagine, Octavo, coins being thrown in a fountain with your name on the rim. And each coin a wish."

"Well, when you put it that way."

"That's better, isn't it? For now, the desert is waiting."

By the next evening they were done with the bones, and with the curling, white roots. Happy to have all that behind them, they stopped to make a fire. Another five days, Remy said, of spinning sand cartwheels in their wake, would see them across the border. Octavo said he would be thankful for that, and for all the good food that awaited them.

They became quiet and watched the thin column of smoke rising from the fire. It rose into the sky, where their next problem waited.

"Tell me, Remy. Do you know a moon like that?" Octavo asked.

"Not a pretty sight, is it? Where I come from, we call it a ghost moon. The ghost of a one-eyed God. Staring."

"Yes, I've heard that before."

"But my father tells me that a moon like that is really a sore. A bedsore, Octavo, on the body of God, pressing through."

"I thought your father died. While taking this same census."

"He did. But he still talks to me in my dreams. He says he's hungry. And very cold. He comes in my sleep, begging for a blanket."

"I see. Tell me, Remy, have you noticed how cold it's gotten?"

"I have, Octavo. I have."

"Yes. So cold. So very, very cold."

Project
by Adele Cosgrove-Bray

"Rafe, wake up. We're here."

Rafe's eyelids fluttered softly in response to Gabe's quiet voice.

"Dreamy head, come on." Gabe gently blew into Rafe's ears. The pillow sank a little deeper as Rafe's bare arm raised then folded over a perfectly smooth forehead. Gabe laughed softly and added, "I know you're awake. We're orbiting the project now."

"Let me sleep."

Gabe frowned slightly. "You know I can't. If it was left to me . . . But we all have to witness this fragment of history. I understand how you feel, but it's our job. And it's Captain Lucy's orders."

Rafe sighed and opened pale grey eyes. Silk sheets slid from exquisite shoulders as Rafe reluctantly sat up. "I don't see why Lucy needs us. I have so many other things I could be getting on with right now."

"Like sleeping?" Gabe smiled and moved away, allowing the gossamer silver veil to fall back into place around the bed.

"I was not sleeping. I was meditating. Many of my ideas develop this way, as you well know." Rafe's long, athletic legs swung free of the bed. Exquisite hands combed through tousled tawny hair. The veil did little to shield Rafe's beauty.

Gabe looked away to give Rafe privacy. Many would have dismissed this gesture as redundant after their prolonged familiarity, yet Gabe felt small gifts such as this made life more agreeable. Soft sounds of dressing reached Gabe's ears. To cover such beauty with cloth seemed almost criminal, but this too had been Captain's Lucy's order. Business first, always.

Gabe carefully picked up an old book that had been resting on Rafe's console desk. The unfamiliar texture of its crumbling leather binding felt repugnant. The fragile, yellowing pages possessed a strong musty fragrance. "How can you bare to touch such things? They're so unclean. Look, now I have the dust of a dead animal on my hands."

Rafe laughed softly and indicated towards a silver basin where Gabe might wash. "Books were powerful once. People both revered and feared ideas contained within books. Conquerors throughout history destroyed whole libraries simply to deprive the vanquished of a valuable resource of power."

"But these grubby relics . . . All the old writings are on the database, perfectly clean and readily accessible. I don't understand why you want to actually touch these primitive, decaying things. How can you endure it?"

Rafe walked towards the door. "For the same reason that looking at a photograph of a painting is not the same as looking at the original canvas. To touch is another way to experience."

Gabe's hands quickly dried under a jet of warm air. "So many ideas . . . How do you hold them all?" It wasn't really a question, but an expression of admiration.

Rafe opened the door and watched as Gabe came closer, Rafe's pale grey eyes meeting Gabe's azure blue. A faint smile was Rafe's only offered reply as they walked along the pristine corridor side by side, Gabe's blue robes swaying in companionable rhythm with Rafe's silver.

When they stepped onto the main deck, Uri and Mike were already there. Uri was combing over long strings of hieroglyphic code as fast as the console screen could display them. The skin of Uri's muscular arms gleamed like burnished onyx. Simple green robes hung carelessly from Uri's powerful shoulders as if dressing had been accomplished in haste, or perhaps in distaste, as it was not in Uri's nature to be overly troubled by sartorial aesthetics. For the same reason, Uri's glossy black hair was shorn in a militaristic style.

Mike acknowledged Gabe and Rafe with a formal nod. Mike's curling ginger hair had been carefully groomed to compliment square yet delicate facial features. Mike leaned casually against the golden railing edging the raised dais which housed the main viewing screen. The screen was on but little could be seen, as this solar system's nucleus had yet to emerge from behind the project planet's horizon. As usual, Mike didn't seem to be doing much but little escaped those eagle eyes, no matter how seemingly insignificant—in Mike's opinion, at least.

Rafe and Gabe took seats and waited.

Gabe said, "Is Captain Lucy going to join us?"

"Of course," said Mike. "This project was Lucy's baby, after all."

Uri mumbled something too low for Gabe and Rafe to clearly hear, but Mike smiled knowingly. Their dislike of Lucy was legendary.

Mike's elaborate red robes sported golden tassels on the shoulders, a new addition in recognition of the occasion. Mike did not like to see any project close down, especially when the experiment had seemed so promising.

"Captain on deck," announced Mike dutifully.

Rafe, Gabe and Uri rose to their feet and in precise unison with Mike they all executed crisp salutes.

"At ease," said Captain Lucy, gliding with sublime confidence to the largest and most comfortable chair on the main deck. Only Lucy could wear dark purple robes of such transparency and yet retain an aura of aloof nobility. Lucy's hip-length silver-white tresses formed a more effective veil than the robes could ever provide.

Even acute familiarity with the Captain could not diminish the crew's awe. Lucy radiated beauty like a lone star in the purple robes of night. As gloriously androgynous as each of them truly were, they would forever remain in Lucy's shadow. Both for beauty of form and majesty of mind, Lucy had been hailed as the highest expression of creative perfection yet to have been made manifest.

Captain Lucy said, "Have you run a systems check?"

"Yes, Captain," said Uri. "I ran a full analysis. All systems are fully functional. Data is already being gathered."

"Excellent," said Lucy, settling back elegantly. "Mike, have you run a surface scan?"

"No, Captain."

Lucy raised one eyebrow.

"I'm on it, Captain." With as much dignity as possible, Mike walked to the appropriate console and set the scan in motion. Trust Lucy to be aware of the one task which had not yet been completed.

Gabe and Rafe sat down again and waited. There was nothing for them to do but watch the main viewing screen as the glowing nucleus slowly became visible from behind the project planet's orbiting mass.

"Sunrise," said Lucy quietly.

The crew had become accustomed to their Captain's use of vernacular terms when speaking of this project planet. It was understandable. Lucy had actually dwelt there, whereas they had merely been occasional visitors. Some considered it unprofessional to become too involved with a project planet. Uri and Mike strongly believed that distance was required to maintain an impartial attitude. Gabe and Rafe, however, liked to personally sample ideas and experiences arising from the creation of a project planet. This balance of attitudes made them a formidable team.

"Uri?"

"Captain. Nothing conclusive to report, as yet."

Lucy nodded once, very slowly. A faint hint of tension could be seen in the way Lucy's slender fingers gripped the chair arms but, otherwise, Captain Lucy maintained faultless poise.

A long beam of light smoothly arched across the main viewing screen. All five travelers stared at the restless green-black waters which daylight had revealed. Before them lay an ocean like any other glittering ocean, where restless waters surged and swirled to the moon's magnetic pull. Below this lay what had once been called Nebraska.

Lucy's slender fingers instinctively reached forward, as if by touching the screen personal connection to the terminated project might be renewed. A single tear slid over Lucy's alabaster cheek.

"The scan reads negative, Captain," said Mike. "No human life."

"Run a wider scan."

"I did."

Gabe slipped a hand into Rafe's.

"Then scan again. And keep scanning." The cold anger in Lucy's voice made them all turn. Lucy's amber eyes glowed with fury.

Uri said, "All data so far confirms this conclusion: no human life."

"Keep looking."

"Yes, Captain." Uri turned back to the strings of hieroglyphs flowing over the small console screen. Lucy's reaction prompted only silent contempt from Uri. This was why impersonal distance from all project planets should be studiously upheld. Emotional attachment always became a hindrance when Central closed a project down. The alternative to shutting down projects was to leave experimental debris drifting without proper guidance or purpose, a concept that Uri and Mike considered detrimental to the established order which Central had imposed.

"Captain, I have a school of blue whales on screen."

"Good, Mike. Rafe, check for other marine life. Mike, get back to scanning for humans."

"Yes, Captain." Rafe reluctantly slipped from Gabe's discrete touch and moved to a nearby console.

"Gabe, scan for birdlife."

"Right away, Captain." Gabe quickly walked to a vacant console.

Uri thought the likelihood of tracing much surviving birdlife was remote. The creatures could only remain airborne for so long.

"Uri, set a new course for the nearest mountain range."

"Yes, Captain." Uri disliked being reminded of Lucy's telepathic skills.

And so it was that, after much prolonged searching, one tiny pocket of human life was found to have survived the deliberately engineered cataclysm which had engulfed the project planet that Lucy had named Earth.

Uri gazed calmly at the main viewing screen. "Should I activate the cleansing beam, Captain?"

No reply came.

"Captain?"

Lucy rose from the chair and walked slowly towards the large screen, purple robes flowing with Lucy's graceful, curiously feline movements.

A jagged circle of snow-capped peaks had protected a high, wide valley from the raging seas, sitting like a crown on the roof of the water-gowned world. A huddle of tents stood together, their multi-coloured fabrics having never seemed so precious. And around the tents and smoky cooking pots were people, ordinary everyday people staring at the seemingly miraculous craft hovering high above them.

Uri said, "Captain Lucy, the cleansing beam is ready. Should I activate?"

Rafe's pale grey eyes were blind with tears. This part of the job was abhorrent. The humans' exhausted faces were filled with hope.

Mike said, "Our brief was specific, Captain. We have to . . . . "

"I am entirely familiar with the procedure for closing down a planetary project, thank you." Lucy's clipped words stung Mike's pride. How ironic, when it had always been Lucy who'd stood accused of being the proud one.

"Captain?" Uri pushed for Lucy's command. "Captain Lucy, the rules specifically state that final cleansing is required."

"Do they, indeed." A playful smile began to curl over Lucy's sensuous lips. "And who wrote those rules, Uri, if not our own colleagues in Central who have long since tired of these projects? I am not tired."

Mike sighed heavily and folded muscular arms, the posture expressing Mike's dislike of any delay in official procedure.

Uri growled, "We are to return to Central once this is done. Nobody cares about these stupid little creatures."

"I care," said Lucy, still gazing at the screen. Excited upturned faces stared back, seeing only the external glow of the interplanetary shuttle craft.

"I care," said Rafe. "Their ingenuity, tenacity and creativity interest me."

"I care, too," said Gabe. "Their emotions are so complex and contradictory. And they are not devoid of a certain simple comeliness." Gabe and Rafe exchanged grins.

"So what? We have our orders," said Mike, always a stickler for regulations and convention.

"And I am Captain here," said Lucy sternly, "and this planet was given into my care almost from the beginning. My law carries full power here. It is possible that other humans have survived in the highest places."

"But atmospheric alterations were transmitted direct from Central," said Uri, sounding puzzled. "How could the flood have failed to entirely cover the planet?"

Captain Lucy smiled mischievously. "Everyone makes mistakes."

Mike scowled. "Central does not make mistakes."

Gabe and Rafe smiled knowingly.

Mike and Uri simultaneously realized that the only person who could have intercepted and altered the transmission was Captain Lucy. They knew Central would be in uproar over this breach of planetary project protocol. They also knew that they would be held partially responsible.

Lucy's silver laughter filled the deck.

Antiope in Black
by Geoffrey Thorne

"Put down the cat," said a voice from the dark. "Unless you want me to kill you."

The voice seemed to come from everywhere at once, which was, Meldrick supposed, the point of this place. Judging from the echoes, he guessed that tunnels extended out before him in all directions, kilometers of them perhaps. It had taken him two hours to find the entrance to these subterranean catacombs even with the map Baba had given him. Two hours of rain, two hours of dodging Clan *Fortis'* outriders, two hours of hidden cubbies, secret trails doubling and tripling back on themselves, ending finally at the abandoned recycling facility. The place had devolved into a simple waste dump in the years since the Break. Consequently he'd had to dig through a mound of unspeakable refuse just to find the door.

Disgusting, he'd thought as he shoved the clods of oozing rubbish aside. *Safety was one thing, but this?*

Meldrick didn't like the mess. Being a Siroccan, he was biologically predisposed to extreme fastidiousness. As a result his life on this dark, drippy, cacophonous world was as close to a living hell as he ever hoped to come. He almost never felt clean anymore, even when he was.

"Did you hear me, bug?" said the voice. "Put the cat down."

The aforementioned feline, suspended by its scruff in one of Meldrick's anterior talons, had become fascinated with his antennae and was currently batting at them with its tiny white paws.

Meldrick hadn't really been hungry, just curious. It had been a long time since he'd seen a cat, even one as small as this. He lowered the thing gently and watched as it scampered off into the dark.

"What do you want here, bug?" said the voice.

"That depends," said Meldrick. "Depends."

"On what?"

"On who," he said. "On who I'm speaking with."

"Here's a thought," said the voice. "*You* answer what *I* ask and I keep not killing you."

Meldrick doubted very much that anyone on Terra Nova III could kill him easily. His carapace was blast resistant, his strength and reflexes considerably faster than those of the humans who made up the bulk of the colony's population.

"I work for Baba Yaga," he said into the dark. "Baba Yaga."

For a time nothing else happened. He was left with the drip-drip-drip of distant ruptured plumbing and his thoughts. He wondered what these catacombs had been for before the Break.

He was impressed by this choice of safehole. It was difficult to find, disgusting to enter and, once in, an intruder might be forever lost in what was surely a maze of lightless passages.

"What's Baba want?" said the voice suddenly.

Enough time had passed that it startled him.

"Baba Yaga wants to see you," he said. "To see you."

"For what?"

"Job," said Meldrick. "Job."

"Skip," said the voice. "Baba can do her own jobs."

Meldrick was surprised for the first time in a very long time. No one said 'no' to Baba Yaga, not if they wanted to keep breathing.

"Baba Yaga says you come," said Meldrick firmly. "You come. Baba says you owe."

This time, as the echoes died around him, Meldrick felt he could detect movement in the surrounding dark. He raised his venom bearing talons defensively.

"Relax," said the voice, suddenly very close. "I'm coming."

A small figure, its face and body mostly hidden by a hooded charcoal colored cloak, emerged from the shadows on his right. It was humanoid, smaller than expected and carrying multiple weapons—including at least one plasma grenade, if his sense of smell was still good. It held the white cat in one hand and a ceramic pot lid in the other. The human set both cat and lid down on the slime-covered floor. From somewhere in the folds of its garment it produced a small flask and proceeded to empty the contents into the saucer. The cat sniffed at the liquid and began to drink.

"That's it 'til I get back," said the human, stroking the cat gently. "Don't be greedy."

The cat ignored the warning and continued to lap.

"Suit yourself," said the human. Then, to Meldrick, "Let's go."

He turned to exit the way he'd entered and heard the human laugh. It was a harsh thing, like a steel knife scoring carbon.

"Not that way, bug," said the human.

Grateful to have been spared another trip into the universe of refuse beyond the little door, Meldrick turned again and followed the human into the shadows. As the darkness ate them he asked, out of politeness, how the human liked to be called.

"Flint," said his companion. "Just call me Flint."

Baba Yaga had been waiting for Meldrick to return with Flint for the better part of two hours. She'd chosen the big Siroccan for his stealth capabilities and his cool head, but even he might be overwhelmed if taken unawares. Flint was a testy little thing, mercurial, and not fond of unannounced visitors. It was witnessing Flint's defeat of and near murder of a flesh gang leader that had cemented Baba's respect for the girl's skill with a razorline. That little dance had earned Flint a permanent place of distinction in Clan *Alexander's* death ledger, hence the current difficulty in tracking her down. Flint had been in hiding for weeks.

Only Baba Yaga could find Flint when she did not wish to be found.

Still, waiting around for a rendezvous was not the way to stay healthy on Terra Nova III, not even in *Shipley* Bazaar.

"You drinking?" said the spindly adolescent who had apparently pulled bartending duties this shift. Food stores had run a bit short for Clan *Shipley* in the last weeks. The boy looked as if he'd been built of sticks.

She shook her head and watched as he ambled down to the far end of the makeshift bar. Everything on Terra Nova was makeshift these days. The bar, for instance, was nothing more than a piece of metal rad shielding propped on empty fuel canisters. As something having to do with necessity and invention whispered through her mind, her hand strayed to the telemet projector on her belt.

Yes, yes, she thought. *All systems nominal.*

She lived in fear of the day the projector would go inert like most of the tech on Terra Nova III. She would die that day, she knew, or on one soon after.

Baba Yaga was a figure to be feared and respected. Barbara Yasbeck, engineer third class, was just one more eventual corpse. If her enemies ever discovered her secret, they would descend on her like ravenous core dragons. Even her friends in *Shipley* and *Marks* would have a go.

Her current disguise was that of an overweight outrider in the livery of Clan *Marks*, pockmarked and sporting three days of stubble. The image was perfect as were all the others she'd used as aliases.

Telemet technology even made the images tactile, if it came to that. It wouldn't, though. It never did. Aside from Scarecrow the Bartender, no one had given her a second look. Outriders, long-range emissaries and scouts for the various Clans, were common in the bazaar.

Marks was one of the most respected Clans, though not as feared as the others. *Marks* held its territory but didn't go in much for expansion. More importantly, Clans *Shipley* and *Marks* enjoyed a treaty that was still in effect after a year. There were rumors of a full-fledged alliance in the offing. Consequently, she was given a wide berth, but not of the sort that drew specific attention.

The projector had saved her life this way on more than one occasion. The day she'd found it, shining like a diamond in a pile of shattered tech, had certainly been the luckiest in her life.

Most of the tech on the planet had ceased functioning after the Break. In the mad scramble that followed no one in the colony had been able to determine why. Baba guessed it might have had something to do with a shift in the planet's magnetic field. That certainly explained the inability of anyone to contact Terra Primus for help. It also explained the perpetual twilight the planet had endured for the last fifteen years. At least it did to Baba Yaga. That and certain recent events had spurred her search for Flint.

"Damn," said someone on her periphery. "Would you look at that."

The object of the comment wasn't difficult to ferret. The big Siroccan was distinctive even covered by his hood and cloak. He bulged in the wrong places. Beside him, like a ghost or a shadow, was Flint. Despite her few years, the girl moved with the assurance of a seasoned fighter, which, Baba conceded to herself, she was. In a straight out, one-to-one, scrap Flint could hold her own against nearly anyone.

The pairing of human and Siroccan was unusual enough to draw more than one set of eyes. Baba didn't like the potential for exposure they presented but, in this case, it couldn't be helped.

She rose and moved purposefully towards them.

"Hey, bug!" she said in her studied approximation of a masculine baritone. "You selling that kid or what?"

"You give good price," said Meldrick. "Price."

"Why don't we go somewhere private and talk it over?"

Having received all the agreed upon code phrases, the big insect nodded his mandibled head and followed where she led. No one much noted them passing after the exchange. The flesh trade was big in *Shipley* Bazaar.

Flint wasn't happy. This wasn't unusual. She was rarely happy. There was precious little on Terra Nova III to elicit a smile. Baba Yaga and her intrigues were not on the list.

The big outrider had lead her and the bug to a dank little room at the back of the main *Shipley* Bunker where they now awaited the arrival of Baba Yaga herself. The 'rider, his job presumably done, had then disappeared.

Shipley Bunker was one of the larger ones, made of plasteel and stone and containing about a hundred rooms. Firelight flickered in some of the upper windows and thin plumes of black smoke belched from hidden rooftop chimneys. To eyes old enough or schooled in such things, the place might have resembled an ancient earthly castle keep complete with towers and gore stained battlements. To Flint, it was just another husk, burnt and scored from too many skirmishes with the surrounding Clans. She'd heard someone say it had been a library once, whatever that was.

She'd noted that there was only one entrance and one exit and that they were the same. That would make a quick departure more troublesome if things went against her.

The guards, standard issue surly brutes, had waved them in without comment. Either someone had bribed them or their bosses were in on whatever this was. Flint was relieved to see the back of them and the evil-looking flechette guns they sported.

Better safe than dead, she'd thought, placing a surreptitious hand on the razorline hidden in her bracelet.

She had no illusions about her fate should this prove to be some sort of trap. There were too many guards and too few exits for skin-of-the-teeth escapes.

Footsteps in the hall indicated someone was coming their way. Flint glanced quickly at the bug, still motionless in his corner, then back to the door. She didn't like this single entrance business and resolved, Baba Yaga or no, that she'd be the one to dictate the next meeting place.

"Somebody comes," said the bug abruptly from the corner. "Comes."

Flint tensed, ready to spring into lethal action should anyone but Baba Yaga enter the room.

"You look nervous, Antiope." said the dark clad figure as the door opened briefly and shut behind her.

"Don't call me that, Baba," said Flint evenly. "I don't like it."

"As you say, child," said Baba Yaga, chuckling evilly. "Flint it is."

The old woman's hair hung around her face in loose ropes of scarlet and white. That face, what Flint could see of it, was still pale and scarred, and somehow more alert seeming than the average cit. The upper portion, including her eyes, was covered by some sort of opaque band of thick metal. Whether it served some function beyond obscuring Baba's appearance, Flint couldn't guess. The woman was clearly not blind.

She was dressed, Flint noted, much as she had been at their last meeting. Perhaps the dark, multi-pocketed flight suit was her idea of a uniform. People on Terra Nova III seemed to have a thing for uniforms.

"So," said Flint, getting right to it.

"What," said Baba Yaga brightly. "No hugs for Auntie Yaga? No gifts?"

"You're still breathing," said Flint.

The bug flexed something under his cloak, but Baba shushed him.

"Well, we can all be grateful for that, can't we?"

"What do you want, Baba?"

The old woman took her seat in the only other chair, clearly not in a hurry. Then, in a motion that Flint was unable to follow precisely, she produced a small burnished object from somewhere and placed it on the overturned plasticine bin that functioned as their table.

"Know what that is?" she said.

Flint did not.

"Never seen one before?"

Flint had not.

"This was found on a prisoner after Clan *Miller's* last incursion," said Baba Yaga softly. "The man wearing it told us he'd taken it off a corpse. A xeno corpse."

Flint picked up the object and looked it over briefly. It was heavier than she'd expected and rattled a bit when she shook it. Some kind of tech? It had been forged into the shape of an oval pierced by a sort of curved arrowhead. She replaced it on the table.

"So?" said Flint. "Xeno's get morgued all the time. Nobody likes 'em."

"No offense, bug," she added offhandedly.

"None taken," said Meldrick. "Taken."

"Not this kind of xeno," Baba continued, clearly irritated by any off-topic conversation. "This was a *Construct*. Ever heard of them?"

Flint had not.

"Doesn't matter," said Baba. "The point is, until three days ago, there were no Constructs on Terra Nova III, dead or alive."

"How do you know that?" said Flint.

"I'm Baba Yaga," she said. "It's my business to know things."

"What I don't know," she continued, "is how long this Construct was here, what it was doing and what happened to its partner."

"How do you know it had a partner?"

Baba Yaga smiled inscrutably. As she said, it was her business to know things.

"Okay," said Flint after a little consideration. "What's some dead xeno—dead *construct*—got to do with me?"

"Do you know how the world works, Flint?" said Baba Yaga. "I mean, how it really works."

Flint, having no idea what the woman was on about, simply sat and stared from beneath the hood of her cloak. Baba was playing this out according to some internal checklist that made sense only to Baba herself. Flint's fingers traced the edge of her razorline absently. If Baba Yaga noticed, she gave no evidence.

"The world is run by self-interest, my dear girl," said Baba Yaga. "At least this one is. It's the engine of our new society. It's been my meat and potatoes for almost ten years and it is what connects you to me and to Meldrick here, and to this dead Construct."

"The trick," she went on, "is telling just how best those interests might be served."

Flint wasn't following any of this. Self-interest? The world was run by the Clans and by whoever had the biggest stick. If Baba thought otherwise, she was torqued. Baba herself was what connected Flint to whatever this was, Baba Yaga and the Big Favor she'd once done.

"The point," Flint said finally, hoping Baba would just get to it.

"Straight edged Flint," said Baba with a chuckle. "All right, girl. All right. I'll get to it. I'll tell you what I want and why you will do it for me."

Stupid. That's what this was. Marching around the Null, alone, to deliver something for Baba Yaga to someone that prolly didn't exist. Stupid plus. Stupid *nth*.

"You will do this, Flint," she'd said when the girl had protested. "You'll do it because you owe me. For your brother."

That's what things always came down to when Baba wanted something—Cadmus. Baba Yaga had saved Cadmus from a press gang when Flint could not, sent him off to "someplace safe," where even Flint could not track him.

"Safer for both if only I know," Baba had said. "You make a lot of enemies."

That was true. Flint was proud of it. Her list of great enemies kept the lesser ones pretty much off her back. She was a fighter, after all. The more people who knew it, the safer she would be in the long run. Cadmus, by contrast, was just a little boy. He had none of Flint's grit, none of her cool efficiency in a fight.

It was good to have Cadmus hidden somewhere, out of reach of friends and foes, alike. It was less so for Flint to be in Baba's debt. A picture of Cadmus, gray eyes wide beneath his ebony mop of hair, appeared in Flint's mind. She forced it away.

"Do this for me," Baba had said, "and I'll send you to see him."

Flint had jumped at that. She'd missed the little brat more than she cared to admit. Before the thing with the flesh gang, she only thought of Cadmus as a responsibility, a family obligation. The only words she remembered from her long dead father were, "Take care of your little brother."

She had. She'd saved them both, fed them both, clothed them both and found them safe shelter for years until the one day she failed and Baba had to step in.

The guilt she felt over her failure with the flesh gang had wounded her more deeply than the scars she earned during the scrap itself. She wore the shame of needing Baba Yaga's help like a great molten stone on her chest. It was through that shame that Baba now owned her. She knew it and, worse, Baba Yaga knew it. Flint loved her little brother after all. Who would have thought it?

But The Null? No one went into The Null. Not even the flesh gangs went there, not even the Clans. No tech worked there, none at all. Even battery-powered palm lights went dark quickly within minutes of entry there.

"You'll give me the bug for back up, yeah?" she'd asked Baba.

"I need him with me," Baba had said.

Of course. Why waste a perfectly good xeno when you can send little expendable Flint? What difference did it make to anyone if something in

The Null ate her for breakfast? Baba would just find some other disposable cit to manipulate.

She paused for a moment to get her bearings.

Someone had told her once (her father? her mother?) that Terra Nova III had once been a lush world covered almost completely in deep dense flora.

Rainforests, whoever had called them.

That's what had brought the first colonists to this Altworld, or so the story went. The universe was a wheel with Terra Primus at the center, but there were Alternate Terra's spread out along the spokes. Lots and lots of alternates. Too many to count.

Each Altworld was a little like Terra Primus and a little not. Flint couldn't keep it straight in her head, but she did know one thing: Terra Primus had run dry and humanity was hopping the tangential realities to save itself.

Her father's parents had been among a group of scientists who'd thought Terra Nova III might be a good place to settle.

She stopped in a little clearing about a klick into the deep dark forest. Though Terra Nova III had no moon the eternal cloud cover gave off a luminance sufficient for her to see without using her night goggles.

Flint didn't mind the dark, mostly. It had saved her life and Cadmus's more times than she could count. Dark in the bunkers and safeholes was one thing, though. Dark in this twittery, misty jungle was quite another. There were things out there in the flora. Things that no one had ever seen and lived to describe. Bodies of those who'd attempted to cross the Null or use it as a long-term staging area for attacks had turned up with wounds that made them look well—*chewed*.

Whatever the creatures were that lived here, they were big and they ate meat. It occurred to Flint that these animals, whatever they were, were the real natives of this world. She and all the other cits were just visitors.

Somehow Baba had determined how deeply into the Null she must penetrate and an approximate direction for her to point herself. Beyond that sketchy information, Flint had no real idea what she was looking for or how she'd know when she found it.

"Oh, you'll know," Baba had said. "Trust me. You'll know."

She knew what to do when she got there, at any rate: drop off the package Baba had given her and get the hell out.

Something skittered in the dark just beyond her field of vision. She tensed, lowering into a half crouch and took hold of her razorline. These things might have teeth, but so did Flint.

A moment or two passed without incident, though the skittering sounds increased somewhat. To Flint the noises sounded like hundreds of rocks being skipped off a concrete wall.

She slowly drew her razorline out of its sheath and shook it loose. Still nothing leaped out at her from the dark. After a minute or two, though she didn't exactly relax, she decided to press on. Baba had said this job was to be done quickly, within the next few hours, and she still had a way to go. Her directions were to go two klicks into the Null, bearing north. Whatever-it-was would be waiting there.

She was surrounded. Something (several really large somethings) was out there in the flora just beyond where she could see. Even after donning her night goggles she had only been able to catch glimpses of the creatures, whatever they were. She saw the flash of what looked like a pair of glowing pale eyes, the hint of what seemed to be a long, scale encrusted tail, but nothing to indicate the true shape or nature of whatever was hunting her.

Herding, she thought, correcting herself. *They want me to go off to the west.*

They were in for a shock, though, if they thought to scare her into deviation from her chosen track. Flint didn't get scared, not anymore, not for a long time. She just went cold inside and then people got hurt.

She made good progress despite her hidden companions. This thing Baba had sent her in for should be appearing soon. She'd been barely aware of the little package she carried in her back pouch at the outset, but now its weight irritated her. She was going to have a talk with Baba Yaga when she got back to the Bunkers.

All at once the skittering stopped. Just like that, the weird sound of her pursuers vanished from the background noise of the jungle. She'd gotten so used to it that this sudden absence might as well have been a shout.

A freon chill spread through her body.

The thing ripped out at her from the foliage almost faster than she could react. As it reached the apex of its spring, her eyes began tracking it in that adrenal slow-time that had saved so many human lives before. Without thinking she gave her wrist a sharp twist, extending her razorline up and out. The point caught the creature in mid leap and cut a molecule thin line along one side of its scaly torso.

The creature let out a shriek and fell in two pieces less than half a meter short of its intention. Flint watched dispassionately as a pool of thick orange blood began to grow beneath the still twitching corpse.

One, she thought.

She knew what they were now anyway: monsters. Their faces, such as they were, were little more than an excuse for row upon row of jagged teeth. Their scale-covered skin seemed to take on the characteristics of whatever surface they happened to touch. They were fast, roughly the size of a grown human and smarter than a lot of people she knew.

She'd killed twelve of them so far and still they kept coming. She realized by then why Baba Yaga had chosen her for this: her possession of and skill with the razorline.

Most people found the device too dangerous even for practice. Barely visible, able to split molecular bonds, the razorline was a weapon that had killed as many of its owners as it had its enemies. She'd taught herself using whips, first, then steel links and polymer chords until she'd felt confident to take up the razor. For a young girl on a planet like Terra Nova III, a lightweight, easy to conceal, lowtech weapon was a necessity. One that could sever a limb in less than a second was nearly equivalent to personal safety.

Most men used flechette guns, clubs or large knives. These monsters were far too quick for that. They'd tagged her twice already despite the razor.

She was getting tired. They'd started coming at her in twos, working in tandem in an attempt to overcome her invisible weapon.

Something crackled in the jungle on her right. She spun, lopping off both the heads of her attackers in a single motion, and ran further up the path she'd set for herself. As far as she could tell she was still on target for Baba's mystery destination but, due to current concerns, she had no idea now how far away it was or how long it might take to get there.

She felt the flora thinning around her and she smelled something different in the air. Something had burnt its way through here recently and taken a good amount of the forest with it. She'd not noticed, having been underground in her safehole for those few days but, even if she had, she'd have given it little attention. There were always fires on Terra Nova III.

There were not, however, enormous pieces of pristine tech on Terra Nova III. Not anymore.

The thing, exactly where Baba had said it would be without saying what, was the biggest piece of unblemished technology she had ever seen in her life. It was about eight meters long, five high, with what seemed like a huge door at one end and plexi windows at the other. There were some weird tubes running along either side of the thing's base.

Though she couldn't read them, Flint recognized letters, large and small, stenciled at points all over it.

She was so transfixed by the sight that she forgot for a moment why she was there and what was behind her.

Theta wasn't coming back.

The window was nearly closed and she wasn't coming back. She should've returned as soon as she realized communications were faltering. She knew the rules and she was far too stiff to break protocol, so he had to assume she'd been prevented somehow from returning.

She'd left him there with the drop-skiff to monitor fluctuations in the planet's magnetosphere, to keep an eye on their exit window.

"I will attempt to make contact with the colonists," she'd said before marching off into the murky jungle like she was on her way to her duty shift in the command core. "You will stay here with the skiff."

"Watch yourself, okay," he'd said. "These people have been cut off for a long time."

He'd heard of Broken Colonies before. What he'd heard hadn't done much to quiet his unease. Still, Construct or not, Theta was senior officer. It was probably safe to assume she knew something of what she was doing.

Her original was Dr. Lupe Garcia, a geneticist on Terra Primus. Dr. Garcia had been one of the scientists who'd created the first Constructs at the end of the previous century. Some of her genetic material was in all of them, but Theta was nearly a complete clone. Aside from the artificial smoothness of her features and her lack of excess body fat, Theta might have been Dr. Garcia's twin.

He'd enjoyed working with her on the *Gilgamesh*, scanning Terra Nova III for some way to breach the magnetic barrier that had thwarted Terra Primus' efforts to assist the colony there.

He'd seen what passed for excitement on her tranquil Construct face when she'd discovered the *ripples*.

"There may be a way down," she'd said.

That was it. Commander Hewdon had immediately dispatched her in a specially altered drop-skiff to "Get down there and see what's what" as he'd put it.

"Take Mattock with you," the commander had added with that crooked smile of his. "He's been itching for a chance to stretch his legs."

The ride down had been bumpy, despite the skiff's modifications. Theta's ripples had proved to be more of the sort produced in hurricane seas than in tranquil backyard ponds. Their descending skiff had come close, far too close, in Mattock's opinion, to ditching before she'd managed to regain control and set down.

Now they were down, Theta was missing, the window was closing and Adjunct Charlie Mattock was going to have to make a command decision.

Flint didn't scream as the talon sliced her thigh open. In fact she barely felt it. There'd been a little pressure, a sense of impact and then the flow of blood. The sight of the gushing red, staining her cloak and leggings snapped her into action again.

The offending creature had turned, beginning its second approach. Ignoring her wound for the moment, she shot the razorline at the thing, neatly bisecting its drooling face.

Without turning, she dropped to her good knee and unhooked the plas grenade hanging from her belt, flipped off the safety and tossed it into the jungle behind her. Seeing the flash in her periphery and feeling the wave of heat on her back, she smiled. She bent to tie off her wound before the chittering monsters regrouped.

Five left, she thought, listening to them circling her. *Maybe six.*

Hauling herself to her feet, she began to inch towards the big tech thing she'd been dispatched to find. She wanted something solid at her back when the remaining monsters made their play.

Her smile broadened when she saw the tongues of flame licking up the sides of the trees that had been behind her. She knew it had been smart to keep that grenade handy.

Mattock started at the sound of the explosion.

"That wasn't natural," he said to himself, even as he rose from the pilot's cradle.

Moving to the rear of the skiff, he snatched up one of the modified pulse guns (Theta had posited potential technical difficulties once they set down) and checked the charge.

"Skiff control," he said. "Open rear portal."

* * *

Well, this is different, she thought.

There were seven of them left, not six, now all the same slate gray color of Terra Nova III's sky. Their rows of fangs shone in the dim light like slivers of steel. Their eyes, two pairs apiece, glowed with their own seemingly preternatural light.

Flint knew she prolly wouldn't survive anything like a tandem attack involving more than two of them. Not for the first time her options had been reduced to how many of her enemies she might take with her into oblivion.

"Come on then," she said softly through her teeth.

As if in agreement, three of the animals broke from the group, coming at her on the run.

She braced herself against the smooth metal of the object's skin, taking comfort in its relentless artificiality. This was a human-made thing. She was a human being. She could handle these creatures.

She flicked the razorline out to its full length and held it rigid. The lead animal yelped as it impaled itself on the invisible wire and fell, writhing, to the ground. Wasting no time, Flint retracted the wire only to fling it outward again in a wide arc.

It cut the other two animals almost identically across both their slavering faces. The wounds might not have been mortal, but they were sufficient to send the pair yipping off into the forest.

One of the remaining animals barked. The last four monsters surged toward her, a nightmare of flashing teeth.

She whisked the razorline out at the big leader, missed, and had to duck as the creature slapped into the part of the construct that had been previously blocked by her face. It rebounded off the thing even as its fellows converged on Flint.

This is it, she thought.

They pounced. She swung, noting with satisfaction, the yelping cry that followed her weapon's impact. Teeth sliced into her wounded arm, but she barely acknowledged them or the strange vibration that chose that moment to run through the edifice behind her.

She fumbled for her knife but her fingers, clumsy from blood loss, could not take hold. She settled for a fist and began pounding the monster's throat even as it bore her to the ground.

"I am Flint!" she screamed as she pummeled its ugly stupid face. "Flint! Flint! Flint!"

She knew there wasn't enough brain in there for the creature to understand her words, much less remember them, but she was alone, she was dying, and somebody had to know. Even if "somebody" was only this vicious, mindless brute.

Then, suddenly, there was a great bright light where the monster had been, but no monster. As she pushed herself up to her feet she was aware of more of the light and of the weird hollow sound that came with it.

She stared in wonder as the remaining predators vanished into the light and were no more.

Dumbfounded by what she'd witnessed, Flint turned to see what or who the author of this miracle might be. She was surprised to see a boy, scarcely older than herself, standing in the now open doorway.

His skin was like dark polished wood and he had no hair on his head. He was wearing a uniform of silver and black. The gauntlet he wore on one wrist sported a badge that was identical to the little artifact Baba Yaga had shown her.

"I'm—I'm Charlie Mattock," said the boy. His voice was shaky.

Why would someone so powerful have such a tremble in his voice? she wondered.

The boy reached out his hand to her, and then everything went black.

"That sounds like a fairy tale, Adjunct," said a voice in the dark.

"It's what happened, sir," said another, more familiar voice.

"She's waking up now, Commander," said something that sounded like a rumbling steam engine.

Having absolutely no idea what to expect, Flint opened her eyes.

Three faces hovered above her; two human and one not. She recognized one of the humans as Charlie Mattock. He was smiling down at her like an old friend. The other human, the older one with the red beard, she had never seen before.

She was at a loss at first to understand what she found so unusual about his face when all at once she hit on it. He looked friendly. They all did. Even the xeno, who was more like a man-shaped pile of melting rocks than a person, was sporting what she thought was a smile.

All of them, the humans and the xeno, wore similar uniforms albeit with different colors complimenting the black.

"Hi there," said the rock thing in a cheery rumble. "I'm Dr. Brogrym and you are a very lucky young woman. Blood loss can be quite fatal, you know."

The bearded man turned out to be Commander Hewdon, and he said he had a lot of questions for her.

"But they can certainly wait until you're feeling better, Ms. Flint," he said. Then, as he left, "I'll want you in my tac room in ten, Mr. Mattock."

"Aye, sir," said Charlie Mattock.

Who were these people, some new Clan she'd never heard of? What the hell was happening?

"You are in the medical creche of the slideship *Gilgamesh*, young lady," said Dr. Brogrym, sensing her questions. "You've had an ordeal, but your wounds are mostly healed. You'll be right as cake in no time."

"*Rain*, Doc," said Charlie Mattock, chuckling. "Right as rain."

"It doesn't rain on El Ohmbar, Charlie."

"But you have plenty of cake, apparently," said Charlie Mattock, shooting Flint a quick, inexplicable wink.

"Oh yes," said the doctor expansively. "Lovely sulfur and malachite confections, which take weeks to congeal. I've been trying to get the cooks to bake one but they're classified as hazmat."

"Look," said Flint, trying to sit up. "What's going on here?"

The Doctor seemed poised to give what promised to be an even more long winded answer, but Charlie Mattock headed him off.

"The Commander's going to want me for debriefing soon, Doc," he said. "You mind?"

"Ah, yes," said the xeno, understanding. "Of course. Speak with your friend."

The rock creature moved away as Charlie Mattock helped Flint into a sit. His touch was the first truly familiar thing she'd felt since waking in this "slideship."

She was underwhelmed now that she got a good look at it. There really wasn't much to the place, just some beds and tables and some weird flashing lights.

"Thank you for saving me," she said.

"Ah, you were doing fine on your own," he replied. "I've never seen a weapon like that whip thing you were using."

She felt herself blushing and didn't know why. He took her hand, the good one, and held it tightly.

"And anyway," he said. "You may have saved a whole colony, so I'm not sure keeping score is a good idea."

Saved the colony? What? Were these people all insane?

"You don't know, do you?" he said, grinning. "You don't know what you were carrying."

Her mind raced, re-firing synapses, rebooting memories. Yes. Now she remembered it all—Baba Yaga, the mysterious package, the monsters, all of it. None of it added up to her saving the colony.

She asked him what he was talking about.

"There's a woman down there," said Charlie Mattock. "A really, really smart woman. Barbara Yasbeck. She's been tracking the shifts in Terra Nova III's magnetosphere almost since the colony broke contact."

"Magnetosphere?"

"We've been trying to get through for years," he continued exuberantly. "But, with all that atmospheric flux, navigation was too risky"

Her brain just wouldn't accept it. He'd needed to get her in view of a window to prove it to her satisfaction. She'd been surprised at how beautiful the planet was from this vantage.

"The point is," he said eventually, "we've been monitoring Terra Nova III for a long time, trying to find a break in all that interference. No luck."

"But *you* got down," she said.

His expression darkened at that, as if a cloud of sadness had passed over his face.

"My . . . friend . . . my partner, Theta, found a window," he said with difficulty. "It's gone now."

He paused for a moment or two. Flint began to feel uncomfortable.

"So you can't get back?" she ventured.

"Not today," he said, brightening slightly. "No. But, thanks to you, we will soon."

"Thanks to me?"

"You and your friend's book. Her calculations, they're predicting that Terra Nova III's magnetic field is shifting, back to normal this time."

"Five years," he went on. "Ten, tops, and we'll be able to go down there and help."

Five or ten *years?* That's what he was so happy about? That was worth his dead friend's sacrifice? Ten more years of battle, death and anguish for the few who managed to survive? Ten more years of the Clans' brutal control of their various enclaves? Ten more years of Baba Yaga? The enormity of what she'd done, what she'd left behind, began to finally penetrate.

Her knees buckled and Charlie Mattock was forced to support her as she wept uncontrollably, drenching his shoulder with her tears.

Baba Yaga had watched the Terran drop-skiff lift off, zigzagging upwards until it vanished into the mass of luminescent gray that had blanketed her world for so long.

"Good-bye, Antiope," she said softly. "Good luck."

She'd lied to the girl, of course. She lied to everyone about everything. The only person Baba Yaga didn't lie to was Baba Yaga.

It really wasn't self-interest that drove the world, but duty. Duty had kept her alive, kept her strong, kept her going on the off chance that someone someday would find a way down to the planet and put what she'd found there to use. Duty had forged Flint into the perfect instrument to deliver those findings to the appropriate hands.

Poor little Flint. How wretched she must feel, and how relieved. The duality of her current situation must be assaulting her mercilessly right now. Flint was tough, though. She'd survive. As soon as her tears were done she'd begin to learn the other thing that drove the world, which drove all worlds when you got right down to it: hope.

Meldrick appeared in the doorway, clicking impatiently.

"Time to go," he said. "To go."

He was right. She still had many projects that needed tending, not the least of which was seeing to it that the *Shipley-Marks* alliance actually came about.

She waved the Siroccan off and took one last look up at the sky. Though she knew it wasn't physically possible, to Baba Yaga it seemed that things had gotten considerably brighter.

Tiger's Eye View

by Mary Ellen Martin

She had only been on Earth a week, and already she was in an argument. That was a new record for her. She had been trying, once again, to convince Reggie that evacuation to the lunar metropolis was the better answer, instead of staying on a dead mud ball.

"Ya know, Share," the male voice spoke in her headset, "Being here ain't all that bad. I mean, yeah, sure, looking for vitals out here may be a losing fight, but it ain't boring. How'd you get to be here instead of Mars, anyway?" New Jersey was gone with the rest of it, but Reggie sounded like he was from Hoboken.

"Just lucky, I guess." Sharon managed to pull a water probe from the ground.

"Lucky, my ass! Let's see," he hummed thoughtfully. "Trying to make more Trops for people in space, in a clean yet airless environment, or be stuck on this sludge ball trying to find a spot, any spot, where life can exist. Hmm." She could practically hear him wink, and couldn't help but chuckle at his attempt at peacemaking.

"Believe it or not, Reg, the moon Trop was boring. At least here there are fewer politicians."

"Good point. Why couldn't the Bang have made politicians extinct, and left everyone else alone?" Reggie planted a weather probe and activated it, the beeping light hardly visible in the wind storm. "Now I ain't saying it isn't hard here, but it's Earth, it's home. Well, except for you. I don't see how you lived for so long on the moon. Seems pretty boring to me. Do you miss it?" Reggie at his sarcastic best. Sharon found out quickly that despite the harsh conditions, Earth sarcasm nearly matched the sense of humor shared by the lunar metropolis inhabitants.

Looking back, the moon Trop hadn't been so bad, after all. As a result of a very loud, very public confrontation with a Trop review board, and some other minor issues, she had been reassigned to Earth. She didn't have the heart to tell Reggie the Earth, once their home, was now essentially a penal colony. The moon had no scenery, but you didn't have to worry about sinking, or death by lightning.

This location was a different story. The ground they were surveying was a marsh. It was wet and thick, and you could lose a boot if you weren't careful. No earthquake or volcanic activity had been reported in the last five years, and it was believed the Bang was a tectonic last hurrah.

Fifteen years ago, in the course of a week, every volcano on the planet blew. The planet itself held together, but the resulting toxic conditions created by trillions of kilos of lava and ash dumped in an already polluted environment made Earth uninhabitable.

There was a small outpost that monitored Earth conditions, peopled by an optimistic few who believed Earth would make a comeback. They monitored surface and weather conditions, and the data collected was beamed to orbiting satellites, which then sent the information to the moon and Mars. Publicly, there was talk of returning some day. However, it was the quiet opinion of the Trop that humanity would live out its last days within sight of Earth, unable to return. Sharon had tried unsuccessfully to convince the group to evacuate to the Trop on the moon.

"I wouldn't say I miss the Trop," Sharon said, as she dropped another probe into the muck. "I had friends there, but I wouldn't call it home. I evacuated immediately after the Bang, so nothing really seems like home to me." The moon was harsh, but the vacuum was nothing compared to weather.

The weather on Earth was now as violent as the ground was quiet. All the ash and lava dumped into the oceans turned the remaining water into an acidic, tidal sludge, killing sea life. The toxins created from the destruction of oil refineries, the burning of chemical plants, and poisons humankind had buried in the soil, turned the atmosphere into a nightmare. Skeletons of trees erupted from the ground like rotten teeth. There were almost no visible signs of the cities that once dominated the area. What the volcanoes didn't destroy, the environmental aftermath did.

Sharon, despite the ugliness and weather, was entranced. She hadn't been on Earth in fifteen years. There was color here, activity. Real gravity. Biosuits weren't needed, but you still had to wear protection. The local suits were thinner and easier to move in, and goggles and a respirator protected what was important. She had never thought she would relish being here, instead of the quiet order of the Trop.

She would die before telling Reggie that, though.

She checked the probe, wiped off the gunk clinging to it, and placed it back in its sheath. "Readings are nominal. There is water content, but I doubt the purifiers can fix it." She radioed her progress to Base and turned to Reggie. The man had a seemingly endless supply of Bon Jovi shirts his parents had, for some reason, raided during the first days of the Bang. Slowly he wore each one to rags and refused to throw away the pieces. He finished collecting water, soil, and air samples and was placing them in a satchel tied to his waist. He looked up and shrugged his shoulders. "You ready to call it a day? I know a great French restaurant, and it's been at least three hours since—"

"Don't go there," Sharon interrupted. "I don't want to hear about your imaginary love life. Again. I'm starving, and I don't want to throw up my only protein pill." She readjusted her pack and grabbed her climbing ropes, hoisting them over her shoulder while Reggie laughed. "Besides, I want to check out that blip five clicks west of here. You go on. Save me an escargot." Another way to cope; joking about exotic foods they would never eat.

She handed Reggie the samples she had collected, and turned and began walking, not looking to see if Reggie was following. The exercise was good, she supposed, but Sharon missed her lunar rover, another secret. She quickened her pace, something else she hadn't been able to do on the moon.

"Sure you don't want some company?" Reggie called. Sharon waved without stopping. "Okay, but you'll miss it when they declare me as the most handsome man on the planet!" The wind picked up, carrying his voice with it. It felt hot on her face, and she wished she could take off her goggles and respirator and let the wind blow through her hair. Until the results came back from Reggie's air samples, however, the equipment stayed on.

Sharon didn't stop walking until after cresting a hill. She was glad to be rid of Reggie. She never understood why she was so vehement about saving humanity, but hated being around people. Of course, her vehemence was what got her sent back to Earth, fifteen years after escaping from it. She grabbed a tube from her waist pack, took a sip of water, grimacing. This water had a more metallic taste to it than moon water, despite purification. She capped the tube and replaced it, and continued walking.

The taste of the water wasn't the only difference. The moon was dry, covered with gray, powdery sand. There were mountains, valleys, plains, and all that, and Earth practically dominated the sky. The ground she was currently walking on varied every few kilometers. She had been in a swamp, and now she was walking on ground that was cracked and dry, with colors shifting from red to yellow and back again. Reggie and the others told Sharon the area used to be Arizona or Utah, and told of signs saying this area was part of the old Navajo reservation. Sharon's mother had been Navajo.

Geography didn't matter now, Sharon thought. It was all gone. The only thing that mattered was trying to find sustenance. Improving water purification, improving health, improving everything, regardless of effort or cost. Damn Trop politicians, she thought. They should come down here to see that getting people off of Earth was the only solution to saving humanity, or at least putting off extinction for a while. Was she the only one who gave a damn about that?

Small puffs of dust rose up from her feet as she walked, yet the ground was stable and firm. Her skin itched around her respirator and goggles, where sweat and condensation from her breath merged on her nose. Yet she followed her old habits as she had on the moon, looking up when she walked. Sharon didn't see the cliff's edge until she heard a sudden *beep* in her headset.

Sharon looked down and gasped, stopping short, her momentum almost taking her over the edge. She managed to recover and stepped back, breathing heavily. God, what would have happened if she had fallen in? The gravity was real here. She looked over the edge and felt dizzy. Damn, this was no good. She got down on her hands and knees and tried again, looking down into the canyon.

Below her was a stunning view of canyon walls, rich in deep reds, fading down to blue from shadows caused by the setting sun. Wait a minute. Shadows?

She looked up, then down again, forcing herself to breathe, forcing herself to see what could only be a hunger induced mirage. Sky. Blue sky. Not everywhere, but blue sky, just above the canyon and a break in the clouds to the west allowing the sun through. There were bands of dirty gray and yellow clouds swirling on either side of the strip of sky, and she could see one small star shining brightly in the deepening blue of the late evening.

She blinked several times, then cursed her memory. She grabbed for her camera, taking pictures as fast as she could. The sky, the canyon, the vibrant colors. A bird coasting on air currents between rock formations below her. Sharon began taking pictures of the rock formations, and paused to change the data cartridge, hoping the zoom worked. On the bottom of the canyon floor, she could see green. Green. Grass, tree leaves, algae in a small stream. The presence of chlorophyll here was a miracle! Her head spun with possibilities.

Sharon also thought she saw what looked like ruins of old living sites in the canyon walls. She knew she might be wasting the last data cartridge on a hallucination, but she felt she had to get this, in case it was real. She took some more pictures and tried to radio Base.

"Base, this is Sharon, uh, Survey Nine. Do you copy? I have an incredible visual you have got to see!" No answer. "Base, Survey Nine. Base, Survey Nine, do you copy?" Still no answer. She didn't know if they were receiving, or if she was even transmitting. She frowned and inspected the radio. It appeared to be fine. It had checked out before they left. She keyed the mike a few more times, and again heard a small *beep*. It didn't sound like radio static. There wasn't a mag storm coming. Was something in the surrounding rock blocking the signal?

Sharon looked behind her, at the path she had taken. The ground was yellow and cracked, lifeless. It hurt to look at, when she'd rather be looking at the incredible view in front of her. There were some taller rock formations, and smaller rocks and boulders littered the area. She noticed one nearby rock in particular, which she hadn't noticed before. It was irregularly shaped, and the same color as the surrounding yellow soil, but there was a small red ring on the left side. The ring was the same red as the soil in the canyon. Inside the ring was a small yellow, brown, and gray circle. It looked, Sharon thought suddenly, like the view of Earth from the moon.

"Now what are you?" Sharon addressed the rock. She bent down for a closer look. It looked like a normal rock, typical for the region. It was about fifteen centimeters high, and maybe thirty at the base. Sharon thought it looked like pumice, but wasn't sure. She saw what looked like a track leading from the rock and continuing into the desert behind her. It looked like a track a small tire might make, but that was impossible. And yet there was no track in front of the rock. It looked as though the rock had made the trail. She reached out to touch the rock, and thought she heard a slight humming noise.

Without warning, she was hit by a memory so powerful, so real, she didn't realize she was still at the canyon rim. She was in the forest again, with her mother. She was eight years old, and her mother was beautiful, with the sun in her brown hair and the leaves making dappled shadows on her face.

"Now let's see, um, that one's a cedar. You can tell by the lines in the bark," her mother way saying. Sharon touched the tree, running her hand over the rough bark and soft moss. Daddy was on some business trip, and she and Momma had gone hiking. Her mother continued, "And that's a fir, and that one's a spruce. The spruce cones are good for helping make a campfire. That one there is a Tamarack, good for winter burning, according to Poppa Eldon."

"When can we go to the ocean? I wanna get some shells!" Sharon whined. Her mother had laughed (oh to hear her laughter again!).

"We go there every summer, don't worry. When your dad gets back, if his vacation request was approved, we'll be off like a shot!"

Sharon had been impatient, and bored with the trees. "But we go every year. Why wouldn't Daddy get to go?"

Momma sighed. "Well, honey, Daddy had to take care of a problem in San Diego, and it's kind of a big problem. It might take him some time to fix it."

"What kind of problem? And how could Daddy not fix it, he's the smartest man in the world!" Sharon had hopped over a rotten log, and stopped to look for beetles underneath. Sometimes, when you were lucky, you could find worms and mushrooms, but Momma said to be careful about picking mushrooms.

Sharon's mother frowned and looked away from her daughter. Sharon knew her mother enough, even at eight, to know Momma was worried. "How far away is San Diego?" she asked, hoping to get Momma feeling better.

"Ooh, all the way down in California, and we're way up in Idaho. It takes a couple of days to drive it."

"Is it close to where you work, Momma?"

This time, Momma had smiled. "No, I work in Washington, D.C. Remember when we looked at the map and found it? It takes three or four days to drive it, but I usually fly there."

Sharon had looked at a robin in a nearby tree. The robin took off and quickly flew away. Just then, they noticed the sky was filled with birds; robins, finches, crows, bluebirds and blackbirds. She and her mother had stopped, watching the sudden migration. When the sky was clear again, the forest was quiet. Very quiet.

"Momma, what was—"

"Shh!" Her mother held up a warning hand. Sharon saw a look of intense concentration on her face; saw her come to a decision.

"Sharon, let's get back to the car. Hurry!"

"But Momma, we just got—" was as far as Sharon got before the world started shaking. Her mother grabbed her, and they fell to the ground. The trees swayed overhead, and Sharon was afraid they would fall on her. Her bare arms and legs hurt from being poked by pine needles on the ground. After a few seconds that seemed like forever, it stopped. They stayed put, gasping for breath. When a few minutes had passed, Sharon's mother got up and started running for the car, pulling Sharon with her.

Sharon's memory from that point was hazy. They drove, the days blending together until they reached Houston. Her mother waved some credentials at a guard, and was allowed to enter an airstrip, where a space shuttle waited. Other people were running toward the shuttle and jockeying to get on board. By this time, the ground shook more often, and the sky was dark. Sharon's questions were ignored. Others had the same questions, and though she guessed Momma knew more, she wasn't telling.

Sharon remembered everyone pressing themselves to the windows after takeoff, and looking at a changing world. There were red spots of fire all over the place, and you could see volcanoes in at least three places erupting. The sky was turning black and yellow from all the ash and sulfur in the air.

"My God, that's Yellowstone! Yellowstone's erupting! How the hell can that be?" An older woman had asked.

"Yellowstone is nothing but a giant caldera," answered another voice behind them. "It was always a geologic time bomb."

"It looks like a tiger's eye marble," Lucy Crow murmured, tears streaming down her face. Everyone was too engrossed with the view to see when she collapsed, until Sharon started screaming.

Beep.

Sharon was lying on the canyon floor. She must have fallen, she thought, but she didn't remember that initial free fall feeling, or hitting the ground. Nothing hurt, either. She sat up and checked herself for injuries, finding none. She looked up at the top of the canyon. Yellow and red dust swirled in the wind above, but down here, it was calm. She could see the green, lush landscape up close. The moon was dull, gray, and gritty. The surface of Earth was either poisonous marsh or toxic desert. Here, there was *life.*

She had been about to take off a glove to feel the grass when the voice spoke behind her.

"Hello, Sharon."

She turned quickly to see her mother standing before her. She was dressed in the same summer outfit she had been wearing when they made their sudden flight to Houston; a black tank top and denim shorts. Her long dark hair blew gently in the breeze. Now Sharon understood. She did fall, and she was dead.

"No, you are not dead."

Sharon paused, trying to gather her thoughts. She watched her mother die. She saw it.

"How did you know what I was thinking?" Sharon asked.

The mirage/dream/hallucination smiled. "I sense the shock and sadness you feel for her loss."

"You are not my mother."

"No."

"Who are you?"

The dream folded her hands in front of her. "I suppose you could call me a messenger."

"That's no answer!" Sharon yelled. Her voice echoed up the canyon walls. A startled bird took flight from a nearby tree. "Who are you? Answer me!" Sharon looked at the image of her mother. She looked the same. Same hair, same clothes, same voice. Sharon then looked at her eyes, which should have been a warm, laughing brown. However, these eyes were multi-colored: black, brown, and yellow, just like a tiger's eye marble. Just like the Earth seen from space. She then remembered what she had been reaching for before this bizarre memory trip. "You're the rock, aren't you? Somehow, you are the rock."

"I am only part of the whole."

Part of the whole? What the hell was that supposed to mean? Part of the whole. Part of a bigger rock? Part of—oh God. She began shaking her head back and forth. "No, it can't be."

The image of Lucy Crow just smiled, waiting.

"Earth? You mean you are part of *Earth*?"

The image nodded.

Sharon suddenly felt very dizzy, and lost her balance. She bit her tongue as she fell to the ground, yet hardly felt the pain or tasted the blood.

She put her head down until her head stopped spinning, and looked up. The image of her mother had not moved. Oh, where to begin with this?

"Okay," she whispered, "okay. Say for a minute that you are the Earth, and I'm not dead or suffering from a serious head injury. Why are you here? Why me? Why all this?" Sharon stood back up and spread her arms wide. "How is this possible? The Earth is dead! When every volcano on the planet blew, it died. Almost everything is extinct! If you are really Earth, what happened? Are you going to try to tell me this was some, some kind of, suicide?" Her voice had risen again, and a small part of her tried to remind her that she was screaming at a hallucination, but the rest of her wouldn't listen.

The image shrugged. "Self defense."

"What? I'm confused, help me out here. What do you mean, self defense? How is killing every living thing on the planet self defense?"

"I was dying."

"If you hadn't noticed, you finished the job."

The image shook her head. "No. I was dying. Poison was in my air, my water, my ground. Poisons created by you. I merely eliminated the threat, and now life is returning."

Sharon had to acknowledge the truth in that statement. If the pictures she had taken showed the same greenness she was seeing now . . . This small area practically teemed with life. After fifteen years of seeing nothing but a small group of humans in one artificial domain or another, she could really see the difference. Trees, leaves blowing gently, bugs flying past, the soft grass under her hands when she nearly fainted. Life.

Think, Sharon, think, she told herself. How? This—this image isn't very forthcoming. How?

The Lucy-image answered, "There has always been life here."

Sharon groaned in frustration. She was a surveyor, not a scientist! The shock of the encounter was making thinking difficult.

Earth/Lucy explained, "My fire burned away the poisons. You might call if purification. And yes, new poisons were made, but it also contained what was needed for life."

"Microbes," Sharon replied. "Microbes in the ash and lava. But it would take millions of years for the conditions to be right to support plant life, much less animal life. How did this happen?"

Earth/Lucy shook her head. "I have done what was necessary. Now you must do the same."

Beep.

Sharon came to with a start. Her goggles were fogged over, and it was hard to breathe. She was sitting with her legs hanging over the side of the cliff, and she held the strange rock in her hands. That's odd, she thought. She didn't recall picking it up, despite its heaviness. It vibrated for a moment, and stopped.

She ran a finger along the edge of her respirator, removing a large amount of gunk that had collected there. She did the same to her goggles, and was able to see a little better. She looked up, and saw that two more stars had joined the first, and a small crescent was shining low on the western horizon. Sharon gasped, realizing that was the moon. It had been a long time since she had seen it from Earth. How small it looked!

Sharon looked behind her, seeing the cracked emptiness of the desert. She turned forward, and looked at the deepening shadows playing on the canyon walls. She had never wondered about the distance between stars, how lonely it must be between them. All her desire to keep people away, to be alone, and she never saw until now how lonely she was. All the humor and sarcasm used to hide her despair were suddenly gone, like that long-ago forest.

Feeling suddenly so small under the great sky, surrounded by the desperate desolation above and below, and still hurting from the memory, she cried for the first time in ages. Momma, Daddy, Poppa Eldon, movies, pizza, zoos, forests, birds, seashells. The whole Earth.

Oh, how she cried.

Sharon didn't know how long she sat there, but as darkness fell she knew she had to get back. She cleaned up her face as well as she could and stood up, hearing several voices over her headset. At least that was working again.

"Survey Nine, this is Reggie. Sharon, do you copy? Answer, dammit!"

Sharon sniffed and began coughing. When she finished, she lifted her respirator and spat out a wad of mucus the same color as the dust. "Yeah, Reg, I'm here. I'm okay. Where are you?"

"God, finally! We're coming to your signal. Makira's coming, too. You missed check-in, and we've been trying to raise you for ten minutes. What's your situation?" Reggie sounded frantic, more serious than she had ever heard him. It seemed she wasn't the only one hiding behind sarcasm.

"I'm okay. Tell Makira not to worry. I don't need a medic. Just shaky, that's all. I've got a visual here you have got to see. It may be too dark now, but we can come back in the morning for a full scan. I think I found some new forms of life, but I don't think all of it is organic."

"What? Uh, Share, it sounded like you said you found life. Say again?"

Sharon smiled. She looked at the canyon and sky. There were millions of light years between those stars, but there didn't have to be between people. Now that she had something to share, maybe she didn't have to be alone, either. She put down the rock. She didn't need it now. She saw two more rocks had come closer, both with those strange trails behind them. Life had begun again on Earth, and it gave her something she hadn't had in a long time.

Hope.

Something out of Nothing
by Martin Hayes

The yard was old and brown and barren, coming off the back of the house and surrounded on three sides by a high wooden fence. Twelve meters wide by maybe thirty long. The rear fence ran along a row of tall conifer trees that swayed whenever the wind picked up and there was a big hole right at the back where years ago there had been a fish pond. About halfway down the yard stood the dilapidated shed where my granddad kept his tools and his almost-empty tins of paint, his work boots and an old bayonet from World War One.

The ground was loose dry dirt with a half-forgotten footpath running through it. There were no plants. There hadn't been for as long as I could remember. My granddad always said that he would replant the garden next spring, but every year spring came and went, and then in late summer he would say it all over again. He never did.

I liked staying with my granddad; he bought me a comic every day whereas my parents only bought me three every week. He hung out with me when I needed company and left me alone when I didn't. It was an unspoken arrangement, something we both knew but never discussed.

During the summer holidays I would spend hours in that desolate backyard of his, the sun beating down on my nine-year-old self, and me, worried that I might not make it back to the shed that served as lunar base camp before the water that I carried in an old tin bottle on my belt ran out. I had tried rationing it but the heat from the unfiltered sun had made me drink. What would I do if I didn't make it across the barren lunar surface before the sun went down and the cold dead night rose up like a ghost and froze me solid?

Other times I would carry the spark-firing ray gun that my Dad had bought me for Christmas, and sometimes, if I thought my predicament was especially dangerous, I would slide the wooden pirate sword that granddad had made for me from an old two-by-one into my belt for added protection. It was no ordinary wooden pirate sword you see, it was magic, and when held by its rightful owner became a kind of lethal laser beam that could slice through alien flesh and cut through any material in the known universe.

I was glad of that sword on more than one occasion. Like the time when I was trying to rescue the beautiful woman who had fallen into the bottomless pit of the dried up fish pond. I dug the heels of my tattered All-Stars in to the loose earth, pulling, heaving with all my young strength, but it was no good. I could feel her slender wrists slipping through my hands. Heave, I thought. Heave with all your might.

And then I began to pull her out of that dark, unknowable pit, and all the while the screams from the alien hordes beneath rang in my ears.

Finally she was out and ohh my God, you should've seen her. The most beautiful thing in the world. Perfection in pale green skin. She explained to me that she was an alien princess from Jupiter, that her evil father had wished her to marry the Sea King of Europa and that she had fled, but his thugs had caught her and thrown her into the pit as punishment.

And just then I turned on my heels to see three of those hideous aliens coming at me from across the dirt yard, each one of their five eyes bulging with hate. They reached for their blasters. No problem, I thought; I drew up my ray-gun and aimed it with practiced precision at the chest of the nearest alien.

Click! Click! Click!

Nothing!

Ohh no. I'd forgotten to replace the Quintarial Crystals after the fire fight with the giant radioactive scorpion from New Mexico that I'd narrowly survived the day before.

I threw the ray gun to the ground and pulled the sword from my belt. The first alien popped off a few blasts from his gun, but I was able to roll forward and to my left, avoiding them. This brought me right along side the middle alien. I hacked both his legs off below the knee; he fell heavily in a cloud of dust, his blaster going off into his stomach. One down.

They were shocked by this and they regrouped for their second attack. I shouted to the princess to run for cover. She hid behind the shed.

They came at me simultaneously then. Both blasting away, mistakenly thinking quantity would win out over quality. I took aim as they thundered ever nearer. As their laser blasts flashed all around me, I raised the sword above my head and let it fly, throwing it with all my might at the largest attacker. It stuck in his fat, bulbous neck and he collapsed, coughing green blood into the dirt. I leapt towards him, reaching for his blaster but I was not quick enough.

The last attacker had me cornered now. I had no weapon, only my wits.

He began to laugh. Saying that I was a fool to have interfered with Jupiterian politics and that I would pay for this indiscretion with my life. He called on his wrist-radio then for the star-ship to come and take me prisoner. I was to be tried, found guilty and then eaten alive by the triple-mouthed frog beasts that lurk in the deepest, dampest fissures of Jupiter's cloud belts.

There was only one chance, and I knew it was a long one.

I began to arc around to my left, ever so slowly, and at the same time I inched ever nearer to him, so that he had to continually back away from me in order to maintain the distance between us. After a minute he was as close as I would get him, now all I needed was a distraction.

The Gods were smiling on me that day; a burst of static came from his wrist-radio and for one spilt second his attention was no longer fixed on me. I kicked up a cloud of dust, temporarily blinding him, and smashed both of my feet into his chest as hard as I could.

He staggered backwards. Back towards the pit where he toppled over the side and fell to what I hoped was his agonizing death.

I wiped the sweat from my brow and took a long cooling swig from the tin bottle. It wasn't water this time though; it was some powerful alien whiskey which only the truly manly could take. I knocked back another mouthful, just for good measure.

I never saw the alien princess again. I would have looked around for her, but my granddad called me in for dinner. And after an afternoon like that, you can be sure that I was pretty hungry.

I went back out after I'd finished my spaghetti, but the sun was setting on that empty old backyard. The shadows lengthening, the light changing to a deep orange that swept across the bare dirt like the flames of some crazy Martian bonfire.

I dusted off my ray gun and picked up my sword and went back inside to watch *The Twilight Zone* with my granddad. We never missed an episode that whole summer. I loved it when that man came on to talk before the show started. It felt like he was talking only to me and he always told the best stories.

Candhiga's Corpse and the Birds at the Edge of the Sea
by Andrew Tisbert

She felt the shaking of the ground, a surging and receding, the heart of the world pulsing all around her. She heard the thunder of the waves, felt the lilt of wind on her bare shoulders, the back of her legs. She opened her eyes to the coarse gray sea moiling into the coarse gray sky. And the soft grit of sand under her belly, and the harsher grit of sand around her eyes. She knew these things when she woke. But nothing was right.

She raised her head, slid her tongue over rough lips. Meaning to sit up, she only lurched toward the receding tide. She was warm, but she shivered, a single overpowering convulsion. Trying to sit again, she reached the plateau of hands and knees then sagged back on her haunches.

The air was too thick. The edge of the sun, a hazed red arc emerging from the edge of the sea, was four times the size it should be, but not bright enough. It seeped blood into the darkness around it to her left. Farther left narrow beach disappeared in shadow water around a root-infested ledge that turned to crumbling stone. Above the ledge a tilted stand of trees rippled in the wind. To her right blue sand ran into sharp black rock, then sand, then more rocks gradually curving toward—and then jutting into—the sea. Behind the beach dark forest brushed the sky. She couldn't tell the color of its foliage, but the swaying limbs in the dark were covered with what looked like jagged fish scales the size of her head.

I don't know where I am, she thought. Or why I'm naked. Veins along her arms stuck out as she brushed sand from her body. Her skin was dark beef jerky. Her thighs were thin but strung taut with muscle. Am I usually that skinny? Have I been fasting? Starving?

As if in answer she felt the burning acorn of her stomach. She looked again to the sea. Have I been shipwrecked? That seemed silly. She scanned the shore again for clues. An uneven wave collapsed, casting foam up the sand. Her eyes lost focus for a moment. I don't know my own name, she whispered. Then louder: Who am I? Her throat burned, and her voice—sand sucked through a straw—startled her.

Warm wind stirred along her skin, fanning an ache of panic.

Something flittered in the corner of her eye. Two shadows flaked from the woods and glided toward the beach. They arced around her, gliding low along the water, then lit, one after the other, a few meters beyond her. Birds, raven-black, about the size of eagles, with square heads like great horned owls. They retracted their wings against smooth, featherless bodies. Their claws dug into the packed wet sand and they regarded her with blank, beakless faces. You've arrived, one of them said.

Her breath snagged on fear. Her hands clutched sand.

You've taken the journey over, said the other. Now you will be the first. Dizzily, she rose to her feet. One of the birds repeated: You will be the first. They took hopping steps toward her.

Stay there, she said hoarsely, and coughed.

We must merge with you, said one. But they stopped. The wind raised the hair on her nape as she took a step backward, toward the trees. Behind the birds, the bloated sun's edge had been rising imperceptibly, deepening the pool of blood on the horizon and solidifying their shadows in front of them.

She considered running to the trees, but no. She'd seen them fly and knew she couldn't outrun them. What, then? Fight? She glanced around for a weapon. There was nothing.

We won't hurt you, said the birds. We only want to merge with you, so you can remember.

I'll rip you to pieces with my hands if you come any closer, she said. Then she paused. Remember what?

Everything, said the nearest bird. It fluttered its wings and hopped forward and her heel sank in the sand as she took another step backward.

Where am I? she said.

You made the journey over.

She wondered if she was dead. This seemed as silly as the idea of a shipwreck, but her pulse still throbbed in her wrists with irrational panic.

The closest bird's wings flared upward as it launched toward her. You will understand when we merge, it said.

She threw up her arms and, instead of retreating, charged the approaching bird. A fist caught it on the chest. With a hiss, it lurched sideways, one wing sweeping across her shoulder. Then she did run, past the other bird and along the beach toward the crumbling ledge.

Come back, they cried as she neared the rocks. Then all she heard was the sea's roar as she passed around the ledge on a swath of sand only two meters across. The roots of the trees exposed in the ledge wound like the coils of enormous snakes. The scales pointed upward with razor edges. She rounded the ledge, sinking to her ankles, to find the beach curved on beyond it, the sand almost turquoise in the thickening sunlight. Panting, she fell to her knees. The air burned in her throat, smelled vaguely of sulfur dioxide. The rising sun had splintered the bluish gray sky with cracks and fault lines of vermillion, its hulking shoulder rolling over the horizon. She wiped stinging tears with a wrist, and then looked further down the beach. Something lay there in a heap just beyond the woods, about a hundred meters away. She forced herself to her feet and started toward it. The slivers of black from the sky, the birds, followed her; she felt their shadows on her back. One swooped ahead, glided in front of her.

There is the one you're looking for, it said, and circled above her. As she approached, she realized she was looking at the body of another woman, stiff, her skin dried to old wrinkled canvas. Her side had burst open and her organs spread along her twisted haunch; now they were dried and hardened too.

The smell had settled. There was only the faint putrid must of months-old decay. Somehow the near absence of death's oily smells was more horrifying than the fetor she'd anticipated. The eyes were a dull glaze. She wondered, as the birds landed once again around her, if she couldn't recognize this corpse because it had been transformed by all the oils and fluids having long since leeched out of it. Something told her she should know this woman, she should mourn her. But there was only the lack of these emotions, just as there was a lack of blood in this heap, as the sun continued to hemorrhage into the sea.

You've found your friend, said the nearest bird.

It was too much. She sank to her knees, growing darker and emptier as the sun brightened and filled the sky. She suddenly understood she saw the world only in approximations. This was not the sun, only *like* the sun she knew; that was not the ocean, it was too thick and warm; the forest was not what she knew to be forest. And the birds, they were only birds by default, by degree, extensions of her expectation.

But this dead woman was not approximate. She was unknown, but real.

She is the last of the others, said a bird to fill the silence.

What do you mean—the others?

The journey team. The ones who failed.

It was a broad knife, prying just under her lungs: she didn't know what the bird was talking about, but it connected with an internal pain. She felt somehow responsible for this woman. And there were others? Were there more corpses to be found along this beach? She stretched suddenly between the need and fear of memory. The only way to cross over that staggering abyss was to question the birds.

What do you know of it? What do you want?

We know only what you know. We want only what you want.

What I want is for you to leave me alone.

The closest of the birds hopped backward. But you must merge with one of us to be whole. You need to make it right.

I need you to go away, she said viciously, hoarsely, and the birds sprang into the sky like startled crows.

She was vaguely aware the sun arced the sky too quickly, so she couldn't be sure how long it took to walk the beach around the entire island. But by the time she recognized the finger of rocks pointing into the water, the crumbling ledge, and then finally her dead woman, the sun hung directly over her head, heavily, as if ready to fall at any minute and suffocate her. She had found a bright orange pack filled with packaged foods, clothing and camping supplies. The birds had watched from a distance as she opened the supplies, ate the dried meat, drank bottled water, and dressed. The light cotton trousers and shirt seemed like some kind of uniform, navy blue, with a tag across a front breast pocket with thick block letters: R. Candhiga. There were boots, too, but she carried them with the rest of the supplies in the pack, and let the shirt hang open. Although the sunlight was not bright to her eyes, she was awash in a constant sweat. As she walked, she spoke the name to herself again and again, Candhiga, Candhiga; at least now she knew the woman's name, even if it spurred no recognition.

The birds followed her as she walked, never let her get more than a few dozen meters from them, and she spent the time deep in thought. She was not shipwrecked, not dead. She did not know how, but she was clearly on another world but what exactly that meant was beyond her. On the other side of the island a continuing arc of islets formed the flailed arm of an archipelago. She felt entrapped, stifled in the thick air, closed in by the syrupy ocean.

She reviewed again and again all the birds had said to her since she woke. Nothing added up. Yet the sum of it oppressed her. Why didn't she remember anything? It almost seemed as if she were responsible for her own amnesia, had shed herself like old skin. Now, nothing appeared before her scrutiny but rising apprehension. Could the birds really make her remember? Is that what she wanted? What if she learned . . . what? What did she fear? It was like a child's panic in the dark. What was not known terrified her most. It was the possibility that you would *see* what was hidden from you, that it would become concrete and real. And she became more convinced the more she thought about it that she was responsible somehow for that woman—and maybe others.

Not a memory, but a bruise where a memory had once been, tender now to her touch. And yet, by the time she found herself standing before Candhiga again, she realized that in spite of the scab of vague guilt that had grown over her dread this desiccated corpse was the only familiar, comforting thing in her world.

The birds settled around her again, like shards of night. She suddenly and desperately needed to know what they could tell her. But not about Candhiga. The dead woman was the spike in the center of everything hidden, at once the most important and the least speakable question.

What do you mean by the journey over?

The journey is a theoretical transition between folds of space and time.

I don't understand.

You can't move fast enough to travel among worlds. The journey is your company's method to jump from one world to another. A mathematical model is created and you are sent to a hypothetical destination. If the destination turns out to be real, then you appear there. Or your appearance makes the destination real. Your own team hasn't agreed on that yet.

So that's what I've done. I've gone to another world.

That's not really agreed on either. You could be on a planet in your own galaxy and we just haven't located it yet. Or you could be in another universe. It depends on which string model you use.

We can show you everything if you merge with one of us. The birds shook their wings.

How can I trust you?

We remember for you.

Somehow that did not persuade her.

Let us take you to the base.

The base of what?

The Hummin Project. In the forest. The machinery arrived before you. We bring things to the base as they appear. The company can't seem to aim more accurately than four kilometers or so. One of the birds hopped closer. We won't hurt you. You're too important. You're the first and the last. If you don't succeed, the project will be scrapped. The company can't afford that.

She sank to her knees in the sand, then sat on her heels. She did not know what to do. It was too much to be alone, too much without even the blanket of memory to secure her. What do I have to do? She said, raising her face to them.

Just relax, they said, and a set of wings wrapped around her. From the underside of their rubbery black surface she felt cilia-like connections around her head, probing. She was immediately dizzy and would have fallen if not for the bird's grasp.

Fragmented memory assails her. Images materialize and shift, disappearing into each other before they quite focus. Her senses kaleidoscope uncontrollably; she smells music, tastes a summer sun on her face, hears the sweetness of roses, strawberries. Snarls of perception adhere, patches of realized memory resonate a moment, then vanish. She watches five men and women appear naked on a metallic dais. They share the same blank expression that slowly disintegrates into terror. She knows there should be one more, and at least one of the men is deformed; one side of his body has melted like heated plastic and then hardened again. She tells herself they knew the risks before they made the journey over. They knew they might not survive. She suppresses a defiant, self-righteous glee as she sees how her husband has been punished, standing there in the middle of the group, eyes darting around the control room like a lost child. Then the memory disintegrates on her. She sees only swirling shadows. She grasps phantoms until they knot into clarity again.

She is talking with a technician, pleading with him. He stands there shaking his head as she talks; he's not even listening anymore. He throws up his hands against her, tells her she's trying his patience. You already know this, he says, you know we can't separate and splice memory for your convenience. We can't leave something out just because it bothers you. Your mind is too valuable.

Every component of a complex system is equally important to the whole. Your mind is a house of cards. We'll need you to function properly, as yourself, if we're going to succeed. We're risking enough as it is and you know it. They've done their best to revise the governing equations, but we still don't even know if you'll make it across in one piece. You saw the first team. We're not leaving any memories out, that's the final word.

Anger floods her like liquid nitrogen. But she can't explain to him how important her need is. Her need to forget. She sees the look on her husband's face again; it haunts her now. She can't face his dull emptiness. So blank, so scared, like all the survivors of the journey team, their minds stripped, bare as husked corn. She remembers her impulse to gloat. It's your fault, she tells herself. Her only hope is that everything goes wrong when she makes the journey, the project closes, leaves her stranded with only half her mind. Forgotten and forgetting. The company will have to recoup its losses through somebody else. She doesn't want to know herself anymore.

Bile, acid, terror. She burst from the bird's embrace thrashing elbows and knees, head spinning, and rolled through the flutter of black wings. She landed face down, mouth full of sand, and heard the birds screech as they beat the hot air over her, rising toward the heavy sun. Spitting, she raised her head. Candhiga's corpse lay there a meter away. Her eyes filled with tears and she sobbed.

Stay away from me, she said, and sat up, trembling.

Please, called the birds, circling. Please, if not for yourself, then for the mission.

She looked up. *What* mission, she screamed. Why is the mission so important?

We can help you remember why.

Just tell me.

The mission is for the growth of mankind. The expansion of the human race. For the intrinsic need to explore, to roll back the edges of the known. For patents to the journey over. For rights to new lands, new resources, new assets. And the company, your company, is at the forefront of the race for new worlds. The company is your family. You owe your life to the company. If you fail here they will close the Hummin project; no one will ever make the journey over again.

That's fine with me, she said.

A bird landed across from the corpse. You don't mean that.

Oh no?

Candhiga . . . .

She looked at the body again. What about her? What about Candhiga? Tell me about *her.*

The other birds settled. Candhiga is the head of the Hummin Project.

Was, she said.

And also the head of the Journey Project before it.

All right, tell me about that.

Mechanical devices were projected first, unmanned probes. They returned undamaged, with pictures and data from a world that appeared moderately safe and habitable, although there were hints of a hostile environment, such as trees with odd defensive scales. After many experiments and probes you eventually sent an experimental crew, six people, to make the journey over, with a pre-timed retrograde pulse to bring them back within fifteen minutes. Previous experiences with animal flesh fusing into protective suits and mechanical devices made you worried about contamination of disparate objects, so everyone and everything, supplies, clothes, everything, was sent across separately. And it worked, at least partially. All but one team member came back alive. But they had been changed, too. The journey had sloughed off their memories, given them some kind of irreparable amnesia. You don't know how or why it happened, just that it's an apparent side effect of the journey over.

Well one thing is clear to me, she said. I came across because I wanted to escape something. Maybe it was the company. Maybe it was my own past. But you aren't touching me again.

She rose and padded through sand toward the forest.

The birds flew over her, dipping by her shoulders, landing in front of her, lifting back into the air. Where are you going? they cried. What are you doing? She ignored them.

In the shade of the trees the ground was carpeted with a reddish growth—a moss, she supposed—with coiling tentacles that quivered and seemed to sense her presence. Afraid to step on them, she sat on a damp rock and finally put on the boots from Candhiga's pack. Then she picked her way through, avoiding the longer worms that undulated all the way to her lower thighs. She crushed coils under her boots and left footprints of squashed jelly with the writhing, broken worms around the edges, squirting bloody saliva.

She shuddered and rested a hand on the trunk of a squat tree, then cursed. The razor bark had sliced her palm. Wiping blood on her shirt, she looked around. The forest was so thick she could see only about twenty meters in. It was damp and hot, a sinister womb. She wanted to turn back to the sea. But she needed materials to build a shelter. She didn't want to sleep the night without something shutting out the birds. She looked down at the strange moss and almost despaired at pulling out any fallen branches; everything was covered by the soft coiling stuff.

The forest smelled like curry and cinnamon mixed with rot. Let's go, she told herself, no one is going to do it for you. She bent down and began pulling up rocks and broken branches. She wasn't sure if she imagined it, but the moss seemed to smell her bleeding hand; the tentacles moved like sentient flatworms on her skin whenever she stopped moving. By the time she had collected enough materials and dragged them just beyond the trees, her hands and forearms were cut in more than a dozen places and the sun had pushed shadows down across the ground with its colossal weight, then begun to slide down behind the forest, smearing the edge of the sky.

She worked as the sky thickened crimson to black, and by the time she was done, her shelter looked more like an oversized coffin than anything else. She had stacked stone for walls and used the branches to make a thick roof studded everywhere with razorblade scales. She turned on the flashlight from the supplies pack, crawled inside, and blocked the doorway with more rocks. She could sit up inside her enclosure and with the flashlight illuminating the jelly stained rocks with an amber bull's-eye she burrowed in the pack until she found a first aid kit. She cleaned her arms with gauze and alcohol then rubbed antibacterial cream into the cuts. The birds swooped around the enclosure, calling to her.

Come out, they said. We will complete you. We won't hurt you.

She heard them settle, one by one, on the sharp roof over her head. She felt as if she would suffocate.

Come out, they said. Or let us in. Or we will fail.

Then fail, she said. She used the pack as a pillow and lay back. For a long time there was silence. But every once in a while she heard the birds shift their weight, perched overhead in the dark, waiting. Finally she turned off the flashlight and fell to sleep with her shoes on.

Every turn of his wrist, every twitch of soft brow, cries out how superior he thinks he is. It doesn't matter that she is his boss, that he must do everything she commands. In fact, that makes him seem to feel even more superior, as if the need to follow her orders gives him a higher moral authority. He turns his back on her, a new scorn apparent in his posture. And at that moment she wants to kill him, more than anything, more than reconciliation, more than happiness, more than the desire that he turn to her and touch her cheek and murmur soft words and kiss her forehead like a tender, patient, father. But it's almost as if he already has been killed, because her husband, the man she has loved and shared this company flat with for the last three years, the man who rubbed her shoulders tenderly when the project worried her too much, who smiled at her with that crease along his cheek, whose eyes glittered with the deepest knowledge of her, that man is dead, and she mourns him, she misses him more than she has ever missed anything. She is alone, now, cut off from everyone. And he doesn't have the decency to evaporate. His body continues to occupy their home, eat their food, even screw her from time to time, as if still alive, a ghost reminding her of her loneliness. Everyone follows your orders, he says; it kills you that you can't make me feel what you want me to feel, doesn't it? You can't control me anymore.

She is shaking. She remembers walking in on them: he is taking her from behind, savagely, sweat running off his back, their eyes locked in the mirror behind the bed. It's the frank intimacy of that gaze that hurts the most. Now, confronting him, she can't decide what she feels. She only knows that she is shaking. She strikes her own chest, oblivious to the pain. If not for me, why couldn't you maintain appearances for the company, the project? We're supposed to be a team. We're supposed to be professionals. How is this going to look?

He turns to her. I suppose it's going to look like a failed marriage.

Something like grief expands in her. Or humiliation. Or rage.

She was my friend, Jake, my friend.

You don't have friends. That would entail a relationship beyond the bonds of domination and control.

Her throat burns and feels like she's tried to swallow a rock. She stares at him long enough to start him fidgeting, then shakes her head. I'll see to it you are on the first journey team. You, and her too. I don't want you around anymore. And if it works, if the equations are right and you bounce back to this world, you'll both be with the first group of settlers, too.

She knows him enough to recognize the fear shift briefly in his eyes. But he manages a smile. He looks so much like the man who once loved her. The smile lingers in her memory, haunts her, oppresses her. That brave smile.

At first all she saw was the smile, fading into nothing, into the shadows around her. Some of those shadows had weight, substance. They formed into wings around her head, embracing her. Screaming, she shook them off, her arms swinging wildly. The bird made a whimpering noise, the tips of its wings flittered against her face as it lurched back against the wall.

She sprang up and sliced her forehead against the roof. She dropped to her side, clutching her bleeding temple, and squirmed around to face the bird. It was sliding down into the sand where it had dug its way under the wall. Dim morning light filtered from the hole as it disappeared. She kicked out the stones of her doorway and crawled outside into the blossoming red sky and the surging shore. One of the birds spun away from her in the air as she rounded the enclosure. The other one emerged from the hole, shaking sand from its wings.

She jumped at it, kicking viciously. The bird fell beneath her feet. She jumped again, stomping on its chest. It whirred as the bird above her screamed. She brought a foot up a third time, and when her heel connected, the chest tore open.

Stay away from me, she yelled into the sky, stepping back from the ruined bird. It lay mashed into the sand, one wing trembling. Where her heel had ripped its body open, circuit boards and wires twisted in disarray. What are you? She said. She looked into the sky again. She squinted against the flow of blood into her left eye. What in Hell are you? But the other bird had fled into the forest.

She swatted angrily at the blood on her face and walked toward the water. Wave edges glittered vermillion in the distance. They're machines, she murmured. Designed to carry memory across the gap in space-time, and then collect and reassemble her like another piece of machinery. The team before her had jumped across the dimensions and returned without memory, their minds stripped. They had been the bare hands of the company, reaching into the darkness. But sometimes fingers got broken. She pictured them again, the ones that made it back, her husband, shivering naked on the control room dais. Some of them horribly disfigured, one of them missing altogether. Their lives were ruined. The company was going to close the project. Candhiga must have come up with this new plan, to send mechanical downloads across so that body and mind could reconnect on the other side. And even with the mathematicians revising their guiding equations there was still inaccuracy in the journey, some distance a person would have to be prepared to traverse to become re-united with the reprogrammable pieces. So Candhiga made the downloads mobile and problem-solving.

But why was *she* sent? Did she volunteer out of a sense of guilt? After all, she'd wanted to hurt her husband. Maybe she even spoke to Candhiga to get him on the journey team. It was Candhiga, though, who was ultimately responsible for the team and her husband's brain damage. Not her. Candhiga sent them to their ruin. And then sent her with the birds to save the project.

She glanced at the corpse. Maybe Candhiga had gotten what she deserved. She unlaced her boots, kicked them off and stepped into the surf. Crouching down she splashed oily water on her face and cleaned away the blood. It was a mistake; the cuts on her head stung and the water felt uncomfortably slick on her skin. She straightened and walked back up on the drier sand. Her conclusions still did not satisfy her. Why did the thought of retrieving her memories still turn her heart cold? What was she hiding from? And what was Candhiga's corpse doing here in the first place? She picked up her boots and returned to the body.

Maybe if I look, really look, I can make myself recognize her face. Maybe then I'll understand. Maybe I can find some memory without the birds. She knelt there and considered the empty, gray face, dead, like her memory. Once again the feeling of responsibility overwhelmed her. But there were no answers in those clouded dried out eyes, only questions, only recriminations. And another thought occurred to her. Maybe she was wrong. Maybe she'd been fooling herself. Maybe this wasn't Candhiga at all.

Maybe the corpse was from the first journey team.

It was as if she'd been punched in the solar plexus. She gasped, and filled with terror all over again. And the two birds were back, circling above her.

It's me, she said. I'm Candhiga. And this is my husband's lover.

The bird landed in the sand.

You are the first, it said.

I sent my husband and this woman, knowing I might be sending them to their death—wanting that to be so. For her, it *was*.

You are the company's last hope for this project. All the sacrifices before you are meaningless if you fail.

Sacrifices, she said. This woman, whose name she couldn't remember, was dead because of her as surely as if she'd murdered her with her own hands. And her husband; she didn't want to think about that blank face again. The entire sum of their lives together, shucked off him in the darkness between worlds. Maybe she could bear the idea of her guilt now, with only these slim shards of broken memory left. But she knew she couldn't stand the full knowledge of the birds, the inexorable truth recorded there, the full memory of her motives, her bitter rage. She did not want to face that. There was a tender spot inside her, a bruise where the memory of her broken heart once lived. She had escaped the deep knowledge of her blackest soul. She didn't want it back.

Merge with me, said the bird. And make things right. You need all your memory to run the base, to bring over the rest of the new team.

You could guide me like this, the way we are now, she said.

No, said the bird. I don't have the ability to guide you as yourself. Every component of a complex system is equally important to the whole. You are a house of cards. To be successful you must understand everything and act upon your own instincts. Without all the pieces you will crumble, and fail.

Candhiga closed her eyes. The company cared obviously little for any individual. What did she care if its project failed? She had escaped the horror of her deepest thoughts. She could make *new* memories, give herself the chance to start over in her own head. This tragedy could be a vague marker, easily left behind. She wouldn't have to worry herself about what had happened. Oh, once in a while she would see his uncomprehending face in a dream, remember the vision of his infidelities. But she could bury this nameless corpse and it would be over forever. What did she owe them, anyway? Who had betrayed whom?

She opened her eyes again to the rising monster sun. Indeed, what did she owe them? The loss of her husband—and the woman's death—were meaningless, except as the result of her impulse for revenge. Meaningless. They were empty sacrifices if the project failed. All they had worked for would be lost. Candhiga wondered if she could live with that. But to take back the pain, the certain wisdom of her own weakness and failure? She *knew* she couldn't bear that.

Had she come here to forget, or had she come to make things right?

She shook her head, tears stinging her eyes. Yes, she told herself, deep down, she had come here to forget. Designed the birds to fail. She was a coward. She clenched her teeth.

Slowly she extended her hands to the bird. Closing her eyes again, she listened as it shuffled toward her.

The woman's name had been Carol. Jake had been attracted to her delicate smile; a smile that was almost always followed by laughter. And the way she listened to him so intently, as if what he had to say really mattered—Candhiga had forgotten how to listen like that. And how she smelled like tulips.

Candhiga buried her beside the forest, and then stood quietly over the grave. She didn't know what to say.

The three men appeared on the beach on a windy morning, clouds raking across the sun like bloody claws. Candhiga watched from the forest's edge as they sat up, trembling, looking at each other with a mixture of confusion and awe. Their birds had arrived the day before, six in all, a back up copy for each man, and they circled Candhiga silently, waiting for her command. She shifted the pack on her shoulders and whistled to them, then gestured with her hand. The birds swooped toward the men and she followed.

One man stood as the birds landed around them, raising an arm defensively.

"It's all right," Candhiga called. "They aren't here to harm you." She stepped past the birds and grasped the standing man's hand.

"Where am I?" he said. "What's . . . happened?"

She smiled at him and the others. "You've been very brave," she said. "Now you need to trust me just a little longer." She motioned once again to the birds. "You are heroes, today. You've made the journey over." Then the birds embraced them with memory.

Later, as she led the team through the forest to their base, one of the men grasped her elbow.

"Candhiga," he said. "You called us heroes."

"You are," she said, and stopped.

He blinked. "We're nothing compared to you. You crossed alone, when no one had succeeded before. You sacrificed yourself for the company. You turned a dead end venture into the first true discovery of another world. I stand in awe of you. We all do. We're honored to be here with you, on Candhiga's World." The other men were nodding.

Candhiga smiled sadly and didn't tell them the truth. She knew who she was. She knew what she had to pay for.

"I did it in memory of the others who weren't as lucky as I was," she said. The men returned her smile. She led them along the path she'd cut in the wormy moss.

"Be careful," she said as they passed through the shadows. "The trees are sharp."

Bad People
by Gene Stewart

"But surely you can see how the world has darkened since 9/11. Surely you can see the bad people have taken over."

Her words haunted him.

She would not marry him because she knew they were doomed. Worse, she aborted the child they had made in her belly to protect it from the empty future she saw so clearly.

She walked away from him to find, as she had said, a place to hide until the bombs come, and Malcolm knew now she had been right all along, in everything.

He stood gazing into the crater.

The bomb had obliterated the house, lawn, and two thirds of an oak tree that had stood for 200 years. The remaining third of the tree looked like a surreal artist's parody. Bright white inside, strips of bark curled at the edges, and branches spilling to the ground as if caught mid bow, the remnant mocked the memory.

Worse, it gave Malcolm a mental image to model his thoughts of Jenny on. Had she been two-thirds blown apart? Would he find a one-third husk of her in the rubble, her skin hanging in curling strips and her limbs frozen in a scorched bow?

He skidded and slid into the crater, leaning back to brace himself with one hand. At the bottom, amidst the debris, he spotted a hand. Squatting, he looked more closely at it. It was a human hand, neatly cut off at the wrist. It looked like a woman's hand, too, but there was no way to tell if it was Jenny's. He did not feel a tingle of recognition. It did not wear her rings.

Had other women been living in the house with her?

Standing, Malcolm made his cautious way around the debris. He did not see any further sign of death. Several hot spots smoldered and smoked, and he avoided those, even as, the gods help him, he savored their warmth on the chilly Autumnal day.

"You about done, professor?" a voice called from the rim.

Malcolm looked up and squinted to see Selliers, a grad student who had adopted him as a kind of father figure after the bombs had blotted the boy's relatives. Malcolm nodded and raised a hand.

"I ask because there's a storm coming."

"Okay, I'll come up now." Snatching the rope Selliers tossed down, Malcolm climbed back to ground level. Once at the top, he brushed off his clothes, then glanced back down.

"Did you find her, sir?" Selliers asked.

"No sign," Malcolm said.

Selliers gestured westward, where a huge thunderhead glowed ominously green and purple in the gritty gray sky. "We better find some cover."

"Okay." John Elliot Malcolm, erstwhile professor of English literature at a midwest community college, bachelor, with relatives in the midlands of England, if any survived, followed his grad student, as he affectionately and jokingly called Selliers, to the horse-drawn cart they had commandeered in Omaha's Old Market district. Since many of the bombs were nukes, cars did not work. EMP had also knocked out communications, so Malcolm and Selliers had heard no news since September eleventh.

The horses nickered and flattened their ears. They shifted nervously. "They sense the storm," Selliers said, already in the cart and leaning to give Malcolm a hand up.

Malcolm winced inside at Selliers's touch. While the lad had proven a great comfort on a few of the darker, colder nights, the growing tenderness and solicitation with which Selliers treated him made Malcolm feel old suddenly, frail. He might have been willing to take comfort where it was offered, but damned if he was ready to concede being a helpless or even feeble old man.

To cover his annoyance, Malcolm gestured forward, then coughed as he took his seat. This drew only another soft pat on his shoulder and a wide-eyed inquiry as to his health.

Both knew illness could mean death, in a desolate world without medicine, doctors, or hope.

"You know, professor, if you didn't find her, maybe it means she wasn't there. When, well."

Malcolm looked at Selliers, who kept his gaze on the horses as he flicked the reins to hurry them along.

"Maybe," Malcolm said. The cart had a leather covering, a kind of fold-up convertible roof, stretched over a metal frame on hinges and joints. He reached back and pulled this up over them, as the first drops of rain splashed.

Around them the flat landscape west of Omaha darkened. They drove along the highway now, most of it left uncracked, unheaved, or unmelted. Now and then they had to skirt around craters or rubble. Once they came upon a multi-vehicle pileup, burned-out shells and charred skeletons visible in an odd yellow fog they had been driving through, and Selliers had wanted to get out and scavenge for anything useful that might remain.

Malcolm had stopped the boy with one word: Rads.

"You think this was nuked?"

"Can we take the chance?"

They had ridden on, the pair of horses patiently clopping into the steady breeze, which did not seem to move the yellow fog around them at all.

Next morning the fog had gone and it was flat nothing as far as the eye could see.

They came upon farm houses set a few hundred meters to either side of the road. Most were burned out or cratered.

The bombs had been thorough, seeking out any and every obvious human enclave, settlement, village, town, or city. They had rained down from and zoomed across the sky like a new plague.

Malcolm thought about religion the first few nights. How it had both prompted all the destruction, and offered not a blink of comfort.

"Think the space aliens will come down now?"

"Now that we're gone?"

Selliers ducked his head and smiled. "Was just thinking."

There was not much else to do but scrounge for water, food, and shelter. And those activities became automatic, allowing thought at the same time.

What creeped Malcolm out was the utter lack of others. How could he and Selliers be the only two left? It seemed impossible to him. They had decided to leave Omaha because of the lack of people. While the city provided much to scrounge, it grew steadily eerier without people. Without even hints of people.

Even stranger was the lack of bodies. Now and then he or Selliers had found a few skeletons. Mostly, though, they found no sign that humanoid primates had existed.

Like so much else, this lack mocked expectations.

Malcolm, for instance, had been expecting the shaking, weakness, and diarrhea to start any time now. He had been bracing himself to notice skin sores, or blisters in his mouth, or the taste of copper.

No radiation poisoning developed in them, though. He and Selliers remained healthy and normal. It puzzled Malcolm.

"Maybe Hell's full," Selliers said one day as they filled their water jugs from a fallen water tower. "Maybe we're the ones who didn't fit."

Malcolm had chuckled, for the boy's benefit, but he had felt a chill, too. It was a thought he did not want to pursue.

Avoiding survivor guilt was not easy, though. Why them? What had they done to deserve such isolation from the pack?

"I keep expecting zombies to pop up," Selliers said another time, as they picked perfectly good apples from an orchard that stood untouched outside Nebraska City.

"Or mutated ants the size of a lorry," Malcolm said, recalling those 1950s movies.

Selliers narrowed his eyes and smiled. "Can I get a lift in your lorry?" he asked, bringing up an old conversation they'd had about how British idiom differed from American.

When he slipped like that, reverting to British speech patterns, Malcolm knew he had probably been feeling nostalgic. If this tremendous, wide open country had suffered so terribly from the bombs, how much worse had Britain fared?

No way ever to find out, he thought. Not now.

Not unless radios started working again.

"Barn," Selliers said, pointing.

Through the rain and gloom, Malcolm made out a large dark shape and took the boy's word for it. Younger eyes worked better, and his professorial glasses were steaming.

They left the highway for a dirt track that led in a meander through plowed, unplanted fields. Mud sloshed. Rain pelted the leather roof like sticks on a drum, making talk difficult. Water soaking through it now to drip, too. Malcolm thought: How miserable we are.

The irony of that brought a smile. How petty human suffering was. How selfish and small a thing human discomfort could be, even in the face of devastation. Yes, the world is gone but I hate cold water dripping down the back of my neck.

He wondered if Mozart's feet had hurt, or Bach's fat belly had rumbled, as they had composed their magnificent music. Of course they had. Rising above such tyranny of the body was their whole point.

As they reached the barn Malcolm noticed how it leaned to one side and wondered if a gust of strong wind would blow it down while they crouched in it.

The horses, as if everything were fairly normal, entered the marginally warmer darkness of the barn and at once found a manger full of sweet hay.

There was fresh lain straw in the stalls, too, Malcolm noticed. Pointing this out, he said, "Use handfuls of it to wipe down the horses so they don't catch cold."

The boy sprang down with youth's enviable energy and did as bidden. The horses, let out of their harnesses, seemed to relax and whickered companionably as they ate. They accepted the boy's ministrations like royals soaking up respect earned mostly by their ancestors.

"Hey professor, look."

Malcolm finished getting out of the cart, then glanced over his shoulder. Selliers was holding up a lantern and said, "There's fuel." He sloshed it, then looked more closely at it. "The mantels are intact, too."

"Light it up."

They had some scrounged candles but a lantern would be welcome.

After Selliers pumped and lit the lantern, they inventoried the barn. They found a couple cans of white gas, for the lantern, and stashed those in the cart. There was a work bench, so they took some tools.

"You know," Selliers said, "I didn't see a farm house when we drove up. Just the barn."

"There's probably a crater nearby, then."

Both nodded, and dropped the subject. The barn and its many small items was better than any hole full of wet ashes.

Malcolm pulled open a drawer under the work bench and found a couple of pens and maybe a third of a sheaf of paper. For a moment he stared down as if he had found pornography featuring his parents.

"What's wrong?" Selliers asked, his hand at once between Malcolm's shoulder blades to offer comfort, human contact.

Malcolm shrugged away from the touch and lifted the entire drawer out. He carried it to the cart and climbed up, then sat with the drawer on his lap.

He had been aching to write for days, weeks. He had wanted the civilized feel of sitting at a table with a pen in his hand marking down words in ink.

"You going to write something, prof?"

He nodded and said, "Why don't you scrummage up some food for us, if there are any cans left."

"No problem. Beans and toast?"

Malcolm nodded, not even noticing Selliers had chosen an old British favorite from the Blitz, when meat had been so scarce.

He lifted a pen, thinking, Maybe it doesn't even work.

It did, and he wrote his name, then began writing his address under that, in the upper right corner of a page.

Address? he thought. He shook his head, feeling like a doddering old man, and scratched it out, aware as he did so of wasting precious ink.

He paused, then, before he could stop himself, asked, "What date is it?"

Selliers looked up, his Victorinox Swiss Army Knife poised from opening a can. "Uh, wow. I don't know, professor. Must be, what, middle of September at least, maybe October by now? How long we been on the road?"

"Doesn't matter. Never mind."

Selliers gave him a concerned look, then went back to preparing the meal by lighting a can of Sterno and getting out the cast iron skillet they used for most cooking.

Sighing, Malcom thought about what he had wanted to write all those days. The story of the end, he thought. How it all blew up and how everyone went away. His search for something to hold onto, even if it was only a lonely community college student who would never graduate. His visit to the last known place Jenny had called home, and his slide into its crater.

The severed hand.

He hung his head, closed his eyes, then opened them and, with a single tear tracing a path unnoticed through the dust on his face, Malcolm began writing.

He was not happy to be interrupted for dinner, and ate abstractedly, eager to get back to writing.

After clean up, when Selliers offered a shy kiss, Malcolm gently eased him away and continued his writing, squinting when the lantern's glow went low, and waiting impatiently when he or Selliers pumped it back up to full glare again.

Sensing not to ask, Selliers, whose curiosity was palpable, restrained himself until the next morning at breakfast. "Wish we had some eggs," he said, offering half a can of sliced pears and some bread scorched on Sterno flame, called toast without any apparent irony. "Bacon. Coffee, oh god. I'd kill for some fresh brewed espresso."

The days of Starbuck's hegemony were gone, Malcolm joked.

And Selliers couldn't contain it any longer. "What were you writing, professor? You were still at it when I nodded off."

Malcolm hesitated. Ordinarily, he did not show writing until it was finished, and disliked discussing it, for fear of souring himself on it with the sound of his own voice.

That morning belonged no longer to the ordinary, though, and he knew it. "I was intending to write down what had happened. The bombs, the lack of people. Everything we've found, and haven't found."

"But?"

He smiled and hung his head. "It seems a children's story is flowing from me, at the moment."

"A story for little kids?"

Malcolm nodded. "It's called 'The Bad People.'"

"But what for? There aren't any kids anymore."

Malcolm shrugged. "In case there are. Somewhere."

"A kid's story . . . " Selliers seemed to be trying hard to fathom this strange confession.

"I thought it might be of more use than a history."

Selliers looked at Malcolm and smiled. "Let's hope, huh?"

"Yes. Let's."

It was no longer raining. They finished breakfast, cleaned up, packed, and hitched the horses for another day's walk.

Living Amongst the Lizards
by Lawrence R. Dagstine

An unordinary, middle-aged man. The strange one, the different one, goes forth into his caverns. He walks along his streambed and sees his aquatic life in the shallow pools. He sees outside its walls the Tartabacks eating the mild grasses. He looks up and sees the high protective rock walls of his cave marching around him, the hole which provides him with a glimpse of the night sky when sheltered. "My mind now lives too long in the light of the three moons of night," he mutters in contemplation. "Let it be in the rays of the two suns by day."

Nothing changes though.

Time to move forward.

An unordinary, middle-aged man goes forth into the moonlight out on the open plain. In that vast wideness, limitless and alive, breathable and evenly temperate, he inhales the fresh air and finds the perfect spot, then bends his knees and sits cross-legged in the thick growth. He knows that he is part of a great quietude that lives and breathes about him; in the silence he hears wind whispering among the grasses. The ancient magic of an animal species' beginnings is there, and long before his arrival.

According to him, winds whispering through grasses are the voices of faraway spirits to a mind that knows such spirits exist. On this planet, the unseen spirit of a life form can bridge long miles—especially for one who is stranded there—and be with a man who has faith in the divine powers of such friendship: a rushing of winds, a leaping of lightning, a glimpse of an outlandish creature or undocumented animal in a flash between darknesses. Such are signs to a man on the brink of losing his sanity, some times, by merging himself into the natural forces that currently surround him. Those are the things that led his ship to this forested world. Those are the things that led him to live amongst this very spot.

1) Arrival:

Dry methane rainfall. The chill drops brought consciousness back to Jared's tortured flesh. Only a lizard's flesh, like tough leather, can endure this storm naturally. He stirred and pain swept through him and he was unconscious again. The rain eventually stopped, and two blazing orbs ascended over the horizon. Dawn spread over the plateau and crept into the cavern, filtering phosphorescent light. Slowly awareness crept through him. He lay sprawled on his back on a thick carpet of old needles under a pine-like tree. His black jumpsuit was ripped and clotted blood clung to his body in many places. His left leg was doubled under him. It was broken a little above the ankle. Pain swelled in his chest with each breath. He wondered how long it had been since the crash: two-three days? Five-six at most?

He stared upwards at the needled branches for a long time. The suns were just about overhead when he moved. An agony streaked through his whole body but life was a kind of movement and he moved, and it hurt. He pushed up a little and looked around. He did not know that he was Jared—not at first—some geographical society's astronaut who had come to this animal-festered wilderness of a world for the purposes of habitat and domain study and future colonization. He was out of memory, a man starving, a simple elemental creature like everything else there, searching for the means of survival.

His eyes found the pieces of the escape pod where it had fallen. He dragged himself to it on his belly and tried to eat the freeze-dried rations that were tucked away inside, but he could not swallow. He eventually sat up, regained some step and momentum. Staring downwards, he saw a streambed leading into the cavern a short distance away. He rolled onto his belly once more, the bag of rations in his teeth, and crawled wormlike to the very edge of the water. Head down, he gulped at the water, unsure at first. It was the same as Earth water. At least the filtration for it here was. Also, he could swallow liquid. Slowly he lifted his head and the water trickled down his throat, and the dry muscles in his mouth soaked in the moisture. He swallowed a little bit more. His jawbone ached, but the crude meat in the bag, pounded into a fine powder, needed very little chewing. He crammed it into his mouth and convulsive constrictions of his throat forced it down. He reached for more and in reaching, a blackness dropped on him.

Once again unconsciousness took over.

When he awoke, there was water in his stomach. There was a little food. Finally the chemistry of life in this new place worked in him . . . .

Daylight dwindled into darkness. The moons—there were three of them, satellites of all shapes, sizes, and colors; that much he remembered—

rose silently out of the mountain ranges and tree-covered hillsides. Their pale lights slid down the canyon walls in succession and moved slowly across the cavern floor. The soft blue radiance touched the limp figure outstretched by the stream. The figure heard strange insects *cricking* in some underbrush right outside the cavern's walls. The figure stirred and its eyes opened. Unconsciousness had passed into sleeping and the sleeping into normal dreaming at last into awakening. A moment later, the gray eyes looked up at the traveling moons. He knew who he was now. He was Jared Pouter, a geographer who had crash-landed some weeks before, and he was lying on the ground of a cave on some strange other world. It hummed with mammalian, reptilian, and amphibious life forms never before documented in human historical annals. Some of these animals were descended from other breeds of normal Earth creatures, upon first glance, at least, but at the same time a few of them had alien-like qualities, humanlike features, and even some resemblances to the cretaceous and protozoa eras. Another small memory resurfaced: he had minored in alien zoology at the university back home. Those were the days of old though, a time when a young man wanted to learn something that, he felt, could be taken with him to the stars.

But he was still hurt in many places, and his leg still broken. He crawled forward; to move even the slightest was to summon the pain. But at least he was human again and he could fight the pain. He drank from the streambed in small swallows, and ate the rations but not much, because the pouch was small and already almost empty. He dragged along the ground to a big stone on the bank and pulled himself up against it on his good leg. He looked around. Everywhere, on all sides, he saw sheer rock wall rising. The three moons swung symmetrically overhead and now their pale lights gleamed dully on nickel near the broken-branched tree. So there are nickel compositions here, he thought interestedly. He dragged himself there and reached and held out his cutting laser. To survive in this place, he needed pieces of nickel and wood to build a sturdy fire, a fire that would light—stay lit in such an environment. He hunted further and further and found one of the fire sticks he would need, a pointed one of hard greasewood. That was appropriate, he felt, as he could not find any others suitable. He crawled to gather small branches, pushing them ahead of him on the ground into a pile; the nickel deposits would act as a rocky base. His muscles ached as he moved, the pain in his leg mounting with torment. He tried fighting it as best he could, while continuing to gather wood. He fought it and fought it and was defeated at one point until he was finally still.

2) Hunger:

When daylight came again Jared knelt by his pile of wood, his weight on his right leg rather than his left. He saw strange fish at the edge of the water, which was a good sign, seeing that his rations were gone. He was still unsure though if the aquatic life there was edible. He revolved his greasewood stick rapidly between the palms of his hands and the point spun in the hole in a flattened piece of softer cottonwood and spacesuit materials he had shaped together with the cutting laser. Tiny wisps of smoke came from the powdered needles encircling the hole. He leaned low to blow gently on the powdery residue, and it gradually smoldered into a glowing red. He nursed the embers into a small fire, churning it, feeding it from his pile of gathered wood. The column of smoke rose straight upwards and far beyond the canyon, a slender plumed signal rising into the sky. All morning, and into the afternoon, he waited but no one came. Perhaps he really was alone on this world. The only human . . . In some respects, an unordinary, middle-aged man.

"I could live here," he said, as if he were talking to someone else. "The air and water is consumable, the creatures I've seen outside these cavern walls bear meat. It's peaceful and without much ado about science and society, technology and traffic. Yes, I *could* live here . . . " He thought about the things that would help him achieve that new life: the many survival courses he took before becoming an astronaut, his university schooling, where he had picked up all that valuable zoological-geographical experience. Such knowledge was beneficial, he felt; now present to contribute to his upkeep.

In the soft radiance of the waning moons, Jared worked on his swelling leg. He took hold of the distorted flesh. The pain was so intense that he knew he must have everything ready before he did more. He used what he could find left of the escape pod's first aid kit and found and trimmed six short pieces of branch from what remained of his small pile of wood. He cut away what was left of his gauze on his leg and took part of the worn cotton and sliced it into thin strips. He added some leather from his spacesuit, put small strips of it into his mouth and clamped his teeth into it. He took hold of his left leg with his hands, one hand below the break in the bone and the other above it. It was a clean break but the ends of the bone were pushed past each other. He slowly wrenched apart with both hands and ground his teeth into the leather piece in his mouth. He heard the bone ends grind on each other and his mind screamed wordless sounds at the pain, the bone ends having been finally put together and the leg straight from ankle to knee. Quickly, before the darkness should take him, he bound the six branches along the leg with the strips of leather, pulled, and tightened the knots. The pain was overwhelming and he fell back and was still. The next morning he fed his new fire and hoped. He held a stout stick in his hands and pulled himself up and about. He used one of the longer, weaker branches from the night before to fish. He laid all his fishing utensils side by side and his bizarre catches in a small heap by the streambed. He could do no more because the swelling in his leg was growing and the acute pain was an agony that crowded his mind. His flesh festered beneath the skin as it swelled outward with evil fluids. Fever burned in his blood, and his extremities held an excruciating stiffness. But he knew it was not gangrene. The skin was purple, not black.

He forgot to feed the fire and it went out. He fell on the ground, clutched at the grass and rocks, drifted in and out of awareness. Dark shadows claimed the cavern and mighty winds of evening wandered over the plateau and the unseen spirits—something intangible and alien-like he had sensed for quite some time—of the canyon rocks floated like ghostly mist out of their hiding places. They threw shadows—or at least to his spent mind—that took the forms of lizards, leaped at him and mocked him with a haunting laughter. "Look at this one," they said. "All alone on our world and he fights a festering within him and is afraid. Just look at him!" Their laughter jangled in the night air. "Hah! The festering is not in his leg alone," they said. "There is a fear that festers in his spirit."

The pain throbbed and his mind raced; he could no longer tell the difference between what was real and what was hallucination. The lizards laughed and far back in his mind a great anger grew. A shout sprang forth and fought outward to his lips. "The laughter of a man gone crazy is in my mouth! I don't believe in you!" And the lizards faded into shady mist once more and he was sitting up with the cutting laser in hand, the same laser he had pierced open an infection with and which was not alien to his flesh. He quickly raised his arm and pointed the tip of the laser at his swollen left leg. An intense pain raced through him as he turned on the beam and widened the cut. The evil fluids gushed from the open wound. He dragged himself to the streambed and thrust his leg into the water. Fresh and cold and clear of methane, the current at that end washed over the leg and moved onward, the corruption of the flesh dissipating with it.

Three days Jared remained there. He was very weak and drank of the running water. He ate of the small heap of fish by his side, slept much, washed his leg often and saw the healing process begin. He studied the whole expanse of the canyon around him. He saw the rock walls rising everywhere. He knew it was time to go outside.

3) Life:

It was early on the first of these days that he saw a giant reptile, a lizard-like creature that he decided to call a "Tartaback" because of its strange tartan hump. The creatures looked very much like giant geckos, but with human-like eyes and the skin of iguanas. He wondered if such an animal was edible, like the fish. There were other breeds, of course, during his time outside the cavern that had shaggy-humped shapes among the wilderness at the wide lower end of the plain. His memory significantly improved, he drew a map of the region that surrounded him and noted its geographical breadth. Also, he noted a great many species—seventy-five percent of them reptilian—that inhabited its plains. He even counted them. There was an old Tartaback and a young Tartaback, five Salamandites and four Snake Crabs, eleven in all. His heart leaped. As soon as he was stronger, he would follow their trails and they would show him the way out of the plain. But by the next day a worry fretted in him. They were always there, staring back at him, and always the same number.

On the morning of his tenth day he unbound his left leg and reset the sticks and made a crutch. There was improvement in the swelling. Straight to the near rock wall he went, began a circuit of the cavern's interior and, from outside, the exterior. The Tartabacks in the fields watched him and grazed again, kept a distance from him. They seemed wary of the man, for he was a new strange thing on their world.

Jared came on the fissure where the stream disappeared. It was not like his small bed of water, his end, where the full extent of methane particles could taint it. He understood how the filtration worked. Some strange moisture from the cavern itself had filtrated and detoxified it, thus making it consumable for humans. However, if he had drunk the water out in the plains, he would most likely be poisoned. As he sat atop the fissure, he saw the other end was small and the stream almost filled it. A man could force his body only two or three feet in, no more. And there could be no open wounds or ingesting it. He came to a pool and waterfall at the upped end of the plain, green waters falling straight down from a high lip of rocks. It made a mist in the air and regardless of the green tinting, a rainbow floated in this. It was very beautiful; once more, he took out his pen and paper and began mapping the area.

He finished the full circuit. It had taken him all day. He would have pushed himself further, but the rocks behind it were smooth and sheer as the other rocky crests. Nowhere was there a trail leading up to a high plateau. Nowhere was there a place where a middle-aged man, even a young man with two strong legs, could climb up to the tall rocky edges. There was no way out.

Jared sat on the flattened top of a boulder by the pool and waterfall. His left leg now itched and peeled, and that was good. It meant that the leg was improving some more. It also meant, in time, that he would no longer need the timber brace or crutch. He wore his black fatigues, ripped and worn, and the stringy belt around his waist on which his papers and cutting laser hung. The distant suns were warm on his body. He had food to survive: an assortment of strange berries where plenty of tapering thistles whose stalks, when the thorny skin was peeled, was soft and sweet; he had fish from his streambed, taken as boys back home took them, by thrusting long branches into the bottom mud in a semicircle but down at the edge so close that they could not pass between them and then shoveling them out with quick hand flips before they could escape. He had all this and once a rodent that he snared and still a proper strength would not return to his muscles. He eventually knew it would not return, for he did not have the real food of a man. He did not have the meats he required, essential for maximum protein. And there, captive outside the canyon that housed him, meat walked and grazed and stared curiously at him.

He watched the Tartabacks moving about and saw the strong limbs that could outrun any man no matter how long his legs. He saw that, aroused to anger, could squash a man, the sharp horns and teeth and talons that could thrust into a man like a lance. He gathered all of his leather, what remained of his leggings and his tattered spacesuit. He sliced it all into thin strips, knotted and braided it together, as he knew these would make a good rope for lassoing. A rough and bumpy rope, but nevertheless a strong one. Then he looked up at the escape pod, hanging stilted on the top ledge of the cavern. A strange moss had now grown over it. He climbed up there to see if he had more supplies available. He found an old audio recorder given to him by his sister. She had given it to him as a gift, for when he landed on that "new world," and so he could keep a geographical voice record. Inside the toolbox were wire cutters and a chisel, and other than the cutting laser, he knew that these were the only things that would be useful to him. Lastly, he found a book covered in soil and dust. He smiled. It was his favorite classic: *The Adventures of Robinson Crusoe . . .*

"It would be nice to get in some reading," he said to himself. "There's no one else to talk to, not much else to do." He put the book down on the ledge.

Maybe later.

4) Hunting:

In the morning he went downstream, carrying the new rope coiled about his waist, as well as a lance he made from a thick branch, the chisel tied to the end of it. Farther down the canyon trail he stopped, watched the Tartabacks for many days and eventually picked up their habits. Every morning they grazed in the open. Afternoons they collected by the stream to drink and wade into the water, where other, more *amphibious* animals, fed with them. By studying this habit, along with the orbital symmetry of the suns, Jared was also able to work out the planet's daily cycle. It had forty-nine hours in a day and the seasons never changed. The Tartabacks had paths where many bushes ringed a pool, and they had paths through the bushes to other pools leading out to the grasses again. Where the other paths emerged the bushes were thick and arched over so that it was like a tunnel opening, and there were a good many trees, tall and thin, close by.

That was where Jared stood. He made a small loop in one end of his rope and passed the other end through it. He had a running slip noose. Carefully he hung the noose in the tunnel bushes so that it framed the opening. Carefully he led the loose end away through the bushes and tied it around the base of the tree. Carefully he knelt down behind the tree and the chisel-pointed lance lay beside him.

He was very patient. The morning passed and the suns were high overhead. Nearby, he heard the Tartabacks going into the water. He heard them splashing in the pool. "I bet they taste like chicken," he muttered to himself, watching and waiting. "They eat fish, the grains and wildlife of this planet, but not insects." He found this strange. He waited and a moment later heard them coming up the second path. The male Tartaback would be first, then the female with their younglings. They would come single file because of the dense, thick foliage. They would pass right through the loop. The one female with no offspring would be the last, lingering behind the others. There the males would wait for her. In the wilderness all that has life must fight for that life. Any planet, the rule is unchanging and eternal.

They stopped. Jared prepared himself. One after another down the line they stopped and stood motionless. For a while he could not see them through the bushes and he could hear no sound, but after waiting some more, the horned head and forequarters of the male appeared in the bush-tunnel opening. He saw the massive head with its long snout and its great and wide, leathery-humped shoulders. The Tartaback stood still, searching the open plains ahead. It smelled the alien human scent and was troubled. The herd, motioning to its leader, was worried too. This did not mean danger to them, not yet, but it was caution. The male took a step backward and snorted; another step and it would be out of the reach of the noose. Once turned away it would not lead the other lizards along that path again.

Jared dared not wait any longer. Swiftly he pulled back and up on the rope. The tree shook and the noose ripped out of the bushes and encircled the massive head. Frantic, the male Tartaback leaped—like geckos or salamanders do—crashing in the bushes to escape and the rope slid to grip around the long neck. Jared seized his lance and pushed up onto his left leg. Beyond the tree the male battered the bushes into the ground. It struggled up and down and pulling back, and the rope tightened around its neck. It leaped and plunged and bellowed, and with each leap the noose worked deeper through the leather of its skin, closing tighter and pressing upon its windpipe. Soon the bellowing died away to a hoarse gurgling in the throat. The bloodshot eyes glazed over. The Tartaback fell to its side, but as the weight eased forward the noose relaxed. The immense body heaved and the breath whistled in through the nostrils. The Tartaback staggered to its feet. The eyes brightened and it reared and again the noose bit deep.

Jared watched. He felt a fear that the rope would not endure such repeated battles, as one smart moment by the lizard and it would either tear or break free. With the aid of his lance, he circled behind the creature. He waited until it stood again with its head swaying and breath whistling past the slightly eased noose. He hopped forward swiftly and a little to one side. Then he lifted the lance and pointed it and drove it into the Tartaback's side, just back of the big shoulder. The male reared in one great shuddering movement and the rope snapped. Jared was flung into the air clinging to the lance, his grasp broken. He fell and rolled backwards with the thought of the talons and horn in mind.

There were no feet trampling him. There were no claws, horns or teeth thrusting into his body. He sat up and looked. The beast lay on the ground and a bloody froth bubbled from its giant nostrils. He had planted the lance as any professional hunter would, firmly and deep in the flesh. When the rope snapped suddenly, the Tartaback, rearing high, had fallen back and sideways, the end of the lance hitting the ground and the great lizard, with its own massive weight, had driven the edged point tearing deeper inward. The kill was a long one, but successful.

Time to eat.

5) Habitat:

The fire that night was a brave brightness. It threw its light upward into the darkness in flickering happy flames. The carcass of the Tartaback was a green and brown humped shape on the ground. Jared sat and watched the flames rising. He was full. And only the food he feasted on, that of an otherworldly animal, could cause his head to nod forward in drowsiness.

Winds of night wandered over the plateau. And the shadowlike lizards of the cavern rocks floated out like mist. They filled the upper air with their presence and they laughed softly, but they did not mock him. "This is the man," they said, "who has killed the lizard. With one leg of bone and one leg of wood he fought hungrily. With the homemade spear and the cunning of mind . . . the courage of heart, he killed the mighty Tartaback." Soon the mist floated higher and higher and drifted away up the cavern, the echo of their laughter now faint and fading.

Jared turned on his recorder. He began to do research, voice mental notes. The carcass of the full-grown Tartaback, he saw, contained nearly all flesh and hide; it looked smaller in bulk now that it lay on the ground and the strength and power of its movement long gone. Already a subtle degeneration began in the once vital organs. Yet it was life, not just food; if a man knew how to prepare it, every part could be eaten. As for the hide, if scrapped clean and tanned with a mixture of the brains and liver and the easily found soap plant, it made a tough leather; then it is *clothing.*

It was all these things and many more. It was the basis for a way of life for a middle-aged man who was stranded—one who had long hours in which to work and to think and to dream while the days and nights drifted over him.

Alone On This Chance Planet
by Shane Nelson

In the final days, the rockets were going.

"Hurry up!" Mama shouted from the sunlit kitchen a floor below.

Kevin Healy looked out his bedroom window. The bus was lumbering to a stop at the roadside. Through the window, he could hear the breathy hiss of air brakes.

Kevin went to his bed, where a single suitcase lay unopened. He had been sent to his room to pack his essentials—shuttle rockets to Mars were crowded and passengers could bring only one suitcase. How could a boy of twelve fit his life in a suitcase? And what about Max?

Max, a ten-year-old dog with a grey muzzle, lay in the hallway. Like baseball games, the backyard hammock and the treehouse, Max would be left behind.

He's too old, Pa had said the night he'd come home with four Interspace Rocket tickets, one for every member of the family. Pa had put a hand on Max's shoulder and said, *Space travel is arduous and animals aren't adapted.*

Kevin's response had been simple: *If Max can't go, I won't go.*

Pa was a practical man who knew about following the rules, especially when it came to Mars. The regulations were *set in stone.* Kevin had gone to bed with tears on his cheeks. After midnight, he had gone outside with Max. Kevin had watched the sky and seen a faint purple spark, like a shooting star. That had been one of the Mars rockets throwing itself free of Earth's hold and plunging headlong into eons of dark space.

Kevin could not leave Max behind.

But now the day had come. The bus was outside. Families sat within, staring through polarized glass. They had to leave—pollution, war, famine and global warming had dealt the Earth a deathblow. The only solution was to populate another world. For years rockets had been carrying men and women to Mars. First went engineers and scientists. Next doctors and 'indispensables.' Now, in Earth's final days, the last inhabitants were being whisked away.

Kevin hurried to the end of the hallway. He could hear his parents downstairs. Pa said, "That isn't going to fit, Annie!" and his mother replied with an exasperated, "It will if you help."

"C'mon," Kevin said, tugging Max's collar.

At the bottom of the stairs, the hallway ran left and right. Beyond, on the screened-in porch, Grandma Healy rocked in her rocking chair and blew notes on her harmonica. Kevin's parents were in the sitting room, piling things into a steamer trunk. Every family was allowed one trunk for heirlooms and memorabilia.

If Kevin tried to slip out the back door, his parents would see. Through the front door would bring him past Grandma. She was blind, but she saw better than most.

Kevin led Max into the bathroom. The window was large enough to accommodate a twelve-year-old boy, or a ten-year-old dog. Kevin lifted Max to the window.

"Okay, boy," Kevin said. "Go . . . on."

Kevin pushed. Max slipped out the window and fell to the ground.

Kevin pulled himself through the window. Max was waiting, tail wagging. From inside the house, he heard Ma shout, "Kevin! Get a move on!"

"Let's go, boy!" Kevin said, dashing toward the fence. Max bounded after him, giving an excited bark.

There was a graveyard across the street. Kevin had gone there with Max on summer afternoons and lay on the grass, swatting at mosquitoes and watching for the silver flash as one of the rockets zipped away from Earth. Now he slipped into the shadows behind a tall headstone. Max came with his agreeable old lope, eager to please.

"Sit," Kevin said. Max sat.

Kevin peered around the edge of the tombstone. Grandma was on the porch, playing music. The front door opened and Pa came out, dragging the trunk. It scraped down the sidewalk. Pa left it by the bus and headed back to the house.

He reappeared, a suitcase in each hand and one under his arm. He deposited them beside the trunk and returned to the house. Ma met him in the doorway.

Ma said, "I can't find him anywhere."

Pa went inside. Kevin imagined him thumping upstairs, throwing open closet doors, demanding that Kevin *come out right now*. Pa emerged a short time later, running a hand through his hair. Over the chugging of the bus, Kevin could hear his mother.

"He knows we have to go."

"It's that dog," Pa said. "Get Gram to the bus." Pa stormed around the house, bellowing. Then he changed tactics, shouting, "Max! C'mon, Max! Let's go!"

Kevin wrapped his arms around Max, who whimpered and squirmed.

"Stay," Kevin said. "If you go, Pa'll make me leave you behind."

Pa and Ma were standing next to the steamer trunk. The bus driver emerged, said something, and pointed at his watch. Shaking his head, Pa pointed at the house. The driver stuck his head into the bus for a moment.

"Kevin!" Ma yelled. "Please, come out!"

The bus driver stepped away from the bus and a second man emerged. He was tall and ramrod stiff, wearing a black uniform. He stepped up to Ma and Pa, a looming man in dark sunglasses, a shiny leather holster on his hip.

Pa began to explain, his voice frazzled and angry. "I don't know where he is," he said. "But he's here somewhere."

The man replied, something low and indistinguishable. Ma put a hand to her mouth and shook her head. Pa had gone scarlet.

"We're *not* leaving without our son!"

The uniformed man spoke again. Kevin couldn't make out the words, but the man's voice was like a piece of flattened iron. Still, Pa refused to back down. He spoke in short, agitated gasps, both hands clenched into furious fists.

"This is our *son* you're talking about, not a piece of furniture! We'll find him and you can damn well wait until— "

This time the man's words were clear. "You're not giving orders, Mr. Healy. We will *not* wait. Your name is on the register and that means you *will* get on this bus, one way or another. This is an evacuation."

"What about my son?" Ma asked, her voice ragged. "What about him? Please, he's my son . . . "

The man in the sunglasses paused, head tilted. Finally, he said, "I'll alert the authorities. Men will pass through here. We'll find him."

"What if it's too late?" Ma asked. "What if we're already gone, what if our rocket leaves and Kevin misses it?"

"There are other rockets," the man said. "Now . . . get on the bus."

"But—" Pa began.

"We *may* make an exception for your son, but if the two of you don't get on board, you won't get another opportunity."

Silence fell like a heavy blanket. Pa and the man in the sunglasses exchanged more words. Ma shook her head, but Pa held her firmly with one arm. Voices went back and forth, raised, desperate, pleading. When the man's hand touched the holster at his side, Pa turned toward the house.

"You have thirty seconds, Kevin!" Pa called, voice unsteady. "We can't wait!"

Kevin's stomach tightened as his mother sobbed.

"Fifteen seconds!"

The bus driver fed their luggage into the underbelly of the bus.

"Kevin!"

Tears rose in Kevin's eyes but he remained hidden, even as Grandma Healy tottered onto the bus. Then Pa took Ma by the shoulders and forced her inside. To the driver, Pa said, "Wait." Then he hurried into the house. The man in the sunglasses waited, arms crossed. Pa emerged a moment later and marched to the waiting bus.

Within seconds the bus was rolling down the road to where another family waited, suitcases pooled around them. The bus's brake lights flashed and the bus stopped. The door on the bus opened. Pa and Ma stepped out, looking toward their house.

"Kevin!" Ma shouted.

The driver loaded the other family's suitcases and ushered everyone onto the bus. The taillights flashed, the brakes wheezed, and the bus lumbered to the next house. It was far enough away that Kevin couldn't tell Ma from Pa as they got out of the bus.

At the next stop, Ma and Pa were two small shapes.

At the final stop, no one got off the bus. Perhaps the man in the sunglasses would no longer let them. The driver loaded up the last family. Then the bus lurched onto the highway and picked up speed. As it departed, the whine of its engine became more and more faint. At last the bus disappeared over a distant hill.

Kevin drew a breath.

Except for Max, he was completely alone.

* * *

Max loped to the shadows of the porch, lying in his accustomed spot by the front door. Kevin stared at the house. *Everyone's gone.*

Maybe not *everyone.* But everyone within a thousand kilometers. Pa had shown Kevin the way in which the government was emptying one square of land after another. Pa had said: *We'll be among the last to go. After we've gone, there won't be many rockets left.*

The wind blew around Kevin's face, tugging at his hair, bringing the dusty, dry scent of abandonment.

"Hello?" Kevin shouted. His voice boomed. He cringed, fearful that someone might hear.

Kevin walked through the house, listening to the sound his feet made on the floor. The house felt much like it did on days when Pa was at work and Ma was out with Grandma Healy. Doors swung open with the same lazy groan and rooms held dust motes in bands of sunshine.

Kevin opened the refrigerator. Ma had been desperate about leaving so much stuff behind, but Pa had shrugged it off. *We aren't about to stuff ourselves to the gills just so we don't leave behind some bread.*

And there was bread. And milk. And a six-pack of soda. Kevin grabbed two cans from the refrigerator, grinning. Then he strolled through the house. He could imagine playing in the empty rooms, not having to listen to his parents, not having to worry about school.

He opened a can of soda and stood at the end of the upstairs hallway, in a long slant of sunshine.

Why wasn't he afraid?

"Nothing to be afraid of," he said. "Not with Max. Not in my house."

That's right. Everything in the house belonged to him. Everything in the neighborhood. Soon . . . everything in the world!

Kevin and Max ran throughout the house banging doors and knocking over lamps. Kevin tumbled over his parents' bed, which had been neatly made before being abandoned, and fell to the floor laughing. By late afternoon he grew hungry. In the freezer he found some pre-made hamburger patties. He removed four—three for him and one for Max—and set them into a frying pan on top of the stove.

When the food was ready (slightly charred on both sides and pink in the middle), Kevin found buns in the pantry and laid out his burgers, layering them with cheese and ketchup. Max devoured his own burger in a few bites, tongue lapping grease from the porch.

The sky was beginning to dim as the sun edged toward the horizon. Across the street, the houses began to darken, windows becoming black squares.

"Let's go inside, Max."

There were three television stations still broadcasting as Earth's last inhabitants headed for Mars. One featured a twenty-four hour news feed. The second showed movies and TV programs, commercial-free. The third kept track of Interspace Rocket flights. Kevin turned on the commercial-free station. When he rose to use the bathroom a few hours later, night had fallen.

"Max?"

Kevin felt warm comfort as Max came to his side. Together, they went through the house turning on lights. Kevin thought of his father saying: *Don't turn on every light in the house! We aren't made of money!* He switched on lights until the house glowed. Then he sat back down in front of the TV.

He didn't get up again until Max scratched at the door, eager to go outside. Kevin let him out. Darkness blanketed everything. For the first time he noticed how black things were. He walked to the end of the sidewalk and stared at the night.

When he became aware of the stark glow of his house, his stomach fell. If there *were* any people left, they would see the house for miles.

Kevin found his father's flashlight and went room-to-room, Max at his side, turning off lights. Finished, he locked the doors. Max usually slept on the porch, but tonight he could sleep inside.

Kevin lay on the sofa, Max at his feet. Then he switched off the flashlight and turned his attention back to the television's flickering glow.

Kevin woke up to Max's nose rubbing his cheek. The house was dark except for a lamp and the TV.

He switched off the TV and got to his feet. Max padded down the hallway, taking up a patient position by the door. Kevin opened it and Max slipped outside. Kevin followed.

The darkness was like a living thing. The Earth seemed to sigh and whisper, perhaps dreaming. The wind blew soft, warm breath against Kevin's cheeks. He walked across the lawn and stopped near the sidewalk, craning his head skyward.

The constellations swarmed. Kevin blinked. As he did so, he saw a tiny spark just above the horizon, in the west. A moment later he saw the bright orange-white streak rising in the sky, carving a furrow in the darkness. *That's a rocket*, he thought. Perhaps the very one upon which Ma, Pa and Grandma sat. Were they watching Earth disappear beneath them?

Kevin went back to the porch. Max lay down in his usual spot, muzzle on his paws.

Dragging a blanket and pillow from the house, Kevin curled up next to Max, flashlight near at hand.

Kevin cooked bacon and eggs for breakfast. The bacon was burned and the eggs runny. He put his dirty dishes in the sink and wiped his hands on his shirt.

Upstairs, he threw his old shirt on the floor and chose a new one from his closet. As he was pulling it on, his eye fell upon the nightstand. Sitting next to his clock was a rectangle of paper. Written on the front was *Government Interspace Council.* Next to it was the department's official seal. It was a rocket ticket. Destination: Mars. Departure: August 15th. Four days.

When Pa had come back into the house, he must have left the ticket.

Kevin looked at it. His breakfast sat lead-heavy in his guts.

Leaving the ticket behind, Kevin headed outside. He couldn't worry about rockets, tickets and trips to Mars. He had the world to himself.

For three days, Kevin explored the neighborhood. He tried doorknobs and found them unlocked. He stepped into homes where the silence was heavy. In a few of the houses things creaked overhead, unsettling his nerves. A thunderstorm rolled in on the third evening. Kevin held Max and watched as rain crashed down. He was glad he had stayed. It broke his heart to imagine Max, cowering alone during this storm. The storm blew out before dark, leaving behind the fresh scent of renewal.

Kevin turned on the TV. The commercial-free channel was running an action movie. He changed the channel and found himself staring at the Interspace Rocket Program Information.

Interspace Departures as of: 14 August

15 August:	*H4 Sector*	*Departure Time:*	*0800 HRS*
16 August:	*H5 Sector*	*Departure Time:*	*0800 HRS*
18 August:	*I4 Sector*	*Departure Time:*	*0900 HRS*
20 August:	*J9 Sector*	*Departure Time:*	*1100 HRS*
21 August:	*T5 Sector*	*Departure Time:*	*0800 HRS*
23 August:	*H8 Sector*	*Departure Time:*	*0700 HRS*
27 August:	*U7 Sector*	*Departure Time:*	*1400 HRS*

Interspace Departures Remaining: 7

Next Broadcast: 15 August 07:55 HRS

Each day of a departure, the launch was broadcast. Usually it was over within minutes. Then the list of departure times would return.

According to the ticket his father had left, their flight would depart tomorrow morning at 8 a.m. That would be the rocket that would carry Ma, Pa and Grandma to the red planet.

The alarm woke Kevin at seven-thirty. He let Max outside, then made some toast. Carrying it into the living room, he sat down in front of the TV.

Interspace Departures For: 15 August

H4 Sector Departure Time: 0800 HRS

Present Time: 07:36 HRS

Departure in 24 minutes

Kevin crunched down on his toast. When Max scratched to be let in, Kevin got up and opened the door.

Departure in 16 minutes

When the countdown reached six minutes, the screen went blank. A moment later the screen showed one of the Mars rockets sitting on a wide, barren piece of land. It was an immense silver needle pointing toward the stars. Its engines were idling, creating a thin halo of white smoke. The ship's hull was smooth; near the top it was dotted with tiny porthole windows.

The rocket shone in the August sunshine. This was the rocket that held Ma, Pa and Grandma.

Departure in 4 minutes

The rocket trembled. The ground ran with ripples, as if something enormous was waking up under the earth's crust. As Kevin watched, the seconds began to tick. 50, 49, 48 . . .

Kevin put a hand on Max. "They're going."

In the final ten seconds dust and smoke swirled as the engines blew fire and pressure. Then, with one explosive thrust, the rocket threw itself free of the earth. After a few seconds it rose out of frame and a huge, billowing wall of smoke and dust roared over the camera, blinding it.

The screen went blank.

A moment later, the list returned.

Interspace Departures as of: 16 August

16 August:	*H5 Sector*	*Departure Time:*	*0800 HRS*
18 August:	*I4 Sector*	*Departure Time:*	*0900 HRS*
20 August:	*J9 Sector*	*Departure Time:*	*1100 HRS*
21 August:	*T5 Sector*	*Departure Time:*	*0800 HRS*
23 August:	*H8 Sector*	*Departure Time:*	*0700 HRS*
27 August:	*U7 Sector*	*Departure Time:*	*1400 HRS*

Interspace Departures Remaining: 6

Next Broadcast: 16 August 07:55 HRS

The basement was small and dingy, with a single light hanging at the bottom of the stairs. Kevin hated it. It was dark and fetid and festooned with cobwebs whose architects scuttled through the shadows.

But the cellar held the freezer, and the freezer held the food.

Kevin stood at the top of the stairs, staring at the lightbulb. It tossed haphazard shadows on the cellar floor. His heart rose in his throat and rattled against his windpipe, making it difficult to breath.

"Max!"

Max limped toward Kevin, moving with arthritic slowness. Taking him by the collar, Kevin began downstairs. The risers creaked and groaned.

The basement was small enough that he could see everything. The furnace, dormant in the August heat, hunkered in the corner. Shelves of preserves lined one wall. Kevin grabbed a jar of pickles and set it on the second-to-last step.

Max edged away from him, sniffing cracks in the wall.

Kevin raised the lid on the freezer. Inside were packages of hamburger and fish. Two turkeys. A ham. Pre-packaged items that Pa referred to as 'junk.' Kevin only ate them when his Pa wasn't around and Ma was feeling generous.

Kevin loaded up on these items. Closing the freezer, he hurried upstairs with Max at his heels. It was a relief to close the cellar door and turn off the light. He had forgotten the pickles, but that was fine. They could sit on the second-to-last step, quiet in the darkness, until the next time he had to go down.

On the morning of August 20th, Kevin awoke to find the bed empty. Max had gone downstairs and fallen asleep next to the porch door. Kevin moved sleepily into the kitchen, calling Max's name three times before Max raised his head.

"Want some bacon?"

Max's tail thumped.

Kevin cooked bacon, dropping three pieces in Max's bowl. Then he turned on the TV. What he saw on the screen gave him an unexpected jolt.

Interspace Departures as of: 20 August

20 August:	*J9 Sector*	*Departure Time:*	*0900 HRS*
21 August:	*T5 Sector*	*Departure Time:*	*0800 HRS*
23 August:	*H8 Sector*	*Departure Time:*	*0700 HRS*
27 August:	*U7 Sector*	*Departure Time:*	*1400 HRS*

Interspace Departures Remaining: 4

Next Broadcast: 20 August 8:55 HRS

Could that be right? After today's launch, would there only three more?

Kevin glanced at the clock. It continued ticking, oblivious to the world's fate. It was almost 8:55.

Kevin turned to the news station. It was blank. Across the screen it said: *This Station Has Ceased Broadcasting.* He switched to a sitcom. He tried to let his mind escape into the TV show, but his mind kept turning his eyes to the clock. Finally, when the clock said 8:57 a.m., he switched channels.

Interspace Departures as of: 20 August

21 August:	*T5 Sector*	*Departure Time:*	*0800 HRS*
23 August:	*H8 Sector*	*Departure Time:*	*0700 HRS*
27 August:	*U7 Sector*	*Departure Time:*	*1400 HRS*

Interspace Departures Remaining: 3

Next Broadcast: 21 August 7:55 HRS

The launch was over.

He had missed it. His clock was wrong. How could he have lost three minutes so easily?

The clock was an old one that Pa wound twice a month. Kevin opened the clock's face and nudged the hands ahead three minutes. Then, using a small brass key, he wound the clock.

He went to the kitchen. Max was waiting to go out. As he went, Kevin noticed that he hadn't touched the food in his bowl.

On the porch, Max turned in a tired circle before lying down. With a shuddering sigh, he closed his eyes and went to sleep.

On the morning of August 21st, Kevin opened the face on the clock and gently pushed the minute hand ahead. Just enough that he could be certain he wouldn't lose any more time. Then he wound the clock again, the key moving barely a quarter-turn. It was 7:45 a.m.

He looked at the television. The screen held his distorted reflection. He looked almost transparent.

He went outside, Max following, and stared at the lawn. It was beginning to brown. Kevin went to the back of the house, unrolled the hose, dragged it to the front lawn and set up the sprinkler. Within minutes water was sparkling in the sunshine.

He went inside, tracking wet footprints on the porch boards. He passed Max, sleeping, his side rising and falling. He walked upstairs, the ticking of the clock heavy and loud in the empty house.

Just before noon Kevin moved the sprinkler into the backyard. The sun was reaching its zenith, baking the air. Returning to the front yard, Kevin noticed that Max hadn't moved from his spot on the porch.

Kevin stopped, one foot on the bottom step. Max lay beside the door, head on his paws.

"Max?"

He didn't stir.

"Max?"

A breeze ruffled Max's hair.

Kevin knelt beside him. Before he put his hand on Max's side, he knew his best friend was gone. His fur was soft, his body warm, but he was no longer breathing. Kevin held his hand against Max's side, fingers working back and forth through the soft fur.

"Max."

Kevin pulled Max into his lap, crying while he held him. After a few hitching sobs, he got to his feet, cradling Max in his arms.

He carried him into the backyard and laid him in the shadow of a large tree. Then he took the shovel out of Pa's shed and began to dig. The soil under the tree turned easily. While Kevin worked he continued to cry.

I didn't go without you, Max, he thought. *Why'd you go without me?*

When the grave was finished, Kevin placed Max inside. The idea of shoveling dirt onto Max was too much, so he went inside and removed the blanket from the back of the couch. Once it covered Max's body, he was able to fill the grave. The tears came on even stronger as the final few shovelfuls were put in place.

With a final glance at the grave, Kevin walked to the front porch. He stood next to the spot where Max had spent so many nights and afternoons. The boards seemed to bear his shape.

To Kevin, the porch seemed very small.

Kevin tried to figure out how he would get through the night without Max. He flipped on the flashlight. The beam darted left and right, making spooky shapes on the walls. He directed the beam upstairs, where his bedroom waited. The thought of bedding down in that vast, lonely darkness was unimaginable.

Instead, he curled up on the couch. He left the lamp burning. When he finally fell asleep, it was to the slow and ceaseless ticking of the clock.

The next morning Kevin gathered rocks from the roadside. When he had plenty, he piled them in the center of the road and stood on the white line that divided the lanes.

He selected a nice sized rock and held it in his right hand. It felt hot. *He* felt hot inside.

He looked across the road to Mr. Popowich's house.

Kevin threw the rock and struck the house, a few feet to the left of the big picture window. He hurled a second rock. It hit the picture window. A crack appeared in the glass. He threw a third rock. A fourth. That one broke the window and sent pieces of glass tumbling onto the lawn.

Kevin continued throwing rocks until his arm hurt and the windows in Mr. Popowich's house were shattered. Then he moved to the house next door. And to the one next to that. By the time he had finished his hands were raw and his eyes were red from crying.

Kevin thought: *Max, I need you.*

The single bulb burned at the bottom of the basement stairs. A fresh cobweb had been strung from the curve of the bulb to the shadows in the corner. Kevin could see the web's owner sitting on the fine silken strands.

Kevin put his foot on the first riser. The wood creaked.

All he had to do was walk downstairs. Just grab the jar of pickles that he'd left on the second-to-last stair. That would give him confidence. Then, tomorrow perhaps, he could go down again.

Still, he remained stranded on the fourth step. Even switching on the flashlight and playing the beam through the shadows didn't help.

Silence built in his ears. It was a booming sound, like the surf crashing against the beach. Kevin took two quick steps back and clutched the doorframe.

I can't go down there alone, he thought. *And if I can't do that, what am I going to do?*

He left the cellar and stood in the kitchen, listening to the swollen stillness. Had the silence been this loud before?

He went up to his room and lay on his bed. The sunshine that fell through the window was warm and put him to sleep. He woke up an hour later and grabbed the flashlight. Marching to the kitchen, he gritted his teeth and opened the cellar door.

Darkness rolled out at him, thick and earthy. Kevin frowned. He had left the light burning, he was certain.

He touched the light switch. It was in the 'on' position. He flipped the switch up and down. The cellar remained dark.

Probably a breaker, Kevin thought. He knew where the breaker box was. Downstairs.

He headed for the living room. Dropping down in his father's favorite chair, he grabbed the remote control. A little TV might help him face the idea of going downstairs with just a flashlight.

He pressed the 'power' button on the remote control, but the TV remained dark.

Was it the main breaker? The power for the entire house?

Kevin began turning on lights. Nothing happened. The refrigerator was no longer making its familiar, soothing hum.

Tears rose in Kevin's eyes as he realized that he would have to spend the night in complete darkness. It would be like sinking into the depths of a dark and silent ocean, slipping deeper until there was nothing. Drowning.

Then he remembered the television in his parents' room. It was a battery-powered set that Pa had for emergencies.

The TV was a twenty-inch model that Kevin carried downstairs without difficulty. He set it down on top of the thirty-two inch television and carefully attached the cable from the back of the big TV to that of the smaller. He found a switch on the back of the set and slid it over to *battery*. Then, stomach dancing, he turned on the TV.

The TV crackled and the screen jumped to life. There was a burst of static and then the screen flickered. The picture looked small and dull compared to the thirty-two inch, but seeing it lifted Kevin's spirits.

Interspace Departures as of: 22 August

23 August: H8 Sector Departure Time: 0700 HRS

27 August: U7 Sector Departure Time: 1400 HRS

Interspace Departures Remaining: 2

Next Broadcast: 23 August 6:55 HRS

Kevin quickly turned the channel, not wanting to be reminded of how little time remained.

That night Kevin fell asleep to the sound of the world holding its breath. Never before had he heard so much *nothing*. The house creaked and groaned as the night cooled and Kevin imagined the cellar door scraping open and bringing out something even darker than the night.

He came awake at sun-up, wondering how long the food in the freezer and refrigerator would last without power. How long would it be before he had nothing to eat? And what would he do come winter, when cold clamped down on the house?

Kevin looked at the clock on the mantle. It was pushing seven a.m.

He turned on the TV and sat down in his father's chair, still wrapped in a blanket. While the sun came up on another warm, empty August day, Kevin watched the second-to-last rocket launch. When it was over, the screen jumped and said:

Interspace Departures as of: 23 August

27 August: U7 Sector Departure Time: 1400 HRS

THIS WILL BE THE FINAL LAUNCH

Interspace Departures Remaining: 1

Next Broadcast: 27 August 13:55 HRS

Kevin went outside and lay down on the grass next to Max's grave.

* * *

On the morning of August 27th, Kevin picked up the ticket from his bedside table. He stuck it into his back pocket and grabbed his backpack from the bed. Downstairs, he put on his sneakers and lifted a set of keys from the pegboard by the door.

No one had come for him. Not even the authorities the man in the sunglasses had talked about. That had been a lie, Kevin knew, to get his parents onto the bus. But that didn't matter because *someone* had to still be here. Pa said that the government couldn't evacuate a town during a flood. There was no way that they could pull this off on schedule.

Kevin raised the garage door and looked inside. Parked nose out was the family car. Kevin climbed behind the wheel. He had never driven before, but he had watched Pa do it.

Kevin had turned on the TV that morning and found a message waiting. It had brought everything crashing home, from the empty silence of the house to the wide-open, breathless quiet of the world.

Interspace Departures For: 27 August

U7 Sector Departure Time: 1400 HRS

Present Time: 0800 HRS

Departure in 6 HRS

THIS WILL BE THE FINAL LAUNCH

Kevin drew the seat as close to the steering wheel as he could. He inserted the key into the ignition, envisioning everything Pa did.

Kevin buckled up.

He turned the key. The engine caught.

He grabbed the gearshift with one hand and slipped it out of PARK. The car made a hesitant *thump* and moved forward. Kevin stepped on the brake and held it down until he found DRIVE. Then he lifted his foot.

The car started forward, gliding out of the garage. When it reached the road, Kevin turned left. The car lost its momentum and Kevin put a foot on the gas pedal. The car surged forward. Kevin lifted his foot and the car coasted.

With experimental taps of his foot, Kevin was able to get control. He felt a rush of pleasure as the car moved down the road. For a moment he forgot about his fear and loneliness. But when he looked out the windshield and saw the long, flat, empty stretch of road, the hollow feeling returned.

Maybe I can find the launch site, he thought. *Pa said it was close.*

Kevin adjusted the wheel, keeping the car straight.

Will someone be there to let me in? Will I have to show them my ticket? He had a flash of fear. Perhaps they would tell him he had missed his chance.

The car gave a sudden, violent lurch. Kevin squeezed the wheel. The car lurched again. Without warning, the engine died and the car stopped.

Kevin tried to turn the key but it wouldn't move. Thinking quickly, he put the car into PARK and tried the key again. The engine strained, but did not turn over. He let go of the key and his eyes wandered to the dashboard, where the idiot lights glowed. *Oil. Engine. Seatbelt.* They were all burning.

His eyes found the gas gauge. Empty.

"No!" Kevin said. He turned the key again, but the engine merely coughed. "Please . . . I want to go! I don't want to stay." He threw off his seatbelt and climbed out of the car.

The sun hung low on the eastern side of the world. Kevin looked back the way he had come. He could no longer see his house.

He suddenly thought of Ma and Pa, stepping off the bus and looking back for him. This is what they had seen. But unlike Ma and Pa, Kevin could not keep going. So, head down, tears coursing down his cheeks, he trudged down the middle of the road, heading home.

In the center of the frame sat the final Mars rocket, glorious, shimmering silver, nose pointed toward the heavens. A halo of white smoke curled around its engines.

Kevin watched as the seconds counted down onscreen. On the mantle, the clock ticked. The seconds synchronized, finding one another in some unspoken harmony.

29 . . . 28 . . . 27 . . .

Kevin hugged his knees to his chest.

The Mars rocket was a glorious thing. A gigantic steel needle that would pierce the skin of space and break through to the other side.

15 . . . 14 . . . 13 . . .

Kevin tried to imagine that he was onboard. Was there a window he could peer through, down to the ground a hundred stories below?

5 . . . 4 . . . 3 . . .

The white smoke blossomed into golden fire as the engine fired. Kevin closed his eyes. His body shook. The house shook. The vibrations of this final Mars rocket carried around the planet, through the foundation, up into his bones, blood and brain.

The rocket rose effortlessly, tearing the sky asunder with sound and fury. Everything trembled.

The clock ticked. Kevin counted seconds. They kept coming.

At last he opened his eyes and looked at the TV screen.

This Station Has Ceased Broadcasting

Kevin crossed to the mantle, where the old clock sat, ticking with infinite patience.

He looked at the slender gold hands. Hours. Minutes. Seconds. He reached up and found the key. He put it in his pocket.

Then he opened the clock face and gently touched the minute hand with his finger. His finger was vibrating, as if holding onto the echoes of the last launch. Drawing a breath, he stilled his finger.

Then he carefully began to turn back the minute hand, one revolution at a time.

The Secret Life of Mars
by Geoffrey Maloney

When he crept out of his hovel that morning, Max Milligan felt he was at the end of his tether. Despite the dust filters in his oxygen mask, he could feel his sinuses swell immediately. The familiar throb began behind his eyes. With cold chalky fingers, he groped in the pocket of his dungarees for a blister pack of anti-histamines only to find he'd popped the last one the night before. He sighed and surveyed the sad sight of the burnt and patchy grass on surface of his hovel. The seeds had been genetically modified for the thin Martian atmosphere and the hard frosts they experienced. He had nurtured them painstakingly, yet still he had no lawn in place.

The professional croquet equipment, complete with genuine Dawson balls and *lignum vitae* mallets, had arrived from Earth three months ago and proved useless in the dust. He was supposed to be an artist reveling in the sweeping barren landscapes before him, but he spent most of his time worrying about his second job as a regional sports coordinator. In the two years he'd been on Mars he'd had not one inspirational moment. He hoped he'd make it through to the end of his 'tour of duty' and not end up in St. Dympna's up in Clementine. He'd heard its padded cells were starting to get a little full.

Just then a patch of red dust stirred on the other side of Stan-Walkertown's only street and his neighbor, Jim McDonald, flung open the front trap of his own hovel.

"My, what a bright shiny Martian day it is," Jim said, with such spontaneous enthusiasm that Milligan immediately felt somehow inferior for not sharing it.

Jim McDonald, despite the dust and grit that clung to everything around him, was his usual neat clean self. He was freshly shaven beneath his face mask, and his blonde hair had been slicked back and given a crisp part on one side. As his neighbor emerged fully from his trap, Milligan was surprised to see he was wearing a pair of red shorts and a yellow singlet over his skin-tight thermal suit, and he had extra oxygen bullets strapped to the belt around his waist.

"Hey, Jim," Milligan called out, "looks like your up for something."

Jim strolled across the street. "You bet I am. This is a new day dawning for me, Max. I woke this morning and just knew I needed to get fitter than I've ever been before. I'm going to power on today and defy everything Mars has to throw at me. So I'm running out to Hellas and back."

"Jim, that's like twenty kays, round trip. You shouldn't overdo it. You've been kind of sick lately . . . "

"So you don't want to come with me? Is that what you're saying? I thought you'd be up to it, Max. I really did. Or do you feel one of your artistic moments coming on? Maybe you could paint me jogging in the desert. It'd be an inspiration to the youth of Mars and you could fulfill two of your job contracts at the same time."

"I really need to get my sinuses sorted out first," Milligan said. "You don't happen to have any spare anti-histamines, do you?" Milligan sneezed. "Besides I need to check my VW units."

"Checked mine already," Jim said, "before the sun was up and, boy, are they pumping the good gas or what? Next year I reckon we'll have this whole planet up to a balmy 12 degrees C in summer, and there'll be a lot more oxygen in the atmosphere as well. Then we can all breathe easily and get rid of these damn masks."

"Weather report said that we'd struggle to reach 1 degree today, so I'm not about to abandon my thermal suit just yet," Milligan said.

"See, Max, that's your problem, buddy. You need to think more positively about things. Go see Serena; she's got a stack of anti-histamines buried away. The trap's still open." Milligan watched Jim McDonald head off down the street, little red dust devils rising up and spinning away from the soles of his shoes as he ran. He wondered briefly if Jim was fit enough to do such a big run, then crossed the street.

Descending into the McDonald's hovel, through the airlock, Milligan found Jim's wife in front of the vid glued to the Marsnet. "Serena," he said quietly, "Jim said you might have some anti-histamine stashed away."

Serena turned from the screen. Her eyes looked half-dead. There were big dark rings beneath them, like she'd been up all night following the community news reports on the Marsnet. "The Riverman's back," she said in a flat washed out voice. "A child was taken north of Clementine last night."

At that time of day and feeling in the shape he was, Milligan wasn't about to enter into a debate about the existence of the Riverman or otherwise. The fact that some people wanted to believe in some supernatural being to explain why their children had disappeared was fine by him. Mars was a dangerous place. People went missing all the time. It was easy enough to fall into a crevice, or get lost in the desert, and never be seen again, but then it was just as easy to imagine some malevolent supernatural being lurking over the horizon. Mars was kind of creepy, too.

Milligan kept his thoughts to himself and nodded sagely, as if he understood everything there was to understand about the Riverman and the children that had disappeared.

Serena pushed herself away from the screen saying, "I've got a pile of loratadine somewhere. I think I've used most of the pseudo-ephedrine; I like the little buzz it gives."

"Loratadine's fine," Milligan said, thinking, as he watched Serena disappear into the depths of her hovel, that she was a fine looking woman: nice slim waist, such a gentle sway to her hips.

When Serena returned she was completely naked. Milligan felt a lump rise in his throat when he saw her. Brazenly she waved a couple of blister packs in the air. "Loratadine *plus* pseudo-ephedrine, a delightful combination for those of us who are nasally disadvantaged. But there's a little something I'd like you to do for me, Max . . . "

"Just hold it there," Milligan said. "I want to paint the perfection I see before me. Let me grab my oils and a canvas. I'll be right back."

Serena winked. "I appreciate the thought of being immortalized for all time, Max, especially by an artist with your talent, but you haven't painted anything in months, and just now that wasn't quite what I had in mind."

In the cramped bunk of the spare room of the McDonald's hovel, Serena said, as she traced her fingernails across Milligan's back, "Sweet Jesus, I needed that."

Milligan grimaced. For the last thirty minutes he had forgotten about his sinuses, but now they'd started to throb again. Serena's sharp nails felt like the claws that were digging into the back of his eyeballs. "How's Jim going?" he said and felt guilty as soon as he said his name.

"Jim is Jim. You know what he's like. The black dog gets him for a while, but then he blasts it off and he's almost back to his normal self. Except he's not interested in sex anymore. So you being the most attractive single guy in this town, I thought we might come to an arrangement."

"Sure, any time," Max said, "just as long as the Riverman's not watching." It was a lame joke, but he was feeling grumpy all of a sudden. He really needed to get out of that bunk and get some of those anti-histamines down his throat before his head caved in.

Serena dug her nails in deeply. Max howled. "Sweet Jesus, Serena, what the . . . ."

"You really don't even try to understand the Riverman do you, Max?"

"Serena, I should go and check my VW units and maybe look for Jim," Milligan said. "He's probably sitting at the edge of Hellas trying to figure out how he's going to make it back."

"You didn't answer my question," Serena said.

"I really need to go," Milligan said, climbing out of the bunk and beginning to dress.

"And I really need to know, Max," Serena replied.

Milligan walked towards the door, picking up the blisters from the bureau as he went.

"You're leaving me feeling like a prostitute," Serena said, stretching herself out on the bed like a cat.

Max looked back at her: dark hair, dark eyes and such beautiful ivory skin, and so many wacky ideas in her head. He wanted to paint her, like she was just then, to capture the intensity of the moment. "Serena, I think you're gorgeous. And if anyone's the prostitute here, it's me. But when you ask me about the Riverman, I don't know what to say, except I just don't know. Maybe he exists, maybe he doesn't. Maybe he takes the children, but there are also lots of natural and logical reasons for why those children disappear. Mars is a geological nightmare. It hates life. It was pure madness to send people here."

"Max, if you really believe that, why did you come?"

Max chuckled weakly. "I thought the desolation might be inspirational."

Back on the surface, Milligan sucked down three of the anti-histamines and walked rapidly to the community buggy park at the end of the street. He waved to his neighbors who were out struggling with their gardens in the early morning chill as he went, but moved fast enough to let them know he wasn't about to stop to pass the time. He was feeling anxious now. He should have never let Serena seduce him like that, and he had the obsessive thought in his head that he needed to get out into the desert and make sure Jim was okay.

There were only a dozen or so buggies in the buggy park, all big ugly machines, shiny and black from the solar panels and tinted windows that made-up their exteriors, and with huge tractor tires deeply-treaded to get a grip on the Martian dust. Most of the townsfolk were out checking their VW units, and others, finished with their checking or not even bothering, had taken the six hour drive up to Clementine to do some shopping beneath the city's milk-white dome, or to simply sit in one of the bars in the canal zone and pass their time in more hospitable surroundings.

Milligan climbed into his buggy, clicked the engine over and drove towards Hellas Basin. There were no roads as such, just bright blue markers positioned every half-kay and the tracks of previous buggy's to show the safest route. The landscape red, flat and desolate with only an occasional mountain, crater rim or hill rising in the distance. Otherwise there was nothing but sand and rocks and dirt. And that was the problem Milligan realized as he drove. There were no trees, no birds, no rivers, lakes or oceans. There weren't even any lizards scurrying about in the desert sands. He knew now that it was life that had inspired him back on Earth, but on Mars the only life was humans and the parasites in their guts.

Five kays out of town, Milligan got sick of the silence and the tedious view. He turned the radio on. Jack O'Cash's lively early morning show, broadcast from Clementine, sparkled out of the buggy's speakers.

Well, good morning all you Earthly Martians. Wasn't the old mother big blue and beautiful last night, hovering there just above the horizon. Anyway folks that's enough for nostalgia; right now there's another Martian day that's gonna make you pay. The big news of the day is that the big old bogeyman, the Riverman, is back. So lock up your sons and daughters, coz the Riverman's coming for them. According to that font of all wisdom, the Marsnet, where ordinary folks like you and me get to dump any old rubbish they like into the information freeway, the Riverman was sighted 150 kays north of Clementine at 2:40 a.m. this morning. The sightee, Jay Stokes, admits to being inebriated at the time, that he'd just had a barney with his wife, and he was quite possibly suicidal when he drove his buggy out to the edge of the Debois plateau. Then large as life, according to Jay, the Riverman pops up out of nowhere, skinny as a scarecrow, an old bag of skin and bones, in an old gray weather-beaten cloak –

just like all good bogeymen should be—and with a long shaft he draws a line in the sand and says "this is where the river runs".

Ooh, ah, spooky, but wait it gets spookier. At the same time according to Helen Boris, from Uhart, a VW town thirty kays north of Clementine, her 3 year old son disappeared from his nursery . . .

Milligan killed the radio. Normally he enjoyed Jack O'Cash and his ironic comments about life on Mars, but that morning he'd had enough of the Riverman. He drove on for another ten minutes, thinking that maybe he was going crazy and he really needed to get back to Earth, sooner rather than later. He tried to remember what the penalties were for those who failed to serve their full three years. Then he spotted a figure in the distance, wearing a bright yellow singlet and scarlet shorts. Jim's still running, Milligan thought, and breathed more easily. But as the buggy drew closer he realized he was mistaken. Jim wasn't running at all. He just looked like he was. Milligan hit the brakes, and when the buggy came to a standstill, he turned the vid recorder on and adjusted the camera angle.

Jim McDonald was frozen in mid stride, the whole weight of his body balancing on his left leg which was as rigid as if it was made of bronze and had been cemented to the ground. His other leg, stretched behind him, was suspended in the air. As Milligan studied him closely, he could see Jim's eyes were half-open, as if they had been stopped in mid-blink. He waved his hands all around Jim's body, over the top of his head, down his shoulders, over his arms, and around his suspended leg, as if to reassure himself there were no strings attached.

Delicately, Milligan moved his hand up to touch Jim McDonald's cheek, wanting to know if he felt cold, needing to know if he was dead. But as his fingertips touched Jim's cool skin, it was as if he had animated a robotic creature, as if he had inserted a fresh battery into some child's immobile toy. In a flash Jim activated again. His right leg swung through its suspended motion and came down upon the ground. His left leg came up and he was off running, straight into Milligan's buggy, bruising his shins on the cruising bar as he collided with it. "What the hell?" he cried. "Where'd this stupid buggy come from?" Then he looked up and, when he saw Milligan approaching him, collapsed in a dead heap.

"Sweet Jesus," Jim said, sucking on a fruit juice tube as the buggy bounced its way back to Stan-Walkertown, "what got into you out there? You just about ran me down with this stupid buggy of yours."

"Sorry, Jim," Milligan said. "You came out of nowhere. It must have been the dust haze. I managed to stop the buggy in time, but you just seemed to stagger into it."

It was clear Jim had no recollection of what had happened to him, and Milligan wasn't about to tell him the truth; not until he got him back to Stan-Walkertown and checked out by their resident paramedic.

"That juice was great," Jim said, grabbing another tube out of the buggy's fridge. "Boy, what a run! It was so invigorating. I feel energized, like I could climb Olympus Mons. How's your sinuses, by the way?"

"Serena delivered on the anti-histamines," Max said, swallowing hard. "The sinuses are doing okay now."

"You know what, Max, I was thinking as I was running out there – a guy like you needs to settle down. About time you made the big commitment, started to look after yourself. I've noticed that Luba Loft's got the vacancy sign out and she's been waving it in your direction. She's a nice decent woman, Luba is. You and her, Max, could take some of the loneliness out of each other's lives. I'm sure you'd start to think Mars was a better place if you two hitched up."

"Yeah, Luba's a nice lady," Max said to be agreeable, but he was thinking he couldn't wait to show somebody what he'd captured on the buggy's vid. He could still see Jim frozen as a flesh and blood statue framed by the lilac sky.

Milligan burst through the airlock of the McDonalds' hovel, saying, "Serena, you have got to see this; it's amazing."

Serena was on the Marsnet again. She sat in front of the vid as naked as he'd left her. Somewhere in the hovel there was smoky incense burning and he immediately found his nostrils twitching.

Serena swiveled around in her chair. "You come back for some more, Max, or do you really have something amazing to show me?"

"Wait till you see what I captured on the buggy's vid," he said, taking care to look straight into Serena's eyes. "It's like the most incredible thing."

"And this morning wasn't?" Serena said, swiveling back to the Marsnet. "You disappoint me, Max. I've been sitting here thinking about nothing else since you left."

"I found Jim out in the desert, frozen like a statute. I dropped him at the Nelson's hovel for a check-up. Don't worry, he seems fine. He was even trying to talk me into marrying Luba Loft."

"Sounds like Jim's back to his old self, playing happy families. He's got this big thing about getting more babies born on Mars. Although just now he seems to have forgotten what it takes to make a baby. Which is where you come in. Like I said before you're . . . "

Just then the hovel's comlink buzzed.

When Serena answered it, Milligan could tell from all the 'sweethearts' and 'darlings' in her conversation that she was talking to Jim. He started to feel guilty again.

Serena closed the call off with a "Bye darling," and turned to Max: "Nelson's told Jim he's got some minor irregular electrical activity in his brain. He's under observation, but I'm not worried. Like you said, he seems fine. Nelson's a panic merchant anyway. So why don't you show me what's so amazing about the stuff you got on your buggy's vid."

Serena ran the buggy's vid three times before she made any comment, then she let out a short sharp breath.

"I told you," Milligan said.

"Yeah, you told me," Serena said. "But what do you think happened to him out there? It's freaking weird."

Milligan shrugged. "Maybe Nelson's right and it's some freak electrical activity in the brain that seized him up and I just happened along at the right time. Jim's got no memory of it all."

Serena ran the vid again and played around with the zoom. "I'm sure when I ran this thing the first time I saw a movement in the background like something else was going on. You probably didn't pay any attention to it because you were worried about Jim. Just like this morning when you left me so quickly, you were more concerned about Jim than me. Or were you thinking about Luba?"

"I was feeling guilty about what happened between us," Milligan said. "I still do."

"I'm not. If Jim's no longer interested and I am, what's a girl to do? Besides Jim's a big boy; he knows how to take care of himself," Serena said, as she continued to manipulate the video.

"Yeah, well," Milligan said, "but if I hadn't gone out there and brought him back, he'd probably still be there, frozen just like I found him, and maybe . . . "

"And I'm not saying I'm not grateful, Max." Serena cut and zoomed the vid again. "It's just that every now and again, I'd like to think, even in some small tiny way, I was the most important thing on this planet and if

Jim wants to run out to the Hellas Basin and . . . oh shit, look at this! Whoa, this is amazing! Max, I don't know how you could have missed it."

Max moved closer to the screen, so he could get a better look at the background of the buggy's vid. Serena had re-focused and sharpened the outlines nicely, but still it was only a very vague image, yet it seemed obvious now that somebody else had been out there when he'd rescued Jim. He watched the vid closely and saw what looked like some old guy in a shabby gray cloak with a long stick in his hand, walking across the background, using his stick to trace a line in the sand. Milligan placed a hand on Serena's bare shoulder.

This is where the river runs, Milligan thought to himself, recalling Jack O'Cash's radio show and feeling a cold chill creep up the back of his neck. He wondered if Serena had felt the chill as well, because just then she shrugged his hand away and seemed to become more somber. "I better get dressed and go and see how Jim is," she said.

Back in his hovel, with the morning still not yet done, Milligan sat in front of his own vid and tried to organize his job portfolio. He realized he still hadn't checked his VW units and, for all he knew, they could be sitting out there pumping carbon monoxide into the fledgling atmosphere. While he'd been out, he'd received a voicemail from Nixon Macloud, the director of sport and recreation on Mars. "Hey, man, there's a whole group of little children down by way of Sans Sou who wanna learn to play that there croquet game you're such an expert in. Their parents, they already build them a nice grass lawn, so take your balls and mallets and teach them well, brother."

Milligan loathed Nixon's exaggerated Jamaican accent. He was about as Jamaican as Milligan was Irish and there were rumors about whether or not his skin was synthetically tinted. Milligan recalled the time Nixon had told him he'd be delighted if all the little Martian children grew up with lovely Jamaican accents; it'd be a distinctive Martian voice he had argued. Milligan had told him he'd be delighted if they all grew up and wanted to go home. Still, Nixon was his boss and, if it was true that they had a decent patch of lawn then he should load his croquet balls and mallets into the buggy and head on over to San Sou straightaway. But at the same time he knew he really should be painting something. Pretty soon the Arts Council of Mars was going to start asking when he was going to deliver on his long awaited exhibition. Instead, he loaded the buggy's vid and watched himself, once again, circle the frozen figure of Jim McDonald.

He had almost decided, after he had watched it for the fifth time, that there was hardly any movement in the background at all, and what movement there was, a sudden and indistinct blur, could easily be explained by a dust devil suddenly blowing up. He was convinced right then that Serena had edited in those hokey images of the Riverman into her copy of the vid just to prove a point.

Milligan was wondering exactly what the point might be when the bell to his back trap rang. He found Serena standing there and looked past her, down the long tunnels of the airlock that connected their hovels beneath the ground, expecting to find Jim jogging along.

"How's Jim," he asked, as he ushered her in.

"Worse," Serena said. "He's gone into a delirium, keeps mumbling all the time. Nelson suspects some sort of weird viral infection. A high speed flitter from St Dympna's is on its way. There'll only be enough room for Jim and Nelson. I'll need to drive up to Clementine."

Milligan saw she was shaking, that her face was pale and the rings beneath her eyes seemed even darker than before. He put his arm around her shoulders. "I'm sure he'll be okay. Apart from an occasional bout of depression, Jim's the fittest guy I've ever met in my whole life. I'll drive you up to Clementine. I'm supposed to be on my way to Sans Sou anyway, so I can take you to Clementine and drop in at Sans Sou on the way back."

Following the same markers out of town as he had earlier that day, Milligan suddenly realized they were approaching the spot where he'd found Jim.

"It was here wasn't it?" Serena said. "I recognize the terrain from the vid."

"It could have happened anywhere," Milligan said. "I bet Jim's thermal suit failed. It's as simple as that. It's minus five out there now. It didn't get past one degree all day. I bet Nelson didn't even think about checking his thermal suit."

"You and I watched the buggy's vid together," Serena said. "We both know the Riverman was there. Jim met him. He told me he did in his delirium. He said the Riverman had a long staff in his hands and he traced it along the ground saying, "this is where the river runs". But he told Jim to go back, that he wasn't ready yet, told him to bring the children. And Jim told him there were no children to bring, and the Riverman smote him with his staff. That's why you found Jim all frozen like that."

Milligan sighed, wondering how he had got himself into this. God knew he had enough problems of his own. "I studied the original vid from the buggy again. The only thing moving in the background was a dust devil. When you were fiddling with the vid at your place, you cut the images of the Riverman in, didn't you? I guess they were symbolic representations you picked up from the Marsnet."

Serena was silent for a moment, neither confirming nor denying what Milligan had said. "You can't accept the Riverman, because you can't accept Mars," she finally said. "That, Max, is your problem. Jim always said that you had "I hate Mars" written all over your face."

Milligan said nothing. Jim was right. He drove on through the cold red dust, wondering what there was he needed to accept about Mars. Ten kays later, he finally replied. "Yeah, well, my muse has flown. Why do you think I'm working for the sports department otherwise?"

"Because you don't know the real Mars," Serena said, reaching out and touching his hand.

Milligan let hot breath escape his lips. "The real Mars is out there, all around us," he said, gesticulating with his left hand through the front window of the buggy, while he drove erratically with his right hand. "Mars is WYSWYG. What you see is what you get and that's all there is. But I need people, I need culture, I need great soaring cities and I need trees. Lots of trees, whole bloody jungles and forests full of trees. But above all I need water: oceans, seas, lakes. And rain! Even a muddy puddle would be nice. Not this dry dead desert, not all these rocks in every direction you look."

"It's an illusion," Serena said calmly. "It's taken me a long while to understand this, but I know now in my heart it's true. The Mars we believe we know, the Mars we have measured and calibrated and tried to conquer is not the Mars that really exists."

"Okay," Milligan said, "try explaining that to me." Serena smiled enigmatically and Milligan immediately regretted what he'd said. It was an open invitation for Serena to expound on her wacky theories again.

"Mars is revealing itself, little by little, here and there, to those who want to know her, to those who believe there must be something beyond this barren landscape that we are confronted with day after day. The Riverman, psychic vulture, the vampire jackal, are just a few of the Martian creatures we have made contact with so far . . . "

"Urban myths," Milligan said. "The place is dead, old and worn out, and we should forget about living here and go back to Earth."

"I don't think so," Serena said. "When we first looked at Mars we saw canals. We imagined it full of life—different to Earth but still thriving. What happened to the canals? What happened to the rivers that fed the canals? Where did they go?"

"I read somewhere," Milligan said, yawning, "that the canals were an optical illusion popularized by some guy called Lowell. Later with Mariner and the other probes, we got all those images of a dead planet. And those images haven't been proven wrong yet."

Serena rubbed her forehead. "Have you ever thought that maybe we got it right the first time? And it was only later, after we started to send up the probes, we got it wrong, and even though we're here now, we're still getting it wrong. Because we see what the Martians want us to see."

"Oh yeah, like we're talking about Martian mind control or something like that," Milligan said, smiling to himself.

"Something like that," Serena said. "Imagine this. On Earth we discover an alien race has been studying us, probing us. We already know from our own probing this race is inclined to be predatory; they are aggressive and expansionary by nature . . . . Actually, it's a lousy example because we'd just go out and fight them, blow their probes out of the sky and kill them when they tried to set up colonies, if we could. But the Martians haven't done that. They fed our probes false data; so all we would find was a dead world. But still we came and now they feed our minds the same false data."

"Okay," Milligan said, "but what happens when they find out humans like you know this stuff, what do they do? Keeping it theoretical, my best guess is that they'd probably kill people like you."

"No, Max," Serena said, "I believe they assimilate you. They let you become part of their society. They lift the veil of illusion."

"It's a nice story, Serena, but you left out the scary bit. What about the Riverman and all those kids who disappeared? The guy's like a pederast bogeyman, isn't he? He always wants the children."

"I've been thinking about it all day and I can see how it all makes sense," Serena said. "The Riverman takes the children first because they have fresh young minds open to accepting different cultures. He doesn't kill them, or molest them, like we used to believe. He helps them understand the true nature of Mars."

Milligan wanted to laugh out loud, but he kept that laugh to himself. There was something wonderful and tragic about Serena. He liked her, and knew that he could never laugh in her face, no matter how cynical he might become. Jim was also tragic and wonderful in his own way. He was beginning to understand their relationship.

Several hours later Max Milligan dropped Serena outside St. Dympna's beneath the milk-white sky of Clementine's dome. As Serena climbed out of the buggy, he said: "I hope Jim's okay. Tell him I'm going back to Earth as soon as I can. I've decided that. You and he should go home as well. It's better there. It really is."

Serena smiled at him as he drove away, blew him a little kiss and mouthed the words, "I love you, too."

Milligan drove through orderly streets of Clementine, paying little attention to its drab government buildings and apartment blocks, his eyes on the lookout for the first pharmacy. There was no way he was going to get hooked into any of Serena's crazy new age Martian mythos stuff. Better, much better, to throw in the towel, admit defeat in the face of the lifeless desolation, and head back home.

Half-an-hour later, with a new stash of anti-histamines onboard, Milligan left the Clementine airlock and drove the buggy out into the Martian desert once more. When he reached Sans Sou, he pulled his croquet balls and mallets from the buggy's boot, and was pleased and envious to find it was true what Nixon McLoud had said. They had managed to craft a fine croquet lawn. Certainly not up to the standard of a croquet lawn on Earth, but still a lawn where the balls had a chance of flying true and straight.

He stayed at Sans Sou much longer than he'd expected to. He had become temporarily enthralled by the enthusiasm of the kids in the local community and, when he departed late in the evening, he left behind his mallets and balls, promising to return in a few days.

As Milligan climbed into his buggy, he felt something akin to a sense of satisfaction. It had not been his best day on Mars, but neither had it been his worst. Out in the desert once more, following the tracks and markers back to Stan-Walkertown, he flicked the radio on. It was Jack O'Cash's evening cruising hour:

Hey, isn't that just great news about little Tommy Boris from Uhart, found safe and well, secreted away in a neighbour's larder scoffing a big bag of potato crisps. Hey, Riverman, there's one that got away from you, ya big old bogeyman, you. But if ya listening don't feel so sad, coz' I got a song for ya, a little something that I picked up out of last century's vaults and here on Mars it's making a big comeback. It's by some old dead guy called Nick Drake. It's number one on the Martian Hit Parade this week, and it's called . . . wait for it . . . River Man.

"Yeah, you big old bogeyman," Milligan said and chuckled as the song began to play. He was glad that the kid was safe and hadn't wandered off and fallen into a crevice, but then as if hit with a sudden sense of déjà vu, he caught a frozen figure in the buggy's headlights. Milligan swore and hit the brakes, too late. He saw the look of surprise in the old man's face as the buggy powered over him.

Bringing the buggy to a halt, he flicked the rear spotlights on and stumbled out into the desert in a panic, wondering what the old fool was doing out there in the dark, and where the nearest VW town was.

Milligan approached what looked like an old gray sack-cloth all crumpled on the desert floor. He touched him where he thought his shoulder was, saw a face emerge from the cloth and look at him.

"I know you," the old man said, climbing to his feet. "You're Max Milligan. The tortured artist. You hate Mars. I've been watching you."

Milligan backed away. He looked around, wondering if he was hallucinating. He'd been pumping the pseudo-ephedrine down his throat ever since he'd left Clementine. He studied the old man in his shabby cloak, realized he wasn't wearing a thermal suit beneath it. Impossible. The temperature had plummeted as soon as the sun went down.

"You must be cold," Milligan said. "How far's your town from here? Let me get you in the buggy. I'll take you home."

"I've come to take you home, Max Milligan," the old man said. "This is where you belong." Then he whipped a sturdy stick out from beneath his cloak and traced a line in the sand. "This is where the river runs."

Milligan felt a cold chill rush across his body, beneath his thermal suit. "You're the Riverman?"

The old man nodded. "Do you want to come with me, Max Milligan, or do you want to stay? I can show you the real Mars."

"You're an illusion," Milligan said, "an illusion. Nothing more."

The Riverman nodded slowly. "It is your choice," he said and walked away, disappearing quickly into the black folds of the desert.

Back inside his buggy, Milligan felt glad the hallucination was gone. He sat in the driver's seat, his hands on the controls, ready to go. The song Jack O'Cash was playing was nearing its end.

"What if I believed?" Milligan asked himself. "What would I lose?" Nothing he decided. Nothing at all, except a dogged determination to return to Earth.

He almost jumped out of his skin when he heard the thumping on the buggy's door. When he opened it, the Riverman was standing there. Milligan nodded and the Riverman put his arm around his shoulder and drew him in close beneath his cloak. "I will show you things you have never seen. Take your mask off, breathe the air."

Milligan hesitated. This might be the moment when he died. There wasn't enough oxygen in the Martian atmosphere. That's what he'd been told. They needed to keep the VW units pumping. But if he believed, if he truly believed. He pulled his mask from his face and for the first time in the two years breathed warm sweet air into his lungs. It tasted like the air of Earth. "I want to see the rivers and the canals. The water and the jungles. I want to see it all."

The Riverman kissed him on the forehead. "Come," he said, "let me show you."

Allotment
by David Tallerman

For some reason that the shuttle crew didn't bother explaining they couldn't drop me directly over DeLambre; instead we came down to the south, near the Zöllner crater.

By the time I'd disengaged myself from the landing module the Holier had already unpacked itself and was squatting on a rock nearby—the moment it saw me it leapt high into the air and disappeared over a rise to the east. It was pre-programmed with its destination and didn't need me while its self-diagnostics were giving the green light. From then on I saw it as a fast moving silhouette against the sky, or occasionally sat folded into a crouch, head rotating as it scanned and plotted route-markers.

So, the journey down to DeLambre was a lonely one. There's something unsettling about the moon—something to do with the silence and most of all with the emptiness. Maybe you think it isn't so barren these days? There are the pipes carrying water from the mines at the South Pole-Aitken Basin, there's the solar farm around the equator stretching all the way from the southern rim of the Mare Tranquillitatis to around the Reinhold crater. But understand, most of the time those huge pipes look like distant rivers, and the panels like lakes that are always on the horizon. By the fourth morning I was starting to feel that another day of tramping through that lunar desert would drive me crazy.

So maybe you'll believe me when I say that when I saw a house sitting right in the middle of DeLambre, I thought I'd finally snapped.

I stood there on the cusp of the crater looking down for perhaps half an hour, feeling like at any moment I'd wake up.

But the more I looked, the more real it seemed. It was something like an igloo, a dome of metallic fiber slung over a large framework with an airlock jutting from one side. It was built partly over the water pipe that runs through DeLambre, while power appeared to come from a nest of solar panels on the nearest rim and oxygen recycling to be handled by scrubbers jutting from the side opposite the door.

It all seemed sensible enough—except that it was on the moon, in the middle of the DeLambre crater, perhaps eighty kilometers from human contact and with no visible means of communication.

Maybe the loneliness had got to me after all.

Except that I wasn't quite alone; the Holier was squatted half a dozen meters from the shelter, its head steadily circling. And it was then that it hit me. I glanced at my map, just to be sure, but there was no question—this was the site. The dome sat in the center of where the DeLambre hotel was going to be built, just to the left of the lobby so far as I could tell.

A number of ideas ran through my head then: that this might be some kind of industrial sabotage, perhaps Nescorp trying to buy time for a second attempt; or perhaps the dome-house was left over from some early NASA experiment; perhaps it was an independent research station . . .

I broke into a run. Actually, forgetting about the low gravity I tried to run, leapt ten meters off the rim of the crater and ended up sliding and stumbling the rest of the way. But I kept going, staggering along until I was within about fifty meters of the mysterious shelter.

Then I stopped, almost tripping up as I did so.

My first thought was that there was a ghost standing outside the entrance of the igloo. The ghost was wearing a dilapidated moon-suit, and it was waving something at the Holier, some kind of tool. As I skidded to a halt the apparition's head turned, and obviously I'd been spotted because it began to drift towards me. I'd never seen anybody move so naturally in a moon-suit, old and battered as this one was, and the figure reached me in seconds.

It was only then that I realized the object it was carrying, the thing it had been pointing at the Holier, was a gun—an old shotgun, a museum piece.

Just as I was starting to recover slightly, there was a crackling inside my helmet. It took me a few moments to realize that it was the intercom, which I hadn't used since I'd landed or even realized was turned on. When a voice followed the static, I nearly jumped out of my skin.

The voice said, "What do you think you're doing on my land, son?"

The speaker was male and the accent was English, but thick and slurred, as if he hadn't had to make conversation in quite some time. The best reply I could think of was, "What?"

"My land, what are you doing on it? Come on; don't play silly buggers with me."

"The whole of the DeLambre crater is the property of Fennick-Ward. What are *you* doing here?"

"This is my home, son, and I don't know anything about any 'Fennick-Ward.'"

"I assure you," I said, "Fennick-Ward Inter-Global Holdings have bought up this whole crater. I'm here to do a survey of the sight. Well, the robot," and I pointed to the Holier, "is here to survey it, I'm here to baby-sit the robot."

Sounding a touch less aggressive but still training the ancient gun on me, he replied, "Perhaps we'd better discuss this inside?"

Pointing cautiously at the shotgun, I asked, "Would that thing work out here, do you think?"

I could just make out a grin through the tinted mask of his helmet. "I haven't the faintest. Do you want to try it?"

"No. No, I don't."

"Well then, come on in. I'll make us a cup of tea and you can tell me about this 'Fennick-Ward' bloke who thinks he owns my house."

Once through the airlock, my new acquaintance began to struggle out of his antique suit. I followed his lead, taking the opportunity to have a look around—easily done since there were no interior walls, just a single open-plan space. The only door was opposite the entrance, and I guessed must lead to a toilet. There was a shower cubicle near the door, with pipes leading out to the water recycler, and next to that a simple kitchen area. The center was obviously the main living space, with a table and chair and around that a hydroponics garden, providing fresh food and presumably also helping the scrubbers clean the air. But what struck me as pretty strange at the time was that most of the remaining space was taken up with bookcases. Fully half the wall housed a huge library, made up mostly of classic fiction with a few science texts thrown in apparently at random.

I was thinking about having a more thorough look when my host called out to me, his voice completely different without the backdrop of radio hiss, "Tea's up, son." And I turned around to the sight of an elderly man in faded jeans and checked shirt proffering a battered cup in my direction.

This was more of a shock than you'd think—that he was so old. The idea of this grey-haired old man living all alone on the moon stopped me in my tracks. I took the cup and stood there holding it at arms length, as if I wasn't sure what to do with it.

Eventually he said, "I hope you're not going to waste that. Do you know how hard it is to make a proper cup of tea on the moon?"

I laughed awkwardly and took a careful sip, trying not to spill boiling liquid over myself in the low gravity. It tasted good and brought me round a bit. We stood there in silence, drinking our tea, for perhaps five minutes. When I'd finished the old man took my cup, offered his hand, and said, "Richard Berrick. Since you're a guest, I suppose you can call me Rick."

"John Harcourt," I replied, shaking the hand.

"And the thing outside?"

"It's an AD Holier, model 09 batch 11, a surveying robot designed for low gravities. It's harmless. It doesn't do much except jump and sit, and it won't be doing any jumping now that we're here."

"Which brings us to my earlier question, Mr. Harcourt—what *are* you doing here? And what makes you think you own this land?"

"Not me, Rick, I'm just a contractor, a Robotics Engineer. Fennick-Ward Inter-Global Holdings brought me in because there aren't many specialists in off-world robotics around. They want to build the first lunar hotel—"

Berrick cut me off in mid-sentence. "A *hotel*? Oh, bloody hell. Who on earth would want to come here?"

"Well, tourists. And—you did."

"Does this look like a hotel to you, son?"

I had to admit it didn't.

"That's because it's a hermitage. I came here to get away from it all, catch up with my reading," and he waved towards the library, "not to show around a bunch of bloody sight-seers."

"A hermitage?" I didn't know what to say, the whole situation suddenly seemed too insane for words. Finally, I began, "All right. You're here, there's no point arguing with that. What I want to know is why you think you own the DeLambre crater?"

"Not the crater," he said, "just this house."

"Just the house?"

"No, that's not quite right. Four acres, I think it was, but I'm not sure exactly where the—hold on, I've got some papers somewhere." He walked to a small cabinet by the bookcases, opened the top drawer, and began rummaging through a mound of paperwork inside.

"Wait," I said, "Rick, could you please just tell me what you're doing here?"

Now, the whole of Richard Berrick's long-winded and tangential answer to that question occupied most of the rest of the day. We sat drinking tea until my bladder felt like it would burst, and he explained how he'd come to be living all alone on the moon. I wouldn't want to bore you with a verbatim account of that conversation even if I thought for a minute I could remember it, but the gist goes like this:

In his former life, Berrick had been astonishingly rich. It hadn't done much for him. He'd been born into more money than he could ever have needed and had worked out pretty early that it was never going to buy him happiness. Happiness for him meant peace, quiet, a good book, not having to worry about properties and businesses that he didn't want or care about.

He'd muddled along like that for nearly sixty years, living alone, trying to ignore his wealth as much as possible. Then one birthday an acquaintance, who had probably spent months puzzling over the question of what you buy for someone who literally has everything, gave him the deeds to four acres of land on the moon, along with the mineral rights and a map showing their location.

It's not quite as ridiculous as it sounds. Back then, before anybody had given much thought to land-rights for an extraterrestrial body that only a dozen or so people had ever set foot on, someone had hit on a novel scam. They'd filed a declaration of ownership for the entirety of Earth's solar system. Then they'd sold it off in one-acre packages, starting with the moon and working outwards. Legally it just about held water, but nobody had paid much attention, or taken it seriously; it was a joke, a gimmick. Who was ever going to use a of plot of land on the moon?

But Rick had the money, and the resources, and he had fingers in enough pies to work out pretty quickly that what he had in mind was possible, though it might take years. He'd poured his finances into research and new technologies, he'd bought or manufactured or had invented everything he was likely to need.

And eventually he had booked a one-way flight on a private shuttle. He'd paid extra and they'd dropped him and his equipment in DeLambre, near his four acres. That had been years ago—Rick was pretty vague about dates, and he couldn't tell me exactly how long he'd been there. But he told me that he'd read about two thirds of that huge library, which gives some indication.

The next day I left Rick and DeLambre. We had a window booked in on a comm's satellite so that I could report back and set a time for my recovery, but the nearest transmitter was at the Tranquillitatis solar station in Sabine crater. That meant another four days travel, alone this time—the Holier had finished its survey program and turned itself off. I figured that the presence of a large dome in the middle of its survey region had confused it, but there wasn't much I could do about that. Rick, meanwhile, refused to accompany me, insisting that the whole affair was 'none of his business.' But I suspected that he was actually a little lonely, for all he said about his hermitage. When I left he told me I was welcome to stay with him while I waited to be collected, so long as I kept out of the way and didn't make any fuss. I didn't even consider it at the time. One night with the old lunatic had been enough, and I was convinced that I'd be getting off this rock as soon as was humanly possible.

That thought made my second journey easier than the first. The traveling was still tough, still exhausting, and lonely, but the thought of home kept me going. I could always see the solar station, as well, a wall of light rising up from the lunar rock, growing fractionally nearer with each passing hour. I made good time, reaching Tranquillitatis station at mid-afternoon on the fourth day.

The station itself was some distance from the nest of solar panels that it controlled via landlines sunk in the regolith, a flat grey building almost hidden inside Sabine crater. The staff were expecting me and even seemed pleased to see a new face. My satellite window wasn't until early the next morning so we sat and talked, played poker, and finished up a bottle of scotch that someone had smuggled in. I asked them about Rick Berrick but they hadn't so much as heard of their neighbor and were as surprised as I'd been to find out about the crazed hermit living out in DeLambre crater. They promised to look in on him and take over some fresh supplies. Finally, they took me to the comm's room, which was tiny and obviously doubled as a store cupboard. They'd pre-programmed the console, so they left me alone to wait. At one in the morning exactly, the screen blinked to life and a voice said, "Mr. Harcourt?"

The picture was distorted by interference but I recognized the face. "Mr. Colpeck."

"We have fifteen minutes, Harcourt. Give me your sit-rep please."

"It's a little complicated—"

"Fifteen minutes and that's it."

So, I launched into an explanation. I tried my best to keep it short and I'd planned it in my head during the walk, but somehow it ended up being pretty garbled anyway.

Colpeck's response, when I finally reached some kind of conclusion, was, "Damn it, Harcourt." He glanced away from the screen. "We've only got a minute left. I'll try to buy another window for tomorrow. Damn it, we only asked you to survey the site. We only asked you to look after the robot while the robot surveyed the sight! Be here tomorrow at the same time." And the screen flickered and went dead.

The crew understood about my staying for another day, even though I was using up valuable food and space; but I felt that I was beginning to outstay my welcome. The next morning I made my way back to the comm's room. But it got to one o'clock and nothing happened. It was half an hour later, just as I was beginning to think about giving up, that the screen flickered on and Colpeck's voice said, "Harcourt? You'd better be there, this cost the company a lot of money."

"I'm here."

"Then listen very carefully. We've been making enquiries. The legality of this moon-selling deal was questioned at the time but nobody found a hole in it, and we haven't either, yet. Some swindler called Hope logged a claim with the US and Russian governments, and what was then the UN General Assembly. He argued that the legislation on owning interstellar bodies covered nations and governments, but it didn't say anywhere that one person couldn't own the whole solar system. The Outer Space Treaty in 2011 changed that and nobody gave a thought to Hope—but his claim still stands."

"What does that mean for Rick Berrick?"

"That we don't know yet. Our lawyers are onto his lawyers, but it looks like he thought something like this might happen. He left them a sizeable amount of money to make sure he was left alone."

I sighed. "Look, can't you just build somewhere else?"

"We've already bought that site."

"Illegally."

"That's a matter of opinion, Mr. Harcourt, and very much open to contention. And, as I believe I just finished telling you, we *are* contesting it."

"Anyway," I said irritably, "what has any of this got to do with me?"

"Ah, well I was coming to that."

There was something in his tone that I didn't like. "Colpeck—I've done the survey, I baby-sat your robot. I'm out of this now."

"The thing is—we need a man on the ground, so to speak. You know Berrick, you know the site, you can maintain the very expensive robot that we're paying you to look after."

"No! Whatever you've got in mind, no, I've done my job; I've done what I came out here to do."

"That, Harcourt, isn't *strictly* the case."

"What the hell do you mean?"

"What I mean is you were contracted to watch the Holier while it surveyed the DeLambre crater. Now, as long as there's a house there, the Holier can't do that. As long as the robot hasn't done its job you haven't. And since this is the case, and given that your further employment remains at the companies' discretion, and particularly taking into account that your contract runs for five years . . . "

I gazed at the screen, aghast. Five years! I had to contact my lawyer, find a way to get out of it. But then the enormity of the situation hit me. I was on the moon—I couldn't contact anyone or anything. I was the indentured slave of Fennick-Ward for the next five years of my life. "When I get back, Colpeck—you'll pay for this."

"That's as may be, Mr. Harcourt."

I gave a long and very bitter sigh, and asked, "What do you want me to do?"

"Try to talk him into moving. We'll pay for it and do the work."

"He won't go for that."

"Then convince him."

"He's a stubborn old nut, Colpeck, he's been there for god knows how many years and he's not going to budge for you or me or anyone."

Colpeck looked as if he was about to tell me what he thought of my opinion. But instead, something seemed to occur to him, and he said, "He's over ninety, you know."

"That doesn't surprise me."

"And he's been living alone for years, with no medical care. How does his health seem to you, Harcourt?"

"I don't know. Good, I guess, considering."

"Still, he isn't going to live forever."

"I hope you're not suggesting what I think you're suggesting."

"I simply mean what I say—he won't live forever. He's probably not likely to last another five years, wouldn't you agree? You might be home sooner than you think."

"I'll be home by Christmas, Colpeck. I'll find a way."

"And where have we heard that before? In the meantime I'd try to make the best of it if I were you. And I'd convince him to move. Because when he goes—so do you."

And the screen pulsed and went dark, leaving me alone with my thoughts.

You can imagine how pleasant they were.

I couldn't stay at the Tranquillitatis station; they barely had room for themselves. They were sympathetic, they said they'd try to get a message out and maybe even get me a place on the shuttle at the next rotation. They told me to keep in touch. Finally, I managed to talk them into arranging me a short comm's window, so that I could upload this message—and we left it at that. I set off for DeLambre around lunchtime. The journey back was the most depressing of my entire life.

When I arrived in DeLambre everything was how I'd left it. The Holier was still sitting in the dirt, turned off, although at some point Rick had thrown a tarp over it to protect it from micrometeorites. I made my way through the airlock and found Rick slouched in a chair, reading a huge tome that turned out to be a complete works of Shakespeare. His first words to me were, "I had a feeling you might be back."

I stayed with Rick for two weeks before starting back to Sabine crater to send this. We got on okay, I guess, you might even say that we've become friends—he's amazing in his way, incredibly intelligent and freethinking, and of course uniquely well-read. But there was always the question of him moving. At first I tried subtle hints, then gentle persuasion, and eventually our conversations ended up as full-blown arguments. The upshot of it is he wants to stay where he is, and nothing I say or do is going to move him. He's probably the most stubborn man I've ever met. And I was wrong, by the way—his health isn't 'pretty good,' it's amazing. He may well outlive me.

So there it is: Rick Berrick won't leave, he won't die, and he left enough money with his lawyers to tie any legal case up in red tape for at least the next five years. There's nothing I can do here short of killing the man—which isn't something I'd consider, by the way, before Colpeck gets any ideas.

The company is paying me to live on the moon with an insane old hermit, drinking tea and reading works of classic literature; it's paying me to go slowly mad on this cold, barren rock. There's nothing else I can think to say, except that I hope someone has taken the time to read this—because I really would like to come home now.

Rats
by Graham Fielding

"No point in reading 'em, they'll be years old," Tush said.

He stood atop a pile of bricks patting the rusty neck of a bent streetlight like it was a giraffe. Little Vern ignored him anyway, pulling the magazine out of the strongbox. He pawed at the well-dressed men and alien females ignoring the print he couldn't read anyway on the pages that had lasted such a remarkable amount of time.

"Is this how it looks in Australia, Mr. Tush?"

Tush slid carefully down the slag heap and balanced on the protruding armrest of a sofa next to Vern. This way they were face to face. He pulled the magazine from Vern's hand and tossed it aside.

"It's something like that, but in Australia they don't bother with the magazines because everybody gets a place in the spotlight, not just a chosen few. That way no one feels left out. You'll see soon enough when the planes come."

"Is the sky brown over there?"

"No, it's blue believe it or not. Blue, and you can't even look at the sun. Too bright."

He feigned squinting at the sun but they were both able to look at the pale white ball in the sky without problem. Drums beat in the distance and Tush said, "Come on."

The drums were coming from the north so Tush led them along the railway lines, now clearer than the roads. But they had not come this way in a year or more and Tush had misjudged the state of the lines, and where the still intercity carriage sat in their path brambles had grown through the rusty wire fences and pushed up against its sides blocking them right through. Somebody had stenciled a marker over the train's intercity logo: XO

And daubed underneath in primary colors: COC

The first marker was at least twenty years old and from the rescue crews after the original outbreaks: Scores dead, entry sealed against contagion. The second marker, from more recent times: Property no longer viable. This was in the parlance of the scavengers who liked to set clear territorial boundaries. Their drums were now much louder.

"Up and over," Tush said.

He placed Vern's limbs on the bottom rungs of the service ladder, frantically staying *mogadon* calm despite the drum beat. The carriage windows, remarkably unbroken, had been misted over by time.

On top, Tush took the lead and Vern clutched on his lower back. The going was slow, he kept them to the middle, probing each step with his toe for weak panels. One false step and they would be sitting amongst the rush hour business types who had taken this last journey decades ago.

Vern's foot crashed through the shell and he disappeared up to his waist.

"Help me please help me, don't let me fall in with the dead people, don't let them touch my legs. Please help me, mum, mum, mum."

Tush looked at the Torso and arms and big red face for several seconds, thinking how he might hush it all. Then he gripped him up, cradling Vern's big head to stem the bellows.

"I won't leave you. I have nowhere to go. Hush now. Do you want the scavengers to find us?"

Vern would only descend the ladder at the other end with a sack over his head. Tush carried one of these as a matter of course. He mentally noted that the brambles were on the cusp of swallowing the tracks for good. Dry and dead they still grew. The last clear route from the city almost gone.

He moved Vern along by the scruff as the sun crept lower to prevent him stopping to gawp at the dark tower in the distance. The stumps orange and green with rust and lichen. The Arndale Centre still had a drape around the top that said in thick red lettering: Healthy Survivors at the M.E.N. Arena, some sick. No radiation danger. Air men please help.

The Arena had burned down long ago.

They reached the Suburban Semi just as the dusk turned obnoxious black; obnoxious because it served as invitation for a million bow-legged scavengers to try it on. But they got in safely and Tush drew the thick black curtains before lighting the oil lamps so they would not draw attention to themselves. Vern took it on himself to get on the roof and Tush could hear him thumping around up there lining up the letter 'H' Tush had created from stones and rope and Vern believed was a helipad. This was harmless in its way, and gave Tush a chance to prepare dinner. Whilst he boiled a pan of water and apples on the *calor* gas he skinned and gutted a rat he'd pulled from his tin traps. Vern was terrified of rats, which was unfortunate in this day and age. Tush wasn't exactly enamored by them either, but they had to eat and rats always fell in the traps.

"Rabbit," Tush said handing a bowl to Vern.

" . . . but what if the Australians come at night and can't see our helipad?" Vern asked, mouth full of rat goulash.

"The Aussies prefer to travel by daylight, they don't like the night."

"I don't like it either. Do you think that drumming sounded close before?"

"No. Don't be silly, the scavengers only dare come so far out."

"I hope the Aussies come soon."

Vern went to his nest of sacking and sheepskin. Tush sat on his wooden chair and took his carving knife and a block of wood from his box. He was carving the Sydney Opera House from memory. He had never been to Australia. He had planned to go once. His wife and child were there. He closed his eyes for a minute. When he opened them he saw stars, but he hadn't cried. His memory wasn't so good and the thing didn't seem to look how he wanted. So what? It probably didn't exist anymore, either. He'd have heard something. Vern stirred in the night and Tush soothed his brow, but the hulk was having a good night tonight, often he would shout out names and places Tush didn't recognize or say phrases in an accent that was more cultured and eloquent than he used in the day to day. Tush gave up on the model. He wasn't going to finish it. The drums were there in the background. That was a first.

He got his hour of sleep, and coughed up the spools of bile into a hole in the floorboards. Another day to fill. This was Vern's alarm clock and Tush heated up the remaining goulash. He added all the Paprika they had left.

Vern's ears pricked up at the continual drumming.

"Eat up. It's a special day. In fact, we best stay around the house. You should go up and light the beacons on the helipad after brekky."

"You mean?"

"Yep, I heard them sweep over last night in their spy planes. They flashed their lights to say they would be coming today. About time if you ask me."

Watching Vern lighting the big candles with his tinder box Tush thought: twenty years old and just look at what he is.

"Make it as bright as you can, Vern. No need to worry about the scavengers today. The Australians will fly over and scatter them."

Tush placed the mutant Sydney Opera House on the chair in the center of the room. He put the knife back in the box. He removed a small bronze revolver. He drew the curtains. He extinguished two of the oil lamps but left the last to burn.

"Vern, come and see this a second."

Inside: "What is it? It's dark."

"I just want to show you something. Look closely at what's on the chair."

Vern looked in the box, kneeling.

At Lunchtime the lights from the Stone Helipad lit up and caught on the dry trees and fences. Soon the house began to burn. No one came to help.

Gift Time

by Lawrence M. Schoen

Every year on the morning of his birthday Michael visits a rented storage room in Chicago and uses one of the time machines he keeps there. He unlocks the door, picking up a large parcel that had been left on the threshhold. A motion detector triggers the lights as he enters, and he sets the package aside before pausing to gaze upon the objects of his collection. The big ones fill most of the space, like the Wellsian Chair o' Time and the fuel efficient chronocycle. This year he squeezes his way past them, whacking a blue-jeaned shin on one of the fins of the phonebooth-shaped Chronstanzer. Hopping in pain, he nearly topples the tank containing the fourth-dimensional specters that can be worn like intangible opera cloaks to let you slip between the ages. Nearly, but not quite, and Michael manages to right it with minimal sloshing of heavy water.

He makes it through to the back, removing his leather jacket along the way; the room is warm and he won't need it when he's going. Before him a shelf overflows with the more conveniently sized devices in his collection. Here are the designer time belts, the travel rings, the headbands and medallions and ear cuffs that respond to spoken commands or thought projection or a dozen other biofeedback-style manipulations. Michael ignores all of these, and instead opens the lid of a headstone-sized box carved from the molar of an animal that would be extinct for a million years if its initial existence hadn't been wiped from the time line even earlier.

The box contains the smallest elements of Michael's collection. Here is where he keeps his packet of temporal suppositories, a vial of nanites that shouldn't exist in our reality, a grain of proto-matter stolen from the Big Bang, and similar artifacts that can be used to bend, warp, or otherwise manipulate time, and which might get lost if he left them out on one of the shelves.

He selects a tiny bottle and pops the cap off, revealing an ochre dust within. Michael licks the tip of one finger and shoves it inside, shaking the bottle so he gets a good coating. Then he removes his finger, sucks it clean, and puts the bottle away in the box. And waits. He doesn't have to wait long. The bits of alien virus transform from their dormant spore form in the warm wetness that describes Michael's trachea and stomach lining. Tendrils of thought reach him, helpless but daring to hope that perhaps this time it will end differently.

Set us free, the virus's cellular group mind pleads. *Do not do this thing.*

"We'll see," says Michael as his body acquires new senses and abilities. He reaches out, tugs on some kind of quantum strand that didn't exist within his perceptions moments before, and plunges elsewhen to celebrate his birthday.

"It works," shouts Guangyi. She says it in Mandarino, a tonal language that is politically forbidden on Earth. But that makes sense because she's standing in her clean lab at the university in New Chengdu, deep below the moon's airless surface. She's the Linus Torvalds chair of Unanticipatory Physics. The year is 2223 and she has good reason to be shouting. She's just invented time travel.

"Are you sure?" asks Michael, stepping out from behind the strands of the past. The telepathic powers of the viral colony that has taken up residence in his duodenum provides him with the means to speak and understand a Chinese dialect that doesn't yet exist in his world. "Have you tested it conclusively?"

"What? Who? How did you get in here?"

Michael smiles sheepishly, "The Provost sent me. I'm to report on your results, to determine if your funding is to be cut."

"Are you insane?" Guangyi's expression leaps from its recent elation through disbelief and into fear. "I've just made the greatest breakthrough in the history of human endeavor."

"Show me the device," Michael says, and he holds out his hand.

He's met with a quizzical, confused look, and realizing his mistake continues the motion of his hand and arm, indicating that the scientist proceed.

Guangyi nods slowly, perhaps taken aback by his strange attire of denim and cotton, extravagant materials not readily available on the moon, let alone in ther sterile enviornment of her lab. She leads him through a door into a painfully bright room that vibrates with light and sound. A meter wide magnetic Klein bottle hangs in mid-air, all corruscating bands of green plasma and radial gravities. Inside the bottle, swimming in nutrient saturated water, a school of guppies lives and grows and reproduces and dies, each generation flashing by in under a minute.

Michael nods. It's not time travel per se, but it can lead there easily enough. "So, you've excellerated a portion of the time stream. Congratulations."

Guangyi beams, and nods vigorously, clearly pleased that her work has been grasped so fully and quickly. "Thank you, thank you very much."

"I'm going to need all of your notes," says Michael. "All of your apparati, and computer records." He points to the cycling fish in their bottle. "And of course I'll be taking this too."

"You're not from the Provost's office," says Guangyi, and there's no question in her tone, other than the usual tones of Mandarino.

"I'm not even from this century," says Michael. He takes a gaudy, golden bracelet from the pocket of his jeans and hands it to her. The costume jewelry is adorned with knobs composed of paste gemstones. "Put this on, and press the ruby."

"Who are you?" says Guangyi, even as she dons the bracelet. The fake ruby depresses and surrounds the twenty-third century physicist with a nimbus of atmosphere and gravity.

Michael takes her hand and extends his temporal manipulations to encompass her. "I'm someone who's trying to keep you from destroying humanity."

Then the lab is gone, and they are standing on an open plain of dried and pitted mud. The sky is a sickly, jaundiced hue that defies color, neither sunlit nor dark. Nothing moves, nothing appears to exist, except Michael in his blue jeans and button down oxford and Guangyi in her university regulation clean suit.

"We're not on the moon!"

"This is Earth," says Michael. "Earth of the future. The future created by your work. People will take your research and destroy everything. The atmosphere is unbreathable, the very soil toxic. Nothing lives here anymore. There's no one left. Not here, not on the moon, not on any of the outer colonies. You destroy it all."

"I've done nothing!" Guangyi wails, the marvel of her bracelet keeping her healthy and whole, unnoticed. "I've only just completed the initial trials. I've done nothing."

"Yet," says Michael. "But in time, you will." He steps away, his feet kicking up clouds of dust or ash or radicalized polymer molecules big enough to be seen by the naked eye. Whatever it is is death, and it billows after him as he walks across the desolation that he says is the future.

She runs after.

"Wait! Why have you brought me here? Time is immutable. If this has happened, then there's nothing I can do to change it."

Michael stops. He turns in place, allowing the particulate to settle, letting her catch up to him. "Math is immutable. Physics is immutable. Time is just . . . Time. It only seems to be otherwise because you're using those tools to apprehend it."

"But how else could one—"

He waves her questions away. "That I'm here, that I've come and shown you this, has to answer everything. You must stop your research, give me your notes, your records, and your prototype. It's the only way."

A thousand explanations run through Guangyi's mind, and Michael's virally enhanced perceptions capture fragments of them. Alternate reasons, justifications, excuses for keeping her research, for denying him. But in the end they fall away, as he knows they will. He sees it in her eyes when she decides. With an act of will Michael lets the natural inclination of Time pull Guangyi back to the moment and location of her lab in the instant he plucked her out. He's carried along in the current, sparing his relucant viral allies the effort.

Silently, Guangyi begins powering down her gear. She disconnects the magnetic Klein bottle from the monitoring equipment and hands it to Michael. The bottle itself continues to run, the guppies within racing along at a faster flow of time. He lets it hang in the air, supported by its own energies.

"Your records," says Michael, and follows her back into the outer lab. A few buttons are pressed and soon she is giving him a carbonized sphere containing compressed nitrogen isomers that code terabytes of informaton. It's roughly the diameter of his nostril. Michael lacks the hardware to decode, or the intellect to comprehend, any of it. It doesn't matter, so long as he takes it from her.

He leaves her the bracelet. Its power supply has burned out the components that provided life support, but it will serve as proof that all this really occurred, a souvenir to remind her to keep her word.

"What am I to tell the Provost?" Her tone is understandably plaintive.

"Are all your notes and other physical records here?" he asks, and when she nods he continues. "Destroy the lab. Let it all be consumed by fire or plasma or what you will. Blame whom you please, or let it be a mystery. The work will be gone, and no one will fault you for being too distraught to start over. But you'll know you've saved humanity."

"Will I see you again?"

Michael shakes his head and taps the bottle he has positioned and tethered on his shoulder. "When I leave with this, the timeline closes after me. I couldn't come back, unless you built another machine. And I wouldn't, because that would mean I'd already failed."

Deep in his alimentary canal the viral intelligence responsible for Michael's godlike abilities begin their internal journey toward his colon; time is running out. He smiles at Guangyi, a warm and weary expression. Smiles are hardwired into primates, they span all cultures and times, and Michael's communicates sorrow and gratitude and the acknowledgment of sacrifice. He's spent many hours practicing this particular smile in front of a mirror.

Guangyi's own expression is less subtle, more tragic. But Michael turns away before he has to see it, not trusting to his diverticulitis to slow the viral beings that desire nothing more than to strand him in this instant of timespace.

It's not simply a matter of returning to the moment he left. The sloshing guppies in their bottle pull against the flow of time, anchored in that other when by no fewer than seventeen dimensions. Time has its own brand of inertia, but by his own point of reference today is Michael's birthday, and the collection in his storage room is proof that even temporal inertia can be overcome.

In actuality, Guangyi's artifact exerts less pull than expected and Michael overshoots slightly in time and space. Either that, or the virus manages a minor coup as it succumbs to attacks by the bacteria in his large intestine. He arrives a week before he left, in a strip mall somewhere in Philadelphia, hundreds of miles from Chicago.

No one notices his arrival. It's late afternoon, and there's one of those packing/shipping shops within shouting distance. Michael repositions the weightless bottle so it appears as though he needs both hands to carry it, and walks into the shop. Ten minutes later he walks out, unencumbered. He hails a cab and takes it to a hotel near the the airport, gets a room, and then retires to the bar. He orders two drinks. The first kills off any lingering traces of the intelligent virus in his system; the second serves as a vehicle for the GABAergic pills he takes from his front pocket and dissolves in his glass.

The cocktail will play havoc with the glutamate receptors in his brain, disrupting consolitation of memory. He watches people come and go, buys drinks for several of them, and eventually invites a woman back to his hotel room, telling her it's his birthday. When he awakens in the morning, he remembers nothing of the day before. There's a strange woman in his bed. He showers, dresses in yesterday's clothes, and leaves the woman sleeping.

Michael checks out of the hotel, and takes their complimentary shuttle to the airport. Instead of returning to Chicago, he flys to California to visit his mother like a dutiful son. Uneventful days pass, six of them, and he returns to Chicago, his flight landing early in the afternoon of his birthday.

Friends are throwing him a party that night, but before heading home Michael detours to visit a storage facility where he rents a small room. It's where he keeps his collection of time machines. He unlocks the door, and as the motion detectors light up the room he finds a large parcel waiting for him.

Michael grins as he opens the box. There's some kind of enormous bottle inside, folding in upon itself, with tiny fish hurtling through it, around and around. To his practiced eye the telltale signs of temporal mechanics are obvious. He has nothing like it in his collection. Michael pulls the thing free of its wrapping and Styrofoam jimmies. He marvels as it hangs there in midair, the fish swimming obliviously. It's easily the best present he's ever had.

"Happy birthday to me," he says.

Author Notes

Drew Arrants is a retired psychiatrist and military flight surgeon. During his 21 years as an Air Force officer, he was stationed in Europe, Asia, and the Middle East, and became fluent in two foreign languages. He is currently living on the outskirts of Phoenix, Arizona, where he occasionally writes short stories. His fictional works have been published in genre magazines and anthology collections in the United Kingdom and America.

Adele Cosgrove-Bray began writing poetry at the age of fourteen. She went on to write and illustrate a monthly dream analysis column for *Your Future* magazine before becoming more interested in Dark Fantasy fiction. She was elected Chair for Riverside Writers in 2003, a post she still holds. Adele has worked as an editor, a library assistant, a photographer and a potter. She has lived on the Wirral peninsula in Cheshire, England, since June 2000, where she writes full-time and shares life with her husband Richard, two cats and two dogs. Visit her website: www.adelecosgrove-bray.com.

Geraint D'Arcy lives in Cardiff, Wales, where he divides his time between his job, poetry, Ph.D. studies, and science-fictional flights of fancy. He has had science fiction published by *All Possible Worlds, Jupiter SF* and *Twisted Tongue.* Geraint performs poetry regularly wherever and whenever he can, being most recently published in the prestigious British literary magazine *Roundyhouse*; his poetry and prose collection *Poetry in a Louder Voice* was released for general purchase in August this year by Spiral Bound Press.

Lawrence Dagstine has been writing dark, pulpy tales of science fiction, fantasy, and horror since 1996. His short fiction has graced *many* a paying, print, and on-line venue within the genre field. Over 310+ publication credits in twelve years, but he still calls it his little side hobby. Sam's Dot Publishing is releasing his first collection in late 2008-early 2009. Considered by friends a die-hard scifi geek and horror fanatic, he comes from Brooklyn, New York, where he lives with his beautiful wife and son, dreaming the great writer's dream... Visit his website at: www.lawrencedagstine.com.

After a couple of years spent traveling in central Europe and Turkey, **Tristan S. Davenport** has returned to the womb of the university. He is pursuing a doctorate in cognitive science at the University of California, San Diego. His fiction has also appeared in *Chiaroscuro* (www.chizine.com) and *Postcards from Hell.*

Graham Fielding lives in Derbyshire, England. When not reading the entire SF Masterworks range, he's trying to broker a reasonable deal with the devil for his soul.

Ginny Gilroy is an IT professional living and working in New York City. As a certified expert in both Mac and PC operating systems, she refuses to take sides in the great computer debate. She is currently employed by a major corporation. Any accidental resemblance to any person, or situation in "The Secret Life of Jane Gray" is purely concidential. Visit her website at SingularStories.com.

C. E. Grayson has been a gas station attendant, sold violent video games over the phone, hunked moldy cheese at a dairy plant, and most alarmingly, taught middle school. He is currently trying to transform himself into the kind of geek that can actually do the world some good. His website is at cegrayson.wordpress.com and his online serial is running at meremortals.wordpress.com. He lives in the Superior region of California (a.k.a. the State of Jefferson; look it up) with his longsuffering wife and two energetic children.

Erin M. Hartshorn is a desert rat transplanted to a humid climate. Her ideal home has bookcases in every room. She is a moderator at Forward Motion for Writers, an online writers community. Each year, she also indulges in NaNoWriMo, acting as regional Municipal Liaison. Her fiction has appeared in a chapbook from Carnifex Press and has placed in the PARSEC short story contest. She also appears in *Ruins Metropolis* from Hadley Rille Books.

Rob Haines is an English marine biologist living on the coast of Wales. He lives with his American fiancée—who moved across the Atlantic to study Egyptology—in an apartment overflowing with dolphins. He has been writing short stories for publication for a year and a half, and his work has previously been featured on the Drabblecast podcast. When he's not writing, he's working at his day-job in cancer research.

Jasmine Hammer earned a B.A. in Creative Writing from the University of Wisconsin, Madison, and currently lives in San Francisco. She can be found online at http://jasminehammer.livejournal.com.

When **Martin Hayes** was eight years old he dressed up as Rod Serling for Halloween. None of the neighbours knew who he was or who he was meant to be. Taking him for a middle-aged male smoker trying to ingratiate himself with a group of children, the police were called and at one point a small lynch-mob was formed. He lives in Ireland and also writes comics. You can visit him at www.paroneiria.com.

Geoffrey Maloney has had over seventy short stories published in anthologies and magazines in Australia, the US and the UK. He grew up in Sydney, Australia but now lives in Brisbane with his wife and three daughters. A collection of his short stories, *Tales from the Crypto-System* is available from Prime Books in the US. A small collection of thematically linked absurdist stories, *Six Silly Stories*, will be available soon from Elastic Press in the UK.

Mary Ellen Martin has enjoyed writing her entire life, but didn't realize until 2005 that it was more than a hobby. She writes in several genres, including poetry, science fiction, fantasy, and Christian. She and her family call north Idaho home. "Tiger's Eye View" is her first published story. You can also check out her blog at http://mehub.livejournal.com.

Tracie McBride is a New Zealander who, at the time of this writing, is preparing to move to Melbourne, Australia, with her husband and three children. She completed a diploma of creative writing in 2005 and won the Sir Julius Vogel Award for Best New Talent for 2007. Her poetry and short stories have appeared or are forthcoming in over 30 print and electronic publications including Pulp.Net, *Gambara*, *GlassFire*, *Fictitious Force*, *Electric Velocipede* and *Edge of Propinquity*. Although she also writes mainstream and literary fiction, speculative fiction remains her first love.

Ken McConnell was born in Nevada, Iowa. Growing up he was fascinated with making Sci-Fi movies with his Super-8 movie camera. After spending a few years working on independent films as an Assistant Cameraman, he enlisted in the Air Force. A marriage and two young boys later, he still enjoys all things science fiction. He currently works in Information Technology as a software test analyst. He writes whenever life permits from his home in Boise, Idaho.

Kevin James Miller lives in Illinois. Dozens of his stories and poems in the horror, SF, fantasy, and crime genres have been published. *Cemetery Dance* called his *Rain on a Stranger's Eyes* a hard-hitting and a solid noir masterpiece with chilling irony. *Publisher's Weekly* wrote that *Stealing Klatzman's Diary* was a morbidly amusing caper with a Shakespearean body count. The *Crazy Colored Sky and Other Tales* is an anthology from Silver Lake Publishing of sixteen of his stories. He blogs at http://geocities.com/kevinjamesmiller2001/blog.html, in Kind Supplanter: Notes from a dreamer, realist, and writer.

Shane Nelson has been writing full and part time for the past eight years. His passion for writing has been part of his life, however, for as long as he can remember. He has published stories in various places, including *Green's Magazine, Brew City Magazine, Abyss & Apex, Storyteller Magazine, The Prairie Journal of Canadian Literature* and *Dreams and Visions.* He is a three-time Journey Prize nominee and the winner of the Harding Prize. When not writing, he spends his time as a substitute teacher. He lives in Indian Head, Saskatchewan, Canada, with his wife Jolene and their exceptionally large cat, Bogart.

Michael Obilade is a resident of western Kentucky. His stories have appeared in Fantasy Magazine and TQR. Link: michaelobilade.50webs.com

Sue Penkivech took a convoluted path toward actual use of her English degree, with jobs ranging from information technologies to human resources. She's now a mom, a volunteer school librarian, and a part time bookseller, and has aspirations of becoming a full time writer. Sue is happily married with two daughters and a cat who likes to pad across her keyboard. In addition to this story, she's had another accepted for *The Infinity Swords* anthology (due out this fall by Carnivah Press), and is shopping for a publisher for her first children's novel.

Shauna Roberts is a biomedical writer and copyeditor and has won many awards for her consumer-health magazine columns and book. Her fantasy, science fiction, and romance short stories have appeared in the anthology *Pleasure of the Heart and Other Stories,* Fables.org, *Andromeda Spaceways Inflight Magazine,* the anthology *Clash of Steel, Book One: Reluctant Hero, Continuum Science Fiction,* and SpaceWesterns.com. She has finished a fantasy novel called *Shrine of the Heavens* and is working on its sequel and a fantasy/romance called *Ice Magic, Fire Magic.* She invites you to visit her blog on writing at http://ShaunaRoberts.blogspot.com and her Website at http://www.ShaunaRoberts.com.

Lawrence M. Schoen holds a Ph.D. in cognitive psychology, spent ten years as a college professor, and when not writing currently works as the chief compliance officer for a series of mental health and addiction treatment facilities. He's also one of the world's foremost authorities on the Klingon language, as well as the publisher behind Paper Golem, a new speculative fiction small press. He lives in Pennsylvania.

Ted Stetson's fiction has appeared in *Future Orbits, State Street Review,* and the anthologies *One Evening a Year, Mota: Truth, Ruins Terra* and *Ruins Extraterrestrial.* His published books include: *The Computer Songbook* and *Night Beasts.* He has given workshops at Florida First Coast Writer's Festivals and been honored with several writing awards, including first place from the Florida Literary Arts Council and the Lucy B. MacIntire award from the Poetry Society of Georgia.

Gene Stewart has lived in Japan, Germany, and all over the United States. He currently lives near Omaha, Nebraska, where he is researching and writing a horror novel of ancient sins, modern lies, and eternal truths. Recent credits include the magazines *Tales of Moreauvia*, *Talebones*, *Pan Gaia*, and *All Possible Worlds*, and the anthologies *Ruins Metropolis*, *Magic and Gothic Erotica*, *Love & Sacrifice*, *Hell's Hangmen*, *Jigsaw Nation*, and *Cold Flesh.*

Geoffrey Thorne is the author of multiple short stories including the critically acclaimed *The Soft Room* (Pocket Books). He has written scifi shorts and novellas for Simon & Schuster and Phobos Books and was a finalist in the prestigious *L. Ron Hubbard Presents Writers of the Future* contest. His first novel, *Star Trek: Titan: Sword of Damocles*, debuted in bookstores in December 2007. He lives in Los Angeles but thinks his lawyers may be able to get him out soon.

Andrew Tisbert currently lives on the west side in Los Angeles, where he writes science fiction, performs and records with his alternative "metal" band "Attic of Love" and advocates for the homeless. His novel *The Rise and Falling Out of Saint Leslie of Security* was released in February. He recently won the Mary Shelley Award for speculative fiction in *Rosebud* Magazine, and was shortlisted a year ago for the Sidewise Award for his story "The Meteor of the War," about Malcolm X, John Brown and elephants.

David Tallerman spent four years at York University studying English Literature, specializing in the literary history of witchcraft—an education that left him ideally suited to be an English teacher, a witch, or some unlikely combination of the two. Ever one to confound sensible expectations, he's currently employed as an IT Contractor. Last year his stories appeared in *Andromeda Spaceways Inflight Magazine*, *Pseudopod* and *The Willows* amongst others; this year he has work forthcoming in Night Shade Books' *The Living Dead* anthology and webzines *Chiaroscuro* and *Flash Fiction Online*. He can be found online at http://davidtallerman.net/.

William Blake Vogel III, southern darkness with a poetic edge, writes a unique brand of Classic Horror that bleeds with an old school grit. Influenced by the likes of Poe and Lovecraft, Vogel's style of Dark Horror reflects a deep love for the genre. He currently is working on his zombie opus, "The New Normal." He is the most published poet in *Champagne Shivers Magazine*'s history, and his work is often seen in *Night To Dawn Magazine*. W.B. Vogel has sold pieces to *Grafika* Magazine, *Champagne Shivers Magazine*, *Abyss & Apex*, *Night To Dawn Magazine*, *Between Kisses Magazine*, *Hungur Magazine*, *Black Satellite*, *Scavengers*, *Fantasque*, *Horror Carousel*, *T-Zero*, *Twilight Times*, *Wanderings*, *Down In The Cellar*, etc. He has also appeared in various anthologies including *Open Graves* (2004), *Potter's Field* (2005), *Zombies* (2007), *Potter's Field 2* (2008), *Abominations* (2008), *Age Of Blood And Snow* (2008), etc. William also writes a column, "Theories In Chaos," for THE ETERNAL NIGHT website (http://www.eternalnight.co.uk).

Christopher Woods is the author of a prose collection, *Under a Riverbed Sky*, and a collection of stage monologues for actors, *Heart Speak*. His plays have been produced in Los Angeles, Chicago and New York. He lives in Houston and in Chappell Hill, Texas.

Also from Hadley Rille Books

Desolate Places

The companion volume to *Barren Worlds.*

www.hadleyrillebooks.com

Printed in the United Kingdom
by Lightning Source UK Ltd.
131721UK00001B/375/P

9 780978 514822